now these have been replaced with dentu
punched me, he didn't know but burst out
thought I looked a lot better with the false
    It took me another three months before ⌐   ⌐ı
him. It was when we were stood in the entra   .⌐ı smith tube
station, he was staring at my face. I glared baც_ while telling him what a
shit he was. I don't think he could believe what he was hearing.

"I don't know what the hell you're talking about - you stupid bitch. I
wouldn't hurt a fucking fly."

"You bloody well hurt me, you know very well you did."

"When was that - you silly cow. I can't remember ever hurting you."

"You ought to remember, you were a real shit you punched me in the
mouth when we came out of the pub, then you had to ring for an
ambulance as my two top front teeth were on the pavement looking up
at us."

"Oh yeah, I remember, what a laugh that was, you fucking deserved the
punch in the mouth, you wouldn't stop yapping while we were in the
bloody pub. When we got outside I gave you something to shut you up
and shut you up it did - the punch did the fucking trick, thank God."

"I've had enough of your stupid nonsense, I'm off. I hope I never see or
hear from you again, you stupid obnoxious bloke."

I ran back to my flat which was only half a mile down the road. I had a
feeling that Derek would follow me from a distance - he didn't. After
arriving in my front room I sat myself down in the armchair and had a
good cry. I was crying with relieve at getting rid of this stupid twit so easily
- at least I thought I had.

My relationship with Derek was fragile, he appeared to have a problem.
I think it was my looks, other men used to give me the eye and it made
Derek lose his temper, then when we were alone he hit out at me. My
problem with him was when he was nice he was very nice and I would give
into anything he asked. On one of his nice days I would have given into
marrying him - thank God he never asked me. I can't think why I agreed to
go out with him in the first place as now I realise he isn't any good for me.

We met in an Irish pub when I was out with a girlfriend. Derek and his
mate came over to our table and like a couple of fools we invited them

both to join us. After a few Gin and Tonics I believed Derek when he told me that he worked in the city and lived in an up market flat in Chelsea. It didn't occur to me to ask why he was hanging out in an Irish pub in Shepherds Bush when life in Chelsea should be more exciting and upmarket. I agreed to have a date with him, daft really, as I soon became hooked due to his charm and good looks. Now I need to get shot of him.

At around ten o'clock I got myself ready for bed, once the light was out and I was laying down I could hear stones being thrown up at my bedroom window. I decided the best thing to do was to hide under the bedclothes and pretend I couldn't hear the stones. The stone throwing went on for at least half an hour when suddenly there was banging on the main door to my flat. I started shaking and wondered what was happening. Once I'd pulled myself together I jumped out of bed and hurried along the hallway pulling my dressing gown on as I went.

"Who is it and what the hell do you want?" I asked.

"I'm Steve the chap from downstairs." he shouted from the other side of the door.

"What do you want? I was in bed trying to go to sleep."

"There's a bloke outside throwing stones up at one of your windows. The thing is some of the stones are landing on my bedroom window and I'm fed up with the noise. I'm trying to get some sleep, as I need to be up and running by five."

"You can't blame me for the stones they're nothing to do with me, in fact I haven't heard them. I'm going back to bed. Don't bang on my door again. I suggest you put cotton wool in your ears then you won't hear the stones, that's what I'm going to do."

"You've heard the noise, you're admitting you've heard the din by saying you're going to put the cotton wool in your ears because of the stones."

"Alright I've heard the stones on my window. The bloke is nothing to do with me."

"I bet he is."

"Go before I come out and push you down the fucking stairs."

"Hold your hair on girl, I only came to ask if you knew anything about this bloke and the stones."

4

"Well, I don't, good night."

I went back to bed and slept until morning when I was woken by Steve at five, banging on my door and shouting into my flat that the bloke who was throwing stones last night was asleep on the door step. I unlocked the door to see what this Steve looked like.

"I told you last night that I don't know him." I said looking Steve up and down. "I've been outside and had a chat to him and he says you're his girlfriend, he refuses to leave until you go and see him."

"That's one thing I'm not going to do, see my mouth without my front teeth?"

"Yeah."

"Well, if he says that his name is Derek, he's the reason why my front teeth are missing and why I have dentures in a pot at the side of my bed. I've finished with him, I finished with him bloody weeks ago. Tell him to piss off"

"He says you were out with him yesterday."

"What if I was, in my mind I finished with him the day he punched me in the mouth. Yesterday was the day I plucked up the courage to tell him to get lost, not the day that I finished with him."

"I'll go back down to see him and tell him you won't be going down to the door as you don't feel too good. If he won't leave I'll threaten him with the police that should get rid of him."

"There's one big problem for me, he lives in the block of flats at the end of this blinking road. His flat is out the front on the ground floor, he can easily see me from the window when I walk past."

"So."

"I can't get out from the other end of the road as it's a cul-de-sac, this means that every time I leave here I have to go past his flat. If he doesn't leave me in peace I'll have to move. Whatever else you say to him for God's sake don't tell him that I may be moving flat's."

"I wouldn't dream of it. By the way there is an opening at the other end of this road, it's by the large detached house on the right, haven't you seen it?"

"No."

5

"Well it's there, if you go down to the detached house the opening is on the right hand side by the garage. It goes out onto a path, if you walk along you eventually come out by the Odeon."

"I'll go and have a look when I've time, but I'm going to think about moving flats especially if he won't leave me alone, I'm going back to bed." I banged the door shut.

Before getting into bed I peeped out the window and saw Derek stood on the curb on the other side of the road looking up at my flat. When he saw the curtain move he put two fingers in the air, whether it was at me or Steve because he had been down to the front door to tell him to move from the doorstep, I don't know. I got back into bed and slept like a baby until eight o'clock when I went along to the bathroom for a lick and a promise. After this I quickly put on clothes suitable for work, ate my cereal then I made my way to the office in Oxford Street.

On the tube I went into a world of my own. I dreamt about leaving my job as I'm bored out of my mind due to it being so mundane. If I give in my notice I don't know what I'll do for a living as the only job I know other than typing is working as an escort and I've only ever done that for a few weeks which was when I left home broke. By the time I got to the typing pool I'd decided to write out my resignation. I put it on Mr Morgan's desk where he would see it as soon as he arrived. I then settled down at my typewriter and got on with typing the letters from yesterday. It was at least eleven o'clock before I realised I hadn't seen Mr Morgan – the office manager.

"Joyce have you seen Mr Morgan?"

"No."

"Has anyone seen the boss?" I shouted out so all the girls could hear.

"He isn't in today." shouted Marg

"You usually try and avoid him, what's up? Have you suddenly taken a shine to him after all these years that you've been working here?" the girls started laughing.

"No I haven't, I don't fancy him, never have and I never bloody will."

"What's up then, why do you want to see the boss? We won't let it rest until you tell us."

"You'll all hear soon enough If he's in tomorrow morning at nine you'll know by five past." by this time all the girls had got up from their desks and were stood around me.

"It must be quite serious especially if he's going to call you into his office as soon as he arrives."

"Yeah, I guess it is, you'll have to wait until tomorrow."

"I'm going to guess, you're pregnant by that dick head you go out with?"

"I'm not going out with him or anyone else."

"If you've given him up, I bet you've had a one night stand and got caught so you're up the duff."

"I'M NOT BLOODY PREGNANT. FOR GOODNESS SAKE SHUT UP THE LOT OF YOU, move away from my desk now. Go and get on with your bloody work, before I lose my temper completely."

Without hesitation they all moved, peace reigned for the rest of the day, no one spoke to me, the girls didn't even chat amongst themselves. Five o'clock soon came around, I called out goodbye to the girls they looked towards me then just turned away and carried on with what they were doing.

Once I arrived home the first thing I did was rummage through all the cupboards to try and find the flat contract. The trouble is I've lived at this flat for a number of years, also I'm not the tidiest of people so the contract could be anywhere but where it should be. I needed to read it to find out how many weeks' notice I had to give the landlord. The landlord's phone number was in my rent book, if I phoned to ask he could say any old rubbish to me and may suggest that I should get out by the end of this week as I only needed to give him a few days' notice. I turned the flat upside down but couldn't find anything resembling a contract.

By this time I was so fed up that I decided to go to the chippy as I was hungry and too exhausted to cook. Being a Tuesday there wasn't a queue, just one person in front of me, he was buying a bag of gribbles along with a small bag of chips, I'd never eaten gribbles so I decided to have some to go with my large piece of cod.

"Chips as well?"

"No thanks, cod and a bag of gribbles will do me fine."

"That's not much of a supper for a growing girl." came a voice from behind, I looked over my shoulder and there was Steve,

"Let me buy you some chips?"

"No thanks."

"I know I'll get a large bag of chips to go with my cod then perhaps you'll eat your supper with me and also share some of my chips as there'll be too many for me. How about that?"

"How about what?" I replied.

"You coming to eat your supper with me."

"I'll think about it while I walk home."

I left the chippy, crossed the road and quickly started to walk along the path towards my flat. Steve caught me up and chatted away to me as if I was his best friend - of course I'm not. I'd only seen him once before, that was the other morning when I was half asleep. Seeing him in the clear light of day I notice he's quite good looking, mind you Derek wasn't bad in the looks department. Anyway I've made a decision I'm not going for looks ever again, this means Steve can forget about making a pass at me.

Outside of Steve's flat he asked where we were going to eat our fish and chips in his flat or mine.

"I want to eat my food quietly on my own in my flat."

"I've bought extra chips to share with you."

"Bad luck, I didn't ask you to buy them. If I wanted to eat chips I would have bought some. I'm not hard up. I can afford to buy my own. I don't need you to buy chips for me."

"We're not going to eat our supper together then?"

"No, I'm eating mine in my flat on my own."

I turned and started to run up the stairs, Steve shouted after me,

"I only wanted to get to know you so we could be friends, no hanky panky. I'm not into that, now I've too many chips."

"Serves you bloody well right, you shouldn't have bought them, I didn't ask you to." I turned around and walked back down a few stairs.

"Before I go up to my flat I've a serious question to ask, do you have any idea how much notice I need to give on my flat?"

"How the hell would I know, I have to give four weeks, the bloke that used to live over the way only had to give two. You must have a contract."

8

"Before I went out I turned my flat upside down, I can't find it."

"If I were you I'd have another look, it'll be there somewhere."

Looking towards me in a strange way Steve continued chatting. . "Are you sure you don't want to come in and eat your supper with me? If you insist on not coming in I'll put a few chips in a dish and hand them to you out here."

"Okay Steve I'll give into you giving me a few chips in a dish." Steve turned to open his door, then suddenly turned back on his heel and held out his right hand towards me, "I know what the problem is, we haven't introduced ourselves, I'm Steve Peterson from up North." we shook hands.

"I'm Mary Huggins from anywhere you want me to come from. Now we know each other by name it doesn't mean I'm coming in, it just means we've introduced ourselves. The thing is you can tell me any old name, to encourage me through your front door."

"So can you, in fact I think you may have. Come on Mary tell me which part of London you come from? I'm guessing you come from London by your accent."

"I was born and brought up in a grand first floor apartment in Whittaker Street near the Royal Court theatre. Steve you must have heard of the Royal Court – it's very famous. It's where John Osborne's Look Back in Anger was first staged. Mum and dad still live at the flat. I've named the flat "snooty" because of where it's situated and their stupid snooty manner."

"Why the hell are you living in this dump if you come from there?"

"It's a very long story, I may tell you some time but not now as I'm both hungry and tired. Go and get the chips?"

"Okay."

Steve soon returned with a cereal bowl full to the brim. I took the bowl and went up to my flat without saying another word.

After I'd finished supper I had another scurry around for the contract but it didn't turn up. I began to think the landlord hadn't given me one, but I'm sure he must have. I went to bed wondering what to do next as I was determined not to stay living here. The thing is I paid a deposit of twenty pounds, I know I did as it's written inside the front cover of my rent book. If I disappear without trace on a date suitable to me, I won't get my deposit back also I'm banking on this money to put down on a different flat.

I tossed and turned for most of the night. When the morning arrived I felt I could stay in bed and sleep all day, of course I had to get up for work. I hurried around and eventually arrived at the office wondering what was going to happen when Mr Morgan read my letter. I was sure he would try and persuade me to stay by making out that the typing pool couldn't run efficiently without me. After hanging my coat in its usual place I went straight over to my desk, "Morning everyone." No one replied. I'd obviously upset the girls so much that they wouldn't even say good morning let alone goodnight.

Eventually the typing pool door went bang and there was Mr Morgan, the office manager going into his office. I kept my head down and hoped he didn't scream out as soon as he read my letter as he usually did when anyone gave in their notice. Most of the girls in the pool had given in their notice at least once and he had managed to persuade all of them to stay - I'm not for staying.

Bang went something on his desk, it was so loud it could have been a hammer that he banged down.

"Miss Huggins, I need to see you now." the girls sniggered.

"There's no need for you lot to laugh because I'm having to go and see the office manager."

"It's a laugh from where we're sitting, we've been waiting all morning for him to arrive and call you in." laughed Ruth.

"I can hear you, Miss West, you better come in as well then you can tell me what's so funny about Miss Huggins having to come into my office." Ruth looked in a state of shock as she got up from her desk, pulling her pencil skirt down to cover her knees.   "It's not funny now you have to join me in the office. This serves you bloody well right, you should have kept your big mouth shut, you've never been good at doing that have you Ruth West?" Her head went in the air as she pushed past me to go into see Mr Morgan first.

"Sit down the pair of you. Miss West I want to know what's funny about Miss Huggins having to come into my office?" silence "come on, hurry up and tell me, you don't seem to find it funny now you're sat here." silence reigned "Miss Huggins do you know why Miss West was laughing?"

"No, I've no idea Mr Morgan. For the record you sound just like my old headmaster when he got cross." Miss West started to giggle at my comment.

"I don't mean to. The thing is Miss Huggins you've upset me by giving in your notice and I'm cross with Miss West for laughing at me." He immediately put his head in his hands and just sat at his desk without saying a word for a good five minutes.   "I'm going back to my desk Mary, you'll have to sort him out." said Ruth nodding towards Mr Morgan. "Don't leave me Ruth."

"I have to leave you, I've got work to do." Ruth walked out of the office banging the door behind her.

"Mr Morgan what's the matter? I haven't meant to upset you, all I want to do is give in my notice and leave."

"You giving in your notice on top of everything else that's happened to me this morning has just about finished me. My fourteen year old daughter has run away from her boarding school. The house mistress phoned my ex-wife last evening and told her that Susanne had disappeared. The staff seem to think she got on the bus outside the school gates at four o'clock yesterday afternoon. I've had a terrible night. Margaret that's my ex, rang to tell me all the details. As well as running away Susanne apparently cut off her long blonde hair, now she looks like a boy."

"One good thing her hair will grow again so there's no need to worry about that. Her running away from school is another matter, I don't know what to say, perhaps she wasn't happy."

"I haven't seen her for over three months, in fact I haven't even had a letter from her for a couple of months."

"Mr Morgan you stay put and I'll see what I can find in the way of a cup tea, do you take sugar?"

"Yeah, two please."

I left Mr Morgan sat looking as if his world had completely fallen apart. The girls cheered as I went into the typing pool "What the hell's the matter with you lot?"

11

"We're cheering because you're helping our manager, we always thought you fancied him and it seems as though we're right."

"I can assure you I don't fancy him. I'm making him a cup of tea as he isn't feeling too good."

"Is it in your contract to make a cup of tea for the office manager?"

"No it's not."

"Why make tea then, unless you want him to give you a quick poke as a thank you. Mary that makes you sound desperate and a little sick. Sorry I shouldn't have said that." Said Marg.

"Shut up the lot of you or you may have me spewing up on the floor, if that happened I wouldn't clean it up, I'd leave it for you lot. Before any of you say another word about me and vomit, just remember that I mean what I've said and it will be one of you cleaning the floor because the office cleaner doesn't clean up spew." I don't think the girls could believe what I said as they immediately turned away to get on with their typing. I went out into the hallway to boil the kettle and make the cup of tea. I was about to carry the tea back when the door opened and there stood Ruth starring across the hallway at me.

"What's the matter, you look like you've seen a ghost?"

"Mary you watch it when you go back into old Morgan's office with his tea. It seems that he can be quite handy with his hands. If you remember Mildred, who was asked to go into old Morgan's office, she didn't hesitate to go and was quite excited about seeing him on her own. When she went to leave he stood over by the door to stop her. Mildred pushed him aside to get out then he started to be handy with his hands. There was a terrible who ha. She was in some state when she eventually came out, since then some of the girls have named Mr Morgan, Handy Andy. Mary I remember it like it was yesterday. Mildred left her job immediately. We girls don't want anything like that to happen to you. If I were you I'd hand in the cup of tea and come away immediately."

"That's what I intend doing, or you could always take it in for me." I said laughing.

"No I'm not doing that for you, in fact I wouldn't do it for anyone. I find Mr Morgan creepy, his eyes get to me. All the girls say the same, they think he undresses them when he looks towards them."

"In a minute I'll go back to my desk without taking him in his tea. Yeah, that's what I'll do. I can always say that I forgot to make it, what do you think?"

"That's what I'd do. He may have forgotten that he asked you to get him a cuppa."

"Thanks for coming out to have a chat." Ruth hurried back into the typing pool, I followed and went over to my desk. I didn't see old Morgan again that day, like the others I kept my head down. The girls and I decided that perhaps he left his office and went home after we all left the typing pool to go for lunch.

Chapter 2

I arrived home at around six feeling completely exhausted and fed up.

I didn't know whether I was coming or going, due to the fact that I was hungry and tired and also I hadn't found the flat contract which I needed so I could give in my notice to the landlord.

I was starving and needed a meal. I had to cook something quick as I couldn't go and get fish and chips or gribbles again as I'd been to the chippy twice this week already. I finished up eating baked beans on toast, for pudding I had ice cream. Once eaten I was determined to have an early night so I settled down in bed by nine with a book. I didn't hear a sound outside.

Once up and running Thursday morning I found a note pushed under my door, addressed to me. It was from Steve inviting me out on Friday evening to the pub. This cheered me up no end as I'd been worrying about what I was going to do on a Friday night. For the last year I'd always gone out with Derek. When I was with him he'd persuaded me to give up all my girlfriends, like a fool I did. Now I haven't anyone to go out and about with unless I ask one of the girls at the office if they fancied going up the West End with me, I doubt if anyone would as they seem to find me a bit snooty. I replied to Steve's note, saying I would meet him in the hallway at eight.

Thursday went quicker than I thought it would, old Morgan was nowhere to be seen, it was as if he had disappeared into thin air. The girls seemed to think he'd taken a few days off, as they weren't expecting him into the office until Monday morning. How they knew this I don't know. I guess that he accepted my resignation and I'll be leaving in four weeks' time, unless I hear differently from him. Where I'm going to work or live I don't know. One thing I do know for sure is that I don't want to stay in this awful mundane job or go back living at home with mum and dad. My parents drive me potty what with their snooty ways and the snooty friends they have in for cocktails. I must keep remembering that it was my parents and their friends that made me leave home in the first place.

Friday arrived and I found it difficult to concentrate on anything as I was excited about going to the pub with Steve. It sounds stupid as I promised myself I wouldn't get involved with anyone and now I seem to be turned on at the thought of meeting up with Steve. I don't know a thing about him except he lives below me and his bed may be undermine which makes me feel even more excited.

The office closed at four on a Friday so I was on the tube by four fifteen. I had plenty of time to get ready once I arrived home. As soon as I walked into my flat I was worrying about the contract. At least I'd given in my notice at the office and if I leave my job before I find my contract for the flat I have some where to live, except I don't know how I'll pay the rent. When I left home I didn't have a job, I went on the game for a couple of weeks - I don't fancy doing that again.

All day I've been wondering what to wear, the trouble is I only have a few things suitable for wearing to a pub, the rest of my clothes are more suitable for going out to a hotel. I looked in my wardrobe, the first thing I saw was the black mini skirt which I bought from a local boutique along with a white skinny rib top.

"These will do, I'll wear these with my one and only pair of stilettos. I hope I don't look like a tart." I said out loud to myself.

Once ready I looked over the banisters, Steve was sat on the bottom step waiting patiently. He must have heard me as he immediately looked up the stairs smiling. "You look a bit of alright." he shouted up. I tried to look demure as I walked down the stairs but I found it difficult in my stilettos.   "What do you mean by that?" I called back,

"What I said, you look a bit of alright – you look good."

"Thanks."

"Where do you fancy going? I usually go to the pub down the Queens road on a Friday night."

"Before we set off what's the pub called it must have a name?"

"I always call it the Queens, I don't know the pub's real name, most people call it that."

"Is it far?"

"If you're worrying about walking in those shoes I can always call a cab, or you can take them off. I'll carry them for you."

"I'm not used to going in cabs, I walk everywhere."

"Even when you're wearing stilettos?"

"Yeah, they pinch a bit but I'm used to that. I walk along slowly but surely, eventually get to where I want to go."

"We'll walk then as long as you're happy."

We set off, it took a good half hour with me having to stop and start, at one point we sat down on a bench, I took my shoes off and Steve massaged my feet.

Inside the door of the pub I realised that I'd been to this particular one before, "I know this pub, in fact I know it quite well, the twit used to bring me here most Wednesday nights."

"I've never been here on a Wednesday but a mate of mine told me that the barmaid that works here on a Wednesday night is well endowed and worth coming to look at."

"I don't know about things like that. I must admit I did notice the men standing at the bar as if they were looking at something other than the beer pumps."

"That's what it must have been the barmaid with the low cut top, they were looking at her tits." laughed Steve

"Must have been, the twit used to come back smiling to himself after going to the bar, yeah it must have been the barmaid that made him smile, as it definitely wasn't me."

"Getting back to going up to the bar, what would you like to drink?"

"Nothing to strong, I'm not used to alcohol. I know I'll have half a beer shandy and a packet of peanuts, if you can run to that."

"Are you sure, about having a shandy, why not have a G and T?"

"Okay if you insist, a small G and T and a packet of peanuts."

"It wasn't difficult to persuade you to have something stronger. You find a table for us and I'll go up to the bar."

The table I found was just inside the main door. It was a bit draughty but it was the only one available. Steve soon returned with our drinks. After settling ourselves down we had a good old natter. He told me about his job at Ealing Broadway, the only thing he didn't like about it was having to get up at five in the morning Monday to Friday, to get to work by six thirty but he was home again by two thirty. I explained to him about how I left home without a proper job and how I worked for an escort agency. He seemed shocked and got quieter and quieter as the evening went on. After he had a few brown splits with whisky chasers he came to life "Mary, are you telling me that you worked as an escort or glorified tart, have I got that right?"

"Yeah, afraid so." I could feel myself going the colour of a beetroot.

"How long did you work as that?"

"Only a couple of months, the money was very good, much better than working in any office." I smiled.

"Where did you hang out?"

"Around the West End for meals during the day with clients from the escort agency. In the evenings I had a couple of hotels I went to where I picked up men, this was separate from the escort agency. One evening I got caught by my dad's friend. He was out and about and came into the bar of this particular hotel. I was sat on a bar stool on the lookout for clients, he turned up and stood next to me. I was looking away from him when he asked if I'd like a Gin and Tonic, I turned around and nearly fell off the stool. I don't know who was the most shocked him or me." We both laughed,

"Did you give it up because you got caught by your dad's friend? Mary I bet you'd still be an escort and working the hotels if this particular man hadn't turned up."

"I suppose I would." I could feel myself going bright red again.

"I never dreamt in my wildest dreams that you of all people had been an escort or tart or whatever you want to call yourself."

"Looking back on my life then makes me smile. Dad's friend made me promise I wouldn't tell my parents about his behaviour. He was married to my mum's best friend and was completely fed up with the sex he had with her, it was far too mundane for him. He visited different hotels every week to pick up women. He said he wouldn't tell mum or dad about what I was doing if I gave the escort/tart job up straight away. That's what I did. He was very good to me and gave me a wad of notes to tide me over till I got a proper job."

"I bet he wanted something for the notes?"

"Yeah he did, I met him weekly for a couple of months. I gave him what he asked for. I soon got fed up with him, he was a bit old for me and sometimes had difficulty getting a hard. Anyway enough of that I managed to get an office job. I've worked at the same office ever since, now I'm leaving."

"What are you planning to do in a month's time?"

"No idea. But I'm not thinking about going back on the game - far too dangerous."

"That's sensible Mary. I was a bit desperate a while ago and I got involved with a so called tart, I soon gave her up. She didn't care who she went with, as long as they paid enough. I was so concerned about catching the pox, I was like that old man you've been telling me about, I couldn't get a stiffy so that was the end of that relationship."

"Most men seem to have difficulty at times. Let's change the subject as I don't want to talk about how difficult men find it to perform."

"Yeah let's, I'll get us both another drink, do you want another G and T, you realise it'll be your third?"

"That's Okay, I'm used to drinking four or five in an evening. The fifth is usually for Dutch courage." I laughed.

"You stay here I'll get them in. This will be the last round tonight." Steve soon returned. "Once we've finished these we'll have to go or at least I'll have to go. I'm having to get up early tomorrow as I'm doing an extra shift. You can stay on if you like but I'll be going."

"I don't want to stay here alone, I'll come with you."

"We'll get a black cab together then, better share the cost as I've nearly run out of cash."

"I've plenty of money, you don't need to worry about cash." Once we'd drunk up we went out on to the pavement and waved down a black cab. It wasn't long before we were jumping out at the flats.

"How much do you want cabby?"

"Five bob."

"What?"

"Five shillings I said."

"Can you help me out Mary?"

"How much do you need?"

"Five shillings, I've only got a bob."

"Here you are, your company wasn't worth the full price of a cab but the G and T's were okay, in fact the Gins were very tasty."

"Well you'll have to wait till I've been paid if you're thinking about me buying you another."

"I wasn't thinking of anything other than going to bed, I've had it, I'm exhausted."

We both staggered up the steps to the front door. Steve was trying to find his key.

"Have you got yours?"

"My what?"

18

"Front door key."

"It's in my bag somewhere."

"Hurry up and find it, I need a wee."

"Don't get annoyed with me, if you want a wee go over there and wee against the wall, I'll look the other way, then again I may watch, I haven't seen a bloke wee against a wall for years."

"Mary, you come over quite brash, no wonder you were able to work as an escort." Steve went back down the two steps and wandered over to the wall where he organised himself to have a wee.

"Found the key, I'm going in." once inside the door banged shut, leaving Steve weeing. Once he'd finished he howled and screamed through the letter box and banged on the door "Let me in, open the door, open it now."   The screaming was so loud that a side window from the next house opened   "I saw you weeing against my wall if you don't go indoors immediately I'll phone the cops." shouted the man.

"I haven't a key."

"That's not my problem, as I've just told you I'll ring the cops if you don't disappear indoors." I could hear all this commotion going on outside, as I didn't want to get involved I opened the door and left it ajar then ran up the stairs to my flat.

Chapter 3

Saturday and Sunday came and went with no sign of Steve. I have a feeling Steve was shocked by my past so decided to keep out of my way. I'm sure he made up the story about himself having a tart as a girlfriend. I don't blame him as I think I would have said the same if I'd been him and got myself in a spot.

Monday came and Mr Morgan was in his office long before I arrived. I found a letter on my typewriter it was from him replying to my resignation. When he saw me arrive he rushed over to say he was having a meeting with all the staff at ten o'clock, then he was going home. At the meeting he explained how he was taking a few weeks off as his daughter was still missing from school.

"I've been out on the streets looking for Susanne and I've handed out leaflets. If anyone would like some leaflets there are a few in my office that you can take to hand out. My doctor has put me on the sick as he thinks I'm on the verge of a nervous breakdown so I'm taking a few weeks off." The girls looked shocked and upset, there wasn't any laughing in fact a couple of them looked like they were about to burst out crying as tears welled up in their eyes.

Before Mr Morgan went home he came over to my desk to say goodbye, he wished me well and hoped I would get a job that suited me, then he kissed me on the cheek and went on his way. The kiss on the cheek was the last straw for the girls, they soon forgot about feeling upset for Mr Morgan. The kiss set them off barraging me with questions about why he should be so familiar with me as he'd never kissed anyone else goodbye.

"We all reckon you have been having a bit of hanky panky with the old man." shouted Ruth, this of course encouraged the rest of the girls to cheer and shout, what I call rubbish at me.

"Shut up all of you, you lot are one of the reasons I'm leaving, I'm fed up with you all shouting rubbish at me. You seem to shout it at me most days."

"Hang on a minute, when we shout at you we usually have a very good reason for doing so. Today it's the kiss on cheek, the other week it was the love bit on your neck, then the punch in the mouth from that dick head of a boyfriend. The punch must have hurt and to finish up with two false teeth would have been the end of him for me. I hope you've told him where to go."

"Course I have, I would rather be without a boyfriend for the rest of my days than go out with him."

"Sense at last." called out Marg.

"Let's shut up for the rest of the day and get on with our work. Mr Robbins will come up in a minute if he hears us mucking about, then we'll all be in trouble. I wouldn't put it past him to sack the lot of us."

"You must be joking Mary, he'd be left here doing his own typing. I can promise you lot that he won't sack us. We can play around as much as we like, remember old Morgan has gone home, he's not here to tell us off."

"Seems like you know Robbins better than we do, what have YOU been up to Marg?"

"Nothing." Marg blushed

"Your face has gone the colour of your red lipstick." I said laughing at her

"Shut up Mary."

"No I won't shut up. If I were in your shoes Marg I'd go out to the cloak room and wash my face in cold water to cool myself down. If Mr Robbins comes up he'll definitely ask you what the matter is, he couldn't ignore your face, could he girls?"

"No." all the girls shouted in harmony.

I turned away and went back to my desk where I busied myself for the rest of the day. Luckily for all of us Mr Robbins didn't come up to see how we were getting on without old Morgan. The other girls spent most of the day on a high chatting about what they'd been doing over the weekend. I didn't join in as I didn't want to tell them about my trip to the pub.

Five o'clock arrived and I was just about to put my coat on when I decided to ask the girls what they were doing this evening. "Not a lot." answered Ruth "I'm a very dull person. I'm going home to have supper, watch a bit of telly, then go to bed."

"What are the rest of you doing?"

"Same as Ruth, It's Monday, we never go out on a Monday, we go home and wash our smalls then go to bed early." called out Marg.

"We usually go out on a Wednesday evening. Anyway what's it to you Mary Huggins, you never come out with us?"

"I thought I'd join you this evening as I'm fed up with my own company."

"On Wednesday we're planning to go to the new club that has opened at Trafalgar Square. The idea is to meet up at Nelson's column, go for a drink in a pub then get into the club by ten. Quite a few of our friends are going with us. Think about it."

"I will, most probably the answer will be yes."

"That'll be a shock to my system, in fact it'll be a shock for all of us." shouted Marg who always thought she was in charge

"Yeah it will be, if you come." they all yelled.

"Well I'm going, I'll see you all in the morning."

As I wanted to stay away from my flat for as long as possible I walked to Marble Arch - window shopping. Then I caught the tube to Shepherds Bush, where I walked the rest of the way to Hammersmith Broadway then on to my flat, it took a good hour. Once inside my flat I felt bilious, whether this was due to lack of food or the worry of having to find my flat contract before I could give in my notice I'm not sure. The thing is I hadn't eaten much all day, just a couple of sandwiches from the sandwich bar. I'm not a very good cook, I'm far too tired to attempt even a simple meal. I finished up eating another snack along with a G and T - my favourite tipple. I went to bed early and slept well considering the worry about me finding the contract.

Wednesday soon arrived and the girls along with me spent most of our spare time discussing what we're going to get up to this evening. Some of the girls lived out in the sticks so they'd bought their glam rags into work and had arranged to wash and change in the cloak room - not very hygienic but it saved them the tube fare. I went back to my flat for my wash and brush up, I glammed myself up in one of my slinky dresses that I wore when I visited the hotels. I hope that no one mentions the year I bought the dress or ask if I'd borrowed it from mum as it looked dated.

I was first to arrive at Trafalgar Square. I'm sure I must have only been stood under Nelson's column for five minutes but it seemed more like half an hour before Ruth arrived. While waiting quite a few middle aged men kept giving me the eye, one in particular kept his distance but kept walking backwards and forwards in front of me. As soon as

Ruth arrived he moved away and went and sat over by one of the fountains but still looked in our direction.

"See that bloke."

"Yeah what about him? He's a bit ancient for us, he's old enough to be our father, Mary."

"He's been hanging around all the time I've been here. I have a feeling he thinks I'm on the game." Ruth looked me up and down.

"Perhaps he does, it must be the dress it's a bit slinky for a night out with the girls. Where the hell did you get it? Mary were you on the game before you came to work in the office?" I blushed.

"No I wasn't, well not exactly. I belonged to an escort agency."

"I can't believe what I'm hearing. Are you saying you used to be an escort? Am I right if I say you used to go out to dinner with different blokes, arranged by the agency then if the bloke asked for sex you decided whether you'd perform or not?"

"Yeah that's about right, the money's very good, especially when you work on your own. I used to go to the hotels up the West End in between working for the agency."

"Perhaps that man is an old customer as he's still over their staring. He may have recognised the dress, there can't be many girls wearing a dress like that one."

"I don't recognise him, mind you it was a few years ago that I was a so called escort. Going back to this dress it's a favourite of mine, I only wear it on special occasions, like when I'm on the loose."

"If you're not careful you'll pick someone or something up tonight wearing that, I hope you've brought some rubbers with you?" said Ruth nodding towards me.

"I always carry them in my bag, I wouldn't dare leave home without them." Ruth looked at me as if I was a dirty little slut. "No need to look at me like that, It's better to be safe than sorry, you can't rely on blokes carrying rubbers."

"I've never thought of that. I must remember to go to the Ladies in the pub to get some, how much are they?"

"For goodness sake Ruth, cheaper than having an abortion or keeping the baby then having to feed and water it until it leaves school. They're two bob for a pack of three at the last count - cheap at the price."

"I suppose that is cheap." Replied Ruth.

"Don't be stupid girl of course it's cheap, ten shillings for a pack of three would be cheaper than having to keep a baby."

I looked at my watch "Ruth do you realise it has gone half eight, I wonder what's happened to the others?"

"I don't know, perhaps they've gone somewhere else, let's give them another five minutes then go. That man is still looking over at us."

"Just in case he comes across in the next five minutes remember neither of us have seen him before. I'll tell him to clear off, unless you want him, because I don't." I said sounding annoyed.

"You must be joking if you think I want him, I'm not hard up, he must be at least forty."

"Time's up, let's go to the nearest pub. I hope it'll be half decent."

"Come on Ruth, for a laugh let's walk past the bloke, then go to the pub we can see from here."

"Mary, do you think the bloke will try and speak to us as we walk past?"

"I doubt it, if he does pretend to be deaf, keep talking to me."

"Don't you worry I will."

It was strange, once we started to walk towards the bloke he got up, turned and walked in the opposite direction. "He was odd, I was looking forward to having a closer look at him, not that I'm interested in any man over thirty. We need to remember we're only twenty four and going out with someone of forty would be like going out with our dads."

"How old was your dad when he got your mum pregnant Ruth? If you think it would be like going out with him, your dad must have only been around sixteen when you were born."

"No, that's wrong he was twenty one when I was born."

"That's still pretty young to get someone pregnant."

"I agree with you, I wouldn't have wanted a baby at twenty one. Imagine if we had been pregnant at twenty one we would both have three year olds' now. One thing we wouldn't have to go to work ever again, but then we would be spending our time washing nappies in some God forsaken place like a bedsitter down the East End."

"I'd rather go to work than spend the rest of my days looking after a baby and living in the East End."

"So would I, babies aren't for me."

We arrived at the pub door "Mary, are you going in first?"

"Yeah, okay here goes." I pushed the door open. The bar was over flowing with people, you wouldn't have thought it was a Wednesday night. "I didn't think it would be this full, if we can't find a seat we'll have to stand at the bar, what the men will think of you in that dress I dread to think. Mine is the opposite too yours, they won't be interested in picking me up in this old thing." Said Ruth laughing at me.

"Ruth, I'll try and find a table."

"Okay, I'll get the first drinks in, what do you fancy?"

"G and T please." I managed to find a couple of stools at a high counter over the far side of the lounge bar. The stools were okay but were quite difficult to get up on, once up I was showing all of my legs along with my knickers as the skirt part of this particular dress was tight and short that I couldn't pull it down very easily. Ruth soon arrived with our drinks "From where I was stood at the bar I could see your knickers, I couldn't understand why the men were looking over here from the bar, I turned around and there were your knickers staring at me."

"I don't believe you."

"It's true."

"What colour are they?"

"Navy."

"That's a good guess, I doubt if you can see them from right over there, you're teasing me. I know you're teasing as my bra is navy and you can see the navy straps, you're guessing that my bra matches my knickers." we both laughed out loud.

"How are you going to get up on the stool, clever clogs?"

"Easier than you, my skirt is longer to start with and is flowing, I don't have the problem of a tight skirt." Ruth jumped up laughing to herself.

25

We soon finished our first G and T, it's my turn to go and get the second round. I hoped that no one was watching while I slide down from the stool. I soon returned with the drinks "I was being eyed up by a bloke that was sat on a bar stool. He may suit you as you're into young men he must have only been our age, when you go to get the next round you'll see him."

"There's a man stood behind you Mary, he followed you from the bar." I turned and who should it be but the bloke that was sat at the bar.

"What the hell do you want?"

"Thought I'd follow you."

"Whatever for? If you're thinking of trying to pick me up you've got the wrong woman, you're too young for me. My mate may suit you, I'll introduce you to her, this is Ruth."

"Hello." he said holding out his right hand to shake Ruth's.

"Aren't you going to tell us your name?" I said sounding annoyed.

"Andrew."

"Andrew what?"

"I'm, Andrew Wills."

"From?" said Ruth looking him up and down.

"Chelsea."

"You're from the posh part of town not like us two."

"Where are you both from?"

"Where are we from Mary?"

"Let me have a think Ruth. At the moment we're living under Waterloo
Bridge."

"That's where the down and outs hang out."

"Tonight we're down and we're out."

"You don't look like you live there to me, your clothes look to up market anyway you wouldn't be able to afford a G and T if you lived with the homeless."

"You shouldn't be so nosy, then we wouldn't tell you a load of rubbish, we didn't invite you join us, piss off." He didn't appear to have any intention of moving, he just stood looking stupid drinking his pint of

26

brown split. "Didn't you hear me, I told you to piss off. We don't want you here. You're spoiling our evening." We carried on talking to each other as if he'd gone back to the bar, knowing full well he was stood behind us listening into our conversation. Eventually I got annoyed and turned around to face him, "Piss off before I go and ask the barman to get rid of you."

"He won't send me packing, I'm the manager of this joint." We both looked shocked,

"If what you're saying is true, get yourself a stool."

"I'm happy standing here chatting, I've only come over because I've a feeling you're on the game and we don't like to have your type in here."

"You've got that wrong for a start because we're not on the game at least I'm not. Anyway tell me why you think that?" I asked sounding annoyed.

"It's the dress, you're wearing" he said pointing towards it.

"What about it? It's my favourite. Ruth and I were chatting about it earlier as it seems to attract men."

"It would attract men. Short and tight calls out come and get me."

"You're embarrassing me, I can see I'll have to put it in the back of my wardrobe and pretend I've lost it."

"That's a good idea unless you want some old man to pick you up."

"The answer to that is definitely NO."

The three of us carried on chatting and laughing together for quite a while, we managed to find out a bit about this Andrew, such as where he lived who he lived with and how long he had worked here. During the conversation he offered me a job behind the bar if I couldn't find an office job.

"I may take you up on the job, the only trouble is I've never worked behind a bar, I wouldn't know how to pull a pint let alone serve someone a Gin and Tonic."

"It's easy enough - I'd teach you. Mary I reckon you would be good behind our bar, you'd attract a lot of customers. It would be far more interesting for you than working in any office. There's just one problem, I wouldn't want you turning up in that dress."

"I told you I'm going to hide it away for life, in fact I may throw it in the dustbin."

"Good." Said Ruth looking at her watch. "We need to go, as we've arranged to meet up with a few girlfriends then go to the new club that's opened up down the road from here. We can get in for free as it's the first night"

"Why don't you wait for me, I'm going their later?"

"No we can't hang around. The thing is we've got to get up early for work, we just want to go and suss the joint. If it's any good we'll be going back at the weekend, then we'll be staying until the early hours." Andrew looked over at Ruth and eyed her up and down.

"That's the same with me, I'll be leaving the club before midnight." said Ruth jumping down from her stool.

"Perhaps both of us will come back here another night. Yeah I'll come back Friday even if Ruth doesn't."

"I'll come back with you, I haven't anything better to do."

"See you both Friday night." Andrew walked away looking as if he was up to mischief. We finished our G and T's and went on our way.

We found the club no different from any other, instead of being given a ticket on the way in, our hands were stamped. While in the queue we were warned by the doorman that they wouldn't put up with any nonsense from the pair of us.

Chapter 4

"You two girls can come in but remember no picking up blokes, especially you in that dress, I've seen girls like you before." he pointed towards me.

"What do you mean this dress is perfect to wear for a night out on the tiles."

"That's what I mean, it's great to wear when you're on the pickup."

"I'll remember that, I couldn't understand why men were looking at me in the pub. I must be thick."

"Yeah you must be." the girls in the queue burst out laughing, while the blokes looked me up and down then cheered.

"That's enough ladies and gents we've had our fun." with that Ruth and I with a few others were allowed in. It was dark inside, we could hardly see where to put our feet let alone where the bar was. Once in the main area I asked a waitress where the toilets were.

"You passed them on the way in, you'll have to go back down the passage, the Ladies is first on the right, mind the step as you go in, especially wearing those shoes. I've warned you as we aren't insured for people tripping over."

"Thanks."

We both went back down the dark passage, there was at least ten females in the queue for the Ladies. We all stood chatting together, a girl that was stood in front of me was passing around large pieces of cotton wool, she gave me a couple of pieces.

"What do I need these for?"

"To stuff in your bra to make your tits look bigger."

"Mine are naturally big." I said pushing my chest out in front of me.

"Well hand the cotton wool to your mate, she looks like she needs some."

"You've got that wrong, she's big enough, without having to use cotton wool."

"Well hand it along the queue, some of the other girls will definitely appreciate me bringing along cotton wool. The thing is most men enjoy a bit of tit, they always seem to make a beeline for the large tit brigade. The girls without tits seem to be left stood around the room wondering why they don't get a dance, even though they're better looking than the ones with the large tits."

"I've never thought about having large cotton wool tits, tell me, what happens if you get picked up, do you run to the loo to take the cotton wool out?"

"Yeah that's what you do, I remember catching someone in the Ladies at another club taking cotton wool out of their bra. Once the cotton wool was out she was as flat as a pancake. What the bloke that picked her up thought, I can only dream."

"Hurry up you in there." said the girl who was at the front of the queue and banging on the toilet door.

"I'll wet my knickers if you don't hurry up."

"I don't wear knickers, they're so inconvenient, take yours off join the clan." shouted a girl from the back of the queue. I turned to look at her, she looked a right little scrubber. Suddenly the girl who was desperate for a wee lifted her skirt and started to pull her knickers down when the toilet door opened. I've never seen anyone look as shocked as the girl that came out of the toilet.

"What the hell do think you're doing?"

"Getting ready to wee, I'm desperate."

"You're telling me you're going to wee where you're stood?"

"Don't be daft, I'm getting ready by taking my knickers off here, I've told you I'm bursting, get out of my way or there'll be a puddle on the floor" The girl pushed her way into the toilet. She seemed to take longer than the girl before her. We all remained quiet and calm because if we started shouting and ranting to make her hurry we were sure one of us would be cleaning urine off the toilet floor, due to her being a bit tipsy and not being able to aim straight.

Once Ruth and I had been for a wee we were ready to attack the dance floor. We sat ourselves down on a couple dining room type chairs when a waitress came over,

"Sorry you can't sit here, you have to find yourselves a seat at one of the low tables. After you've sorted yourselves out I'll come and take your order."   She went on her way, we sat for a few minutes to decide what to do as most of the seats around the tables were taken, so we went on a walk about and finished up sharing a large sofa at a table with a crowd of club goers that looked very boring.

"Is it okay if we plonk ourselves down with you lot?"

"Suppose so." answered one of the girls looking a bit glum.

"I'm sorry we're female, perhaps if we were male you'd smile. I'll tell you something if you sit here with a long face, like you are, no man will come over and join you so we may as well sit down."

"Don't take any notice of what my mate is saying, she's not an expert on men, in fact she's useless where they are concerned." said Ruth looking down at the floor and grinning to herself.

"What do you mean she's useless with blokes, she looks quite glam to me and should be able to get anyone. In fact her sitting with us may encourage blokes to come over and join us, with a bit of luck they may even buy us a drink."

"Mary always manages to pick up the wrong type. The last bloke she had punched her in the mouth, guess what, she has dentures."

"Ruth shut up and stop talking about me, if I want these strangers to know about me and my false teeth I'll tell them myself." I shouted at Ruth.

"Sorry, I won't say another word." said Ruth looking stupid.

"Have you decided what you'd like to drink?" asked the waitress.

"I'd like a large G and T please, what do you want Ruth?"

"Same please." The waitress went on her way to the bar.

"Ruth you realise that these will be our forth G and T's tonight?"

"Good, I feel like getting pissed, I'm fed up with being sober." said Ruth

"I'm not getting pissed. Girls and boys let me introduce myself and my mate, I'm Mary and this is Ruth."

"What do you do for a job Mary?" asked one of the boys, laughing with his mates.

"We both work in an office at Oxford Circus. Why are you all laughing at us, you seem to be laughing at me in particular, is there something wrong with me?"

"Nothing's wrong." answered the boy who was trying to stop laughing.

"First of all tell me your name and where you live, then you can tell me what's wrong with me. I'm not laughing at any of you so tell me

what's so funny about me that makes you laugh so much." I said
sounding annoyed

"I'm John I live in a bedsitter behind Selfridges."

"Right John from behind Selfridges, please tell me what's wrong with
me that makes you laugh so much?"

"It's not you as such, it's that dress you're wearing."

"This damn dress makes most people laugh. Tell me why you're
laughing about me wearing it?"

"It's the type of dress someone would wear for a pickup."

"Well, I'm not on the pickup as you call it. This is one of my favourite
dresses, everyone that I have met this evening thinks I'm on the game
because of this damn dress. I'm not going to wear it ever again. When I
get home I'll take it off and throw it straight in the dustbin."

"Three cheers. Mary I'm fed up with people thinking you're a tart
because of this stupid dress and I know damn well you're not, I'll be
glad to see the back of it." the boys continued to laugh while the girls
just looked me up and down.

"You're what I call a tease." called out the bravest of the boys.

Once we settled ourselves on the sofa and started chatting we found
that we had quite a bit in common with our new found acquaintances,
which included music and clubs. Eleven o'clock soon became midnight,
when Ruth and I had to decide whether to go home or stay until the
early hours.

"Mary, what are we going to do as it's past midnight, I'm expected
home before one?"

"You decide what we should do. The reason I left home was because
I was fed up with having to let my parents know the time I'd be in every
time I went out the front door. Now I can stay out all night if I want to.
The thing is Ruth you still live at home and your parents will be
wondering where you are. First things first can you ring them, are they
on the phone?"

"No, we don't have things like phones, we're not millionaires."

"I suggest we leave here as soon as possible as you can't get hold of
your parents. I'll never forget the night I didn't get home until three, my
mother was waiting at the top of the stairs, looking down at the main

entrance to all the flats. I was in big trouble and was grounded for quite a few weeks. Seeing her looking down at me from the landing gave me the fright of my life, you see she was stood there in the dark, all I could see of her was a shadow. That's how I came to leave home, I couldn't stand being grounded and having to account for all my actions. I looked in the Evening Standard for a cheap bedsitter and left without even having a job to pay the rent, the rest is history as they say."

"How the hell did you pay the rent without a job?" asked one of the girls,

"Don't ask, that's my business." I tapped my nose

"We better leave immediately. Come on Mary." said Ruth looking down at her watch.

At the tube station Ruth and I said our goodbyes. I caught the tube to Hammersmith and walked back to my flat, Ruth went on her way to Bethnal Green. She had to change on to the central line at Oxford Circus which was a worry for her as it was past midnight and sometimes strange men slept on the tube. All I could do was hope that they weren't on the tube tonight, if they are she'll be telling me all about her eventful journey home when I get into work tomorrow.

By the time I got home it was a quarter to one, very late for me especially midweek. I crept up the stairs without bumping into any of the other tenants that were returning late. Once inside my flat I poured myself a large glass of cold water to have before going to bed. I'm hoping that this water will stop me from waking up with a hangover. It must have been the Gin and Tonics I'd drunk because it suddenly occurred to me that I hadn't looked in the cardboard box that was on the top shelf in the sitting room cupboard for the flat contract. Instead of waiting until Thursday evening I pulled the armchair over to the cupboard and climbed on to the arm, in my tiddly state I pulled the box down and fell off the chair onto the hard floor, the glass of water went everywhere. I laid on the floor stunned for a few minutes when there was banging on my door.

"What's happened Mary?" I laid still for a few more moments, "Mary are you okay? I heard a loud bang above me, it was as if you were

coming in through the ceiling. Please answer me, are you okay?" I tried
to get up but couldn't so I crawled along the floor to the door.

"I'm not too bad, I fell off the arm of the chair, the chair landed on
top of me. Hang on a minute Steve, I'll try and unlock the door. The
thing is I'm a bit tiddly and I can't get up from the floor." Eventually I
managed to stretch up to unlock the door.

"What the hell have you been up too?"

"Not much, I've had a few Gin and Tonics, obviously one too many." I
said looking up at Steve from the floor.

"I can tell that, it must be the one to many that's done this, in fact it
has done it very well indeed."

"I can't get up."

"Give me your hand and I'll try and help you, up you get my dear."
with great difficulty Steve pulled me up on to my feet.

"Thank you Steve, come in, close the door behind you then I'll make
you a cuppa." I said slurring my words.

"A cup of what?"

"Tea, coffee or you can have a glass of water in fact you can have
anything you fancy as long as I've got it."

"I'll make us both a mug of coffee, you go and sit down in the chair."
Steve wandered into the kitchen, I waited to hear him scream and he
did.

"What a bloody mess your kitchen's in Miss Mary," shouted Steve "I
don't reckon you've washed the dishes or cleaned anything in here for
weeks, you're what my mum would call a messy pup."

"The dirty dishes are there because I'm a very busy person, look at
tonight I've only just got in." I replied hiccupping, "You can't expect me
to start washing dishes at one o'clock in the morning then get up for
work the next day. I only wash up once in a while and that's when I've
run out of clean dishes. I'll tell you what I do, I spend a Saturday
morning every fortnight washing up. If I had somewhere to plug in a
dish washer I'd buy one. I shouldn't be talking to you about my dishes
and the state of my kitchen as it is none of your damn business. I
wonder what your place is like?" silence reigned. I sat quietly in the arm

chair and waited for my coffee to arrive. The next thing I knew, Steve was nudging me awake.

"How long have I been asleep?"

"Only about ten minutes."

"You've made the coffee, thanks." I said looking around "Where's the box that fell out of my cupboard with all my bits, what have you done with it?"

"I've put it on the worktop in the kitchen, your flat contract is in the box."

"You're telling me that you've been looking through my private papers."

"No I haven't read any papers, the flat contract was on the top of everything else. I recognised the paper it's written on, it's the same as mine, blue."

"Are you sure you haven't been reading my private papers?"

"Promise, I haven't read anything."

"Move out the way I'm going to spew up, let me through, please, to the kitchen sink." up it all came G and Ts' along with the coffee. "That's better." I said looking ashamed of myself, "let's get back to you, why are you here Steve?" I said plonking myself back down in the chair,

"Because you fell over and disturbed me with the bang on the ceiling, I thought you were coming through."

"It's almost two o'clock and you're not in your pyjamas, have you just got in, where have you been?"

"I haven't been anywhere, you woke me up, I had to dress to come up here, as I sleep in the buff, I'm sure you wouldn't want me to visit you naked, I'm not a pretty sight."

"I haven't seen a man naked for years. I can't remember what a man looks like in the buff."

"Pretty grim."

"You better go before I invite you to stay, you look quite fanciable in my drunken haze."

"Meaning?"

35

"I wouldn't mind having sex with you, you stupid dick head." Steve looked shocked, it was as if he had never been spoken to like this before.

"I'll have to go away and think about what you've said, I only wanted you to be a pub friend and now you're telling me that you fancy me."

"Because I've said that I fancy you, doesn't mean that I love you, it just means what I have just said, I fancy you." With that Steve left in a hurry leaving me sat in the arm chair.

Chapter 5

Thursday came, Ruth was in the office long before me. By the time I arrived she had been in full flow telling all the girls about her night out with me and what they had missed by going elsewhere. Marg was explaining to Ruth how they had met a group of rugby players in the pub down the street from Oxford Circus, apparently they were game for anything and were the reason for the girls not turning up at Trafalgar Square. I burst out laughing and went on to ask what time they got home because I was quite sure they'd made up the story as they looked quite perky for having a night out with rugby players. They all looked a bit surprised to be asked this and one girl let it slip that she was home in bed before midnight.

"In other words you all had a quiet night not like Ruth and I."

"What did you two get up to?"

"Everything you can think of, we were even given cotton wool to put in our bras."

"Whatever for? If it was to make your tits bigger, they needn't have bothered as they look big enough from here, you must be at least a size thirty eight D." I looked down at my breasts.

"I'm not that big."

"They look big from where I'm standing, tell me what size you are then, Mary dear?"

"I have no idea, as I don't wear a bra, I never have and never will, I don't know my size, I haven't a tape measure so I can't measure my tits."

"Ruth did you use the cotton wool?"

"No I didn't, any way they didn't offer me any." said Ruth looking flushed,

"I'm not going to say another word about our night out, I'm going to go over to my desk and get on with my boring typing."

Like any other morning silence reigned until lunch time when we all had to decide whether we could afford to go and get a bite to eat. Ruth and I went across the road to the sandwich bar where we sat on stools and discussed whether we were going back Friday night to the pub to see Andrew. Ruth was upset as her parents were like mine waiting for her to return home last night and threatened her with being grounded for two weeks.

"Can you imagine me being grounded for two weeks at the age of twenty four?"

"I told you what I did, I left home immediately when my parents suggested I stayed in for a couple of weeks."

"Going back to tomorrow night, if I can come out for the weekend, do you think I could come and stay at your place?"

"I only have one bed we'd have to sleep top to toe!"

"What the hell do you mean, top to toe?"

"You up one end and me down the other, with our toes meeting in the middle, unless one of us pick's someone up. Ruth I have my eye on Steve who lives down under, if I play my cards right I may be able to sleep with him then you can have my bed to yourself. Remember, I don't want you bringing some strange bloke back to my bed."

"I'll make sure I don't do that."

"Right you arrange to stay over with me tomorrow and Saturday night. When you go back home on Sunday your parents will have missed you so much, they won't ground you."

"I'll tell them I'm staying the weekend with you when I get in tonight. Tomorrow I'll bring my weekend bag to the office."

"I look forward to the weekend."

"I hope the weekend will be as good as I'd like it to be, in other words, brilliant."

I arrived home Thursday evening and tidied up the best I could. After looking and reading the flat contract I plucked up the courage to phone the landlord from the hall phone. I gave him my four weeks' notice. He didn't sound very happy as he would have liked me to have given in my notice on the last day of the month or the first day of the following month. He seemed to think it would be easier to find someone to take over the flat at the beginning or the end of a month.

"I can give in my notice any day I fancy, there's nothing in my flat contract to say anything different."

"Well if you insist on giving it in tonight that's okay with me but you'll have to give me something in return for me giving in."

"What the hell do you mean?"

"Sex is what I mean and need, I understand you're quite good at performing." he shouted down the phone.

I was shocked, "That's not true, you're talking a load of rubbish." I screamed at him.

"I know all about you, I'm a close friend of your Derek, he's told me all about your antics. I'll be round a bit later, it's no good thinking I can't get in because I can. I've a spare key to your flat."

"He's not my Derek. You're not having any of me today, tomorrow or any other day." I screamed down the receiver before banging it back down on to the base.

I turned to go back upstairs when the front door opened and there was Steve walking into the hall, having returned from the library. My face must have been a picture because before I knew it he was asking what had happened. I explained about giving in my notice and how the landlord wanted to visit me later tonight. Steve didn't seem surprised, apparently a girl that used to live across the landing from me had the same problem when she gave in her notice.

"Anne lost her deposit because she packed up all her things, called a taxi and was gone within an hour, never to be seen again."

"Do you think he'll come around to see me?"

"I've no idea. I'll tell you one thing I wouldn't leave like Anne did. Mary he'll win if you leave, he'll bank your deposit then he'll be quids in."

"I'm not going to walk out, I've made up my mind about that. I'M GOING TO WORK MY NOTICE ON THIS FLAT." I shouted so everyone in the building heard me.

"Good, I'll keep an eye on you."

"Thanks."

"It's Friday tomorrow, fancy going to the pub?"

"I wouldn't mind but my mate Ruth, is coming to stay."

"The three of us could go out together. Your mate Ruth, is she the one you went out with the other night?"

"Yeah, we both had one to many, we've planned to go back to the same pub in Trafalgar Square tomorrow night."

"If you like I could go with you, what do you think?"

By this time I was a bit flustered "I'll sleep on it, I'll leave a note under your door saying yes or no, in the morning."

"Before you go up do you fancy coming in for a coffee? It will only be instant as I don't have a percolator."

"No thanks, may be another time, I'm going to bed early, also I must organise the door so the landlord can't get in."

"I'll help."

"No, I don't need help, I'm quite able to sort the door out myself."
Steve didn't look happy, he turned and went into his flat without saying another word, I went upstairs.

After having a close look at my door I decided that it was easy to stop the landlord from entering when I was home as the lock was a Yale with a dead lock. The worry I have is that he could enter my flat while I'm out so he could be sat waiting for me when I return. From tomorrow evening and over the weekend there won't be a problem as Ruth will be staying with me. If he's in here when we get back from somewhere one of us can go and phone the police.

Friday morning I wrote a note and put it under Steve's door telling him that I'd let him know after work about him coming to the pub with us as Ruth may not want him there.

I arrived at the office at my normal time of ten to nine, all was quiet, I don't know what was wrong with the girls as they had their heads in their work as if they were workaholics and that's far from the truth. I've worked here for over three years and I've never seen any of the girls so quiet and typing as if they hadn't a minute to spare.

"Morning you lot, what's up? do you realise it's only just nine o'clock and you're working like beavers as if you haven't any time to spare?" Joyce put her finger up to her mouth as if to say be quiet.

"You may as well tell me what the matter is, come on Audrey tell me what's up, you're usually good at spilling the beans."

"I'm not spilling any beans, you'll have to ask the boss."

"We've all had a warning." shouted Marg.

"What about?"

"For not getting on with our work, if we don't settle down we may have to get on our bikes."

"He can't tell me to get on my bike as I have only two and a half weeks' left to work in this dump. Where I'm going to work when I leave I don't know, but no one need ask me to stay, because I'm not for staying."

The girls continued to type without saying another word, before I knew it lunch beckoned.

"Anyone coming out with me?"

"Where are you going?"

"The first place I come to that sells cheap sandwiches."

"Well that will be your normal haunt the sandwich bar."

"I suppose it will be, so who's coming with me?"

No one answered,

"I'll have to go out on my own if no one answers. Ruth are you going to come with me, you usually do?"

"If you want me to but you'll have to wait as I promised to finish typing these pages before lunch."

"I'll sit and wait, don't take too long, I'm starving."

"I don't reckon a boring ham sandwich from across the road will fill you up. It would be better to find a pub and have pie and chips along with a G and T, once I've finished this lot I'll need a strong drink. Mary what about that pub we're going to tonight."

"What about it?"

"We could go there for lunch if it's not far."

"Where are you two going tonight?" shouted Marg.

"Mind your nose, we're going nowhere that concerns you lot." replied Ruth looking peeved

"I'll get it out of you before the office closes. I'm only being nosy, I don't want to go out with you."

"I'm pleased about that, as you wouldn't suit our style. I'm going to get on with this typing, if I don't get a move on I won't have time for lunch."

"Yeah get on with it Ruth, I'll go to the loo and tart myself up especially as we're going for a G and T.

I wandered off to the loo. Marg followed me along with a couple of the other girls. "You realise if you have an alcoholic drink with your lunch you'll be in trouble with the boss."

"We'll only have the one."

"That may be one to many, especially if you don't have any food to soak up the booze."

"Don't be such a spoil sport."

"Well it's true." Said Marg smirking.

"I reckon you're jealous of us going to the pub for a quick one." I said laughing.

"Before you go, you two need to realise that alcohol makes your breath stink."

"Can you smell Gin or is it just Lager and Beer that makes your breath stink?"

"I'm not sure, Gin comes from juniper berries and they have a scent, ask the barman when you get to the pub, he should know, if he doesn't you'll make him laugh. Buy some peppermints to eat for when you get back here, mind you if the boss smells the peppermints he'll guess you've been to the pub as peppermints are an old trick."

"Why don't you lot come with us? Then we'll all be in trouble together."

"After you saying we can't come out with you tonight you've got a bloody nerve to ask us out at lunch time for a drink, anyway which pub are you going to?"

"We haven't decided but most probably one in Carnaby Street, as that's not far from here."

"I thought you may be thinking of taking an extra long lunch hour and go over to Checkers Tavern near Fortnum and Masons."

"You must be joking Marg, we would need to take a black cab, neither of us can afford that, we haven't that sort of money."

"Mary, I've finished the typing are you ready?" called Ruth from the end of the passage.

"Yeah I'm ready, these three are thinking of coming with us."

"We don't want them with us Mary, whatever are you thinking about?"

"That solves that problem, we won't be coming with you." shouted Marg

"Good." called out Ruth. We both left the office and went on our way to the first pub we bumped into in Carnaby Street.

Entering the pub we saw a few customers sat on stools at the bar chatting to the barmen. They didn't take any notice of us in fact they didn't even turn their heads towards us when we walked in. I thought this was a bit strange as I usually receive a nod or a wink from the bar staff but not today.

"This place is a bit odd."

"What do you mean Mary by a bit odd?"

"Odd because the barmen haven't noticed us."

"Why should they?"

"You ought to say why haven't they noticed us. It's not as if they don't like women as they are chatting to the ones on the stools.

"Jealousy gets you nowhere Mary."

"I'm not jealous, the thing is Ruth all bar staff normally give new customers the nod or a wink, forgetting about that, what would you like to drink?"

"I'm changing my tipple to Vodka and Lime."

"That's different, I'm keeping to my normal G and T. I'll see if they've a menu before I get the drinks in." I wandered over to the bar,

"What can I get you?" asked the elder of the two barmen who was smiling away to himself.

"A menu first please."

"We don't have menus, we only sell crisps or cold food like a scotch egg with mustard or chutney. Have a look up at the board that's on the wall behind where you're sat."

"I will, then I'll come up again."

"Don't you want a drink?"

"Yeah of course we do, one G and T and a Vodka and Lime please."

"Go back to your table, I'll bring them over, then you can tell me what you fancy eating."

I went back to the table and discussed the food with Ruth. We decided that coming to this pub was not such a good idea and having an alcoholic drink without having any food was even more stupid, especially having to go back to work. The barman came over with the drinks, I paid up and at the same time explained that we both expected to eat a meal along with our drink, as we could only get a snack we'd be going on our way once we'd drunk up.

"Come and sit at the bar and have a chat with Eric and me. I'll give you a packet of crisps on the house."

"They won't fill us up we need a meal."

"What do you think about sitting up at the bar Mary?"

"Okay, but we can't stay long. I need to get some proper food inside me."

Ruth looked down at her watch.

"We both have to be back at work in twenty minutes, I also need food."

"Where's work?"

"Oxford Circus."

"It'll only take a minute to walk there. Come over to the bar, I'll introduce you to my mate."

We picked up our belongings and went over to the stools which were still warm from the women that were sat on them earlier.

"Right this is Eric and I'm Paul who are you two?"

"Mary and Ruth from where ever you want us to come from." Eric and   Paul looked at us strangely then held out their right hands for us to shake. We settled ourselves on the stools and ate our free packet of crisps and finished our drinks.

"Fancy another?" said Paul taking the glass out of my hand.

"Better not."

"Why ever not?"

"Well we need to get back to our boring mundane jobs, if we arrive worse for wear we may be shown the door."

"It's Friday, I doubt if your boss will notice if you've returned from lunch or not. Most probably he'll be in a pub somewhere getting worse for wear with some old bird he's picked up for the weekend, have another drink."

"I can't see any female wanting to be picked up by our boss with his big fat belly. He must weigh fifteen stone, the thought of him performing makes me laugh. First of all finding his dick would be a job. Sorry I shouldn't have said that, sorry it's the drink talking sorry everyone. Getting back to having another drink, what do you think Ruth, shall we stay or shall we go?"

"Let's stay, as we're having fun, let's chance our luck."

Paul immediately took both our glasses and poured us both a couple of doubles.

"It's goodbye to the afternoon at the office, and hello to the afternoon in the pub." We remained in the bar till two thirty when Eric told us that we had ten minutes to drink up and go.

"What! you're telling us to go after giving us more drinks than you know damn well we should have had."

"Sorry girls but that's how it is, unless you want to spend more time with Paul and myself upstairs in the flat." We looked at each other.

"I wish I'd only had the one." said Ruth slurring her words.

"Well we've both had far more than we should have had so we need to decide what we're going to do."

"Let's go, I don't want to get involved with these two." said Ruth while she started to get down from the stool.

"Are you taking fright after being invited upstairs?" laughed Eric as he walked away to clean the tables.

"Mary I have a problem." Said Ruth looking worried.

"What the hell is that?" Ruth leaned over and whispered in my ear.

"I haven't a rubber or johnny."

"I told you days ago to buy some, two bob for a pack of three. I have some in my bag, I always carry them but I'm not going to let you have one. Go across to Boots in Regents Street and buy some. Anyway Ruth what makes you think you'll need them?" I whispered back.

"The way they're both looking at us, I can see sex is on their minds and I can't see how we can get out of it, unless we run. Getting back to buying johnnies, I've never bought any, which counter do I go to?"

"For goodness sake girl the surgical or pharmacy."

"You coming with me?"

"You must be joking you're a big girl, you just go up to the counter and pick them off the shelf then pay the assistant the two bob, quite easy. Chop, chop." I clapped my hands.

"It might be easy for you Mary but not for me, please come with me." Ruth was nearly in tears.

"Ruth you're behaving like a kid, don't cry."

"We'll be back in a few minutes." I shouted over to the barmen.

Once we'd arrived in Regent's street Ruth told me that she wasn't going back to the pub but she would still go into Boots for the johnnies as she thought she may need them over the weekend. "Whatever's the matter with you, it's not as if you're virgin."

"Mary, I don't want either of those blokes. I couldn't perform with either."

"I wouldn't mind a bit of Paul." I said laughing.

"Eh, that's the drink talking, you're welcome to him. I don't want Eric so I'm going back to the office and pretend to be sober. I'll see you outside the tube station at five o'clock that's if you're not coming back to work."

"At least you're thinking about picking someone up over the weekend which is something." I stood and looked Ruth up and down, "Perhaps you're right about the drink talking, sober, I doubt if I'd give either of them the time of day, I'll come back to the office."

"Three cheers for common sense." said Ruth jumping up and down while clapping her hands. After buying the johnnies we rushed back to the office chatting about what we're going to get up to over the weekend.

"I've got my weekend bag, I've left it under my desk."

"Good."

"I found a dress in my wardrobe similar to the one you wore the other night so I've brought it with me."

"Well, you'll be on your own in the tart dress as I've got rid of mine. I'm going to be little miss prim and wear a frock that buttons up to the neck, mind you it's a bit short, well above my knees, I guess that makes up for the high neck."

"This is going to be a laugh as my dress is three or four inches below my knees but the neck line is very low."

"Where ever did you buy it?"

"In that shop at the top of Regent's street."

"You mean that place around the corner from the office on the left?"

"Yeah that's the one Mary."

"I've only been in there once, I found it quite expensive. Once you're inside the shop, assistants pounce on you. The day I went in I watched one of the customers ask to speak to the manageress. The customer was annoyed about the behaviour of one particular assistant. I overheard her complaining and saying how she wouldn't be going into the shop again to look around let alone buy anything, of course the manageress apologised but the customer was adamant that she wouldn't be going in again."

"That's a bit sad as the clothes they sell are worth having a look at, even if you don't buy any, due to the price."

"Well that's what happened, perhaps I'll go in again one day, yeah I know, I'll go in on pay day."

"If I'm feeling rich Mary I'll go in with you."

"That's a date."

Chapter 6

We arrived at the office door. "Don't say a word to anyone just go to your desk and get on with your work as if you've been sat there all the afternoon, Ruth are you listening to me?" I said poking her in the side.

"There's no need to poke me of course I'm listening, I won't say a word. I know damn well it's best to keep quiet. Mary we forgot to buy any peppermints."

"To late now, one, two, three, in we go." The girls were sat at their desks just as they were first thing. Not one of them looked up or called out hello. We both went over to our desks as planned. I typed away for about ten minutes before I noticed a note on my desk addressed to me from Mr Robbins. I read it, he was asking me to go down to his office first thing on Monday morning, apparently he had wandered upstairs and did a head count and found both Ruth and I missing.

"Ruth," I shouted.

"Yeah, what?"

"Have you got a note from our boss?"

"Yeah I have, he wants to see me before I go home."

"You're joking."

"No joking here, I've got to go to his office at a quarter to five." replied Ruth slurring her words.

47

"It's three thirty, you better try to either sober up or go home. On Monday pretend you didn't see the note because you didn't return from lunch, as you came over all dizzy while out shopping so you went home."

"That sounds a good idea Mary, I'm going to go, are you coming with me?"

By this time the other girls had stopped typing and were listening in, "We're both going home, don't any of you dare to tell the boss that you've seen us."

"Hope you don't get caught on the way out, the thing is the boss has been up here three times this afternoon looking for you two, we're all keeping our heads down. We promise not to say a word don't we girls?"

"Yeah, we won't spill the beans." said Audrey who found it quite amusing. We picked up our belongings including Ruth's weekend bag and disappeared down the stairs and out of the front door without being spotted.

On the way to the tube station I bought the Evening Standard along with the Evening News "What the hell do you want two papers for?"

"To look at the adverts, for a job and a flat. I've only two weeks before I leave my boring old job so I need to find another one as quick as possible. At least I have four weeks to find a flat thank God. Over the weekend you can have a look through these papers and see what you can find for me." I said slurring my words.

Going down the escalator we held on to each other as if we were glued together so we couldn't get thrown off balance. The first tube that came into the station was going to Hammersmith so we hopped on and were back at the Broadway within minutes. Arm in arm we zig zagged our way down the road towards my flat, once indoors we attempted to make our way upstairs. Ruth was in a terrible state, going up two steps and back one.

"Pull yourself together Ruth, hurry up or we'll get caught by Steve or even worse by a stranger from one of the other flats."

"Mary, the drink I've had today is the most I've ever drunk in one session."

"Ruth, you'll have to get used to drinking that amount or more if you're going to be friends with me. You need to try and sober up ASAP as we'll be going out again by eight o'clock. Anyway Ruth getting back to tonight, if you can listen to me without falling over we need to decide if we're going to invite Steve to come out with us, what do you think, will he cramp our style?"

"Let me finish getting up these stairs and into your flat before we talk about tonight and Steve. Mary you should know the answer to that question, you know him, I haven't even seen him at a distance let alone had a chat to him, you should know if he'll cramp our style. A question for you Mary are you hoping to stay the night with him? "

"I don't know, I definitely wouldn't mind a bit of him, if it was offered."

"If that's the case let's invite him, if he cramps' our style we can always loose him. Where will we meet him?"

"Outside his flat. He'll be sat on the bottom step."

"Have you been in his flat?"

"No, I've only been to the door, he never opens it very wide, I've never seen inside."

"Mary you may be in luck tonight, you may see inside more than his flat."

"Stop talking a load of rubbish. I'll write a note and take it down, let's say eight o'clock will that be okay? The thing is Ruth it's nearly six thirty and we have to get ready and also have something to eat."

"Yeah, eight o'clock will do, it doesn't take me long to tart myself up, ten minutes and I'll be ready."

"I take a bit longer than that, I should be ready by eight though. Hey Ruth, do you realise the landlord isn't sat here. I'd forgotten about him saying he may come around, it must be all the G and T's I've had that has made me forget about him. Thank God."

"What the hell would he want to come around here for unless you haven't paid the rent?"

"Of course I've paid the bloody rent, I've no idea why he's thinking of coming round, except he said something daft like he was going to visit me for sex, not that he'd get any, the silly old bugger."

"Tell me is he young or old?"

"Old and fat, far too old and far too fat for either of us."

"Thing is Mary if he had come around he could have come out with us tonight if he was young and thin but not if he is old and fat. Forget what I've said, he's no good for us."

"You've got that dead right Ruth he isn't any good for us or anyone else for that matter as I doubt if it still works."

"Mary we want someone with one that works, not a man with a soft one."

"You've got it, that's exactly what we need, one that works."

I wrote the note and took it down to Steve, the door to his flat was wide open. I called in but instead of him coming out of the door he came up behind me from the bathroom that he apparently shares with two other tenants.

"You made me jump Steve." He explained how he'd just been for a bath as he expected me to say yes about him coming to the pub with us.

"You shouldn't take things for granted, I could have easily said no to you coming out with us."

"Well you've said yes, I thought you would, what's your mate called?"

"Ruth."

"See you both at eight, look forward to it."

I staggered back up the stairs, I don't think Steve noticed that I was a bit worse for wear. Once in my flat and after having a bite to eat we got ourselves organised to go out. Ruth put on her so called tart dress and I found a black and white geometric creation in the back of my wardrobe which was very boring compared to what I normally wore. At least I found a pair of Mary Quant cream tights to wear along with a pair of black patent leather shoes, these went well with the dress.

Eight o'clock soon came around, already to go we went downstairs where I introduced Ruth to Steve, he was all spruced up. The three of us wandered down the road to the tube station, Steve kept looking at us strangely. I could only guess it was because we were talking a load of dribble while walking along arm in arm - trying to hold each other up.

"You two don't half talk a lot when you're together, I can't get a word in edge ways." we both started to laugh "What are you laughing at? I can't be that funny."

"You're not funny, it's us, we're laughing at ourselves, we've had a drop too much to drink."

"You're telling me that you've both been on the bottle before coming out to go to the pub."

"You've got it dead right Dear Steve, we went to the pub at lunch time. I had my usual G and T and Ruth had a few Vodkas and Lime."

"How many did you have for God's sake?"

"Enough."

"Come on tell me, spill the beans, depending on what you had earlier depends on what you can have when we get to the pub."

"You're talking to us as if you're our dad. We don't have to tell you, anyway Steve you'll soon know if we've had too many because we'll fall over. If we don't fall over you'll know we only had one or may be two."

"Thank goodness I didn't have anything to drink before leaving home, I'm boring, and sober." said Steve sounding annoyed.

"From where I'm stood Steve you look very boring, very boring indeed." said Ruth laughing away to herself.

"Just because I haven't come out half sloshed like you two, doesn't mean I can't enjoy myself. When I've had a few drinks, I can enjoy myself with the best of them, wait and see young Ruth."

"I'll wait and see alright. I understand from Mary that you run home once you've had a couple."

"What rubbish have you been telling your mate?"

"I haven't told her any rubbish, she's just guessing that you'd run home."

"You look the type to run home."

"It might be you two running home tonight, it definitely won't be me. I'm game and prepared for anything."

Chapter 7

Silence reigned as we arrived at the station. Steve offered to buy the tickets, I think he thought we were too sloshed to get our purses out. The tube soon arrived and we were on our way to Trafalgar Square. Once on the square we had a look around and to our surprise the bloke that was sat by the fountain Wednesday evening was sat in the same place again.

"That bloke is sat there again Mary." said Ruth pointing towards him.

"Do you two know him?" asked Steve looking shocked.

"Only by sight."

"I'm pleased it's only by sight."

"What do you mean?"

"He picks up anything that moves."

"Well he hasn't picked us up but then we aren't just anything or anyone, we're fussy Mary and Ruth."

"If he'd picked you up I'd go on my way leaving you both to your own devises."

"Steve, how do you know him?"

Steve explained that the bloke used to work with an ex girlfriend of his in a coffee bar on the way to the South Bank. He found it easy to chat up the females when he was serving the coffees or when he was clearing the dirty dishes from the tables. While he was working there a lot of money went missing from the till. The manager was sure this bloke had taken it as he kept turning up in expensive clothes, eventually he was sacked. Weeks later Steve read in the paper that the bloke had been to court and had been charged quite a bit of money.

"I'm not going to look in his direction, he's definitely not my type whether I'm drunk or sober."

"When he was here Wednesday evening he frightened me, as he kept walking backwards and forwards in front of me, while I was waiting for Ruth."

"Now you know about him keep your heads down. Don't give him the eye as he may be after a job and imagines that you work the streets, he may think he can become your pimp."

"You must be joking Steve, I wouldn't have him as my pimp, anyway why do I need a pimp? I'm not on the game. I finish work at the stupid office in a fortnight and I haven't a job to go to but I'm not going on the game. I know for a fact that back along I could have earned more money with an escort agency than working in any office but it's not for me these days."

"I'm very pleased to hear that." giggled Ruth

"So am I." smiled Steve knowing full well that I'd worked for an escort agency in the past.

"Now a days I would have an awful job to get customers due to my two false teeth. I would need to take them out before performing. The sight of me without my two top front teeth would make anyone laugh and also put them off the job in hand. I wouldn't earn much money, I doubt if I'd earn any."

The three of us continued to walk across the square. "Who's going in the pub first?" asked Steve,

"I will." I wanted to be first to walk in the door to show the staff and the locals how I'd changed my image which of course I had but only for this particular evening. My face must have been a picture when I opened the door, as I didn't recognise any of the bar staff, also Andrew was nowhere to be seen. "Mary you look in a state of shock and disappointed at the same time, what's wrong?"

"Nothing's wrong Ruth."

"I know there's something wrong and I can guess what it is, first Andrew is nowhere to be seen, second it's different bar staff from Wednesday, am I right or am I wrong?" laughed Ruth.

"You're right, I suppose." I replied slurring my words and looking embarrassed.

"I don't think I should have come out with you two this evening, it's obvious to me that you are both looking for a man and that man isn't me, also you've had far too much to drink for your own good."

"What, Steve you've got that wrong. I had planned to try and get off with you tonight, Ruth's after the manager of this joint but he's not here. Steve there's one thing I will agree with you about and that is that we've both drunk far too much."

53

I said blushing while trying to grab hold of Steve's arm. He moved out of my way.

"Why are you moving away from me, don't you fancy me Steve?"

"I'll have to think about that."

"Don't think for too long, you either fancy me or you don't."

"I suppose I do fancy you." he answered looking stupid.

"Move back then so I can hold your arm."

"Give me a chance girl, before starting all this flirting let me get you both a drink, nothing too strong - I suggest a soft drink."

"Here you go again, behaving like a daddy, no soft drinks here, I'd like a G and T, Ruth usually has Vodka with Lime."

"Don't you decide what I want to drink as I change like the wind and tonight it's going to be Cinzano with whatever goes with it."

"I don't know what goes with Cinzano, is it lemonade or tonic water?" asked Steve.

"Put lemonade with it, I like lemonade that should taste good."

"I'll get a G and T and a Cinzano with lemonade, the smallest they'll sell me." Laughing away to himself Steve went up to the bar while we found a table with three chairs.

"I won't put you through the embarrassment Ruth of getting you sit up on a stool like I had to sit on last Wednesday. I'd hate to think the world could see your knickers along with your suspenders." I laughed out loud.

"Mary I thought you liked it up on the stool, you didn't complain when you got a lot of attention from a few of the men."

"I did enjoy the attention. I don't think you can handle blokes like I can so we're going to sit at a table with chairs."

"Hang on a minute Mary, I have only been out with you socially a couple of times, you don't know what I can cope with and what I can't."

"I'm not daft Ruth, I have eyes and you appear shy, wearing that dress will make you either come out of your shell or run home."

"I shall be my normal self, Mary - shy." I burst out laughing.

"I have an idea, we could swap dresses."

"Don't be so daft you silly bugger, I'm not shy when I see a man I fancy, I won't waste any time trying to get him." said Ruth sounding annoyed.

"I'll keep my eye on you tonight, remember I don't want some strange bloke sleeping in my bed. If you manage to get hold of someone or something go back to his place then come back to mine in the morning."

"Mary, I told you before we came out I'd do that if I got lucky."

After about ten minutes Steve returned from the bar "I need to go to the bog, don't get picked up while I'm away."

Before we blinked Steve had returned complaining about the corridor not having an electric light and also the lavatory was in darkness. We both laughed as he told us how he had attempted to wee in the trough, as he couldn't see some of his urine had gone down his trouser leg.

"I hope that dries quickly and doesn't stain." I said looking towards Ruth who was holding her hand over her mouth while she giggled away to herself. "I don't find it funny Ruth, it's more embarrassing than funny, it's definitely nothing to laugh at." said Steve sounding cross.

"Yeah Ruth, stop laughing at Steve, he doesn't deserve to be laughed at."

"It's the drink that's making me laugh, I'm sorry."

The three of us sat quietly, it could have been for half an hour but most probably it was only about ten minutes before Ruth started chatting away to a bloke that had plonked himself down at the table next to ours with his pint.

"You look lonely."

"I am." He replied, I couldn't believe what I was hearing or seeing. Ruth immediately invited him to join us at our table. Steve and I sat staring towards them in shock. I leaned across to Steve,

"When you were at the bar Ruth told me that if she fancied someone she wouldn't waste any time, I thought she was saying it to sound clever."

"Obviously she meant what she said." said Steve laughing in my ear.

"Steve, what are we going to do, shall we leave Ruth with this bloke?"

"She's your friend Mary, I think we should stay for a while and see what he's like. We can't leave Ruth with a stranger especially in London."

"I'm waiting for Ruth to introduce us to him. Are you listening to me Steve?"

"Yeah I'm listening to you alright but she can't introduce us until she's found out his name." Steve decided to speak to him. "Hi, I'm Steve and this is Ruth's friend Mary." Steve held out his right hand to shake this bloke's but he didn't take the bait he carried on talking to Ruth, ignoring the pair of us.

"Did you hear me, I'm Steve and this is Mary." eventually he looked across.

"Sorry I was far away talking to my new found friend."

"Who are you, what's your name?"

"Stan."

"Haven't you anything else to say?"

"Not really, my business is nothing to do with you two," Steve sat leaning over towards Stan hoping that he'd get embarrassed that he'd either tell us more about himself or leave.

"I'm sort of getting to know Ruth."

Eventually he explained that he lived above a coffee bar in Soho and worked at the far end of Tottenham Court Road. Steve asked him about his job "It's not much of a job, it's not worth talking about."

Both Steve and I got annoyed as he wasn't making any conversation, he was just answering our questions.

"Come on tell us a bit about yourself, it's my friend you're trying to get off with, we need to know a bit about you, before we go on our way and leave you on your own with Ruth. This is London and you could be anyone."

By this time Stan looked embarrassed that he decided to tell us about his job which was a cleaner in a department store at the corner of Tottenham Court Road, he'd only been there a couple of weeks. I told him that he looked as if he could work at something better than cleaning. He went on to tell us that he had left his wife and had come to London as she had too many affairs for his liking. After the forth he left home promising never to return, he also walked out on his job at the local bank. The reason he decided to move to London was to see the bright lights and start living all over again.

"Where was home?"

"Stevenage."

"I've never been there, have you two been to Stevenage?" I asked.

"No, I don't even know where it is." answered Ruth looking stupid.

"I don't either." said Steve.

"It's in Hertfordshire, not far from London." We went on chatting but Stan was hard work, what Ruth saw in him I could only guess, to me he was what I'd call boring, boring and more boring, some would say that was why his wife had affairs. "I'm off to the loo." I said hoping that Ruth would come with me and she did.

"I need a wee."

Ruth got up and staggered along with me. I was bursting, thank goodness there wasn't a queue. I went in the first cubicle but soon came out. "There isn't a lock on the door and it's dark."

"So."

"I don't want someone to walk in and catch me weeing." Ruth couldn't stop laughing,

"When you've sat yourself down and made yourself comfortable on the throne, whistle for all you're worth then no one will walk in and catch you with your knickers down, in other words Mary, whistle while you wee."

"That's a good one, I've never heard of anyone saying or doing that." back I went and weed for England.

Once we had both finished in the cubicles and washed our hands we had a chat about this new man in Ruth's life. "Ruth to me he's not very interesting, I don't think you're going to have a good time with him, even if he's game, what do you think?"

"The same as you, he's a bore."

"You shouldn't have started to talk across the tables to him."

"I realise that now, the thing is he's quite dishy to look at, a real turn on."

"Derek was dishy and look what happened to me. I lost my two front teeth. There's always a reason why people are sitting on their own, the reason Stan was on his own is because he doesn't look interesting, if you hadn't chatted to him he'd either have gone home or he would still be on his own with his first pint. Now you've got to think of a way to get rid of him as you asked him to join you at our table."

"What you have said about you and your teeth won't happen to me as I'm not going out on a date with him, especially now you've told me that he may not be up to it. What's the use of a man with a floppy dick?"

"No use at all. If we stay chatting here for a while Stan may go on his way. I have a feeling that he may get embarrassed as he won't know what to talk to Steve about so he'll leave, unless something untoward happens, like he gets a stiffy at the thought of performing with you."

We remained in the ladies for at least another twenty minutes, when suddenly a couple of girls came rushing in asking if we were Mary and Ruth,

"Who's asking?"

"Two blokes, they asked us to come and see if we could find you."

"Well here we are, what now?"

"They seem to have had quite a bit to drink. I have a feeling they've bought you both more drinks as there are a few full glasses on the table. If you aren't interested in them we'll go back and take your place."

"You can if you like, I don't think you will get much joy from either of them. Stan is as dull as ditch water, we've decided he may not be able to a get a hard so he's no good. The one called Steve always runs home as soon as it gets too hot for him."

"Hang on a minute Ruth, you can say what you like about Stan but I fancy Steve, I've had my eye on him for some time, I think he's worth bothering with. I'm going back to the table to see what's going on."

We returned to the table where our two chairs were occupied by a couple of girls, they were chatting away to Stan and Steve as if they'd known them for a while. The four of them looked shocked at seeing us turn up, "We thought you'd fallen down the plug hole." said Stan laughing at the pair of us.

"Well we haven't we're here." replied Ruth hanging on to me for grim death.

"What have you been doing?" asked Steve looking us up and down.

"Whatever it was it took you long enough." said Stan.

"We were having a bit of girl talk, while we've been away you seem to have got yourselves organised and picked up these two." said Ruth pointing at the girls.

"Well we're not going to sit here waiting for you two, as you both seemed to have disappeared into thin air. The thing is girls it only takes a minute to have a wee not half an hour. You need to remember females are like buses if you miss one another will come along and as you can see two have." said Stan laughing at us. Steve sat looking into space as if he was fed up and not listening to a word of what Stan was saying. I went on to ask Stan if he wanted Ruth and I to get lost, his answer was yes as Steve and him had picked up these two Australians that were far more interesting than either of us. Steve didn't say a word,

"Did you hear what Stan has just said Steve he wants Ruth and I to get lost."

"I heard him, Stan I don't like your manner."

"You'd better get lost as well if that's how you feel young Steve."

"That suits me fine, come on girls, pick up your drinks we'll find a different table." the three of us went on our way and found a table at the other end of the bar.

"That'll teach you Ruth, don't do anything daft again tonight or Steve and I will leave you on your own to pick up the pieces."

"I've decided I have had far too much to drink, one of you can finish my Cinzano, I'm going to have a soft drink and sit here like little miss prim."

"You'll have a job being miss prim in that dress, I can see your stocking tops and suspenders from over here." said Steve laughing along with me.

"If that's the case I'd better stand up and see if I can pull my dress down so you can't see anything untoward, the trouble is it's a bit short but here goes." Ruth stood up but was saved from falling backwards onto the floor by a bloke from the next table. Steve and I had a good laugh at this but warned Ruth not to show any interest in this bloke because if she did both Steve and I would walk. Ruth immediately tried to become focused on our conversation which was mainly about where I was thinking of getting a flat and the type of job I was considering.

At eleven o'clock the barman called time which meant that we could buy one more drink but we had to drink it up within the ten minutes of drinking up time. Instead of having another drink we left. Ruth was in a bad way and insisted on singing the song "Ten green bottles." as the three of us attempted to walk in a straight line with our arms around one another across Trafalgar Square to the tube and home.

Chapter 8

As I hadn't managed to get off with Steve and Ruth was worse for wear we both had to share my double bed. It was an awful job to get to sleep as Ruth had the fidgets and her feet kept touching mine, making me jump. In between this Ruth had to keep getting up to go for a wee it was just as if she had a urine infection. If she'd been a bloke I would have said he was suffering with his prostate. Anyway the night soon became morning, I was first up and dressed. I left Ruth snoring away, she didn't wake until ten o'clock.

"I've a headache alright, if I didn't know any better I'd think I suffered from migraines but I don't."

"I'm going out to buy some milk, don't you go back to sleep, if you have a headache the Panadol are on the worktop in the kitchen."

"You know darn well how you got the headache, if I have to spell it out, it was from all the drink you consumed."

"I guess we both had a fair bit, the thing is Mary we started drinking at midday and only had a break from the booze when we came back here to get ready to out with dear old Steve. Any way where is he?"

"In his flat I suppose."

"Didn't he sleep here with us?"

"No he didn't. I'm going to the supermarket, see you in a bit."

I arrived at the super market where I bumped straight into Steve who was coming out of the main door carrying his weekly shop.

"You're up early, how's your head?"

"Fine, how's yours?"

I went on to tell him what a rotten night I'd had sharing my bed with Ruth and how she was still in bed recovering from the booze and lack of food. Steve mentioned how he'd only drunk shandies while Ruth and I had been on the hard stuff. My face must have been a picture as it went from cream to bright red. Steve continued chatting away about last evening and even though the pair of us had drunk a lot he said we hadn't done anything untoward unless I thought talking about having sex with every Tom, Dick and Harry was wrong. I felt such a fool that I pushed past him and went straight over to the fridge to cool off before buying the milk and going back to my flat and Ruth.

"You're up then."

"Yeah, I'm up alright, don't you say a word Mary just drink the coffee, two Panadol haven't touched my headache."

"Serves you right, perhaps it will teach you a lesson on how much you're able to drink in one sitting, obviously not as much as me, because I'm up and running."

"Shut up Mary." screamed Ruth at me.

"I don't allow people with tempers here."

"Don't speak to me like I'm a child."

"Don't lose your temper in my flat." Ruth immediately left the room banging the door behind her to sulk in the bathroom. While she was away I had a look through the newspaper for a flat. There were lots available but the prices were out of my league. I decided the best thing to do was to visit my parents and see if they would lend me some money or may be give me a gift of a few pounds as there was no way that I could afford the prices landlords were asking without help. After an hour Ruth came out of the bathroom and apologized for her outburst. I explained that I needed to go over to Chelsea to see my parents and said she could come with me as its safety in numbers.

"What the hell do you mean safety in numbers? It's only your parents you're going to see surely they don't bite plus the fact you haven't seen them for over a year, I'm sure they'll be over the moon if you visit."

"You don't know them, they'll be charming in front of you but once one of them gets me on their own in the kitchen all hell will be let loose, the thing is Ruth I have to ask them for money, flats seem so expensive and I haven't got   enough money for the deposit for even the cheapest place."

"You shouldn't have been in such a rush to give in your notice here. Giving in your notice at the office was a good idea, I'd give in mine if I had the nerve as there are plenty of jobs to be had. Working in an office isn't the best job in the world, you can get a job in a restaurant and earn the same amount of money and you get tips while you work there. I've worked as a waitress up West, the tips were brilliant."

"Why don't you give in your notice?"

Ruth went on to explain why she hasn't and won't. Her parents are poor and are so proud of her for getting a job in an office that she doesn't want to disappoint them by leaving.

"You'll be there for the rest of your days if you don't take the plunge Ruth - I dare you to leave. If leaving your job upsets your mum and dad you could leave home and then perhaps we could share a flat up West. There are plenty going behind Selfridges, the only trouble is I doubt if they're as nice as this one, also we may have to share the loo with other tenants. Steve was telling me that he has a problem downstairs with the other tenants washing their clothes in the bathroom sink and leaving them there all day."

"My parents are so poor that I doubt if they would manage living in their flat without any help from me. Mum can't walk very well, she spends most of her time sitting around in doors. I have to get the weekly groceries on a Saturday morning."

"Today's Saturday, so who's getting the food in this week?"

"Dad, he gave in to me coming here but he wasn't very happy about having to do the shopping, he always spends Saturdays down the pub with his mates."

"He leaves your mum on her own every Saturday?"

"Yeah afraid so, he usually goes out around eleven and returns at about ten at night. In the afternoon he goes to the betting shop, the more he wins the longer he stays away from home the more drunk he becomes. When he does arrive home he's not worth speaking too, he becomes aggressive and talks a load of rubbish, as well as a rubbish conversation he demands food."

"What happens if he doesn't get any food?"

"Don't ask, mum always makes sure there is some. A couple of years ago mum didn't cook any supper for him as she was at the end of her tether, he got so cross he turned the kitchen table over and broke one of the wooden legs along with the china that was on the table."

"I couldn't live like that, the only problem I have with my parents is there snooty ways, I call them Mr and Mrs Snooty."

"Do they know you call them that?"

"No, if they did they'd cross me out of their will - they have loads of money. I wouldn't risk mum or dad finding out my name for them. If they did it would mean me sleeping on the streets for the rest of my days. Anyway forget about them for the minute you need to see their best friends who live next door. He's desperate for it and goes up the West End one day a week to try and pick up a female. He told me that his wife was useless in the bedroom and that he'd only got a hard with her once, that was when she got pregnant." we both laughed.

"You know quite a bit about them, what does she look like? I bet she's fat but then again she may be skinny that it would be like shagging bones."

"You're right there, she's as thin as a pin, him well he's the opposite fat. How the hell they manage to meet in the middle I can only guess."

"Obviously from what you've said they don't or can't."

"Mary, what does your dad do for a living if he has all this money?"

"Dad works in the accounts department of a store in Regent's street. It is mum that has the money, she doesn't do anything she wanders around Chelsea like a lady and holds cocktail parties when she feels like it. Her parents, who were my grandparents lived up north in some sort of mansion they were a Lord and Lady, mum has her own money as they died back along."

"She's lucky."

"That's what I told her, she's never offered me any of it. Mum is strange, she made me go out to work as soon as I was old enough which I suppose is not a bad thing but she's never done a day's work in her life. Today is going to be the day I ask her for a bit of my inheritance."

63

"What are you going to do if she won't give you any?"

"Shoot myself in the foot, sorry I'm joking. If I'm desperate which I'm not at the moment, I'll have to go back on the game but as I've said before I have two front false teeth which will make a difference to how much money I can make. Mind you I could always have a chat with Alan who lives next door to mum and dad to see if he'd fancy me, he pays well."

"How do you know what he pays?"

"I've had him before, he kept me for a few weeks." I went on to explain to Ruth about how I got involved with him, I think she was shocked.

"Mary it would be better if you got yourself a decent job and found a flat without any involvement with your parents friends. If I were you I'd rather scrub floors than perform with a fat man. Working the streets wouldn't suit me."

"I have a feeling you think I used to walk along the streets and show a leg to all the cars that slowed down, that is far from the truth. I used to go into the hotel bars and sit and hope, that's what I would do now."

"I wouldn't have the nerve."

"It's easy enough, you go in, buy a drink, then sit down on a sofa or on a stool at the bar."

"I thought you told me that you belonged to an escort agency?"

"I did belong to one, I also worked on my own. At one point I went to a hotel up the West End where my friend was the manager. I used to go upstairs and walk the corridors. If I caught the night right I got plenty of money. The best nights were Monday to Thursday as reps stayed at this particular hotel on those nights, they were always up for it. I shared the money with the manager."

"Between the pair of you, I bet you earned a pretty penny. I couldn't do that, I'd rather be poor." We went on chatting for the rest of the morning in between drinking mugs of coffee.

Ruth agreed to go over to Chelsea with me. Before setting off for Sloane square I gave mum a call to warn her of our visit. She seemed pleased to hear from me but her voice seemed a bit down in the dumps.

"Is something wrong, you sound a bit down?"

"I'll tell you when you come over. I hope you bring good news."

Chapter 9

Before ringing the doorbell to the flat I explained to Ruth how mum was very good at getting a bottle of booze out of the cupboard instead of offering a cup of tea to any of her visitors.

"Please don't accept anything to drink other than a cup of tea, if mum manages to get you to say yes to booze she'll drink along with you until she's completely off her head."

"If you'd told me that earlier, I would have had second thoughts about coming over."

"Well I've told you now, here goes." I rang the bell, after a while the door opened and their stood mum glammed up as if the Queen was coming to tea, not her daughter plus her daughter's friend.

"Please come in, lovely to see you. It seems ages ago that you were living here with your dad and me."

"It was over a year ago when you kicked me out after a row with you and dad."

We made ourselves at home on the sofa, mum repeated how wonderful it was to see me and how well I looked.
She didn't seem to notice I had false teeth – thank God. It was a shock when she offered us both a cup of tea along with sandwiches and cake from Harrods, instead of alcohol. She went on to explain how she'd fallen down the stairs a few months back after having one too many and how she'd finished up in hospital with a bad back. I asked her why she hadn't contacted me so I could visit, the reason she gave was that she hadn't got my phone number, I looked at her in amazement.

"I did give you my phone number, you should have looked after it. I'm not giving it to you again as I'm moving flats as soon as I find somewhere else to live. Getting back to you and your back, are you better?"

"I have an awful job sleeping, I take pain killers before I go to bed, they only work for a few hours, then I either take two more or get up and spend the rest of the night on the sofa."

"What about the booze?" silence reigned for a few minutes, then she went on to tell me she hadn't had a drop since the night she fell down the stairs.

"What did dad say about the fall?"

"Not a lot, it was partly his fault." she went on to tell me that they were having a row, over an affair he was having with a woman at work. He told mum that it had finished but she had her doubts as he's always going out on his own. "Look at today his office closed at midday and it's now three thirty and he hasn't arrived home."

"Mum if he arrives home while we're here ask him where he's been, I'll know if he's telling you the truth."

The three of us chatted together until dad eventually walked in on our conversation, he seemed pleased to see me but seemed a bit distant towards mum.

"John, why are you late home again?"

He went on to say that he'd been to a travel agent and had booked a holiday for the pair of them to go to the Canary Isles. Mum looked shocked as he had never taken her on holiday, he always said his wages wouldn't run to it. His normal speech is, 'if you want a holiday get your cheque book out then I'll join you on any holiday you would like to take.'

The three of us looked surprised, mum got up and gave dad a kiss on the check then offered to make him a cup of tea. "It's a shock to my system you booking a holiday for the pair of us as you've always said your wages wouldn't run to a holiday. How did you pay for this holiday, John?"

"I can't even arrange to take you away for a few days without you thinking I've been up to something."

"No you can't because in all the years I've known you which must be over thirty you have never booked to go away anywhere so you must have a guilty conscience. What do you think Mary?"

"Mum is right dad." I answered while looking him up and down. Ruth looked at the pair of them then came out with this statement, "This is the first time I've met either of you so I don't know if you've booked this holiday because you're feeling guilty or not. I would like to think it was because you love your wife and wanted to give her a surprise treat."

"That's what it's supposed to be, we're going in a couple of months' time." I followed mum who was beaming from ear to ear into the kitchen to help with dad's cup of tea and at the same time have a private chat regarding money. I explained about the flat and how I needed some money for the deposit on the next. "You give me a good reason why I should give you of all people a few bob. This is the first time you've visited since you left home, in fact today is the first phone call I've received from you in a year. I guess you were only phoning because you wanted something and I'm right, how much do you want?"

"I need the deposit for a flat, thirty pounds would be nice please." Mum looked at me strangely,

"What's happened to your teeth? It looks as if you've got dentures in the front. I'm your mother - mother's notice everything. I'm not stupid so what has happened to your teeth?" shouted mum sounding shocked. I explained about Derek and how he hit me in the mouth. I made up a story about it being an accident.

"I doubt if it was the first time he'd hit you, if you're still seeing him, it won't be the last." I felt stupid. "Let me have a look in your mouth. Your teeth used to be straight and pearly white, now they seem to be set at an angle both sides of the dentures and all of them appear dirty. Do you drink red wine? if you do that is what has caused the discolouration or it could be tea or coffee as they both stain."

"I don't drink red wine but I do drink quite a lot of tea and coffee."

"It must be the tea and not visiting a dentist. If by chance you're visiting one he can't be giving your teeth a polish. I know you're not seeing my dentist as he told me the other day that he hadn't seen you for at least eighteen months."

"I go to Mr Chow at Leicester Square, he's very kind and also very cheap." I said looking embarrassed.

"That's why your teeth are dirty, I doubt if he's ever given them a polish when you've had a check up."

"I have not got money like you for things like that. If I had money I'd still be seeing Mr Diamond, also I wouldn't be asking you for a few bob."

"Your teeth were so nice when you lived here - straight a pearly white. You used to see Mr Diamond every six months. I realise I paid the bill, it was worth it though for my lovely daughter to have great teeth."

"I would see Mr Diamond again if I was treated."

Mum went on to say that she'd have a think about that. "Tell me who organised the dentures was it a NHS dentist or did you manage to go privately?"

"Mr Chow sorted my mouth out, he's a NHS dentist. I'm quite upset about the dentures, I know they don't look very good and my own teeth on both sides of the dentures look awful."

Mum went on chatting about money, my teeth and how I should be able to manage without her help. She told me I wasn't to get excited about having money from her because first of all she had to find her cheque book and that could be difficult as she isn't organised.

"I'm not the tidiest of people as you know, it could be anywhere. Two or three days ago it was in the drawer in the hall. I looked there this morning and it's missing, where it is I don't know."

"I must have got my untidiness from you, I can never find anything. It took me ages to find my flat contract."

"Yes you must have. I hope you're not on the bottle as that is catching and once you've caught it, it's difficult to give it up."

"No I don't drink alcohol never have, I doubt if I ever will. I only drink tea/coffee and soft drinks." I said lying through my teeth.

After that we went back into the sitting room where Ruth seemed happy chatting to dad.

"Here is your tea darling, enjoy it."

The four of us sat looking at each other wondering who was going to start a conversation. It must have been a good five minutes before mum asked dad if he'd seen her cheque book. Dad blushed and nearly tipped his tea down his trousers in fright.

"John you look a bit shocked at me asking you about my cheque book."

"I haven't seen your damn cheque book. I don't understand why you need to ask me. I must go to the bathroom."

"While you're there put your head under the cold water tap to cool off."

When he eventually returned he looked like he'd put his head in a hot oven instead of under the cold water tap as it was still bright red.

"John, your face is still bright red. I bet you took my cheque book and used it to book the holiday that is why your face is red - red with embarrassment. I'll know sooner or later. Mary, back along your father took my cheque book plus credit card then spent money from the credit card on flowers for some woman he was seeing. I was stupid enough to forgive him. JOHN, I AM NOT GOING TO FORGIVE YOU THIS TIME." shouted mum as loud as she dare.

"I have not taken your damn cheque book" replied dad looking daft.

"If you have you know what you have to do, GO AND PACK YOUR BAGS. Behind you is the front door for you to leave by." Mum looked upset as she left the room to look in the drawer, she soon returned with her cheque book.

"I know you put it back in the drawer when you went to the bathroom as it wasn't there an hour ago." shouted mum in dad's face. Dad sat looking down at the floor like a naughty school boy.

"It's time for you to move and start packing."

"Sorry."

"That word doesn't mean a thing to you, if it did you wouldn't have taken my cheque book again. Before you start to pack you may as well tell me what you have used it for and how much money you have spent from my current account."

"I've only spent a few hundred pounds out of your couple of million." said dad smirking to himself. "What I spent it on is my business and nothing to do with you."

"There's no need to smirk or be rude to me. Mary, the last time this happened my solicitor suggested I got shot of your father if he did this again and he has, go and start packing now John."

Dad left the sitting room. Ruth and I sat looking at one another. I made a face that suggested to Ruth that we should leave. "Mum, Ruth and I are going. I'll ring you as soon as I find a new flat, here's the number of the flat I'm in at the moment, don't lose it again. When dad has gone give me a call if you'd like a chat."

"I'll do that. It won't take your father long to move out. Most probably he'll move in with Allan, his mate who lives across the road on his own. They make a good pair. Allan's wife left him back along, she was fed up with him going up to the West End hotels once a week to pick up a tart. His wife never found out where they went to perform, I always thought he paid for a room at the hotel but his wife was not so sure." When mum was saying this Ruth was grinning to herself as she knew I had met Allan up the West End and knew exactly where he took me and other girls to perform. Thank goodness mum didn't notice me getting more and more flushed by the minute.

"Mum we're going before you embarrass us anymore about old men and their performances. I look forward to your phone call"

Chapter 10

While we walked back towards Sloane Square tube station Ruth wouldn't stop yapping about my parents and how mum had told dad to get out while we were sat in their apartment.

"Going with you to the flat was nothing like I was expecting, in fact it turned into a complete nightmare for me."

"What do you mean? I warned you that mum and dad were Mr and Mrs Snooty."

"They're snooty but not snooty enough to be called Mr and Mrs Snooty. I never dreamt in my wildest dreams I'd be with you when your mum had a row with your dad and decided to tell him to get out - it was embarrassing. I thought they were happy living together, if you'd told me that they may be parting company I definitely wouldn't have come to meet them." replied Ruth sounding upset.

"Don't get upset about them. It doesn't worry me that mum told dad where to go, serves him damn well right, it's his own stupid fault, he shouldn't have had a mistress or two. I reckon the last straw for mum was dad taking her cheque book AGAIN and having the nerve to use it."

"I wouldn't have stood for that. It's bad enough him having a mistress but spending your wife's money on one is damn disgusting. I would have told him to get out years ago."

"So would I. One thing's for sure neither of them realised that I had gobbled dad's best mate Allan, thank God."

"Perhaps they were too embarrassed to mention it."

"I know them well enough, mum would have said something or given me one of her looks and she didn't."

We both had a good old chuckle in fact we were still laughing while we were trying to buy our tube tickets. The ticket attendant got quite cross as he couldn't understand what we were asking for due to us laughing.

"For goodness sake stop your laughing, if you can't you may as well tell me the joke so I can laugh along with you."

"We can't do that, it's not suitable for a ticket attendant."

"Hurry up the pair of you and tell me where you're going." he said looking annoyed.

"Let's go to Trafalgar, we can always walk on to Covent Garden or Oxford Street from there."

"Have I got it right you want two tickets to Trafalgar?"

"Yeah, that's what I said." I paid up.

Once out in the open at Trafalgar Square I could see the bloke who was here the other evening sat by the same fountain soaking his feet. "What the hell does he think he's doing." shouted Ruth nodding towards him.

"I don't know, go and ask him." I replied. "I bet he lives on the streets, Steve said he hadn't a job. It looks to me as if he hasn't a home either, if he had he would have washed his feet before coming out."

"Mary how can he have a home if he hasn't a job?"

"He can't."

"In other words he's sleeping rough, most probably under Waterloo Bridge with the rest of them." Out of nosiness we walked towards him, obviously the closer we got the more we could see of him and his clothes. His shoes were not worth wearing as the heels were coming away from the main part and his socks were almost none existent.

"Come on Ruth, I don't want to get any closer he's far worse than I ever imagined. If I get closer I'll have to find a peg for my nose, as most probably he honks."

"When my mum was younger she worked at the local hospital as nursing auxiliary, some of the patients were a bit like that old boy. One old woman arrived with fleas in her hair, mum's job was to help the trained nurse cut the old woman's hair. Mum itched for a week."

"Eh, I wouldn't want to look after someone like that."

"Mum loved the job, she's always saying if she could walk properly she would still be doing it. Not all her patients had fleas in fact this was the only one she'd seen in three years."

"How Steve can suggest that dirty old bugger could work as my pimp. All I can think is the bloke has gone downhill since Steve met him in the coffee bar."

"Let's get back on the tube. I don't fancy staying around here."

"Okay, Ruth where shall we go?"

"To be honest I'm starving, we could get off at Leicester Square then have a meal in Soho?"

"I've never eaten in a Soho restaurant." We bought another couple of tickets and went on our way chatting as if we were the only ones on the tube.

"With all your experience with men Mary, I'm surprised that not one of men has ever taken you for a meal in Soho."

"I don't know Soho at all." I went on to explain that the nearest restaurant I'd been in to Soho was one down the bottom Regents Street. "The men looked ancient and were with young ladies about twenty years there junior obviously on the game. The men kept looking over their shoulders to see who was coming into the restaurant as I guess they didn't want to get caught."

"Who were you with?"

"A regular from the escort agency. I used to meet him every two weeks, he was married and bored with his wife. He told me how feminine I looked compared to her, apparently she'd forgotten how to look like a female. When he took her out and a about he got funny looks from people as she wore dungarees and her hair was cut extra short, like a man"

"It sounds like she could have been a bit of a dyke, in other words Mary she may have been a lesbian."

"Oh my gosh, I hadn't given that a thought. Know wonder he was up West taking out real women from an agency."

"Mary, it makes me feel sick. I know I shouldn't ask but did you perform with him?"

"Ruth, we used to meet for a meal in a posh restaurant. You remember this, being an escort doesn't mean having sex it means the man has paid to go out with the woman socially. If the man asks the woman for sex she can always refuse as it's not part of the agency contract. I only agreed to have sex with Ken the once and he insisted on using a rubber, even though I was on the pill. Thank God."

"I've another question for you Mary. Did he have a place away from where he lived with his wife, to take his women and to wash his bits?"

"Ruth you will make me cross in a minute as it's none of your damn business if he washed or not."

72

"Sorry." replied Ruth.

"Ruth if you need to know more about Ken here goes, if he felt rich apparently he rented a room from his mate for an hour or two - that is where I went with him"

"If he wasn't feeling rich what did he do?"

"How the hell do I know. I only had sex with him the once. Most probably he found some out of the way place to perform and before going to the out of the way place I bet he washed in the public lavatory." I said sounding exasperated.

"Mary, perverts could have been watching him. Someone told me back along about a man looking through the key hole at a bloke sat on the throne in a public lavatory, he was caught red handed by a detective and was arrested." Suddenly the tube stopped at Leicester Square where we got off.

"I've had enough of this conversation, let's find somewhere to eat."

Once out in the open we made our way to Garrick Street where we soon found a Chinese restaurant which looked quite respectable. On entering we were ushered to a table that was being set for four people.

"We only need a table for two."

"I thought you would be eating with a couple of gentlemen friends that's why I have put you at this table." said the waiter eyeing us both up and down. I pretended that I didn't understand what he was on about.

"We haven't come in with a couple of men, you can see we're on our own." I said looking around to embarrass the waiter. If we hadn't been hungry I would have suggested that we left immediately, instead we both put our heads in the menus to sort out what we wanted to eat.

"I think that waiter imagines the pair of us are on the game." whispered Ruth.

"I think he did. We need to remember we're in Garrick Street and it's a Saturday evening not the middle of a shopping centre at lunch time and this is one of the areas that the ladies of the night hang out."

"Mary, you're saying the waiter thinks we're tarts that have called in hoping to be picked up while eating a meal?"

"Yeah, I reckon he thinks that."

"That's a joke Mary as I've no idea how to pick someone up for a bit of the other. It must be you Mary that the waiter thought was the tart, there's no way that he thought it was me - yeah it has to be you – it's the way you look at men when you're speaking to them."

"Ruth, you don't behave like you're Miss innocent, I keep seeing you giving men the eye."

"Shut up Mary, I'm not going to listen to any more of your rubbish."

That was the end of the conversation, we ordered our meal and sat in silence while eating it. After paying the bill we went on our way to the tube station and home. It must have been nine o'clock by the time I put the key in the front door. We both plodded upstairs in silence hoping not to disturb Steve if he was in.

Inside my flat we both had the shock of our lives, sat in my one and only arm chair was the landlord. "Miss Huggins you're home at last. I've been here since three o'clock waiting for you. I've made myself at home by making a cup of tea and eating what I could find in your cupboard which of course isn't a lot. How you survive by eating such a small amount of food, I don't know."

"You've got a bloody nerve to come into my mate's flat, you've no right to be here."

"I have, I own this place and I have a key."

"My friend pays rent to you so that makes it her flat as long as she pays the rent."

"I'm sorry young lady but Miss Huggins has been expecting a visit from me haven't you my dear?"

I explained to Ruth that I was expecting Mr Jones at some point but wasn't expecting him to be sitting here when we returned. I lost my cool and started to shout and rant. I told the landlord to get out immediately and if he didn't I would be calling the police, as he'd entered my flat without permission, also he'd taken food and drink from the cupboard.

"I told you on the bloody phone that I would be leaving in four weeks, it's now down to three fucking weeks, this fucking dump will be empty in twenty one days. I'll need my deposit back by that day, to put down on a different flat. **GET OUT NOW** before I phone the fucking police. Don't you dare come back in here while I pay you rent or your life won't be worth living. If you don't send the deposit by post and you don't fucking phone to tell me how and when I'll get the money back a friend and I will be round at your fucking place knocking your door down for my money. There's no fucking hiding place for you old man. **GET OUT**."

"Not so much of the old."

"Go home and look in your bloody mirror, you look old to me as well as fat. How you can think anyone would want to ride you, I don't know. It's all in your fucking mind fatty," with that I pushed him towards the door. Ruth followed, "Why are you saying all this rubbish to him Mary?"

"Before you leave I'm going to answer my friend's question in front of you. The real reason this old man has come around to the flat is because he wants me to have sex with him before he'll hand me back my deposit. Can you imagine me performing with him?"

"It would be a bit of a laugh. Being serious no I can't, in fact I can't imagine anyone wanting to perform with you Mr. To start with I think it would be difficult to find your fucking dick as I can imagine rolls of fat hiding it." We both burst out laughing and pushed him out of the door on to the landing.

"That got rid of him."

"Thank God we didn't have any alcohol while we were out as we might have had one to many, then when we returned and found fatty here we would have had a job to get rid of him also he may have insisted on us having a three some."

"Eh Mary, talk about something more wholesome. Just looking at your landlord makes me feel sick let alone having to think about performing with him."

"Okay, let's talk about flats and jobs, I have to find both in the next couple of weeks."

"That's a bit boring for a Saturday night." Ruth answered looking a bit fed up.

"I have an idea, while I sort out the newspapers you go and buy a couple of bottles of wine from the off license to cheer us up while we look through the papers. I'll pay for the wine as it's my suggestion." I gave Ruth a few bob and sent her on her way, she soon returned. I'm not sure what she was thinking about because one bottle was Blue Nun the other was Mateus Rose'. "Ruth I didn't think you liked white wine, I definitely don't so you'll have to drink the Blue Nun."

"I thought it would make a change."

"It may be a change for you but not me. I'll be drinking ALL the Mateus Rose' myself"

"Pig."

"Well you made the mistake so you'll have to drink the Blue Nun." silence reigned while I found the glasses.

"Don't you have wine glasses?"

"No, I don't have the money to buy sets of different glasses for different drinks. I only have tumblers."

"I've never had to drink wine out of a tumbler."

"I can assure you the wine will taste the same and have the same effect whatever you drink it out of. I've had to use a cardboard mug before now - the type you take on picnics. Think yourself lucky, I've known people to drink their wine out of the bottle or use a coffee mug. I realise it may not be ladylike enough for you but the wine will taste just fine unless it's corked."

"Oh well here goes, cheers to the wine in a tumbler."

"Cheers Ruth."

"Getting back to the newspapers which am I going to look up, jobs or flats?"

"Flats, sit over there with your white wine. Pen coming over for you to mark the flats that you think look suitable for me." We settled ourselves down, before we realised both of us had drunk both bottles of wine.

"That didn't take long." I said slurring my words,

"What didn't?"

"Us drinking our wine. We must have needed it as we have drunk both bottles in half an hour, perhaps we have become alcoholics." I replied laughing.

"You may be one but I'm not. The thing is Mary it's catching and you have caught it from your mum. She may have given up the bottle but I bet she still has a glass of some thing or other in secret when she feels down."

"What about your mum and dad, you said yourself that your dad comes home drunk most Saturday nights, perhaps you've caught it off him. At least my mum doesn't go down to the local."

"She wouldn't as you call her Mrs Snooty, Mrs Snooty she is. Her type never go to a pub. I imagine if she ever has a drink outside her own home it would be in a friends flat or house of the same calibre as hers."

"Shut your mouth Ruth, I thought we were friends and friends don't normally shout at one another like we are especially about ones' parents."

"We're friends or we were before we started this stupid argument because we have had far too much to drink in a short period of time."

"You gave me the money to go to the off license, so it's your fault dear Mary."

"I didn't think it would cause an argument. The trouble is Miss Ruth people always say the truth once they've had one to many, and you've said a few things that are not very nice."

"You have as well dear Mary. Let's say sorry." Ruth held out her arms towards me to have a hug.

"I'm going down to see if Steve's in. If he is, I'm going to persuade him to come up and make us both a coffee as I'm not able to put the kettle on, at least that's what I'm going to tell him." Said Ruth laughing to herself.

"Ruth, he's my friend not yours. I'll go down to get him." I staggered out the door on to the landing where I sat on the top step and slid down on my bum to the ground floor - like a child. I stayed put but shouted out to Steve, after a few minutes the door to his flat opened. He looked shocked at seeing me sat looking up at him. I explained in my slurred state what had happened. He was a bit peeved but he did agree to come up and put the kettle on for us. To get back up the stairs Steve helped by giving me a bit of a push, half way up I fell back onto him which of course made him more annoyed than he already was.

"How much have you drunk? I bet the pair of you haven't had any food." Steve shouted down my ear.

"Yes we have but I can't remember what we had. We went into a Chinese in Garrick Street earlier this evening, the waiter thought we were both on the game, which was a laugh."

"Hold on to the banister and start walking up the stairs Mary. Try and be sensible, or I'll go back down to my flat."

"We'll both try to be goody goodies especially for you dear Steve."

"Mary, sarcasm is the lowest form of wit."

"I'll remember that, that's if I can remember, as my memory's terrible."

Once on the landing and still holding on to me for grim death Steve opened the flat door.

"Here I am, Steve is with me, he's making us both a coffee."

"I'll show him where everything is." said Ruth getting up from the arm chair as if she owned the place. Pointing out into the kitchen she went on to explain exactly which cupboard the coffee was in along with the sugar.

"Who the hell do you think you are? first sitting in my one and only armchair like lady muck, then explaining to Steve where my coffee is kept. If anyone needs to tell him where things are in my flat it should be me, not you."

"Sorry Miss Snooty."

"Stop it the pair of you. If you don't shut up I'll leave, then you won't have any coffee."

We both looked at one another and grinned. "I don't care if you don't put the kettle on for us, we had coffee before we drank the wine, we just wanted you to come and visit us."

"Now I'm here I'm making coffee for the three of us. I don't care whether you drink it or not - I'm making it. Before you start telling me again where the coffee is Miss Ruth, I don't need your input as I made coffee in this kitchen the other night." Steve went storming into the kitchen and left us both in the sitting room. Ruth put her tongue out at me. "Enough of your silly nonsense Ruth, if you don't watch it you'll be going home to your mummy and daddy after drinking your coffee. I'm quite capable of showing you the door and pointing you in the direction of the tube." Hearing us arguing Steve came back into the sitting room and once again told us to shut up as he thought we should be good friends.

"What makes you think that clever clogs?"

"Well you both have parents that drink far too much. Look at Ruth's dad he drinks and your mum drinks as much as she can get hold of."

"You're right about Ruth's dad but my mum has given up the bottle for a cup and she says that she is tea total. Just to let you know clever clogs she told me that she hasn't had any alcohol since the day she fell down the stairs drunk."

"Do you believe her?"

"I'm trying to but I'm finding it difficult, we all know once anyone drinks daily they eventually find it almost impossible to give up the bottle."

"Look at yourselves, I reckon both of you are verging on being alcoholics. You two may not think you drink a lot but you do, look at the other night and now tonight. Tell me how long it has taken you to drink two bottles of wine between you? Come on tell me."

"Half an hour." I answered laughing

"There you go, both of you drink far too much. Mary you take after your mum who seems to drink gallons if she has the chance. Ruth, well you drink far too much for a little person and take after your father."

"Getting back to our friendship, having drunken parents doesn't mean we have to be friends."

"To me you make good friends especially when you're sober."

"Thankyou." we both replied in harmony.

Steve went on yapping and telling us how I'd find it easy working for an escort agency. He reckoned I wouldn't refuse sex with anyone especially after a few Gin and Tonics.

"Ruth did Mary tell you what she said to me while coming up the stairs?"

"No."

"She could gobble me all night." laughed Steve.

"I don't believe you Steve, Mary would never say or do that."

"Well she did say it, didn't you darling?"

"I can't remember, anyway enough of the darling. I'm no one's darling. I doubt if I ever will be with two false teeth in the front of my mouth."

"One day Mary you'll find someone who'll be your darling as long as he isn't another Derek."

"Go and get our coffee, I'm gasping for it." While Steve was out of sight I rambled on to Ruth.

"I thought Steve had taken a shine to me, now I've found out that he doesn't fancy me. If he did he wouldn't be talking about me finding another bloke, or would he?"

"Mary, it's no good asking me, you keep saying that I'm no good with men. When he comes back in I'll do you a favour and ask him what he thinks of you."

"I'll go in to the lavatory then you can ask him." I whispered.

"That sounds a good idea."

"You two seem to have calmed down thank goodness. Take your coffee Mary and you Ruth." I gave Ruth the nod and left for the lavatory. Ruth explained to Steve that I needed to know if he fancied me. Apparently he looked a bit surprised as I'd asked him this question a few weeks ago. "You didn't give Mary a straight answer and she wants to know if you fancy her."

Steve stood starring into Ruth's eyes,

"I'll ask you one more time, do you fancy Mary?"

"I could if she didn't drink so much. I'm not used to girls that drink like both of you."

"Are you saying if she didn't drink you may be interested?"

"May be." he smiled.

"I'll tell her, if she gives up the drink she may be in with a chance, have I got that right?"

"Yeah, but I quite fancy you."

"What, that's the last thing I expected to hear, I never dreamt that you'd be interested in me." Steve laughed and held out his arms to give Ruth a hug.

"If you fancy me more than Mary, what are you going to do about it?"

"Nothing, I don't want to rush into anything that I may regret."

"Well put your arms down, forget about giving me a hug. I reckon you should drink your coffee and go back down to your dump." Before Ruth could say another word Steve had left, banging the door behind him.

"Mary, come out, Steve's gone." whispered Ruth while putting her head around the corner of the lavatory door.

"Did I hear you say Steve's gone?"

"Yeah." Ruth went on to say he was in a rush as he wanted to watch the telly.

"I hope you asked him if he's interested in me."

"I asked him alright, he would be interested if you didn't drink."

"Are you sure he said that? He's never commented on my drinking habit. In fact when I've been out with him he has bought me G and T's until they're coming out my ears."

"Well he said that today, as soon as I asked the question he shouted at me about all the G and T's you drink. He also said it was okay being friends with you if you drank but if you were to become his serious girlfriend you'd have to give up the drink." said Ruth looking very serious. "Apparently Steve's parents don't keep any alcohol in the house. If they ever went to the pub it would be for a special occasion then his dad would have a pint of bitter and his mum a sherry or port and lemon."

"I reckon this is why he hasn't got a girlfriend because most females enjoy a drink these days, years ago I don't reckon girls drank much. I'm not going to give up alcohol for someone who lives in a bedsitter, works down a factory on the production line and to crown it all he doesn't even own a decent car so that's the end of dear old Steve being my boyfriend."

Chapter 11

Sunday came, at least neither of us woke up with a headache. "Are you staying here all day or are you going home to your mummy and daddy?"

"What are you going to do?"

"Why answer me with another question Ruth?"

"Because I feel like it."

"Well don't, it's very annoying. Getting back to what I'm going to do today, I may read about the flats you marked off in the papers and wash my smalls. At some point I'll sit and dream about Steve sleeping under me."

"What the hell are you on about Mary?"

"Steve's bed, it may be in the same position as mine but in his bedsitter, this means you and I may have been sleeping on top of him."

"Mary, don't be daft."

"I'm not daft Ruth, the only thing that's been in between both of us and Steve overnight is the mattress the floor and air." an argument started.

"I think you've lost the plot you silly bugger. Last night you were not going to bother with Steve ever again because you had found out that you wouldn't be able to drink alcohol if you became his girlfriend."

"For God's sake Ruth, a girl is allowed to have a dream about anyone or anything and I'm going to dream about Steve sleeping under me."

"I think I'm going to say cheers and go home. I need to have a sleep in my own bed. What with you tossing and turning for most of the night and making me jump with your cold feet touching mine. I've had enough."

"Before you go I must tell you what I'm thinking of doing once I leave my stupid office job."

"Hurry up as I'm going. I hope it doesn't involve that silly bugger down under."

"Don't be stupid, it's about me joining an escort agency again as the money is good and I need MONEY."

"What about your false teeth?"

"What about them, I can afford to get them sorted. If I can't, mum may pay."

"You're telling me that you're going back on the game or are you just going to join an agency and go out socialising with up market men?"

"I've been thinking about doing both for some time. The agency that I've found is on the third floor of a building in Noel Street off Wardour Street in Soho, apparently they have up market clients and also the owner/manager is very posh."

"How the hell do you know all this? Have you been around to the office?"

"No I haven't. On the phone the owner sounded snottier than mum as she told me about her clients."

"That doesn't mean she's snottier it just means she's been for elocution lessons."

"Stop arguing with me and causing an upset."

"Sorry, before I go where the hell are you going to work from and also live?"

"I'm going to get an up market apartment suitable for the upper crust. I've been thinking about living in Tite Street, over in Chelsea."

"That'll cost you."

"Yeah, probably it will but the pay from this particular agency is brilliant. All the clients are toffs, they have plenty of dosh for socialising and sex." Ruth sat down to recover.

"This is a shock to my system. If we hadn't decided to give up alcohol I would say give me a Gin."

"I'm not giving up alcohol I never said I'd give it up, also I didn't hear you say you were going tea total from this morning."

"I said I'd think about giving it up." replied Ruth.

"That must have been in a dream as I can't remember hearing you say that. Here's the bottle pour us both a large gin." I handed over the bottle with two tumblers. Ruth went completely over the top and poured us both trebles.

"Ruth that is far too much for me this time of the day, pour a drop back into the bottle please. You're welcome to drink a treble but it's not for me." it didn't take Ruth long to drink hers down, then she started to hick up.

"That'll teach you, drinking the Gin so fast. A few minutes ago you told me that you're thinking of giving up the booze and you're the one drinking a treble down as fast as you possibly can."

"Well I needed it to get over the shock."

"Now you've had the drink and hopefully recovered have you any questions for me or are you leaving?"

"I haven't any questions for you but I have something to say about how you look. I don't mean to be rude but a bit of advice from me you need to spend some of your hard earned money on clothes and a new hair style, you look a bit dated for toffs."

"That's a nerve coming from someone who can't pick anyone up anywhere due to their dowdy clothes and untidy hair, GET OUT." I screamed.

"I'll see you in the morning."

"No you won't, I'm taking the day off."

"Why?"

"Mind your nose."

"I'm going." Ruth turned and opened the main door to my flat rushed out and down the stairs and was gone before I could say another word.

I spent the rest of the day on my own doing all my odd jobs including sorting out my clothes to see if I had something suitable to wear for an interview at the escort agency. Ruth is right about me being a bit dated around the head, also she is right about my clothes, I haven't bought anything new for a couple of years. I know I need some new clothes along with having my hair sorted into a more up to date style before phoning the escort agency as they may wish to interview me immediately and I wouldn't be ready. After a lot of thought I decided a new hair style should come before the clothes so I planned to phone Vidal Sassoon in the morning and see if he can fit me in before lunch.

Whether I can run to Vidal cutting and restyling my hair is another matter but I can always look out my Barclaycard to use if the price is an arm and a leg.

Sunday night I slept well and was up and running by eight. At nine I rang Vidal's and was lucky enough to be offered an appointment at ten thirty with a senior stylist - Vidal had taken the week off. I had the shock of my life when I asked the price, Barclaycard or not I'm not paying Vidal prices. I put the receiver down before the receptionist asked for my details.

After a lot of thought I've decided to ring the local salon and see if they can fit me in later today and the answer is yes. The cut the stylist chose to give me was geometric, the same as I was hoping to have at Vidal's but at half the price, thank God. I have a plan and that is to buy a monochrome dress along with a new pair of patent shoes these should both go with my hair. I don't need to think about tights as I usually wear stockings while working and I'm sure I have a pair of tights the right shade for the dress in the back of a cupboard.

Going back to the stylist she was very focused not like some that yap away then ruin your hair by cutting a chunk out in a prominent area.

An elderly lady had popped in for a quick shampoo and set and was sat next to me, she seemed very pleasant until she was upset by the way the junior had set her hair.

"You've set my hair as if I've had a perm. I want to look like her," she said pointing her finger directly towards me "not like an old woman from the East End, you shouldn't have put rollers in my hair and made it curly." The junior ran away crying. My stylist excused herself and went after the junior. They both returned after about ten minutes but not before the old lady had a good old chat to me about looking modern around her head.

"How can I go out looking like I'm still living in the fifties," I laughed "I don't find it funny, don't laugh at me. I may be in my sixties but I want to look as if I'm forty."

"Are you on the lookout?" I said trying to keep a straight face.

"On the lookout, what do you mean?"

"Are you looking for a man?"

"I wouldn't mind one."

"If you're looking for a man you'll have to look at more than the hair on your head."

"What do you mean young lady?"

"Look at me, I wouldn't mind a bloke, so I'm sorting out my hair first, then it's going to be my clothes. I know mine are a bit dated so I'm thinking about buying a monochrome dress along with black patent shoes. I'm going shopping for both this afternoon."

"Perhaps I should buy a dress once my hair has been sorted."

"Well if you don't get everything sorted it will be difficult to pick up a bloke especially at your age. Getting back to the dress you're thinking of buying, where are you going to wear it?"

"I'm going dancing at the Empire, Leicester Square on a Thursday. Muriel -that's my mate, met a woman my age who was picked up by a man at the Empire."

"How old was the man?"

"Seventy plus. They still see each other, in fact they meet up every Thursday for a dance."

"Any hanky panky?" the woman burst out laughing.

"I wouldn't think so, I can't imagine some old boy wanting a bit of an old woman."

"You never know, funnier things have happened. I've heard of elderly ladies being picked up by toy boys, some young men enjoy older ladies, like some old men enjoy young ladies. I've often seen toy boys out with ladies your age and they were definitely not their wives or mothers because of what I overheard them talking about. I reckon you're in with a chance, especially if you update yourself."

"You may think I'm in with a chance but if my hairdresser doesn't hurry up and come back to change this awful style, I'll miss the boat. The thing is I still have a good pair of legs and men like women with shapely legs. I reckon I'll look good in a mini, what do you think?"

"I can't see your legs from where I'm sitting so I can't say whether they're good or not. A bit of advice from me, if you do wear a mini you'll have to wear a pair of tights as the tops of your stockings will show especially when you sit down."

"I've never bought a pair of tights in my life, I wouldn't even know where to buy them. I'm used to wearing stockings."

I laughed out loud which annoyed the old woman. "Stop laughing it's not funny, at least I don't find it funny."

"I'm not laughing at you. I'm thinking about my gran, that's my dad's mum. Her skirts were short but not as short as the one you're thinking of wearing. My gran kept having to stand up when she was sat on the sofa, to pull her skirt down to cover her stocking tops. My parents found this embarrassing but my cousin and I found it hilarious as we were only kids and we often saw her suspenders."

"Tights it'll have to be, where do I buy them?" said the embarrassed woman.

"Marks and Sparks."

"That's easy enough."

The conversation came to an end just as the hairdressers returned thank goodness, as I suddenly thought that this woman may start to question me about why I'm here on a Monday morning and not at work. Once my hair was finished I paid up, then hurried out of the saloon. I reckon my hair looked like I'd been to Vidal's without the price tag. I felt like a new woman ready to hit the town to buy a new dress plus shoes for my new life.

Chapter 12

I glanced down at my watch and noticed it was almost lunchtime. I needed to find a phone box as soon as possible to ring into the office and explain why I'm not at work. I walked a few hundred yards and there on the corner of Brendon road was a public phone box. It didn't appear to be in working order, a few of the panes of glass were missing and the receiver was hanging down as if it didn't working. I went in, luck was on my side, even though the line was not clear I could use the phone but I had to hold my nose due to the strong smell of what I imagined was urine.

"The boss is waiting to see you."

"What!"

"The thing is Miss Huggins, Mr Robbins left a message on your desk last Friday afternoon for you to see him this morning and you haven't turned up for work, he isn't happy." I almost choked,

"I gave in my notice two weeks ago, I leave in ten days. He can't have much to say to me unless he's going to tell me to leave now." silence reigned. "Are you still there?"

"Yeah of course I'm here, I can't hear you very well. I don't know what to answer except you ought to come in and see him ASAP. Can you hear what I've just said?"

"Yeah of course I can, but it's a terrible line. I'M NOT COMING IN TODAY," I shouted into the receiver. "I'm not well. I have stomach ache, you should know what that feels like." I continued to shout down the phone.

"I do know what it feels like, it has never stopped me from coming into work."

"Well it has stopped me, you're the firm's receptionist not my boss. You ought not to be telling me what I should or shouldn't be doing."

"Mr Robbins asked me to speak to you on his behalf if you rang in."

"Well I've rung in to say I'm not well and I may be in tomorrow if I feel like it." I banged down the receiver.

I stood and thought for a moment before deciding not to go shopping for a new dress but I'd walk back to my flat to look through the wardrobe and my linen basket as both are full of dresses and other things I may be able to wear.

I took all the dresses out of the wardrobe and laid them in a heap on my bed there must be at least twenty decent dresses in different colours, styles and size. I looked at them all and kept half. The other half I put into a carrier bag to take into the office to sell or give away to my mates. All these clothes can tell a story, which shop they were bought in, how much they cost and where I wore them.

The garments I stored in the linen basket I also emptied on to the bed, out fell dresses along with skirts and jumpers which looked worse for wear. At the very bottom of the basket was an old favourite of mine, a jacket. I've had this for quite a few years and have worn it on many an occasion especially when I wanted to make a splash, sadly it only looks fit for the dustbin, as it's full of moth holes. I gave each garment from the linen basket the once-over and decided to keep a couple of the pencil skirts along with a few dresses that were not too dated and could be worn for an interview, the rest I took down to the dustbin.

In the entrance to the flats I bumped into a middle aged man coming out of a room directly opposite Steve's with a dog. The dog waged its tail at me as if I was its long lost friend, I went over to stroke it.

"Don't you touch her, she may appear friendly but her looks are deceiving."

"She should be friendly she's waging her tail."

"Don't say I didn't warn you."

I stood back and immediately the dog showed her true colours and snarled up at me.

"I reckon you've trained her to snarl at people when they stand back from her." The bloke laughed in my face as if I was stupid. "How how long have you lived here?"

"What's it to you?"

"I've lived here a couple of years and haven't seen you before, in fact my mate Steve who lives in there has never told me about a man with a dog living here. I reckon you have broken into the room and spent time in there without paying rent, in fact you may have only stayed last night. I'm sure Steve would have mentioned you as he would have heard the dog bark." I said pointing down at the dog.

"Mind your hand, she'll bite it if I tell her to." I jumped back out of the way of the dog.

"What's her name?"

"Dog."

"You call her Dog?"

"That's what I said."

"What's your name?"

"Man."

"You must think I'm daft and I'm not. Getting back to your dog barking, I've never heard her bark either."

"Dog doesn't bark"

"All dogs bark."

"Well my dog doesn't, get out of the bloody way, I'm coming through." I stood aside while they went out the door. I followed Man and Dog from a distance and went round to where the dustbins are kept. The man stopped once he was out on the public footpath he turned to look at me, and shouted, "Hey you."

"Yeah."

"What are you called?"

"Lady."

"You've got a bloody nerve calling yourself a lady you're no more a fucking lady than I'm a gentleman."

I hurried back indoors and rushed up the stairs to look out of the window to see which direction Man and Dog were going. Man was hurrying towards the tube station pulling Dog behind him which made me think he didn't live in the room I saw him come out of.

Chapter13

After watching Man and Dog disappear along the road I settled down to watch the television, at the same time keeping my ears open to hear if Steve was downstairs banging about. Nine o'clock came and went I didn't hear a sound from down under so I decided to call it a day and take a bath then go to bed early. While bathing I thought about tomorrow, whether I should go in to work or stay home for another day to sort out a flat, plus a job at the escort agency. The decision I made was to take an extra day off.

Tuesday arrived, once up and dressed I was raring to go. I phoned the escort agency and managed to get an interview late morning. This meant I could go over to Tite Street in Chelsea during the afternoon to look at the flats I'd seen advertised in the Evening Standard, apparently they're available to move into in a couple of weeks' time. One of them may suit me fine as long as I can find the deposit, and the furnishings are in good order. My interview seemed to go well at the agency, at least Miss Celia Bates, that's the boss/manager of the joint didn't give me any funny looks due to her noticing my false teeth. To my surprise she thought I'd have a regular flow of customers as I was far more glamorous than the other girls that were on her books. She made a point of telling me I was first and foremost an escort to keep men company when they're out socialising, no hanky panky, if there is and she finds out I'll be given my marching orders. At least I know where I stand. Miss Bates took a photo of me to put in my folder. After arranging the date to start work I said my goodbyes then made my way to the Chelsea embankment where I'd planned to meet the man from Harvey's estate agents.

By the time I got to the embankment the agent was sat waiting for me on a bench. All I could think when I saw him was here we go again as he was eyeing me up and down, I had to ignore the way he's looking at me as I need the flat in Tite Street especially if I'm to work as an upmarket escort.

"Miss Huggins?"

"Yes that's me."

"I'm Mr Harvey, from Harvey's estate agents." he said jumping up from the bench to shake my hand. "Very pleased to meet you." He explained where the flats are situated which is across the road from the embankment on the corner of Tite street. There are two flats both in the same building, one is in the basement while the other is on the ground floor. Mr Harvey explained how it was possible to go down to the basement flat via the lift from the main hall or go down the steps from the public footpath. Apparently there's a small area at the bottom of the steps to sit in the open and in private.

The ground floor flat is just inside the main door on the right, next to the lift. The trouble with this flat would be the noise from the lift motor and not having an outside sitting area. After explaining all this Mr Harvey took me over to the flats to have an internal inspection of both. I quite liked both but my favourite was the one on the ground floor. The basement flat smelt of damp so if I decided to take one of them it would have to be the one on the ground floor even though it could be noisy.

"Now I've shown you both what do you think of them?"

"The basement flat is out of the question, it smells of damp." Mind you it would be more convenient for my customers coming and going, I thought to myself.

"What do you think of the ground floor flat?"

"Okay I suppose. Is anyone interested in either?"

"You're the first person to view them. I can't offer you either without finding out a bit about you. I have a list of questions that I ask all my clients so if you're interested I'll start to ask them." Mr Harvey had at least ten questions but the most important question to him was what I did for a living, he looked me up and down as if my job couldn't be very wholesome. "I work as a typist in an office over at Oxford Circus."

"How the hell do you think you can afford a flat here on office pay?"

"Quite easily, mum is as rich as shit, she'll pay the rent. She's a Lady with plenty of dosh. She told me back along that she'd help me out with the rent, as long as the flat's in Chelsea. Mum hates the thought of me living in Hammersmith - that's where I live now."

"Where does your mum live?"

"Whittaker Street, near Sloane Square."

"I know it, you need plenty of money to live there. Does she rent or has she bought?"

"Bought. I was born there twenty four years ago."

"I'm going to ask a nosey question, how long has the lease got to run on her apartment?"

"Mum wouldn't tell me anything like that, she keeps her business close to her heart. I'm lucky to be getting money out of her for my rent. Now I've answered your questions how long have you been doing this job?"

"Years, since I left school. I own the estate agents, dad died back along and left it all to me, problems and all."

"What problems are they?"

"As your mum would say mind your own business."

"Why mention problems if you won't tell me what they are? Come on tell me. I don't know anyone who would be interested in your firm with all its problems, that's if there are any."

"I know I'll take you for a cup of tea after we've finished here, then I'll tell you about them."

"I'll take you up on the cup of tea. Before we move on how much is the rent, is there much difference between the two flats? I don't reckon the basement flat is worth as much as the ground floor flat. One it smells of fags plus damp, second it needs decorating, the walls and ceiling are a dirty cream colour – that's caused by fags. Mind you a bit of paint wouldn't go a miss in either flat. I noticed the lavatory in the basement flat was so dirty that it needs replacing immediately. The wash basin in the ground floor flat, well that's got a crack across the middle, it will leak as soon as the tap's turned on. I wouldn't be able to invite friends let alone mum around to either flat as they are at the moment. Mum would go mad especially if she was paying the rent"

"About the rent, the price depends on the person who rents it. I own both along with the freehold I can charge what I like within reason."

"Come on tell me what you'd charge me for the ground floor flat in the condition it's in at the moment."

"Depends whether you're going to live there on your own or get someone to share with you. I'm looking for a young lady to be a Saturday girl for me and you fit the bill. If you took the Saturday job living in one of these flats could be cheap, even free if you looked after me."

"What do you mean look after you?" I asked trying to look as if I didn't understand what the hell he was on about.

"You look the type who knows exactly what I mean, don't kid me you don't." answered Mr Harvey with a twinkle in his eye.

"Okay here goes, you're telling me if I become your tart and perform at the clap of your hands I can live in one of your flats for free?"

"You haven't got that quite right, you'd have to help me out on Saturdays in my office."

"Before you get any grand ideas I can tell you definitely that I'm not going to look after you, so you may as well tell me the true rent for the ground floor flat as that's the one I'm interested in."

"Let's go for this cup of tea in my favourite café in Kings Road then we can have a chat about the flats, rent and the Saturday job." Looking annoyed he locked the doors to both flats then walked on ahead of me as if he hadn't a minute to spare. I tried my hardest to keep up but wearing stilettos it was difficult, in the end I had to take them off and carry them. Mr Harvey arrived at the café long before me, in fact by the time I got there he was sat at a table with a pot of tea for two along with a couple of cream cakes.

"Have you bought me a cake to sweeten me up? If you have I can tell you now, it won't but I do enjoy a cream cakes, thanks." Mr Harvey chatted away about the flats in between filling his mouth up with a cake. He wasn't interested in chatting money. To me the money is the most important part of the conversation as I need to know how much I have to persuade mum to lend or give me. The Saturday job is on his mind, he seems desperate to find a young lady to work from 9.30am to 4.30 pm every Saturday. I'd rather rent the flat full price and get on with my life without any involvement with him. I could imagine him losing his temper and giving me notice if I didn't perform to his liking or he couldn't get a hard then I'd finish up homeless.

"I need you to answer a few questions before I decide to take one of your flats with cheap rent and the Saturday job or with full rent and no complications."

"Fire away, I'm waiting for the first question." He said leaning back on his chair.

"Rates are they included in the rent?"

"I'll have to think about that."

"Is there a gas and an electric pay meter in both flats or will I get a quarterly bill?"

"There's a pay meter for the electric in both flats, there isn't any gas in either."

"The walls need painting in both, will you be getting a decorator in to do this before anyone moves in?"

"I'm not sure, I may leave it for whoever rents the flat."

"Paying for painting one of the flats would cost me. It would take at least three coats of paint to get rid of the nicotine. You allowed your tenants to smoke in the flats so you should have to pay for them to be decorated. I'm not made of money. The washbasin is another matter, it needs replacing, I'm not paying for that either. You're the landlord so you have to pay."

"Being the landlord doesn't mean that I need to make everything perfect for my tenants."

"You're telling me there won't be a new basin in the bathroom, so water will go everywhere?"

"Suppose it will unless you buy a plastic washing up bowl to go on the floor under the basin, or you could stick tape across the cracks and hope."

"You're not a very good landlord, in fact you're a rotten landlord. I have plenty more questions to ask but it's obvious that I won't be taking either flat unless you promise in a written contract to do all the things that need to be done before I move in or pay a deposit."

"I'm not rushing to get a painter or a plumber in to sort either flat out without knowing that you're going to definitely take one of the flats."

"How can I say I'll rent either flat when I haven't seen the end result."

"I reckon with all my wisdom its best that you don't rent a flat from me as I have a feeling you'll cause me a lot of trouble and I can't stand trouble makers." He replied loud enough for the other customers to hear.

"I can't stand landlords who try to pull the wool over my eyes, I reckon you're one of them." I shouted back.

"Got anything else to say Miss Huggins?" said Mr Harvey looking me up and down while smirking to himself.

"No, have you?"

"One question, how much do you charge?"

"For what?"

"You know damn well what I mean, what would you charge me for a night with you?"

"You trying to say I'm on the game?"

"You look like you are."

"Well I'm bloody not." I screamed at him. The waiter immediately came over and asked if I was okay.

"Yes and no, he's asking if I'm a tart as he's looking for one, I'm going."

"You don't need to go miss, he's the one that's going. Come on Simon out you go." Said the elderly waiter opening the door, while all the other customers looked on tutting to themselves. Thank goodness he went quietly.   After all the commotion I had an extra cup of tea while the waiter chatted away to me about how Mr Harvey was always bringing young ladies into the cafe after showing them the flats that he'd shown me. Apparently he's been advertising these flats in the Evening Standard most weeks for quite a few months. The waiter thought Mr Harvey hadn't any intension of renting out either flat to anyone and that he gets his kicks out of showing young ladies around the flats then saying the same rubbish to them as he did to me.

"He makes me feel bloody sick, to start with, look at his size and age. I'm twenty four he's got to be fifty. How the hell he can think I or anyone around my age would want him for five minutes let alone a night." The waiter put his arms up in the air exasperated.

"God knows. Thing is I've known him since he left school which was years ago. He has always been the same - stupid."

The waiter continued chatting about Mr Harvey and how he'd been left the estate agents when his father died five years ago.

"As soon as old Mr Harvey died the assistants that worked for him immediately gave in their notice, leaving Simon in the lurch, as they were all sure they couldn't work for him as he behaved just like he does now."

"Why was he left the estate agents, instead of his mum. Are they divorced?"

"No, Mrs Harvey died years ago, she was living in an old peoples' home, she had been living there for years." He went on to tell me about the day when old Mr Harvey came rushing into the café to tell him about how Mrs Harvey had a stroke that lunch time. Apparently she was always complaining of headaches but wouldn't go to see the doctor. One Saturday she fell down on the kitchen floor while cooking lunch, she had a massive stroke and finished up not being able to walk, talk or feed herself. Simon and his dad used to visit her every evening until she died. The waiter seemed to know an awful lot about them and went on to tell me how old Mr Harvey had a lady friend that he used to see after visiting his wife at the home.

"I couldn't blame him for seeing someone else, his wife was a bit like a vegetable by all accounts. If someone had the nerve to tell Mrs Harvey about this other woman she wouldn't have understood what they were on about. To be fair to old Mr Harvey he made sure his wife didn't want for anything all the time she was in the home, he was very good in that respect." The waiter continued chatting to me in between serving the other customers.

"How the hell do you know so much about this family?" I asked.

"Mrs Harvey was a regular for afternoon tea. She used to chat away to me, she often complained about the headaches she had. I kept saying that she should go to see her doctor but she refused, she said she'd rather suffer on."

"Mr Waiter, how long have you worked here?"

"Years, since I was twenty eight and Simon was fifteen."

"How old are you now?"

97

"To old for you, sixty three?"

"To me that's very old. Getting back to strokes, my gran had one quite a few years ago. Gran managed to walk again, in fact she led a nearly normal life for quite a few years, she died a year ago next month. Let's chat about something more cheerful. Mr Waiter I need to find a flat to live in. I'm out on my neck next weekend."

"What do you mean out on your neck?"

"I gave in my notice four weeks ago. Next Friday is my last day at my flat so I'm in a bit of a rush to find somewhere. The thing is it needs to be in Chelsea, down the road from here would do very well." I told him about how mum is going to help me out with the rent as long as the flat is here. "My niece lives down Tite Street and has a spare bedroom in her small flat, whether it would be any good for you I don't know. It's quite up market with an up market rent to go with it."

"It may tie me over."

"Leave me your name plus phone number, if my niece is still looking for someone I'll give you a call. Before you go I must tell you my name it's Jim Small not Mr Waiter." he said laughing and holding his right hand out for me to shake, he handed me over a pen plus a piece of paper for me to write my details on.

"Thanks, here are my details." I called over to Jim while looking at my watch "I must go or I'll catch the rush hour, bye for now."

Chapter 14

By the time I got back to my flat it was gone seven, I was exhausted and in need of a strong mug of coffee to help me stay awake until bed time. The phone didn't ring or at least I didn't hear it. I went to bed dreaming and wondering where I was going to live. I was up earlier than normal Wednesday morning and found a hand written note that had been pushed under the door. It was from Steve to tell me that Jim had phoned last evening but it was not good news, his niece had already found someone to share the flat with. In temper I immediately ripped up the note and threw it in the waste bin before collecting all my things together which included the carrier bag full of dresses to give or sell to the girls at the office.

Once I arrived at my desk the girls started to question me about what I'd been up too. They admired my hair but were quick to tell me Mr Robbins was waiting to see me and they were sure that he'd notice my new hairdo. "Mary you were supposed to be off sick, not taking two days off as a holiday then coming back with a new hairstyle." laughed Ruth.

"I bet he'll notice your hair, old Robbins doesn't miss a trick." called out Joyce from the other end of the office.

"He hasn't seen me for weeks, so he won't know if my hairstyle's new or old."

"Mary, old Robbins looks out of his window when any of us bang the door shut to come and go?"

"I didn't know that."

"Well he does, Joyce is right Mary. I've seen the nets move in his office many times." continued Ruth as if I was daft.

"You lot are trying to embarrass me before I even get into his office."

"No we're not, we're just telling you the truth about what he gets up too. One morning I had to go and see him and I forgot to knock on the door, I walked in on him playing with himself."

"That's not true, I know it's a lie, you lot are trying your hardest to embarrass me. Before you tell me anymore rubbish I'm going down to see him."

"Go then, remember we're telling you the truth. Don't forget to knock on the door and then wait for him to say come in. The longer he takes to say come in - you can guess what he's doing." laughed Marg.

"Whatever you do Mary don't walk in on him, or you may see something you have never seen before and it might be bigger than you could ever imagine." Joyce said while laughing with the other girls.

"Shut up, you lot are disgusting." I held up my carrier bag, "see this?"

"Yeah." shouted most of the girls.

"It's full of dresses for you lot to look at and to decide if you'd like any of them. I'm fed up with them so I'm selling some and giving the rest away. I've priced the ones for sale. Have a look, while I go and see what our boss is up to."

I threw the bag across the room Joyce caught it. All I could think about while I was going down under was what the girls had told me about old Robbins, the thought of seeing him playing with himself made me blush. Once I'd calmed down I knocked on the door and waited, Mr Robbins didn't answer for a good five minutes. When he eventually came to the door I almost fell into his room as I was leaning against his door.

"Miss Huggins come in, I've been waiting for you, take a seat." he said pulling a chair across the office for me. Being the boss he went around the other side of his desk allowing him to look directly at me.

"What has been going on?" he said looking me up and down as if he was going to proposition me.

"What do you mean Mr Robbins?"

"In simple English you haven't been here for a few days."

"I haven't been well."

"You look okay to me, in fact you look remarkably well. I like your new hair style."

"Thank you." I smiled,

"What's the reason for you not coming into work? Did you have a headache due to drinking to many G and T's or did you pick up a bug from something you ate?" he laughed.

"What's it to you Mr Robbins I'm leaving this joint Friday week so you can decide for yourself what the matter was with me." He sat looking over the top of his spectacles.

"Two days off means you'll have to stay working here for an extra couple of days unless you want two days less pay." I was shocked.

"I can't afford to lose two days' pay. I'll have to stay and work the two days which means I'll be leaving the following Tuesday. Mr Robbins, I have a big problem, as well as leaving this job I'm moving out of my flat Friday week then I'll be homeless unless I can find somewhere else to live. Do you know of a flat or bedsitter in the West End that may suit me to rent - not to expensive?"

After a few minutes of thinking and looking at me he said that if he hadn't a wife I could have moved into his place as he'd got a second bedroom. He continued to ramble on about how he and his wife used to take in female lodgers to make ends meet and how he used to sleep with them for a change of scenery.

"Eh, being my boss you shouldn't be telling me things like that. Now you have, whatever did your wife think about you sleeping with a lodger?"

"She didn't mind as long as she didn't catch me. We've had an open marriage until recently. My wife often used to stay out all night with her boyfriend, that's when I slept with the lodger. I always made sure the lodgers were young ladies that would keep their mouths shut. We're both a bit old in the tooth for that sort of thing now so there's no more open marriage."

"Getting back to me needing somewhere to live, surely if you live in the West End and you've a spare room I could lodge at your place until I found somewhere of my own. I'd be good company."

"I can imagine that but I'm too old for any hanky panky, anyway my wife wouldn't like you staying with us."

"Why ever not?"

"I've told her all about you, she knows everything about you. We may have had an open marriage in the past but we've never had any secrets."

"You can't have told her anything about me as you don't know anything worth repeating."

"I've seen you working the hotels. I had to leave one hotel in a rush back along as you were sat at the bar looking for company. I bet you've been working the hotels while you've been off work this week."

"How dare you think I'm a tart in my spare time because I'm not. I wouldn't know which hotels to go in to pick someone up to start with." Old Robbins continued to look at me over the top of his spectacles.

"It must have been my twin sister you saw, yes it must have been her, she's always up the West End working the hotels it's her full time job. If I need money, I ask mum for some as she's as rich as shit." I was getting myself all flustered.

"Calm down Miss Huggins I'm sorry I've accused you of working the hotels. Getting back to your sister, why doesn't she get money from your mum instead of working as a tart, the thing is it's a very dangerous occupation picking up men for a bit of how's your father?"

"My parents and my sister don't get on, they never have. I was lucky enough to be sent to a private school to be educated properly. Marjorie was sent to the local secondary modern as they didn't care how she turned out. You see Marjorie and I may look alike but we're as different as chalk and cheese."

"That's a bit sad as twins are normally sent to the same school and are usually put in the same class especially if they're identical."

"I can promise you that's what happened. Marjorie managed to learn how to attract men while at the secondary modern. I don't reckon she went to many lessons, she arrived at school for registration each day then spent the rest of her time in the lavatories or behind the bike shed. Marjorie earns far more than I do or ever will. She used to come home from school and tell me what she'd been up to all day. One evening she arrived home very excited and told me how she'd had a sex lesson in the girls lavatory with the most experienced boy in the school, it cost her the five pound note that mum had given her for shopping. I was horrified when she told me, thank God she didn't get the pox or even worse get pregnant. Now you know about my sister."

"Miss Huggins I want to believe you but I have a feeling you've made all that up. If it's true I'm sorry for not believing you, if it isn't you've got a damn good imagination." He said laughing at me and shaking his head at the same time.

"You can think what you like, I can assure you it's true. Mr Robbins don't forget I'm going to stay working here until next Tuesday week." I immediately got up off the chair and went out the door before Mr Robbins could say another word. I plodded up the stairs to be greeted with the girls looking through my dresses.

"You all look like you're enjoying yourselves."

"We are. Before you start talking dresses with us, how did you get on with our boss?" asked Joyce.

"Very well, the only trouble is I have to stay working in this dump for an extra two days, due to me taking the days off. If I leave Friday week as planned I won't get paid for the two days. I can't afford to lose that money as I haven't a job once I leave here so every penny counts."

"What the hell are you talking about Mary, you told me that you're going to work as an escort starting on the Wednesday after leaving here." the girls looked shocked.

"Ruth you shouldn't mention my business to the girls. If I want them to know what I'm going to do for a job when I leave here I'll tell them myself. Anyway girls it depends on a number of things. Friday week I move out of my flat and I haven't anywhere to live. The following Wednesday morning I shall wake up SOMEWHERE without a flat or a job."

"What the hell are you going to do Mary?" asked Joyce.

"God only knows. I thought you lot may be able to help me out. I could always sleep on the floor at one of your places until I find a flat of my own." The girls sat looking at one another. Out of the blue Ruth had what she thought was a bright idea.

"Why don't you go down and ask the boss if you can stay on here for another month then you would only have one thing to worry about instead of two. I don't reckon he has employed anyone to take over from you. I haven't seen anyone come for an interview. Girls, have you seen anyone come for an interview for Mary's job?"

"No." they called out in harmony.

"Ruth I'd rather leave this dump without a job then stay at my flat for an extra month. There could be a problem though as I reckon old fatty – that's my landlord – would put the rent up for the extra month."

"Mary, Ruth has told us what you're thinking of doing, so go and be an escort. I bet the pay is better than here so you would have enough money

103

for the extra rent. Have you worked as an escort before?" I tapped my nose to tell Marjorie to mind her own business.

"Of course she has." laughed Ruth.

"We've been wondering why you have so many posh dresses, now we know."

"Going back to where I'm going to live, is anyone interested in sharing a flat with me in the West End?" Liz put her hand up to say I could move into a room in her flat in Westbourne Terrace.

"At the moment three of us live in a four bedroom top floor flat. We need someone to rent the forth bedroom. I collect the rent for the landlord, it's me who decides who comes to live with us in other words I'm in charge. I reckon the room would suit you down to the ground."

"How much would the rent be?"

"Three pounds a week including the electric."

"That's not bad. Can I come and have a look at it sometime?"

"Yeah come home with me tonight if you like. Enid, who is one of the girls at the flat is having a friend around for supper, there'll be plenty of food so you can stay and eat with us."

"If I like the room and we all get on can I move in this weekend?"

"Yeah."

"What about your deposit Mary, fatty owes you twenty pounds, you'll lose it if you don't stay to see him?" said Ruth being miss matter a fact.

"I realise that Ruth but I'd rather get out of the flat than have to pay for my deposit."

"What the hell do you mean pay for your deposit Mary?" shouted Marjorie from the other side of the room.

"I'll tell you what she means," smiled Ruth, "Mary's landlord wants her to perform with him for her deposit if she doesn't agree to have sex with him he's going to bank the money."

"Shut up Ruth, don't tell everyone. Anyway I'm not going to do anything with old fatty I'd rather lose the twenty pounds. I don't want to catch the pox by performing with him."

"I couldn't afford to give away twenty pounds." continued Marjorie.

"I can't either but I haven't a choice. Fatty has a key to my flat. The other night when Ruth and I returned from my mum's place we found him sat in the armchair. He warned me on the phone that he'd be around for a bit of the other and there he was. I managed to get rid of him, with the help of Ruth. If you lot could see him with his great fat belly and everything that goes with that you'd run and lose your twenty pounds."

"I performed with a fat lump back along, I had a job to find his dick. He insisted on laying on me, God he was heavy. Let's change the subject back to these dresses, I fancy this red creation. How much do you want for it Mary?" asked Joyce.

"A couple of quid will do - it's my favourite. I used to wear it on a Friday or Saturday night when I did the hotels, all the men liked it."

"That's the one for me. I tried it on when you were downstairs and it fits perfectly." Said Joyce rubbing her hands.

"Where the hell are you going to wear it?" asked Ruth.

"To a hotel up the West End. Thing is Ruth if Mary can get picked up with false teeth I reckon I can get picked up with a full set of my own. You see I need a boyfriend I haven't had one for months."

"You mean you haven't had IT for months." All the girls laughed and clapped their hands while Joyce went as red as the flowers on the dress she's buying from me.

"Joyce, on a more serious note, I haven't worn the dress or worked the hotels since having the false teeth. The dress is a good choice, I'm sure you'll find a boyfriend while wearing it. I always found a man when I wore it. Girls look at the clock it's almost lunchtime and none of us have done any work today. We'll need to settle down after lunch or we'll be for the high jump."

"I've told you all before including you Mary that old Robbins won't do anything about us mucking about instead of working - he won't sack us. If he caught us playing about he'd join in the fun. I doubt if you know this Mary Huggins but he's performed in one way or another with most of the girls he's employed over the years. He isn't in a position to ask any of us to get on our bikes. I know such a lot about him that I could report him for inappropriate behaviour towards his female staff." Said an embarrassed Marjorie.

"Who the hell would you report him to, dear Mr Morgan isn't here, who the hell would you tell?" I asked Marjorie.

"I'd find someone. The cleaning woman doesn't like him. I could start by telling her she'd soon tell everyone what he's been up to. Let's forget about the cleaning lady and old Robbins and think about what we're going to do in our lunch break. Shall we try on the dresses and have a fashion show? "

"Yeah let's, but we need some food." Said Liz smiling to herself.

"I could go and get us all sandwiches, that's if you want some. You'll have to give me your money before I go, as I don't want to have to get the money from you when I return, you may refuse to pay up. Before I go remember I've chosen the red dress, don't any of you get any grand ideas by seeing if it fits you while I'm out of the way."

We all handed over money to Joyce and sent her packing to the sandwich bar. While she was out the way the girls tried on more of my dresses. Liz and Joan found a couple which were a bit tight but they liked the idea of this so they paid a few bob for them. After the excitement of the fashion show I put the remaining dresses back in the bag to take home.

Chapter 15

Five o'clock arrived and before I knew it Liz and I were walking along towards the tube station, chatting about which station we should get off at. Queensway and walk or change stations at Notting Hill for Bayswater then walk to the flat. The difference in the price of the tickets was considerable.

"I normally get off at Queensway, in fact I have a return ticket to there. The exercise does me good also it saves me money."

"I don't mind saving money and also I don't mind having a walk. Yeah, let's get off at Queensway."

Once I bought my ticket and we were on the tube it was a question and answer game for the first few minutes of our journey - I asked the questions Liz answered. The thing is Liz and I have never socialised together even though we've worked in the same office for over two years.

During the journey I did manage to find out where Liz came from and it wasn't London. Liz was born and brought up on a farm in North Bucks on the outskirts of a village called Swanbourne. Her parents still live on the farm and are still working it.

"Your parents must be getting on a bit for working on a farm?"

"They are. Dad was brought up on the farm. When he was at school he helped his dad out in the evenings and weekends on the farm. When dad eventually left school he worked full time on the farm, he has never done any other sort of job. Once dad married mum they both moved into the farm house with dad's parents. How they got on living together I don't know as grandad was an awkward old sod. Since I've moved away they're always saying that they may sell the farm and move into the bungalow they rent out to a couple in the village. They keep saying that they're going to give them a month's notice - they never do. I reckon they say it to make me feel guilty about leaving home."

"Knowing that you were brought up on a farm I would have thought you'd have married a farmer and had a few kids by now."

"You must be joking farming's not for me. I hate the farming life, I can't stand it. I joined young farmers after being bullied into joining by mum. My parents wanted me to find and marry a farmer so we would take over

107

the farm when they got too old to run it. I wouldn't be any good at looking after cows let alone sheep. I'm a bit like you, night clubs are my thing."

"Your parents couldn't have been very happy with you."

"They were cross. The trouble started when a girlfriend invited me to come up to London for a day, I loved it and was immediately hooked. Life here is completely different from Swanbourne. I couldn't get away from the farm quick enough. The first thing I did when I got back to work from my day in London was to give in my notice at the stupid office job I had at the Cow and Gate factory in Aylesbury."

"It must have been bad for you to give in your notice so soon."

"It was bad alright, life at the office was as boring and mundane as our jobs at Oxford Circus. The only difference is that life outside of work here is far more exciting than in boring Aylesbury. I would never go back to living on the farm or working in Aylesbury. Some of the blokes that worked on the shop floor as operators at Cow and Gate thought they were the cats' whiskers and wouldn't leave us office girls alone. If they had half a chance to come over to the offices they did. None of them were up to much in the looks department - not that looks should matter. They were not worth getting dolled up for to go out with for a coffee let alone anything stronger."

"They were worse than Derek by the sounds of it but he did look okay."

Liz continued to tell me about Aylesbury and how she thought the only thing going for the place was the jazz club on a Tuesday evening, now she goes to the 100 club in Oxford Street to listen to Humphrey Littleton.

"You'll be surprised to hear this Mary, some of the blokes that go to the 100 club used to catch the train to Aylesbury on a Tuesday especially for the jazz."

"It must have been good jazz. Was Aylesbury any better at the weekends?"

"Depends what you were looking for. There were a couple of dance halls and a cinema. You have to remember RAF Halton is only up the road from Aylesbury, some of the apprentices from there used to turn up at the dances - they didn't interest me. I had a girl friend who got off with one of them. I dread to think what's happened to her, the last thing I heard was that this clever dick of an apprentice had got her pregnant."

"Liz, I bet she is in some grotty flat looking after her baby, while the father is on a tour of duty far away putting his dick where ever he fancied. Anyway enough of that do you ever go back to see your parents?"

"Only when I have to, on high days and holidays. Mum sometimes visits me. She catches the train across from Aylesbury to Baker Street where I meet her, she'd never find her way to my place. I love both mum and dad dearly but they're country dumplings. When I take mum out in London I notice the Londoners looking at her strangely."

"Liz, this should make you smile, I've never travelled out into the country." Liz looked at me strangely "that's not quite true, I spent a couple of nights in Kent a few years ago. I couldn't get back here quick enough - I hated it. I was born and bred here and have been here ever since. Even when I'm on holiday I stay in London. There's so much to do and see. I love it."

"I upset the apple cart good and proper the day I moved out from the farm. Mum wanted me to stay - I refused. I left her crying on the door step. Dad took me to the railway station, it was the worst car journey I'd ever taken with him, he moaned all the way to Aylesbury. The last thing he said when I got out of the car was 'if you don't get on in London don't come crying back here because you can't come and live with us again' I didn't let him see me crying but I cried for England on the train. Thank God, I've never regretted moving here."

"How long have you lived here?"

"Long enough to think of myself as a Londoner."

"How long's that?"

"How long's a piece of string?" said Liz sarcastically.

"The way you're speaking I bet you've only been here a year."

"You've got that wrong Mary, I've worked at the dump for five years, I arrived in London at least two years before working there." The tube came to a halt.

"It didn't take long to get here." I said jumping up to get off.

"We're not at the flat yet. We've a fifteen minute walk once we get out of the lift."

"All the years I've been out and about in London I've never got off the tube at this station. I don't think I've ever been to Westbourne Terrace. What type of area would you say your flat's in, up market or low market?"

"Westbourne Terrace is what I'd call the in between market."

"That'll suit me as I'm not very good at up market, to snooty for me, low market doesn't bare thinking about, the in between will suit me just fine, that's if the room is warm and clean."

Once we'd gone up in the lift and were out on the pavement, I stopped, turned and looked back at the station.

"Mary, you look like you've been caught on the hop, or seen a ghost, what's wrong?"

"You'll think I'm daft. I used to meet a boy at a tube station that looked like this one."

"All tube stations look the same in the entrance." laughed Liz.

"I know that but the whole area looks familiar. To start with most stations have escalators not a lift like this station. I used to stand and wait for Tim over there." I said pointing towards the ticket office. "I remember that tobacco shop across the road. I used to watch the customers going in and out of the shop and think to myself thank God I don't smoke."

"I used to smoke, I found it difficult to give the fags up. It took me a good six months, it's a filthy habit my clothes used to stink. It's strange because some people can make up their minds to stop smoking, then immediately throw the last packet they have in the bin and that's the end of smoking it sounds easy but it's not it's bloody hard. My uncle smoked about twenty to thirty a day. It was him that encouraged me to take up the dirty habit. He eventually got a very nasty cough and had to be taken into hospital with what they called a chest infection. The ward doctor asked all the patients that had the so called chest infection if they smoked of course they did. The next question from the doctor was how many a day. Once the doctor knew how many he told the patients how much money the fags were costing them a week then he told them what a waste of money the fags were."

"What a nerve that doctor had, I bet the patients weren't very happy."

"You've got that dead right Mary they moaned like hell. Uncle was so cross he wasn't worth visiting - so I didn't."

110

"Did he get better?"

"No, he died within weeks of going into hospital. It was him dying that made me give up the fags."

"Going back to this chap called Tim, where did he live Mary?"

"Down the road from here on the right hand side, in a bedsitter he shared with his mate."

"Mary, this will make you either laugh or cry, I went out with a chap called Tim that lived down the road from here about eighteen months ago."

"You're joking Liz." I said looking shocked.

"No I'm not joking. I only saw him for a few weeks he bored me to tears. The only thing he wanted to do other than bed me was go to the Irish pub the other end of Queensway. I didn't mind going to the pub but not every time he took me out."

"I'd have soon got fed up with that." I said smirking to myself and knowing full well I enjoyed the pub life like most Londoners. "Like you I only went out with him for a few weeks that's if it's the same bloke, it sounds like it could be. Do we pass your Tim's place on the way to the flat?"

"Yeah, I'll show you where he lived." We started to walk, after about five hundred yards Liz stopped, turned and pointed towards a green door. "That's where he lived behind that door." I looked in amazement as this was the door I used to knock when I visited Tim.

"Liz, that's where Tim lived. It's a shock to my system finding out that you have dated a bloke that was seeing me, perhaps he was two timing us. I hope he wasn't, mind you I thought he was a bit shifty."

"Mary, I never thought of him as shifty but thinking about him I guess he was. I asked him where he worked, he wouldn't tell me, he said it wasn't any of my business, I guess it wasn't as I didn't have any feelings towards him. I knew I was going to chuck him as soon as someone better came along - he bored me silly. After I gave him up I bumped into his flat mate, while chatting he told me that Tim worked on the production line in a factory at Shepherds Bush.
Whether he was working there when I was seeing him I don't know."

"Liz, Tim told me he was a clerk at Barclays bank at Tottenham Court Road." We looked at each other in surprise then burst out laughing. "When I chucked him he just walked out of my life never to be seen by me again. I wonder where he is?"

"God only knows. I told you he bored me silly, I don't care where he is, he could be digging up the daisies for all I care. One evening and after a couple of drinks he told me that he'd bedded more women than he'd had roast dinners. I reckon he went out with a different woman every week. I remember telling him that he was a dirty old ma

"That sounds about right. He used to swank to me about his conquests especially where and how he picked the women up. One evening he couldn't stop laughing about how he met an extra posh female in the Harrods lift. At the time the lift was extra full, the badge Tim had on his jacket lapel got caught up in this woman's hair. I didn't believe a word he was saying but he continued yapping on about how he took the woman out for a meal to say sorry for what had happened and finished up in bed with her. The woman must have been daft. Mind you the one time I agreed to go to bed with him I thought he was a good screw. This woman wouldn't have realised how good a screw he was until he got her into bed. Tim must have encouraged her by giving her extra alcohol surely she wouldn't have given into him without booze. I don't know what you thought about his bedroom attributes, Liz?"

"Not a lot Mary I'd known better, just because I lived out in the country for years doesn't mean I don't know what a good screw should be like. Now I've shown you the green door we'd better get going, my watch says it's half six. Enid is getting supper for seven o'clock. It will take us a good ten minutes to get to the flat."

"Come on then Liz, left, right," I said hurrying along the pavement.

"Slow up Mary I can't walk that fast."

"Nor could I if I was wearing your shoes, if you take them off and carry them we'll get there in less than five minutes."

"How the hell do you know that? If you've never been to Westbourne Terrace." Said Liz sounding annoyed.

112

"The one and only night I got Tim to take me out other than to the pub we went for a meal in the Chinese restaurant on the corner of Westbourne Terrace."

"That restaurant isn't there any more, it closed over a year ago." Liz explained how she'd been to this restaurant on two or three occasions, the third time she ate there she needed to go for a wee.

"The lavatory was out in the back yard, it stunk. I never sit down on any throne when I wee, I always wee from a height. If I'd wanted to sit down this particular time I couldn't have - due to the filth. I started to wee then a rat came running in under the door, I jumped out of the way of it, my wee went all over my knickers and tights. I was so embarrassed I never went back to the restaurant again not that I wanted to. I reported the restaurant manager to the council and told them about the rat and the state of the lavatory within a week it was closed."

"Eh, that's the last thing I thought you'd be telling me Liz. Change the subject, let's talk about your flat mates, I'm sure they're more interesting than the dirty Chinese restaurant."

"I'll tell you about them but to me they're no more interesting than you or I."

"Well fire away, I've got my ears tuned in."

"I'll start with Enid she works as a clerk in an office in the city, she's the one cooking tonight. Tom - her boyfriend may come around for supper, we'll have to wait and see on that. I better tell you that Enid is in love with him whether it is reciprocated I'm not sure as he always seems to be looking at other girls. Now there's Margaret who works in the local paper shop, she imagines that she's a cut above us all, and can work in the paper shop due to the fact that she comes from a wealthy family, apparently they give her a monthly allowance. The money she earns down the paper shop covers her rent for living at the flat. After you have met her and we're on our own tell me if you think she is rich or poor. Getting back to the supper, Enid's cooking spaghetti bolognese for mains and apple crumble and custard for pudding."

"That sounds good to me."

We plodded along in silence until Liz eventually said "Here we are home at last."

"What here?"

"Is something wrong with it Mary? You look as if it isn't up to your standard."

"It looks a bit grubby from the outside."

"Inside it's just fine, the thing is if it looks posh on the outside burglars may pay us a visit and that would never do. I'd hate to wake up in the night with some yob standing over me. That happened to a friend of mine, it took her ages to recover from the shock. Mary a lot of houses are like this tatty on the outside and posh on the inside. I heard of a film star living in London like us, her excuse was the same as mine."

"Liz, let's go in quick before anyone see's me."

"Mary you're a snob."

"You've got that wrong, I'm not a snob. I just don't want to be seen going up to the door of a building that looks like a dump. People that see us may think we live in a squat." Liz was silent, then out of the blue and in an annoyed state she said, "You'd make a good friend for Margaret as she's always saying what a state the entrance is in, she needs a friend she can have a good old moan with."

"I'm not a moaner."

"I'll give you the benefit of the doubt." said Liz still sounding annoyed. In we went up the stairs to the top of the house.

"What I've seen inside so far, I like."

"Good."

"Liz, before I get to excited and I forget is there a phone in the building as I can't possibly take the room if there isn't one that I can use."

"What's wrong with you going down to a public call box?"

"Nothing Liz, as long as it's just around the corner. I don't want to have to walk all the way back to the tube station to use a phone."

"Yeah we have a phone it's downstairs in the hallway, you can use it like it's a public call box. After supper I'll show you where it is."

"Is it okay to use it for incoming calls?"

"Yeah of course it is. Joan who lives downstairs gets a bit annoyed about having to answer the phone for other people but none of us take any notice of her. If a call is for any of us she'll scream our name up the stairs."

"That's good, I can take the phone off my tick list. I only need to see the room if I like it I'll probably take it."

"Mary go and have a look, see what you think of it. The bathroom is across the landing, have a nose in there at the same time." Liz waited outside the kitchen door.

"What do you think?"

"I had a quick shifty around the bedroom and put my head around the bathroom door what I could see seemed okay. If I get on with the girls I'll take the room."

"Good, I'll keep my fingers crossed as you taking the room will save me advertising and showing strangers around. I'll need a deposit of twelve pounds that's four weeks rent. You can let me have it on Saturday, that's if you move in."

"I'll be bringing mainly clothes with me. I don't have any furniture but I do have some plates and mugs along with some cutlery. My food cupboard over at Hammersmith is almost empty, I decided weeks ago to run it down so I didn't have the problem of carrying food to my new abode."

"Let me take you into the kitchen then I can show you the arrangement we have in the fridge. We all have a shelf each which means there should be an empty area for the new girl."

In we went and there was Enid cooking supper. Liz introduced me, what she thinks of me I dread to think as she didn't look pleased to meet me. "I can't talk now. I'm busy cooking we're having supper at seven and it's ten to seven already." she said looking me up and down as if she didn't like what she saw. Suddenly the doorbell rang.

"Who's going down to answer that?" asked Enid.

"Enid it should be you as most probably it's Dear Tom. I'll go, anything to keep the peace with you." answered Liz. Down the stairs she ran as if she hadn't a minute to spare, she soon returned with Tom plodding up behind her. After we were introduced Tom plonked himself down at the head of the table as if he was in charge. Liz and I went and sat in the sitting room and waited patiently to be called in once the meal was ready.

"Now he's arrived supper's bound to be late. Thing is Tom can chat for England and Enid is so overawed by him that she stops cooking and stands looking at him. I often have to go and ask her to get a move on, before now I've caught him with his hand up her skirt."

"Eh, I hope she doesn't touch him up and not wash her hands after, you don't know where he's been before coming over here for the meal."

"Shut up Mary."

"No I won't. I'll put you off eating Enid's food, I have a story I can tell you."

"Sounds like you have been drinking and you haven't, at least I don't think you have."

"Do you drink in this establishment then? I thought you may all be tea total."

"Mary we're not tea total, we drink alcohol quite often. Anyway getting back to your story, I'm waiting to hear it."

"Here goes. I was invited to a bottle party in a posh area of town, there were two sitting rooms in this particular flat with different music being played in each. I went on my own as I hadn't a man and also at the time I was what one would call a bit of a loner. I stood in the room which I thought was playing the best music when this man came over saying I looked lonely, his exact words were 'You look lonely bird' like a fool I agreed with him. After chatting for a bit he fetched me a drink from the kitchen."

"For God sake Mary hurry up with your story I'm desperate for a wee. If you don't hurry up I'll wet my knickers."

"If you're that desperate go now and I'll tell you the rest when you get back." Liz rushed to the bathroom but soon returned.

"That's better, let me hear the rest of the story."

"Once upon a time."

"Don't be daft Mary just continue with the bloody story. I hope it's worth listening to."

"After a few drinks and him chatting me up we went into a spare bedroom for a bit of hanky panky, guess what."

"Tell me." Said Liz looking peeved.

"A woman started to bang on the door. It was the woman that this George had been seeing for a couple of months. He didn't know what to do as he had never been in a predicament like this before. Cutting a long

116

story short I got him to hide under the bed and I pretended to be asleep in the bed when she walked in."

"What ever happened Mary?"

"The woman screamed at me asking if I'd seen her George I said no." Liz sat looking at me as if she didn't believe a word I was saying. "Well if you have seen George I hope you haven't been playing about with him as he has the pox and has to keep his bits and pieces to himself. I nearly died because of course I had been mucking with him."

"Dinner." Shouted Enid from the kitchen door.

"It's a good job Enid shouted or I may have got you to tell me more of your rubbish."

"It's not rubbish Liz it really happened. I had to go down to the pox clinic, talk about embarrassing."

Chapter 16

The four of us sat down for supper, the table was set for five.

"Where's Margaret?" asked Tom nodding towards the empty space.

"Still down the paper shop." answered Liz.

"What time will she be back?"

"God only knows, perhaps she's been picked up." Said Liz laughing.

"Who the hell would fancy a bit of her? I definitely wouldn't." replied Tom.

"She's got to get her money from doing something. I don't reckon her wages at the shop are enough to pay the rent let alone food and everything else that goes with living."

"Liz, you told me that she comes from a wealthy family and they help her out. What do her clothes look like for God's sake?"

"She looks as poor as a church mouse and her clothes - well they're old." Said Tom laughing.

"Just because she looks poor doesn't mean she isn't a nice person, also she may be good at gobbling." I smiled.

"What do you mean by that Mary?" asked Tom looking at me as if he needed an explanation.

"Don't make out you don't know what gobbling is because I know damn well you should."

"Shut up, I can hear her coming up the stairs." Margaret arrived looking like she had been pulled through a hedge backwards, her hair was everywhere. Her clothes well they definitely didn't look like they belonged to someone that had a bob or two.

"You're late." Said Enid sounding annoyed.

"So what."

"You know supper is always at seven o'clock on a Wednesday."

"I've been busy. The boss has given me extra responsibilities which means I have to lock up and take the key around to his place before coming home."

"I can guess what that means, did he invite you in for a cuppa?" asked Tom.

"What if he did, I'm here now."

"You look like you've been pulled through a hedge."

"Well I haven't. Any way if I had it's none of your damn business Tom."

"I'm going to put all my money on you having been pulled through the hedge. Before you sit down go and look in the mirror." said Tom laughing at Margaret. Margaret turned and walked straight out of the kitchen to have a look at herself. She soon returned but was the colour of a beetroot from the neck up. Tom was full of it teasing Margaret at every opportunity.

"I bet you have been up to something with someone. I wonder who the lucky man was, any idea girls?" I looked around the table to see who was going to join in the teasing – no one did, the girls carried on eating.

"Margaret don't take any notice of Tom, he's a tease. He's always teasing me I try not to take any notice but I know what it feels like, it hurts like hell." silence reigned for a few minutes while Margaret watched us eat.

"For goodness sake girl sit down and help yourself to the food, you'll be hungry if you don't." said Tom laughing in her face.

"I'm not hungry, even if I was I wouldn't sit down and eat my food with you." With that she turned away from the table and went to her room but not before slamming the kitchen door closed.

"That was your fault Tom, you've upset Margaret. You need to mind your manners when you're here as you're a guest in this flat, the reason we allow you to eat with us once in a week is because you're Enid's boyfriend. You have to remember that you mean nothing to the rest of us. This meal is paid for by the three of us without a handout from you. If you want to continue coming for supper don't upset any of us. I hope you're listening."

"Of course I'm listening, I think I better leave."

"Good go, get out." screamed Enid. "I've been waiting for this to happen and at last Liz has said what I've wanted to say for weeks." We sat looking at each other while Tom put his jacket on and went on his way.

"That's got rid of him - freedom at last." smiled Enid.

"You could have finished with him weeks ago you didn't need to wait for me to say something. I couldn't understand why you went out with him in the first place and if you had to why for so long. One evening you even sat down and told me you loved him and wondered if he felt the same about you. I laughed to myself when you said it." Enid stood up and brushed herself down.

"Enough about Tom he's yesterday's news. We women are daft at times. I'll go and call Margaret to come and eat her supper."
Enid soon returned with Margaret looking as if she had been crying.

"Tom's comments aren't worth crying over."

"I've just told Margaret that. You have all done me a favour especially you Liz, I was fed up with him. I couldn't think of a way to get rid of him." By this time I decided to join in the conversation.

"I hope for your sake that he has gone for good and doesn't hang around outside to pester you."

"Why should he do that?" I explained what happened to me with Derek, the three girls were shocked.

"One of the reasons I need to find somewhere else to live is because of that dickhead. Mind you I haven't seen him for weeks - thank God."

"Let's have something strong to drink, I'll go and get the one and only bottle of Blue Nun from the cupboard." Said Enid getting up from her chair, she soon returned carrying the wine bottle but it was half empty. Holding it in the air and sounding annoyed she asked who had been drinking it.

"Not me." Said Liz

"Nor me." Said Margaret. The three girls sat looking at each other.

"If we haven't been drinking the wine a visitor must have had a drop when we were out of the room."

"We have only had one visitor in the last week and that was Tom. He may have been a pain in the back side but I can't imagine him helping himself to our wine and I've never offered it to him, he wouldn't even know if we had any booze let alone where we kept it." I held my hand in the air before saying,

"I can imagine Tom drinking it, some men don't have any scruples. When I was going out with Derek, I had a full bottle of Gin tucked away in the back of a cupboard. One evening I went to have a glass and blow me some of it had been drunk. I didn't say a word to Derek I just marked the label and put it back in the cupboard to see what happened the next time he came around. I caught him red handed having a swig when I returned from the bathroom. I'm not telling you what I did or said but I was cross. Derek was a charmer and could charm the knickers off me. If he hadn't been so charming I would have killed him for drinking the Gin, I'd be in prison now, serving time. Always remember that some boyfriends snoop around girlfriends rooms, he was obviously one of them just like Derek. Good job he's gone, I say good riddance to bad rubbish. Remember it could have been your money. My friend Barbara had forty pounds stolen from her hand bag along with one cheque from her cheque book. This chap knew how to write Barbara's signature and managed to get quite a bit of money out of her account on the one cheque. The problem was she didn't use her cheque book very often. It was over two weeks before she realised what had happened and by that time she had dumped him."

The girls looked shocked. "Let us all have a drink, I know there is only a dribble left in this bottle but at least it's something to drown our sorrows with - I'll get the glasses." Said Liz in a fluster.

"If you decide to move in with us Mary I'll buy a few bottles of wine for the weekend to celebrate your arrival." Said Enid looking at me as if she was enjoying my company.

"I think I would find it fun living alongside you three so I'm going to take the room. I'll move in this coming Saturday."

"Three cheers." shouted Liz.

"Unless you're going to offer me coffee I'll go on my way, it will take me a good hour to get back to my dump. I've one problem about returning there on my own, the landlord may be sat waiting for me like he was the other night."

"I've a suggestion to make, knock on your friend Steve's door ask him to go up to the flat with you." suggested Liz.

"That's a good idea. Getting back to staying for a coffee are you putting the kettle on now Liz?"

"Mary, I always make the coffee after our evening meal but I won't be putting the kettle for a few minutes." replied Margaret who seemed to have cheered up.

"Margaret I'll stay for coffee then perhaps we'll be able to have a chat and you will be able to tell me a bit about yourself like what makes you tick. A nosy question for you how many hours a week do you work down the paper shop, is it full time?"

"I work as many as I like, if I'm feeling poor I work an extra hour or two. Only two of us work there along with the boss he's a bit of a womaniser. The other girl and I have to watch our bums, given half a chance he will slap them when he's passing us. Elizabeth has a short fuse and often gets annoyed with him. I can see her walking out one day, if she does it would mean that I'll have to work a lot more hours unless he found another assistant or I knew someone who could take her place."

"A job like that may suit me. If she walks out, please think of me."

"Mary, why would you want to work as an assistant in a paper shop everything about it is rubbish including the pay along with the boss?"

"A week Tuesday I'm leaving my office job, then I'm working as an escort so I need something to do in between going out for meals with clients."

"I thought working as an escort you would be lying on your back with your legs open." Margaret laughed.

"Don't be so crude, I wouldn't have sex with my clients, most of the men are old and past it. Let's get this straight, if I decided to have sex with one of them, God forbid, I would be sacked, that's if I was caught by the agency. In my contract it says sex is not allowed, mind you over the years I have known a few girls that have performed with their clients but it's not for me."

"Now I've told you about my boring job and you have told me what you're hoping to do for a living go into the sitting room while I clear the decks and make the coffee for us all." Having got my marching orders I joined the other girls. Once we were sat down I asked Enid where she worked - it was in the city.

"What's it like working there?"

"Not bad, the same as most offices. I've been working there for a few years answering the phone and typing boring letters that say the same old thing to the customers like - pay up or you won't be covered with your house insurance. You would be surprised how many reminders I send out each week."

"That would bore me silly writing letters like that every day."

"The only time things change is when the boss goes on holiday then we girls have to watch ourselves as the blokes - married or single, attempt to chat us up to see if we're willing to go into the stationery cupboard for a bit of the other. You would be surprised how many agree. They call me Miss Prim as I refuse to play there silly game."

"So would I, you could get the pox. Imagine having to explain to your boss that you needed time off to go to the pox clinic because you performed with Jim in the stationery cupboard. There silly nonsense wouldn't suit me. I would ring in sick the week the boss was on holiday. I'd rather go without pay than have to perform with a man that worked in the same office as me. You need to remember after performing with these blokes you have to work with them five days a week as if nothing untoward has happened. Before changing the subject back to something more savoury do you lot mind if I bring men back for the night once in a while?" Liz immediately looked up from the magazine she had her head in.

"I collect the rent so I'm in charge and bringing men back for the night is okay as long as he's a steady boyfriend and he doesn't use the bathroom for anything other than the loo and preferably only for a wee."

"Understood." I felt a stupid.

"The thing is Mary I don't want this flat turned into a knocking shop. I hope you understand that it's steady boyfriends only."

"Liz, I understand what you're saying. If I get picked up I'll have to go down a back alley for a quickie."

"That's what people did years ago so you'll have to do the same unless the bloke has a flat or enough money to rent a hotel room. I wouldn't go near a man that couldn't afford one or the other." Smiled Liz.

"I bet if I did what you have suggested Liz I would get caught by the local bobby and finish up in a cell. I would rather go without the sex than have it up against a brick wall then into the bargain get caught." said Margaret coming in with our mugs of coffee.

"Once I've drunk this I'll have to go. Its nine thirty already and Steve may be in bed when I get home."

" Mary, you may be in with a chance if you catch him in his pyjamas."

"I don't fancy him."

"That's not true Mary. You know damn well it's not true, Ruth has told me you fancy him. The trouble is girls he won't go out with Mary because he reckons she drinks far too much."

"Join the club." shouted Enid.

"I'm going before I say too much and regret what I've said."

It was past ten thirty by the time I got back to Hammersmith and the front door to the flats. Once inside I knocked on Steve's door and waited. It was a good ten minutes before he popped his head around the door, as expected he was stood in his pyjamas ready for bed.

"What do you want Mary? You've woken me up. You know damn well I go to bed early during the week and I mustn't be disturbed as I have to be up and running by five."

"I need you to come upstairs to my flat to check that old fatty - our landlord isn't sitting in my flat waiting for me to return. In fact I'm wondering if you would do this for the next three nights."

"That means you're going to disturb my sleep for the rest of this week. Now you've got me out of bed I'll come up but first I have to get my dressing gown." He disappeared back into his flat, he soon returned. "If you need me to come up to your flat each evening for the rest of this week you'll have to call in much earlier than this - say six o'clock. If you're frightened of fatty, you'll have to stay in once you are back here as I'm not going to keep coming up this late due to you wanting to go out on the tiles. Mind you if you agreed to come out with me one evening I'd be willing to check the flat when we got back." Steve smiled.

"I'm far too busy to go out with you or anyone else this week as I'm moving out on Saturday, I'll be packing."

"You leaving here?"

"Yeah that's what I said."

"I'll miss you with all your fun and games." answered Steve half a sleep.

"Steve I'm not moving far, only far enough to get away from old fatty and Derek. You can always visit. In fact you could help me move, then you'll see my new abode."

"Hang on a minute Mary, I'm not in the right frame of mind to think about visiting you or helping you move out. I'm half a sleep, remember you woke me up and got me out of bed."

"If you get a move on the sooner you'll be back in your bed - sleeping like a baby."

We plodded up the stairs. I opened the door, Steve entered first and went into each room in turn. "No one here."

"Thank God for that."

"I'm going back to bed. See you tomorrow at six o'clock, remember what I said Mary. Don't knock on my door after six." Steve turned to go then kissed me on the check. "Night Mary." I couldn't believe I was given a kiss on the check, mind you that will be the nearest I'll get to anything passionate from Steve.

The next two days I spent occupying myself with work and packing. Each evening at six I knocked on Steve's door. On the Thursday evening after checking my flat Steve plonked himself down in the arm chair as if he had hours to spare.

"I've a list of questions for you."

"Fire away. I hope they're not too personal." I replied standing on ceremony.

"Question one, is Saturday the day you have to be out of here or is it the day you have decided to move on?"

"My notice on this flat is not up until tomorrow week. I'd rather leave in peace and lose my deposit than have the worry about fatty turning up one night next week. It's bad enough having to get you to check my flat out this week, I'm sure you wouldn't want to check it for another week. I thank God I can afford to lose the deposit. If I couldn't I dread to think what I would have to do to get it back."

"Next question, where are you going to work?"

"I'm going to work for an escort agency. The one that I have chosen is very up market. The clients have plenty of dosh, which suits me fine."

"You still haven't given me your address, if you don't I won't be able to forward your mail."

"I thought you were thinking of meeting up with me occasionally, then you could bring my mail with you?"

"I was thinking about it. That was before I realised you were going back on the game."

"I'm starving, I haven't had any supper yet"

"Mary, If you're hungry I'll go and get fish and chips for the pair of us - I haven't eaten either. I was going to bed on an empty stomach"

"I would love that, I haven't any money in my purse to pay for my share."

"Forget about having to pay, this is my treat, you stay here. I won't be long but I have to get dressed first."

"Thanks."

Steve went on his way. After a few minutes someone knocked on the door, thinking it was Steve I opened it. Instead it was fatty waiting to be invited in. I attempted to slam the door shut but this was impossible as he had managed to put his foot plus leg between the door and the wall.

"Caught you this time."

"What the hell do you mean? You haven't caught me, you never will." I said leaning on the door with all my strength.

"Come on girl let me in, I have something for you." Where I got my strength from I don't know but I kept pushing and hoping that Steve would return before I gave in. As we don't live far from the chippy he should be back within minutes, if there isn't a queue. It seemed like I was pushing for a good half an hour before I could hear Steve at the front door. It was strange because he didn't come up, all I could hear was someone banging on the door. Laughing in my face fatty said, "I've put the Yale lock down on the front door. You're on your own now girl as your so called boyfriend is locked out." He smirked.

"If I let go of this door you'll come tumbling in and it will be the last thing you do before I ring the police." I let the door go, fatty fell over. While he was trying to get up from the floor I managed to clamber over him and get down the stairs to the front door where Steve was sat on the door step.

"Why's the Yale down?" I explained what had happened.

"Come on let's get up the stairs and find the old bugger." We ran up as fast as we could and found fatty sat in my sitting room waiting for me to return.

"Get out now." Said Steve pointing towards the door. Fatty didn't move he stayed put as if he was there for the duration. "Go now or I'll call the police. You have five minutes to get out." screamed Steve.

"This is my flat and I'm staying put."

As we got closer to fatty it dawned on us both that he'd been drinking as his breath stunk of alcohol How much he had drunk we could only guess.

"Old man you stink of booze. It's obvious to me that you've been down the pub. We'll get you out of here if it's the last thing we do. Mary, you take that arm and I'll take this one. Come on old man you have to leave now."

"Don't you call me old man or man handle me boy." Said fatty pulling his arms away from us.

"Well get up and go now. If you don't go Mary will phone the police." "Hurry up fatty, I want you out of here." He seemed to listen to me and with difficulty tried to get up from the chair. Once he was up Steve and I had a shock, the cushion on the chair was wet, it was the last thing we expected to see. I screamed down his ear. "YOU HAVE WET YOUR PANTS YOU DIRTY OLD BUGGER. Now we know why you wouldn't stand up." Fatty looked at us both in a stupid and embarrassed way.

"I can't go, you can't throw me out like this."

"I don't care what state you're in, you're going and that doesn't mean out on the landing, it means out the front door." shouted Steve down his other ear.

"You can't kick me out of my own place."

"You just watch us." we took an arm each and frog marched him out on to landing and down the stairs to the front door. Once we had pushed him outside I banged the door shut.

"That's got rid of him, thank God. Now where are we eating in my place or yours?" asked Steve

"You choose."

"I'd rather eat down here then go upstairs later to sort out the arm chair."

"That suits me. I'll run up and get the fish and chips." I soon returned. "Where are we going to sit? It's a bit small in here and there aren't any comfy chairs."

"This is the reason I've never invited you in and why you find me sat on the stairs."

"Are you saying that we're going to eat our supper on the stairs?"

"It has to be the stairs or sitting on my bed."

"If we sit on your bed we can watch the telly."

"Yeah, we can if you have some change to put in the meter as it's run out of juice and I haven't any money, in fact I won't have any until pay day."

"Steve just now you were inviting me to go out for a drink, in the next breath you're saying you haven't any money. What the hell is going on Steve?"

"Nothing. The truth is I've spent my last few pence on our fish and chips."

"Steve you offered to pay. I've told you before that I don't need any help to pay for anything. The only reason I said I hadn't any money was because I hadn't been to the bank, not that I haven't any money."

"Trust me to get it wrong. Anyway surely we can sit and eat here without watching the telly?"

"Yeah." Silence reigned. I was too annoyed and hungry to chat about anything, I just got on with eating my fish and chips. Once we'd finished Steve broke the silence by asking if I'd like a cup of tea.

"Tea Mary?"

"Yes please." I went into a world of my own.

"Mary you look like you're falling asleep, are you okay?"

"I'm sat here day dreaming about where you wash your dishes as you don't seem to have a sink."

"I don't have a sink I have a plastic bowl where I do everything including having a shave, cleaning my teeth along with my dishes."

"Eh, whatever else am I going to find out about you this evening? I couldn't live like you do."

128

"How the hell did you think I lived? You need to remember that I'm not made of money, I only work down the local factory. Most of the blokes that work with me only live in rooms like this one. I was invited to supper by one chap, he told me a yarn about the rent he paid for his one room it was a dump and cost a lot more than I have to pay. I wouldn't have slept there for one night let alone all the years he'd lived there. He told me how he watched mice running around the room when he was in bed."

"You're making this up it can't be true." I answered looking a bit shocked.

"It's true alright, he showed me a photo he took of a mouse running along the skirting boards. The same chap also told me a story about one of the other tenants who kept hearing noises between the walls when she was trying to sleep. It was the mice running up and down in the cavities."

"For God's sake Steve don't tell me any more I have the itch. Change the subject."

"I'll put the kettle on. Did you say tea or coffee?"

"I'd prefer tea please."

"I'll see what I can find. Keep your fingers crossed, while I look in the cupboard."

"Whatever do you mean Steve everyone has a pack of tea in the cupboard."

"I'm not everyone and I may not have any." I began to think that it was a good job that I hadn't got involved with Steve. If I had, the next thing I imagined him to be saying to me once we were in a compromising position was that he didn't have any johnnies or he couldn't afford them or even worse he was allergic to the rubber and if I wanted to use contraceptives I'd better put a cap up my you know what.

"Found some tea, mind you it looks a bit musty."

"For God's sake Steve as far as I'm concerned you're definitely not a good catch. If I was interested in you, I wouldn't be interested in you now. You don't seem to have the basic things for living in this place or any other place for that matter. I'm going to ask you one question, do you have any johnnies? Don't answer yes and mean no and don't answer no and mean yes, I want the truth. I'm going to have a quick look under your pillow because that's where men normally keep them." I lifted up the pillow." I guessed as much, no johnnies.

Can't you afford them? It's better to buy and use them, than get someone up the duff."

"Well I haven't any. I've never bought johnnies in my life, I rely on females providing them or having a cap up their fanny."

"I couldn't get involved with you even if you wanted me to. I like a man to be in control and that means having johnnies under the pillow along with other things like tea in the cupboard. It seems to me that you like the woman to be in charge so you don't suit me. Mind you, you're a very good friend but don't ask for anything more than friendship. Let's drink our tea then go and look at the chair. Thank God the chair doesn't belong to me, if it did I'd bin it then send fatty a bill." Steve stared across at me.

"Let us get back to your deposit."

"What about it?"

"I reckon you should look around your flat and see what you fancy taking for the price of the deposit. If there isn't anything, break something, like a table leg so fatty has to repair it or buy new with your money, it would serve him bloody well right and he couldn't do a damn thing about it."

"I must be thick as I wouldn't have thought of that. I'd have walked away and left him banking my money."

Once we'd finished our tea we immediately went up to my flat where Steve tried to take the cushion out of the chair but couldn't. "I'll take the chair out into the garden. I'll leave it by the dustbin." suggested Steve.

"I don't care what you do with it, I just want it out of here it stinks of wee - dirty old bugger."

"Mary, once I've got rid of the chair I'll come back up to help you look around for things for you to take or steal whatever you want to call it." Steve didn't take long.

"We could start with that old standard brass lamp in my bed room, I reckon it's worth a bit. I'm going to take it even though I don't want it. I'm not leaving it behind for fatty to sell when he's feeling a bit hard up."

"That mirror over there isn't bad either." said Steve pointing towards it.

"Okay that's two things."

"Let's make it three."

"What about that plant in the pot?"

"Mary I thought that must be yours."

"No it's fatty's."

"Well take it."

"I will."

"All done and dusted it didn't take long." Steve said while clapping his hands.

"It's only eight o'clock. I thought it must be time for bed."

"It might not be your bedtime but it'll be mine by the time I get back down stairs."

"On Saturday are you going to help me move out?"

"Can you tell me why I should?" smirked Steve. It took me a while to decide what to answer.

"Come on girl answer my question, you've pulled my life style to pieces and you still want me to help you - tell me why I should."

"You're the only man I know as a friend."

"Mary I'll have to see what tomorrow brings."

"What do you mean?"

"Well I've a date with a girl from the factory, I may not be here Saturday morning, then again I may be as I've said you'll have to wait and see."

"Steve will you be able to check my flat tomorrow evening?"

"Yeah as long as you call in by six o'clock."

"I'll do that as I couldn't cope with fatty being here and me being on my own."

"I'm going." said Steve smiling to himself.

"I'll see you tomorrow evening at six o'clock." I said leaning over to kiss him on the cheek.

"Night then.

Chapter 17

I tossed and turned for most of the night. It must have been the excitement of moving over to Westbourne Terrace on Saturday that kept me awake as it definitely wasn't anything to do with Steve giving me a quick how's your father because that hasn't happened.

I arrived at the office Friday morning just after nine and found all the girls looking a bit glum while I was on a high. The way I was behaving no one would have guessed that I hadn't had a good night's sleep.

"What's wrong with you lot, you look as if the end of your world has arrived?" No one answered.

"I've asked you a question you haven't answered me?" I said sounding annoyed.

"What was that?" asked Joyce.

"I'm wondering what's wrong as you all look like you're about to burst into tears?"

"I doubt if you'll understand or believe what I'm about to say Miss Mary but we're all upset about you leaving and moving on, we'll miss you." answered Ruth looking down in the mouth.

"Any of you can join me in leaving, in fact we can all leave this dump a week on Tuesday. All you have to do is not come into work the next day which is Wednesday. I doubt if any of you would be missed until at least Wednesday lunch time. Look at today we won't see old Robbins until late afternoon. I dare you all to do the same as me and LEAVE." I shouted.

"I may take you up on leaving. I can't afford to walk out but I may give in my notice." replied Ruth.

"Ruth, you're thinking of leaving here?" I sounded surprised.

"That's what I said, also I may leave home." I sat down to get over the shock. "Don't sound so surprised Mary, I've been thinking about leaving here for a while and I've almost decided to move out from home. The thing is mum and dad would have to manage if I got married and moved to the country."

"Have you got a man on the horizon?" asked Joyce, calling across the room.

"Don't be daft, how would I have a man looking like I do and living with mum and dad." replied Ruth.

"You may have one for all we know. They say the quiet ones are the worse and you're always quiet at least while you're here."

"Ruth's not quiet after she's had a couple of drinks. If you went to the pub with her you'd have the shock of your life. Once she's had a few Gin and Tonics she'll try and pick up any old bloke."

"That's not true Mary. Girls she's making it up." shouted Ruth sounding annoyed.

"Ruth, can't you remember how you picked up that stupid bloke in the pub at Trafalgar Square, after you had drunk far too much alcohol. If you had been sober you wouldn't have even looked in his direction let alone chatted to him and invited him to join us at our table, you'd have told him where to go, instead of that you said 'sit down here with us' when he came over on his own and sat down at the table next to ours, you even pulled a chair over for him." Ruth didn't know where to put herself.

"Ruth, If or when you leave here you could join the escort agency with Mary. Dolled up you may even find a millionaire to socialise with - you never know your luck. Sharing a flat with Mary would be very convenient for the pair of you as neither of you would worry about the other bringing a man home for the night." said Joyce laughing, the other girls joined in the fun by cheering Joyce on.

"Shut up the lot of you before I decide to walk out NOW." Screamed Ruth.

"Ruth, calm down and listen to me please, ages ago I suggested you left home and your job here - you wouldn't hear of it. I even suggested we rented a flat together. Now I'm moving into a room in a flat that Liz rents with other girls at Westbourne Terrace. I would have far rather shared a flat with you on our own. Like Joyce has said we would have been able to do what we liked when we liked, now Liz is going to call the shots. Her style won't suit me, I doubt if I'll stay at her place for long but it will tied me over until I find some where more suitable. Here comes Liz ask her if she has another room at the flat that may suit you."

"Ruth am I hearing right, you want a room?"

"Yeah I'm considering leaving home, in fact I'm thinking of leaving this dump as well. I need to arrange some where to put my head before I move out from mum and dad's."

"I'm going to tell you the same as I've told Mary, if you take a room at my place it's no good thinking about bringing men back for the night as I won't have any of it, ONE NIGHT STANDS ARE OUT OF THE QUESTION. Do you understand what I'm saying?" called out Liz.

"Yeah I understand, any way Liz I'm not into one night stands in fact I've never had one."

"Good as that means there may be a room available downstairs with Joan. Joan is always complaining about how much rent she has to pay for her two bedroom flat. I keep suggesting that she should find someone to share with but she hasn't. I'll have a chat with her over the weekend and see what she thinks of you sharing with her. Monday morning I'll let you know what she's had to say."

"Liz, how much will the rent be?"

"Joan is paying seven pounds a week. If you moved in she'd only have to pay three pound ten shillings as you would be paying the other half."

"That sounds okay to me. Another question for you, do you own the flats?"

"No, I collect the rents for the landlord." answered Liz looking a bit stupid. Everyone laughed.

"I reckon something must be going on with you and this landlord as I've never known any landlord to trust a tenant to collect the rent." called out Marjorie.

"I CAN ASSURE YOU THERE ISN'T ANY THING GOING ON." shouted Liz "if you could see him you wouldn't even suggest there was."

"I've heard that one before." I called out. "I remember mum telling me about her friend Anne who collected the rent from tenants in quite a few flats for her landlord. Every few weeks the landlord would call around to Anne's place for the money. One day for a laugh mum phoned Anne once she knew the landlord had arrived, guess what Anne didn't answer the phone. When mum bumped into her the next day she asked why she hadn't answered the phone, 'I wasn't in, I went out early,' that's not true I saw you answering the

door just before I rang you." The girls laughed.

"What did she say to that?"

"Not a lot, she just looked stupid then walked off down the road in a huff."

"How did your mum know it was the landlord visiting and not Anne's boyfriend?"

"Mum used to see Anne most days as she lived around the corner from her place. On one of the days when they had a chat Anne told mum that she hadn't a boyfriend, apparently she hadn't had one for years. Mum wasn't surprised, as Anne always looked a bit worse for wear unless she was expecting the landlord then she would put on her Sunday best. Mum said Anne wore the same dress every time the landlord called around so mum knew when he was visiting and found it quite amusing. Mum told me that the landlord had quite a bit of money in the bank but he wasn't up to much in the looks department. Mum reckoned Anne had to be desperate to go with him. She also told me that she wouldn't have waited in for this particular landlord to visit and she definitely wouldn't have collected the rents for him, especially if he didn't help her out money wise or let her live in her flat for free."

"Liz, I hope you listened to what Mary has just said, do you live in your flat for free?" asked Joyce laughing out loud, "You must get something for collecting the rent."

"I don't get anything." Liz screamed at Joyce.

"Bigger fool you, at least this Anne lived in her flat for free and also had a bit of how's your father into the bargain. I'm going to go over to my desk and get on with my typing."

"Have you lot got much typing?" I asked after I'd looked at all the letters I have to write.

"Why?"

"Well old Robbins seems to have given me quite a bit. I'll still be here on Monday doing this lot unless one of you helps me out." the girls sat and laughed at me.

"I don't find it funny. I reckon one of you has given me more than I should have." I said sounding annoyed.

"We haven't given Mary extra typing have we girls?"

"No." they called out in harmony.

"I may help you later Mary but it seems like old Robbins has given us all more typing than he usually does." said Ruth.

"I'll help you out if you pass some over." said Marjorie looking shifty.

"Marjorie, you have gone bright red. I reckon you have given me some of your letters to type up."

"It was a good try on my part, sorry Mary, I'll take a few back. The thing is I'm slow at typing and old Robbins wants them all finished by five today."

"What! I'll never finish this lot by then unless I give up my lunch break and stop yapping with you lot." I called out. "I'm going to tell you now that I'm not giving up any of my free time to type these. Ruth about you leaving this dump, I dare you to go down and see old Robbins now and tell him you'll be leaving in four weeks. If you don't go down and see him today you'll never leave."

"That sounds a good idea Mary, in fact it sounds a bloody good idea. I'll go for a wee and organise myself around the head. Mind you I doubt if old Robbins will notice if I've combed my hair or not. Here goes."

Eventually Ruth returned from the cloakroom, Joyce gave her the loudest wolf whistle I'd ever heard from a female, then she called out "Fancy you putting on all that war paint just to go down the stairs to see dear Mr Robbins. I reckon you're hoping for something, if you're not, he'll be asking for something." The girls cheered. "Looking like you do it's no wonder Mary thinks you could become an escort along with her. In a minute we'll hear that the pair of you have opened up your own agency. Ruth remember there is plenty of money to be made." Ruth walked out of the office laughing away to herself while wriggling her bum.

We all got on with our typing until Ruth came back up the stairs - she was full of herself and wouldn't stop chatting about the boss and what he thought about her giving in her notice.

"He wasn't very happy about me leaving, he thinks I'm one of his best typists and he can't understand why I want to leave, as the pay here is good and I won't get paid any more anywhere else. He kept asking the same question 'what are you going to do for a job because no doubt you need a reference but you haven't asked for one?' he asked this question three times while looking me up and down as if he was interested in me." Ruth continued rambling on about the boss and how he mentioned her makeup. "After staring at me for a good five minutes he went on to say 'In my day your makeup would have been called war paint.' I told him straight that my makeup was the fashion for this era and it didn't matter whether he liked it or not as it wasn't put on for his benefit."

"That's a load of tosh Ruth, we all know damn well you put it on for him." laughed Joyce.

"If I did I still don't need to tell him why I put it on."

"Did he make a pass at you, did he try to touch you up?" I asked

"No he did not thank God, well not exactly." said Ruth looking embarrassed. "He sat back in his chair with his arms behind his head looking across at me as if he was waiting for me to sit down on him – as if I would. I have given in my notice and I leave in four weeks' time. While he was putting the date down in his diary, I rushed out of his office."

"I wonder if he'll ask to see you before you leave?"

"I doubt it, if he does I'll do a runner as I won't be going down to his office again. One of you can take my place."

"You must be joking none of us will go down, especially on our own." I looked down at my watch "It's twenty past twelve time to stop typing not that I've done any. I'm going over to the sandwich bar, are you coming with me Ruth?"

"Yeah I'll come but I must take off some of this war paint before I leave the building."

"Hurry up or it will be teatime before we've had any lunch and I'm starving."

Chapter 18

Once we arrived in the sandwich bar we were lucky enough to find a couple of chairs at the far end where we could sit and have a private chat while we ate. "Now we're alone and can't be over heard let's chat about our futures. I know how I'm going to earn a few bob but what about you Ruth, what are you thinking of doing?"

"Well it seems like I have had what one would call the seal of approval from the girls about how I look with all my war paint on. I've also had a quick wink from the boss so I may as well join you as an escort. Before you tell me that I'll be able to go out with you during the evenings to the West End hotels to earn extra cash, I'm going to tell you straight – I'M NOT GOING TO VISIT ANY HOTELS. This evening over supper I'll tell mum and dad I'm leaving home. What they'll say I dread to think, most probably it'll be tears before bedtime for mum as she'll get upset about not having company when dad goes down the pub on a Saturday."

"Ruth don't tell me that he only goes to the pub on a Saturday and that's the only evening you have to stay in. I feel sure that he goes most evenings for a quick pint, people who enjoy alcohol go to the pub more than once a week. If your dad had a dog I would say that when he took it for a walk he'd visit the pub. I know a bloke that did this every evening at seven o'clock."

"Mary I doubt if you'll believe this but I swear it's true. Sunday evenings, dad gets the calendar out then asks me which evenings I'm prepared to stay in so he can go to the pub."

"Ruth, this must be some kind of joke, you're joking, aren't you?"

"No I'm not, this is exactly what happens in our house on a Sunday." I looked at Ruth wondering what was coming next.

"If I were in your shoes, I'd kid your dad that I was going out every evening one particular week then he couldn't waste his money in the pub or I'd tell him I was staying in every evening so he could go out and waste his money."

"I reckon the pair of them would get into a right strop with me, as they'd know damn well I wouldn't stay in every evening. When I leave home they'll have to sort the pub evenings out themselves and mum will have to find something to do when dad's out of the way. One thing is for sure they can't fall out with one another if he's down the pub, unless he manages to get off with some old bird that's on the pickup. Mind you mum wouldn't even know about the old bird unless dad was daft enough to tell the old bird where he lived and she went around to our house." we both laughed.

"Your mum could always join something like Women's Institute but that's only held one evening a month, she'd have another twenty seven evenings to fill in her time with, that's if your dad went out every evening, Mind you she could go with him."

"That would teach him a lesson especially if they got in the habit of going to the pub every evening, it would cost him an arm and a leg - it would serve him damn well right. I don't reckon he would like mum to go with him more than once a week as she would cramp his style. If she laid down the law and insisted on going I bet he would leave her sat at a table while he stood at the bar with his mates. I've seen men do that, it's very embarrassing for the woman. Mary, I was in a pub one evening when a woman was left sat on her own for a good twenty minutes then this woman decided to go over to her husband who was up at the bar with his mate, she said 'I may as well go home as I'm sat on my own.' His answer to this was 'well go home,' she did."

"My dad wouldn't have liked it if mum had insisted on going to the pub with him, as he would have been meeting a lady friend. To stop mum going with him he would have instigated a row. A boyfriend I had years ago told me about a married friend of his who used to have three women on the go. He went out every Friday night with one or other of them." Ruth looked shocked.

"Mary how the hell did he get out on a Friday night of all nights? I always thought the husband normally took the wife out then."

"I don't have an answer to that question. I only know that one particular Friday he was waiting in the pub for one woman and all three of these women turned up together, they were friends with one another and decided to catch him out."

"Mary, what the hell happened?"

"I don't know, we can only guess - what a laugh for the ones' looking on. The bloke must have felt such an idiot, mind you it served him damn well right."

"Let's get back to where I'm going to live. I've decided to wait until Monday to see what Liz comes up with, before looking in any newspapers. If Joan thinks I could share with her I'll go and have a look at the room next week."

"I reckon it will be okay and will tide you over until you find a flat of your own."

"Mary, aren't we going to find some where to live together?"

"Back along you didn't want to share anything with me, that's how I've got into this predicament and finished up going to live in Liz's place. I'm hoping to move out after a month. For God's sake Ruth whatever you talk to Liz about don't you dare tell her this or she may say that she has changed her mind and I'll be out on the streets from tomorrow."

"What do you mean out on the streets? You've still got the flat above dear old Steve."

"Yeah I know, I've paid the rent until the end of the month, I need to get out before then though." Ruth looked at me as if she was going to ask me another question. "Ruth, don't you dare ask me why I have to get out of my flat as I told you the reason weeks ago, if you've forgotten what I said start to use your brain and try and remember."

"I do know why, fatty fancies a bit of you."

"Good, you've remembered and I'm not staying around long enough for him to have a bit of me. I forgot to tell you how I found fatty sat down in my sitting room and how Steve and I had to man handle him out of my flat."

"Hurry up tell me what happened."

"He wouldn't leave, he wouldn't even stand up. When we eventually got him to stand we found that he'd wet his pants."

"What! That's a laugh and a half but how bloody disgusting."

"Let's finish our sandwiches and go back to work, on the way I must get some black bags."

"What the hell do you need them for Mary?"

"I only have one suitcase and I have filled it already. Black bags are cheaper than having to buy another suitcase. If I was a man and I'm not, I would tie the bottoms of each trouser leg with string then put my clothes down them."

"Haven't you got a pair of slacks that you could use?"

"No, I've never bought slacks or jeans in my life. I bet you haven't any either."

"Well Mary, you've got that wrong. I'm more with it than you, I have one pair of black slacks."

"I can't imagine you in them."

"I only wear them at home on a Saturday."

"Ruth, I bet you only wear them at home because your bum looks big in them."

"Mary, most probably that's the reason you haven't bought a pair, fat bum." laughed Ruth. "My parents are really daft, they won't let me wear them on a Sunday."

"Why ever not Ruth?"

"Because dad says girls shouldn't wear slacks and definitely not on a Sunday. If I dare to go down stairs in slacks for Sunday lunch I'm sent back to my room to put on a dress. Mind you this will all change once I move out, it's three cheers for moving out."

"I hope you don't mind me saying this but your parents treat you like a child and you're in your twenties."

"I know, that's a good enough reason as any for moving out. I'll tell them in no uncertain terms especially if they say something daft like, they won't manage without me."

Once we were back in the office we soon finished our typing in fact we all finished by four thirty so we had half an hour to spare before going home.

"About tomorrow Mary, don't come over too early as we - meaning the girls and myself, stay in bed Saturday mornings to recover from our Friday night out on the tiles, we always have far too much drink for our own good." mentioned Liz laughing.

"What about me arriving around two o clock? By the time I've organised myself and said cheers to dear old Steve, I won't be over before then."

141

"That sounds okay."

"Before I go can you give me the phone number for your place." Liz wrote the number down on a scrap of paper which I put in my pocket before saying cheers to everyone.

This is going to be my last night at the flat, I haven't heard a sound from Steve which is very strange. I knocked on his door as arranged - he didn't answer, mind you he did say something about having a date, I thought he would still be around until at least eight o'clock, in fact I thought he was teasing me when he mentioned having a date. I was hoping that he'd come to his door carrying a bottle of Blue Nun to celebrate me moving out – no such luck.

Once upstairs I became anxious about going into my flat alone in case fatty was sat waiting for sex. Thank God he was nowhere to be seen. This meant that I could get on with my packing. I filled all six black plastic bags to the brim, how I'm going to carry them down the stairs without them splitting open remains to be seen. By the time I finished packing it was almost ten o'clock bedtime, but I'm starving. I felt that I needed more food than I have in the cupboard, which is only two tins of baked beans. These were supposed to keep me going until tomorrow when I'll be going to the local supermarket in Westbourne Terrace. A decision needed to be made as soon as possible about going to get fish and chips or go to bed on baked beans. I know if I go to bed hungry or after eating baked beans I won't sleep, I'll lay in bed tossing and turning for most of the night - the fish and chips won.

The people in the queue at the chippy behaved as if they'd been to a pub and were on their way home in a tiddly state. Watching them while sober made me think how stupid I must look after a few drinks. Whether they all knew each other I'm not sure. One of the blokes tried to get me to chat to him, I pretended to be deaf - it didn't work, as he made me smile when he said he couldn't see my hearing aids.

"You're not deaf you just don't want to talk, you're bloody rude. See this sober git over here boys and girls," he said pointing down at me "she's made out to me that she's deaf and she's not. I reckon we should all stand around her and scream in her ears."

"Don't do that, please don't do that. The reason I haven't been speaking is because I'm shy." I called out holding my hands over my ears.

"She's not shy." called out a middle aged man from the other end of the queue.

"Who shouted that?" asked the bloke that wanted to chat.

"Me, I've known her over the years," he replied putting his hand in the air, "in fact I used to meet her up the West End on a Friday night. She's game for anything, anywhere after a few Gin and Tonics. The only trouble is she's a bit expensive and I ran out of dosh so I had to give up meeting her."

I didn't know where to put myself because by this time everyone was stood staring towards me, while laughing at me. Thank God I was saved by the chippy.

"Shut up you lot, get back in the queue or I'll shut up shop. This young lady doesn't deserve you talking about her like you are so I'm going to serve her before you lot, then she can go on her way."

I walked towards the counter where the man I'd met years ago was stood grinning all over his face, while staring towards me as if he was undressing me with his eyes.. "I remember you, half the time I couldn't find your dick because it was hidden under rolls of fat, you were enormous even fatter than you are now. The other times you couldn't get a hard. You were completely useless. Girls you remember what I've just said when he dares to ask you out or mentions having sex, he's not worth bothering with." He looked daft.

I ordered my fish and chips, paid up then hurried on my way before any more rubbish could be thrown at me. Thank God my flat is only a few hundred yards from this chippy as I had visions of the ex-customer chancing his luck by following me home but luckily I was in doors before he had time to think about doing that. I remember him being a bit thick so it would have taken him a while to realise that I must live near or I wouldn't be in the queue.

The fish and chips saved my day - they were yummy.

Saturday morning I had a lie in until nine thirty as there was no need for me to get up any earlier as it only takes a few minutes to get over to Westbourne Terrace by black cab. I would hate to think I had to sit on the door step for a couple of hours before anyone would be up to let me in. By midday I had everything I owned down stairs in the hall along with extra things that Steve suggested I pinched from the flat. I knocked on Steve's door hoping he would invite me in for a coffee before giving me a goodbye kiss on the cheek.

"I thought it must be someone important at the door the way it was being knocked and it's you. If I'd known it was you Mary I'd have come to the door in my dressing gown I wouldn't have bothered to get dressed." said Steve looking annoyed.

"You're late getting up. I thought you would have been up and running hours ago."

"Well you know what thought did, you know damn well that I always get up late on a Saturday. Anyway now I'm here what do you want?"

"I've come to give you my phone number and to say cheers."

"Are you going somewhere?" asked Steve looking puzzled.

"Yes I am and you know where I'm going." Steve began to scratch his head.

"Steve have you got fleas?"

"Don't be daft, of course I haven't fleas - I've never had fleas." answered Steve sounding annoyed.

"Well stop scratching your head."

"Mary I have an itch on my head, it's definitely not fleas."

"I haven't fleas either, but I can tell you about a woman that was sitting in front of me on the bus the other week – before you say that I have made it up it's a true story, I could see a flea crawling in her hair. The woman looked clean enough but fleas like clean places. Once I got back here I stood in the front garden and shook my head for all it was worth. I imagined I'd have an itch all night but I didn't, thank God."

"That must have been terrible."

"It was the thought of me having fleas that made me itch. Anyway Steve are you going to invite me in?"

"I suppose you can come in Mary but whatever you do or say please don't complain about the state of my place, or we'll finish up having a blazing row and that'll be the end of you and me."

"I won't say a word dear Steve. I'd hate to fall out with you."

"Right come in."

In I went and plonked myself down on the end of Steve's bed.

"I'll take the kettle down to the bathroom and get some water from the bath tap as I guess you'd like a coffee."

"Yeah, I'd love a coffee but not made with water from the bath tap. I don't fancy that, Steve how do you know it's suitable for drinking?"

"Because I've been drinking it for years and I'm still here. I used it for the tea you had the other night." I didn't know what to answer, I pretended I didn't hear what he said about the tea.

"Okay, I'll trust your judgment but hundreds wouldn't."

"Good. If you're happy sat here alone I'll go and get the water."

"When you get back I'll tell you another story." Steve soon returned.

"Here goes, once upon a time."

"If you're going to act daft Mary don't tell me the story as I won't listen."

"Sorry, here goes. I heard about a woman who couldn't get out of the bath due to her arthritic legs. She had to stay in the bath until she found the courage to shout for help. The first person that heard her was the man that lived in the bedsitter next to the bath room. He couldn't get in, for obvious reasons, she'd locked the door."

"Mary, I don't believe any of this, you're talking a load of rubbish but carry on yapping as I'm longing to know what happens to the woman."

"The lock on the door wasn't one of those silly bolts that open as soon as the door is pushed in. This particular door was locked with a key so the bedsitter man had to phone the landlord to get him to come out with a spare key. You can imagine the landlord wasn't happy about this but when he saw the woman sat in the bath his eyes nearly popped out of his head."

"Who the hell was the woman, what was wrong with her?"

"Nothing was wrong with her, the landlord used to visit her but they lost touch years ago."

"Is that it?"

"Yeah, afraid so. I'm going to leave the rest of the story for your imagination dear Steve."

"If this woman is anything like you I bet they walked out into the sunset had a few drinks and then had a bit of how's your father."

"You're nearly right but not quite. This woman had been a dominatrix, the landlord used to visit her flat. While he was visiting he did her ironing plus clean the floor in the nude, while this woman whipped him." We both laughed so loud that everyone out in the road must have heard us.

"That was a good yarn Mary. I wish I had your imagination." Said Steve still laughing.

"Changing the subject back to the coffee Steve, it isn't bad considering where the water came from."

"Thanks for the compliment."

"Do you know the time?"

"Yeah, about one o'clock Mary, my watch has nearly given up the ghost but that's what it says."

"I don't need to leave here until about two o'clock. If I get over to Westbourne Terrace before two I'll have to sit on the doorstep and wait."

"What the hell do you mean, wait for what?"

"To get into my new flat. Liz, told me the girls at the flat including her go down to the pub on a Friday night and have a few to many, this means they stay in bed Saturday mornings so there's no one to answer the door."

"Mary, I didn't think you were moving out for another week."

"I'm leaving as soon as I've drunk this coffee." I handed Steve the piece of paper with my new address and phone number. "This is for you in case you want to keep in touch."

"Thanks for that, you never know I may ring." Said Steve smiling to himself.

"Mary I'm pleased you're moving in with your favourite type of friends – boozers. Friday nights you'll be able to go to the pub together and get sloshed."

"I'm not going to stay living with them for years. Once I've saved a few bob I shall move into my own place. I forgot to tell you Steve I may share with Ruth."

"That's a shock to my system, I thought Ruth had to stay living at home."

"She's going to tell her parents this weekend that she intends to move out as soon as possible."

146

We carried on chatting until two o'clock when Steve helped to carry out the black bags plus my suitcase on to the pavement. While I was waving down the black cab Steve gave me the shock of my life by inviting me out for a drink.

"Do you fancy meeting up tomorrow evening for a drink?"

"Are you inviting me out on a serious date?"

"I don't know about it being serious but we could meet up for a drink. What about Trafalgar Square at seven o'clock? We could go across to the pub we went to the other week?"

"Okay Nelson's column at seven o'clock, see you then." Before I blinked I was in the back of the cab relieved to think I hadn't bumped into the landlord but sad that I didn't get a kiss on the check from dear old Steve.

Chapter 19

Arriving at Westbourne Terrace the cabby asked which side of the road the flat was on. I pointed it out to him, to my surprise he immediately turned his head towards me to ask if I was sure that this was the building.

"Of course I'm sure. I've been inside the flat and had a meal with the girls. It's that building."

"It doesn't look very respectable to me from where I'm sat."

"Forget what it looks like outside, I can assure you it's fine on the inside, in fact it's quite posh."

"It doesn't look posh from out here. If you were my daughter I wouldn't be very happy with you living in there. I'd be taking you back home to live with me and your mother."

"Well I'm not your daughter - thank God. Anyway it's none of your damn business where I live."

"I'm going to say one thing and that is the whole place looks like a squat to me. I'll help you over to the door with your luggage then I'm going to leave you to your own devices" the cabby said looking a bit shifty.

"Cabby, I reckon you know more about this place than you're letting on."

"It's not for me to tell you anything about anything."

"Well, don't tell me anything, but I'll be wondering what the matter is all the time I'm living here. Come on Cabby tell me what you know." The cabby looked me up and down as if he felt sorry for me which made a change from someone looking at me as if they were undressing me.

"Okay here goes. I picked a chap up from here the other week who said he'd had a room in that building for the last two years."

"Is that it?"

"No, it's not the end of it. He said he left because the girls came on strong to him. I hope you don't think I believed what he said because I didn't. His looks and clothes were not up to much, I know damn well that no one would fancy him. It was more like he hadn't paid his rent as he looked the type to do a runner."

"Are you sure he came out of this door?"

"Of course I am, I was stood exactly where I'm stood now. I helped him out with one of his two bags." He said pointing towards the ground.
"Where did you drop him off?"
"Waterloo Bridge."
"That's where the down and outs hang out." I said looking shocked.
"I know that. The thing is young lady if he hadn't any money where else could he go and stay?"

"I've no idea. I'd hate to be in that position with no dosh. Cabby you're nothing to me but for what it's worth I'm going to promise you that if I'm not happy with the situation in there." I said pointing towards the door, "I'll leave in fact I'll leave before I unpack especially if I find out that the bloke you're talking about has slept in the bed I'm having and has left it in a terrible state."

"You may as well leave now. I can take you to a hotel or guest house that's if you have that sort of money."

"I'll ring the bell, whoever answers the door I'll get you to ask about the bloke. If I'm staying I'll pay you and send you packing. If I'm not staying you can take me to a respectable guest house or hotel not too expensive as the more it costs the fewer number of nights I can stay." I rang the bell after waiting a few minutes Liz came to the door looking a bit worse for wear.

"Welcome to your new abode."

"I'm not coming in until you answer a question from the cabby." I said looking a bit down in the mouth.

"Did a bloke live in this flat until the end of last week?" Liz looked like she had been shot in the foot.

"No, only females live here. We've never had men living here, at least not while I've been here and I've been here years."

"By the way you look Miss I reckon a bloke did live here and this young lady is taking his place in his old room. Am I right or am I wrong?"

"You're definitely wrong. Come in Mary, don't take any notice of him he's only the cabby. He wouldn't know who lived here or who didn't, he's made it up." Liz pulled in one of my bags.

"I believe Liz because I've known her for longer than half an hour in fact I've worked with her for the last couple of years. Cabby I'll pay you off." I immediately handed over a couple of notes to keep him happy.

"You watch it, I hope there won't be any bed bugs in your bed if there are you'll wish you'd listened to me." Said the cabby walking backwards towards his cab.

"I'm going to chance my luck cabby." I said while putting the rest of my luggage at the bottom of the stairs.

Liz stood to one side, "I'll take the suitcase upstairs for you as long as it's not too heavy." Liz picked it up. "What the hell have you got in here? It's bloody heavy no wonder the cabby helped you over to the door. I reckon there's everything but the kitchen sink in here. I think we should help each other up the stairs with this."

"I've only put clothes and a few plates and mugs in there. If you can't carry it on your own because you're weak, I'll carry it." I took the suitcase from Liz and dragged it up the stairs. "You carry the black bags Liz, they're not as heavy."

"Thanks a lot. I'll have a go, they look as if they've got so much in them that they'll burst at the seams."

"If they burst so be it, all my knickers and bits and bobs will roll down the stairs." Once up on the landing I left my belongings and walked along to my new room where I found the door locked.

"Liz, what's going on here, the door's locked. Have you got the key?"

"Yeah it's in the kitchen at least that's where I last saw it, I'll go and get it."

I waited patiently. "It's not here."

"I reckon the bloke, that's if it was a man who had the room before me, it could have been a woman for all I know - has taken the key." I said sounding annoyed.

"I better come clean with you."

"About what?"

"The room."

"Come on then tell me who had the room. I bet it was the bloke the cabby was talking about. Am I right?"

"Yes, afraid so Mary."

"Liz what is going to happen to me, where am I going to sleep?"

"I don't know."

"Liz, I can tell you now I'm not going back to my old flat at Hammersmith so you better start thinking where I can sleep. I don't really care how temporary it is as long as I have a bed and it's clean. I'm quite willing to live out of my suitcase until you manage to get a locksmith to come around and open the door, then I can go in and inspect the condition of the room. I bet it's in some state."

"No it won't be in a state. Andrew was a respectable chap." Liz looked as if she wished the floor would swallow her up.

"Well this Andrew wasn't respectable enough to leave the key behind. If he had nothing to hide he would have left the key on the side and he hasn't - something's up. Mind you when I went in to see the room the other night it looked okay. I wouldn't have agreed to take it if it didn't." I said getting more and more annoyed. "Liz I'm going to tell you a TRUE story – it's not one of my yarns. I met someone who let out rooms. In one particular room the mattress was left in a disgusting state."

"What do you mean by that?"

"One side of the mattress had dried poo on it the other had urine stains, it was bloody awful."

"That must have been terrible. We'll have to hope that this room is perfect or at least good enough for you. Let's change the subject before I spew up. Mary would you like tea or coffee?"

"Right tea it'll be. Go and sit in the sitting room while I make it." Liz didn't take long before she returned carrying two mugs.

"Mary I can't ring around trying to get a locksmith."

"Why ever not?"

"Because I'm not the landlord and if I arrange for a locksmith to come around I reckon I'll finish up paying the bill so I'm not phoning one. I'll phone the landlord instead and let him know what has happened I dread to think what he'll say as I'm only allowed to rent the rooms to women. When he finds out we've had a bloke living here for the last two years he may send me packing, especially as I'm the one who's in charge of collecting the rents."

151

"All I can say Liz is that it serves you damn well right. It's your own stupid fault." Liz looked embarrassed.

"Any way getting back to me, where am I going to sleep?" I suggested that perhaps I could move into Joan's spare bedroom.

"That sounds quite a good idea as you'd be able to help her out with the rent. Joan is always complaining about what she has to pay each week. I'll go down and have a chat with her once I've finished my tea."

Silence reigned for the next few minutes. Liz looked worried to death as if her world had come to an end. Liz knew that she shouldn't have let the room to a man - she knew the rules before she took him in. Mind you she had managed to keep him under wraps for two years which was pretty good going for her, considering she isn't very good at keeping quiet about things.

"You stay put while I go down and see Joan, I should be back in a few minutes. If I'm not back within ten minutes you know damn well that I'm having difficulty trying to persuade her." I sat patiently, the ten minutes Liz said it may take, took over twenty before she returned to say I can sleep in Joan's spare room.

"Sorry I took so long, the room was full of Joan's junk. I've been helping her clear the bed and a space for your bits in the corner."

"Thanks, before I go down and introduce myself where will I be eating?"

"You can choose, you can eat with us or take everything down to Joan's and eat with her."

"I'll go and meet her before deciding." Down I went I knocked on the door, a middle aged woman answered.

"I've come to meet Joan."

"That's me." I must have looked shocked as Joan seemed to get more and more embarrassed by the minute, it was as if she'd lost her tongue. The thing is I was expecting some one in their twenties and Joan looked like she could be in her mid forties or older. After a few minutes of staring at me she started to talk and couldn't stop.

"Welcome to my flat, come in and have a look around tell me what you think of it. I've lived here for years far longer than any of the girls upstairs. Before you decide to take my spare room I've a problem, which will involve you as much as it involves me."

"What's that?"

"It's the phone that's outside in the main hall. When it rings I have to answer it as the girls upstairs can't hear it ringing and it's usually for them. This is very annoying for me especially when I'm watching the television and it's my favourite programme. Before you agree to living down here you need to think if you can cope with answering the phone when it rings."

"The phone won't be a problem to me, in fact it would very convenient as I have quite a few friends that often ring me."

"That's okay then. Another problem with the phone is that it sometimes rings in the middle of the night and wakes me, this is very upsetting and annoying as I find it a job to get back to sleep. I used to leave it ringing but I find it easier to pick the receiver up then put it back down without speaking but whoever's phoning seems to find it a joke and rings again."

"Why don't you take the receiver off the hook at eleven o'clock and not put it on the hook again until the morning, at least you'd get a good night's sleep?"

"Mary I reckon I must be a bit thick. I've never thought of doing that. You've solved my problem with the phone. Even if you decide not to live down here you've helped me out with that - thank you. Come into the sitting room, take a seat, I'll make a cup of tea."

"Can I visit your loo before I sit down?"

"Of course you can, that's if you can get in there - it's full of junk. You'll have too squeeze in between the junk to see the lavatory let alone use it."

"Thank you. The only thing I have done today is drink tea and coffee. I must have had at least six mugs. I'm bursting, I'll wet myself if I don't go to the loo."

In I went it was in some state. No wonder Joan was having difficulty finding a flat mate, we all know loos should be clean and this one isn't. It's one of the dirtiest I have ever seen, along with the hand basin which only had a cold water tap. Once I'd had a wee I returned to the sitting room holding my hands out in front of me.

"What's wrong Mary, is something wrong with your hands?"

"I want to wash them. I've been for a wee so I need to wash them."

"There's a basin in the lavatory."

"I know, it's dirty, also it doesn't have a hot water tap."

"You're a bit fussy."

"No, just hygienic."

"Mary use the basin in the bathroom, it has a hot water tap." This was slightly better but the twin tub washing machine was in the way of the basin, I had to lean across it to get to the taps. I also noticed that Joan had left her dirty clothes in the bath as if it was a linen bin. By this time I decided the flat was not for me but before leaving and out of nosiness I had a few questions to ask.

"My hands feel a bit cleaner, thank you. I'll sit down and drink my tea while asking you a few questions before I go back upstairs."

"Fire away."

"You appear a lot older than me, I'm twenty four, how old are you?"

"Forty three, I don't understand why my age matters to you."

"Well it does. I'm used to living with girls my own age not my mother's age. The next question why the hell are you living in a place like this, it's grubby, in fact it's bloody filthy?"

"This was the only flat I could afford when I left my husband. He was an alcoholic, I was fed up with his drinking habit so I left. He got up in the morning had a bite to eat then he started drinking by tea time he had drunk at least three bottles of Blue Nun wine."

"Why didn't you join him with a glass?"

"I did in the beginning but I soon got fed up with all our money being spent on alcohol and not having enough for food so I left. I haven't touched alcohol since. If you come and live down here you needn't get any grand ideas about drinking alcohol then coming back here drunk because I'll kick you out. I'd rather carry on paying the full rent and live on my own than smell alcohol around the flat." Joan made me feel uncomfortable as I couldn't imagine living a tea total life.

"Don't you go out with the girls to the pub on a Friday night and have a drink even if it's only a soft one?"

"No I don't. Never have and I never will. If they disturb me when they get back from the pub they're for the high jump on the Saturday morning."

"Joan, I reckon you're too much of a stick in the mud for me also you live in a complete mess, I wouldn't be able to tolerate the mess. I like to have everything in its place so I can find it at a minute's notice. I'm not going to sleep here for one night let alone a few. I have a suggestion to make, you need to clean this flat or you'll never rent the spare room to anyone."

"I'll have to stay living on my own as I'm no good at cleaning, even if I felt like getting my act together and cleaning the joint I can't afford to buy any cleaning materials."

"Joan it's obvious to me that you need to give in your notice here then go and get a bedsitter, which would be cheaper to run and easier to keep clean. Common sense should tell you that someone with more money in their pocket than you ought to live here. Has the landlord seen the state of this flat?"

"No. You're the first person to come in here since I took it on."

"How the hell have you managed to get away without anyone seeing inside before today?"

"Quite easy I just don't let anyone in."

"You let Liz in."

"Yeah but she only saw the spare room, she helped me clear the bed."

"I'm going back upstairs to have a chat with Liz and tell her how I have found your flat. You better be prepared for a visit first from Liz then the landlord."

"Go now and don't return." said Joan looking stupid.

"I'll go but be prepared for the visit."

"If someone knocks on my door, I won't answer."

"If you don't they may be able to get in because most probably they'll have a spare key."

"What makes you think that?"

"Because my landlord had a key and I found him in my flat when I returned from a night out." I left leaving Joan in a state of shock.

155

Chapter 20

"Liz, where are you?" I called from the top of the stairs. After a few minutes Liz put her head around the corner of the sitting room door - she looked terrible. "What the hell's the matter with you? Stop the crying and tell me what has happened it must be something bad for you to be crying like you are, also you look dreadful."

"I phoned the landlord and caught him on a bad day. I explained what had happened and he started to rant and rave down the phone at me. He said that he would be around sometime but it wouldn't be today. I asked if I should get a locksmith to save him having the bother, his answer to that was, 'go ahead if you're going to pay the bill because I won't be paying.'" Liz replied wiping the tears from her eyes.

"Did you tell him that a bloke had been living in the room that you had lost the key for?"

"Yeah."

"That was bloody daft Liz, you shouldn't have told him, you know damn well men aren't allowed to live here. I bet Andrew wasn't worth getting into trouble like this for."

"No he wasn't. My problem is that I'm not any good at making up stories like you are Mary, I had to tell him the truth."

"You should have used your brains and had a think before phoning or waited until I returned, then I could have helped you out. We could have made up some old yarn between us to tell the landlord. Liz try and stop crying."

"Once I start crying I find it difficult to stop. Five years ago I had a mental breakdown due to some silly upset which is not worth talking about. It made me cry, I cried nonstop for over a week. I went to bed crying and got up crying. Eventually I was taken into one of those mental institutions it was awful. I don't want that to happen."

"Well stop the crying. Go and sit down while I make a pot of tea. By the time I get back I hope you'll be smiling."

I returned to find Liz beaming from ear to ear. "Mary I'm pleased you've decided to live here, you're what I need as I'm weak and you're strong, you tell me exactly what I should or shouldn't do. I take tablets for depression. While you were making the tea I took a couple so I feel a bit better now."

"Good. I don't want to see any more tears." I explained about Joan's flat and the state it's in. "Liz, I'm not going to sleep down there for one night let alone a few nights so you better start thinking about where I can sleep."

"I have no idea."

"Before you suddenly have a brain storm about me sleeping top to toe in your bed, I'm not going to. I have a suggestion to make, go down and have an inspection of Joan's flat."

"How the hell can I do that?"

"Quite easily, go down and knock on the door then tell Joan why you're there. The thing is Liz the flat is filthy, it needs a damn good clean, along with the walls and ceilings being painted. Joan told me herself that she can't afford cleaning materials. If she's telling the truth, I reckon she should be given a month's notice. As you collect her rent I imagine you can give her notice."

"Mary, you're a hard soul."

"Someone has to be, if no one tells you what to do you'll get yourself in more of a mess than you're in already with the landlord."

"I'm not in a mess.

"From where I'm standing you are. Everything down stairs is pretty grim and I can only see it getting worse. Joan needs to be given notice. I'll frighten you into going down to have a look. The lavatory is the worst I've ever seen. Liz think about the one at that Chinese restaurant it's worse than that, Joan can't have cleaned it for years. In a minute she'll demand a new toilet seat along with a toilet bowl. I forgot to say that the whole place stinks. I recommend you take a peg with you."

"This is one of your stupid yarns Mary. I can't imagine Joan living like you're saying."

"Go down and see for yourself, if you don't believe me."

157

"I will once I've finished my tea." Liz looked across at me very strangely. "I know what this is all about."

"What's that?"

"You want to take over Joan's flat."

"At least I'd clean the joint and pay the rent on time."

"I'll go down and have a look around for myself. If the flat is as bad as you say it is I'll get rid of her, remember you won't be able to move in straight away. I have to give her four weeks' notice so that takes it up to the forth of May."

"Well give her four weeks' notice, during that time get her to buy cleaning materials and ask her to start cleaning up her shit. On top of cleaning I reckon the place needs a coat of paint. I guess you know she smokes - all the walls and ceilings are stained yellow."

"No I didn't know." answered Liz sounding annoyed. "Joan knows that tenants aren't allowed to smoke, the landlord only allows non-smokers to rent."

"Well Joan smoked at least five fags while I was sat there and I was only there for half an hour – the place stinks."

"There'll be trouble when I get down there."

"Before you go to see her, what's going happen to me? Have you decided where I'll be sleeping?"

"I told you earlier Mary I don't know, I can't say I don't care but I have no idea."

"You better think of somewhere and where ever it is, it better be clean." Liz went down the stairs looking like thunder. While she was away I took stock of myself. At this moment I have nowhere to sleep tonight let alone tomorrow. Even though I have a week left on my flat I've no intension of returning to it. I've said many times before and I will say it again I'd rather lose my deposit of twenty pounds than have sex with an incontinent twit called a landlord to get my deposit back. My sleeping arrangements have to be made as soon as possible especially if I can't sleep here and I have to leave to find a room in a guest house. I don't mind having to do this as long as Liz has given Joan notice and I'm able to move into the flat down stairs in four weeks' time with Ruth.

Liz came back sooner than I thought she would, plonking herself down on the sofa she started to shout and rant at me about Joan and the flat.

"I caught her red handed, she came to the door with a fag hanging from her mouth."

"You believe me now then?"

"Yeah, I believe you. I wish I hadn't got to, the place is far worse than I imagined."

"What's going to happen I need to know. Have you given her notice?"

"I've given her notice alright, she said she'll move out in two weeks. Before she leaves she either pays me to get a cleaning lady plus a decorator in or starts cleaning and painting it herself. By the time I left she was not a happy bunny."

"Liz, I'm going to ask you the same old question. Where am I sleeping?"

"I keep telling you I DON'T KNOW."

"While you were down stairs I had a think. What about me taking over this room at night? I could sleep on the sofa, it should only be for a couple of nights that's if the landlord comes around to open the door and we find the room in perfect condition."

Liz looked at me. "I'll have a chat with the girls once they're up and running. Mary, this is our one and only sitting room where we all settle down to watch the television in the evenings." I explained that I only needed a corner for my six black bags and one suitcase also I go to bed quite late most nights and get up early so I wouldn't need the sofa during the day or evening.

"I'll see what the girls have to say."

"Liz, when will you ask them as I need to know?"

"As soon as they're up."

"Surely they should be up by now."

"They had what we call a good night out. Instead of having one to many they finished the night with an extra one on top of the one to many. Enid drank Vodka all evening and finished off with a G and T while Margaret drank G and Ts' all night and finished with a double Vodka. I was the only one out of the three of us who was half sober. It was a very expensive night out as we had to get a black cab to bring us home. Once the girls

159

have sobered up they'll have to pay me back their share of the cab fare as I'm not made of money."

"Is this what happens every Friday night?" I asked.

"Normally we have three shorts each but on pay day we all have a couple more. The thing is Mary it was pay day yesterday. Enid and Margaret felt rich and continued drinking after I'd stopped. I owe money on a clothes catalogue, it has to be paid off by Monday so I only drank my normal three. The cab is another matter altogether, usually we walk both ways but when we've had far too much for our own good, we come home in style. I could have walked but I doubt if the other two would have made it half way home let alone all the way."

"I'll come out with you next Friday, I doubt if I'll be able to keep up with the three of you but I'm willing to have a go."

"I look forward to that. The girls at the office have told me about your nights out with Ruth, after what they've told me I'll be surprised if you come home sober."

In walked Margaret looking worse for wear. "Margaret, Mary is wondering if you mind if she sleeps on the sofa as I've lost the key to her room. She'll only be sleeping in here until the landlord arrives with a locksmith and we can see what state Andrew has left his old room in."

"Liz, you collect the rent so you should make that decision but if you want me to have an opinion on the subject, I don't mind as long as we can still watch the television during the evening. I would hate to think that you wanted to go to bed at say nine o'clock and we'd all have to move out."

"Often don't go to bed before midnight. I'll be out most evenings once I've finished my office job which is a week Tuesday. From the following Thursday I doubt if you'll see much of me."

"Margaret is Enid still asleep?" asked Liz looking a bit puzzled.

"I think so. I haven't seen her since we got in last night - she was in a bad way even worse than myself." Liz went on to say how she went to bed before the other two. Apparently Enid had to be pushed up the stairs, by the time she was on the landing Liz was completely fed up with the pair of them and went off to bed.

"It's a good job neither of you spewed up, I'm not going to say what I would have done if you had but both of you would have seen the wrong

160

side of me. Getting back to our journey home you two owe me a few bob for the cab. I can't let you get away without paying again as I'm feeling poor."

"Mary, has Liz told you how she fell in love with some sexy underwear in a clothes catalogue? Like a fool she ordered it and now it's pay back time."

"I feel daft as I can't return the bits as I've worn them, my problem is I have to pay the bill by Monday."

"We've all done something daft during our time on this planet. I'll give you something to smile about. My mother bought a pair of shoes when she got around to wearing them she found one shoe was comfortable and the other was tight, she could hardly walk in them - without complaining. Looking closely at them she found that one was a size four and the other a five. The size four was tight and the other was okay. After a lot of deliberation she returned them to the shoe shop, being vain she changed the size five to a four they were never worn again. Every time I visited her she got me to try them on, my shoes are a size five and a half so they didn't fit me. I always reckoned she thought my feet would shrink in between visits." We all laughed, then out of the blue Margaret started to sing the chorus of Carly Simon's song 'You're So Vain,' Liz stood up and joined in the fun, as I can't sing I conducted the pair of them. After they'd sung the chorus three times we all fell down in a heap on the sofa laughing.

"What the hell's going on?" shouted Enid from her bedroom door "you sound as if you've been drinking."

"Yes we have – tea." called out Margaret.

"Enid I've something to ask you." called Liz "Can you come here please?" Enid arrived in the sitting room holding her head, "What do you want me for?"

"Do you mind if Mary sleeps on the sofa for a few nights?"

"I don't I mind as long as I can watch my favourite programmes on the TV. What's wrong with the bedroom Mary why can't you sleep in there?"

"I can't get in, someone has locked the door and taken away the key."

"The key is missing Enid I thought it was on the kitchen table but it's not. Now Mary hasn't anywhere to sleep." Enid put her nose in the air and turned on her heel and left, she soon returned carrying a key out in front of her.

"This must be the key, I found it on my dressing table when I got out of bed."

"Enid you were in some state last night, I bet you picked it up and took it into your room."

"That must have been what happened. Everyone happy now all happy little bunnies." laughed Enid holding her head.

"I'm not happy, I've got myself in a spot. I phoned the landlord to explain about the key and like a fool I told him that Andrew had been living here."

"I've told you before Liz to think before you open your big mouth. That'll teach you a lesson."

"If I were you Liz I'd phone the landlord and shout down the phone when he answers and say 'I've found the key' then put the receiver down. With a bit of luck he won't phone back or think of coming around." I said smiling away to myself.

"You're such a clever clogs Mary Huggins you always know what anyone should or shouldn't do, even if you can't do it yourself."

"Calm down the lot of you. Once I've dressed and I'm up and running I'll go and get a couple of bottles of Blue Nun from the off license." Shouted Enid.

"Whatever for, we had enough last night?" said Liz.

"I promised Mary that I'd celebrate her moving in, I always keep my promises."

"You were in a bad way last night, remember that not all the alcohol you drank then is out of your system."

"Liz you're such a spoil sport. I promised Mary that we'd have a couple on Saturday night and today is Saturday so we're having a couple. At least you lot are drinking at my expense. I may have a lemonade." said Enid still holding her head.

"God, I couldn't drink lemonade after all that booze you poured down your throat. I'd drink water or nothing at all, then I'd sit back and watch everyone else making fools of themselves."

"At the moment girls I'm nursing a headache so I may go and buy the drink then go back to bed."

"While you get yourself up and running I'll take Mary along to see Andrew's old room and see what condition it's in, fingers crossed that it will be okay." After looking at everything including the mattress which was spotless - thank God - I paid Liz my deposit then she left me in peace to sort myself out.

I must have been exhausted as I fell asleep on the bed, before I knew it Liz was knocking on my door.

"The three of us are waiting for you to come and join in the fun." I looked at my watch it was nine o'clock. I had slept through supper and if Liz hadn't knocked the door I don't think I'd have woken until Sunday morning. "I'm coming." I said sounding half a sleep. I gave my hair a bit of a brush and wandered out into the sitting room where the girls were sat waiting to drink the wine which was lined up on the coffee table with the glasses. "I thought you'd be going back to bed Enid, I never dreamt that you'd be here with us opening the bottles."

"I'm going to sit and watch you three and see which one of you drinks the most."

"Which are you going to drink Mary, White, Rose' or red?" asked Margaret.

"I don't mind, perhaps I could have a mixture, a small amount of each in one glass."

"I've never tried that, I bet if I mixed all three types together I'd wake up with a really bad head in the morning."

"Margaret it may have the same effect as drinking one glass of the same type of wine except you'll have a small amount of each type in the one glass, having the mixture may not be as strong. Try it." I remarked.

Liz decided to be the waitress and poured our drinks. What happened during the evening I don't know - I can't remember a thing. The next day the girls told me what a good night they'd had. Apparently after I'd drunk the three mixtures of wine in one glass I fell asleep in the corner and snored the night away. The morning came and that's when I found myself in the corner. I managed to stand up and go into the kitchen where the others were cooking a fry up.

"Morning girls. How the hell can you lot eat that after a heavy night?"

"Quite easily, watch us. We always have a fry up on a Sunday whether we've been drinking or not."

"Don't cook me any, I'm off to bed. God my head's bad. I'm never going to mix different wines together again."

"Mary, it'll teach you a lesson, then again it may not as most people that drink too much say never again and then next time they seem to drink even more."

"Here's a couple of Panadol for your head along with a black coffee." added Enid.

"Enid can you carry the coffee to my room please?"

"We'll be calling you Miss Drunk in a minute instead of Miss Mary."

"That's not a very nice name to call me."

"Well you shouldn't mix your drinks or drink so much."

"It was a one off girls, I hadn't eaten anything all day." I said looking embarrassed.

"Whatever you three do today please don't disturb me unless it's getting on for six o'clock. I'm going out tonight." They looked towards me.

"Aren't you going to ask what I'm up to?"

"Come on tell us or we won't wake you up."

"I've a date with dear old Steve."

"You kept that quiet."

"I'd forgotten all about it as I've been busy yapping, drinking and snoring."

Enid, helped me to my room along the way she told me not to take any notice of the girls and their stupid talk. "I'm in all day so I'll wake you at six if you're not up and about."

I slept well thank God until four thirty when I woke, had a bath then tarted myself up for the evening.

I left the flat at around six thirty to get to Trafalgar Square where Steve was sat on a bench, he seemed pleased to see me and started chatting for England as if he hadn't had anyone to yap to for days. Thank goodness I had piled on enough makeup and blusher to make me look healthy and also so Steve couldn't see how pale I really am after a Saturday night on the bottle.

"Before we leave here for the pub have you eaten?"

"No." I answered looking sheepish.

"Neither have I. If we find a restaurant open do you fancy going in for a meal instead of going to the pub?"

"Depends what type of food they sell - I wouldn't mind going for an Indian."

"Let's go up St Martin's lane into Monmouth Street. I know of a good Indian up there on the right. When I asked you out I forgot it was a Sunday. Anyway we should find somewhere open hopefully it'll be the Indian in Monmouth Street."

We made our way up St Martin's Lane chatting about different things including the state of my room and how I may take over the flat downstairs. Steve mentioned how he'd bumped into his landlord coming down the stairs, apparently he didn't look happy in fact he looked very unhappy. "Good I would hate to think he was smiling. What did he have to say?"

"Nothing to me, mind you I didn't give him the chance to speak. I pretended not to see him and went into my room banging the door behind me. I had no intension of opening it again even if he knocked."

Chapter 21

It didn't take us long to reach Monmouth Street. Keeping all our fingers crossed we went over to the door of the Indian restaurant and gave it a push, luck was on our side it opened, in we went. There were only a couple of empty tables, we chose the one nearest the wall and in the corner so we could have a private chat while eating, it was also away from the customers that were smoking.

The waitress dressed in a sari came over with a menu. Steve explained to her that neither of us had ever ordered an Indian meal before and asked what she could recommend.

"What about a set meal for two?" we accepted.

"That was easy enough. Now we'll wait and see what arrives."

"Steve whatever arrives I hope it won't be to hot. When I visited the Indian at the bottom of Regents Street I had a madras, it was to hot for me so I drank a glass of cold water which made my mouth even hotter. Steve always remember not to have an ice cold drink with an Indian meal. Always have a warm drink not that I think that's correct either but it would be better than an ice cold drink. The best thing to do is ask the waitress which drink she recommends. I thank God that when I ate the Indian in Regents Street I didn't have a vindaloo if I had it would have burnt the inside of my mouth" We both laughed and waited patiently. After half an hour Steve called out to whoever was listening, "Where's our food?"

"It's cooking." called out the head waiter who was wandering through the restaurant to the kitchen. Steve went on to explain that we'd been waiting for a good half an hour. With that a couple of blokes at the other end of the restaurant started to bang their knives and forks up and down on their table, at the same time they sang the song 'why are we waiting' as loud as they dared.

"Stop that noise." shouted the head waiter sounding annoyed.

"Why should we?" replied the blokes.

"Because you're in a restaurant." replied the head waiter.

"We want our food we've been waiting bloody ages." screamed the blokes while they continued to bang the cutlery up and down on their table.

"For God's sake shut up, stop the racket." called out an elderly man from the table next to ours. "The food we're eating is very good, when yours arrives you'll realise it was worth the wait - shut up and wait."

"Mary keep your head down, we'll give them a bit longer then if the food doesn't arrive we'll leave." Steve whispered.

The kitchen door opened and there stood the chef looking flushed, "Quiet please all of you and that includes you two over there." he said pointing his finger at the two noisy blokes. "The oven has broken down. We've an electrician trying to repair it. The manager has asked me to offer you all a drink on the house while you wait. Sorry for any inconvenience."

"Double Gin and tonic for me." I called out without hesitation.

"Shandy please, no sorry I didn't mean that, I would like a bottle of Blue Nun it's my favourite tipple and it should go down well with my meal." called out Steve.

"Mary let's stay here and drink what we can for free, if the food doesn't arrive we can always walk out after having an evening of free booze."

"That sounds good to me, the only problem I can see is that I haven't had any proper food since Friday, I may fall over as soon as I stand up if I have too many Gin and Tonics."

"Mary, once you've drank three doubles and I've finished the Blue Nun and if the food has not arrived we'll leave and go somewhere to get a meal whether it will be an Indian I'm not sure, it may be egg and chips at the local café. Let us hope that the oven is repaired and we don't have to resort to the egg and chips."

"Listen to me Steve, three double Gin and Tonics is a lot of booze on an empty stomach."

"Don't be daft girl, I've known you to drink more than that without food."

"That was last week not this evening."

"Are you trying to tell me something Mary, are you trying to say that you've cut down on your drink?"

"Something like that." I replied looking embarrassed which made Steve throw another question at me.

"I don't think you've cut down on the booze, I reckon you had far too much for your own good last night, am I right or am I wrong?" Steve laughed.

"Steve you always guess right and you're right again. We girls had a couple of glasses of wine to celebrate my arrival at the flat." I went on to explain how I'd mixed the different types of wine together in one glass. Steve was disgusted but before he could tell me exactly what he thought, one of the blokes on the other table started to shout out about a girl he could see looking in the main window of the restaurant having pulled her top up to show off her boobs.

"Look at her John she hasn't got a bra on and she has pulled her bloody top up for the world to see her tits." his mate turned towards the window.

"They're not bad Brian I wouldn't mind getting my head between them." replied John laughing out loud.

"Don't be so crude." shouted the elderly man. "I think you should be asked to leave, I'm going to ask the head waiter to send you both packing." John immediately stood up bowed then announced to the customers,

"Before we're told to get out of this fucking useless joint here is my party trick." He immediately did a hand stand between the tables. Out fell everything from his jacket pockets including johnnies which he informed the other customers he would be using later tonight unless the men in the restaurant wanted to buy them from him at half price.

"Get out the pair of you." shouted the head waiter.

"We have to finish our drinks first sir." replied John bowing towards the head waiter.

"You must be joking go before I pick you up and throw you out the door. If I have any more cheek from you the police will be arriving. GET OUT NOW." The pair turned and ran out banging the door behind them.

"Head waiter" called out Steve "can Mary have another G and T please, make sure it's a double."

"A double?"

"That's what I said, we deserve some thing for the time we've sat here waiting for our food. If you don't hurry up we'll start singing 'Why Are We Waiting' and it won't be the clean version."

"Well you'll go the same way as those two blokes, out the door if you start that nonsense."

"You better hurry up then." he left our table to organise my drink.

"Once we've finished these drinks we'll run as I doubt if we'll get any food here tonight and I'm starving – my stomach is rumbling."

"I agree with you Steve but get a move on as you've half a bottle Blue Nun left to drink."

"Once you've finished the Gin and Tonic they're bringing, you can have a drop of this wine. If you can mix different types of wine in one glass and drink it down you can definitely drink wine on top of Gin."

"Here comes my Gin."

"Enjoy." said the waitress.

"I will, I definitely will." I don't know what came over Steve but he helped me out with the Gin by adding a drop to his wine. As soon as we had finished our drinks and we noticed the head waiter go into the kitchen we got up from the table and were about to do a runner when the waitress came out from the kitchen with our food. "How the hell do you think we'll be able to eat all this after the booze we've drunk Steve?"

"I don't know but we'll have to have a damn good try." We plonked ourselves back down. We must have eaten half the meal when we gave up.

"I don't feel to good, I shouldn't have eaten that on top of the Gin plus wine. I reckon when I get outside I'll spew up."

"Mary, go now if you feel ill, we don't want an accident in here. I can imagine what the staff and customers will say and do if you make a mess in here." Out I went and found an alleyway at the side of the restaurant, up it came – what a waste of money. Steve was stood behind me "Better up than down."

"I don't want to eat an Indian meal again for a while in fact at this moment I wouldn't care if I never saw the inside of an Indian restaurant ever again."

169

"God you must feel bad."

"I feel awful, but I wouldn't mind calling in somewhere for a glass of water. What about the pub we passed on the corner of St Martin's Lane and Long Acre?"

"Mary you never give up on pubs. I guess you know the joint because I don't."

"I know it alright, its right up your alley Steve – boring."

"You told me I was boring before you left your flat in Hammersmith but it hasn't stopped you from coming out on a date so I can't be that bad."

"You're not, I'm teasing. Can I hold your hand?"

"Of course you can." Steve took hold of my hand without thinking twice.

"Steve don't get too excited about me holding your hand. Remember me holding your hand doesn't mean we're going to get married, it means we're holding hands. I thank God you agreed to hold my hand though, if you'd refused I doubt if I'd be able to walk properly or even walk at all."

We plodded along for a bit when out of the blue Steve suggested that I should put my arm through his because I was walking everywhere except in a straight line and pulling him along with me, "This is cosy." I said laughing.

"Mary if I hadn't suggested this I could see you falling head first on to the pavement before we got to any pub."

"Steve, I don't understand why you appear dead sober and I'm on the verge of being called sloshed?" I said almost tripping over my feet.

"Mary, that's quite easy to understand you had more than your fare share to drink with the girls last night. This evening you drank too much alcohol before having a meal, all of this before Saturday's night's alcohol had completely gone out of your system."

"In the restaurant you told me that you hadn't eaten anything all day." I said slurring my words. "If that's the case why are you sober when you should be tiddly like me?"

"Because I'm a man and I should be able to drink more than a woman without getting drunk. Here's a pub, is this the one Mary?"

"Are we at the corner of Long Acre?" I asked.

"Yeah, I can see the sign saying Long Acre."

"We're at the pub, we're at the pub." I sang.

170

"For God's sake Mary shut up or they won't let us in. Pull yourself together."

"I know, you go in and I'll stay sitting on this step and wait for you to bring me out a glass of water."

"You must be joking Mary, if I go in you're coming with me." said Steve getting more and more annoyed and agitated.

"Steve I have a plan. You leave me here and go in and see if there's some where to sit, if there is I'll come in."

"That sounds okay in theory but I'm not going to leave you out here on your own - you may get picked up."

"Me get picked up, never, no one would want me drunk or sober."

"Are you testing me Mary, you seem to be trying to get me to say that I'd pick you up?"

"I bet you would, in fact the way you look at me sometimes I know damn well you would." Steve started to blush and choke with embarrassment. "Come on Steve tell me, I need to know if you fancy me." I've never seen Steve in such a state he always seemed in control of his emotions but he isn't tonight. After a few minutes he looked towards me, "Come on Mary let's go in together and find a seat."

We helped each other up the two steps Steve pushed open the door, I almost fell head first into the bar but was saved by a man that was coming out.   Once inside we were lucky enough to find two chairs at a table where a couple were sat "Is it okay if we plonk ourselves down here?" I asked.

"Suppose so." replied the girl who looked as sober as I'm tiddly.

Steve soon came back from the bar with a coke for himself and a glass of tap water for me. We sat in silence when the girl started to chat to Steve leaving me with only my glass of water for company. After a while she asked in front of the bloke she was with and not caring about me and my feelings.

"What the hell are you doing out with her?" nodding her head towards me, Steve looked embarrassed.

"What's it to you why I'm out and about with my friend Mary." Said Steve looking over at the pair of them. "We haven't sat here for any other

171

reason than to sit on the only two chairs left available in this pub. We're not here to make friends with you two."

"I thought perhaps you had. John is my brother we meet here every Sunday evening. We're both on the lookout."

"I'm not on the lookout and neither is Mary, she's my friend and a very good friend she is. We'll remember not to come in here on a Sunday ever again" Steve leaned towards me. "Come on Mary drink up it's time for us to move." Steve stood up.

"We've only been here five minutes, give me a chance to drink my water."

"To me that is five minutes to long Mary dear. Drink up or leave the damn water, as it didn't cost me anything." We both staggered outside.

"Thank God we got out of their unscathed. Mary don't you ever suggest going into that pub again if you're out with me."

"I thought it was quite a nice pub. I couldn't see anything wrong with it."

"Mary the building was okay. It was the couple at our table that were the problem. I reckon the man was that girl's pimp, he didn't mind her chatting to me in fact he seemed to encourage her."

"Steve you must be joking."

"Couldn't you see or hear her?" replied Steve.

"I sat with my head in my hands as its going around and around. When I did look towards the bloke he didn't look like her brother or her pimp to me"

"If he wasn't her brother and if you don't think he was her pimp she must have been trying it on, to get a foursome out of us not that it would have happened."

"It would have been a way of me getting you into bed Steve, not that I would have wanted to share you with those two - I'm selfish. I'd want you for myself." Steve pretended not to hear or listen to what I said.

"Let's go to Trafalgar Square." Said Steve looking as if he was in a hurry but at the same time trying to get me to walk in a straight line which was difficult.

"Steve stop pulling me along. Before we go any further let me have a look at my watch I must know the time."

"I'll tell you the time ten o'clock, past my bed time."

"Are you going to send me on my way?"

"Why should I do that?"

"You've just said it's past your bedtime meaning you need to go to bed."

"I was only making a statement about the time. If I wanted to go to bed my normal time I wouldn't have come out or if I had come out, I would have met up with you during the afternoon. Think yourself lucky that I'm here and I've had some alcohol to drink on a Sunday evening."

"Steve it is a bit of a shock seeing you mixing your alcohol in the restaurant let alone seeing you drink more than a couple glasses of wine. When we've been out together before you have done a runner after two drinks."

"Well I'm not doing a runner tonight."

"Good."

"I decided before I left home that if I drank to much alcohol I would ring in sick in the morning. I've worked at the factory for over five years and I've never had a day off sick - tomorrow may be the big day."

After getting over the shock of Steve telling me this I went on to explain about a man I knew that worked in the National Westminster bank who regularly took a day off on a Friday especially after he'd had a heavy Thursday night. He was in trouble most Monday mornings. They were fed up with him come the end that they docked his pay which upset him as he often finished up not having enough money to pay his rent or buy food. The manager wasn't stupid and one day out of the blue he took Jimmy - that was this bloke's name – into his office and suggested that he should visit Alcoholics Anonymous - most of the staff knew the alcohol was the reason for him not going into work on a Friday. The shock of the staff knowing made Jimmy change the heavy Thursday nights to a Friday.

"Steve don't look so worried, what I've told you won't happen to you as one day off won't make them think you're a drunk unless of course you're going to make a habit of not going into work on a Monday."

"Mary, let's go and find some where to sit and have a coffee to try and clear our heads."

"I know of a cosy coffee bar around the back of the National Portrait Gallery. I often pop in there when I'm in this area. It stays open until gone midnight, we won't have to hurry our coffees as long as there is somewhere to sit. It's very popular with the locals, one evening I went in and it was full of the down and outs."

"Mary you really know how to upset me."

"It's fun watching your face and seeing you getting cross. I promise what I said was meant as a joke."

The coffee bar only had a few customers one being an old woman who stood out from the others. She was sat in the corner scratching her head and picking her finger nails. Steve's face was a picture when he saw her but he did agree to stay for a coffee as long as we sat at a table far away from the old woman and her trolley.

"I wonder where the hell the old woman hangs out at night?" asked Steve nodding towards her.

"How the hell do I know. Most probably she sleeps in a door way with some dirty old bugger that fancies her."

"You get worse by the minute Mary Huggins it must be the drink that makes you imagine things like that. Who the hell would fancy her, holding her hand would be bad enough for me, giving her a quick poke would kill me off."

We were sat drinking our coffee when out of the blue the old woman got up from her seat and started to stagger in our direction "Here she comes, she's coming over Mary."

"That's alright she must be going to the loo - it's in the corner behind me." I replied. Once she arrived by our table she stopped and lent over to whisper in Steve's ear which made him squirm. "Young man I can hear you talking about me from where I'm sat and what I heard I didn't like." Steve looked worried to death. "For your interest I have got a man – don't look so surprised, we sleep together under Waterloo Bridge every night unless someone pinches our spot then we have to find a doorway. The one thing you aren't right about is my SEX life, if we wanted sex we couldn't perform because of all the clothes I have on to keep me warm - they'd get in the way. My old man would never find my fanny to touch me up, anyway he's a bit long in the tooth for sex also his dick disappeared into outer space years ago. Now I've told you all you wanted to know I'll go back to my table." The shock of the old woman coming over and telling us what she heard sobered us both up.

"The old woman gave me the shock of my life when she stopped by our table and told us about her non - existent sex life. I feel sorry for her I'd hate to be in her shoes. I reckon we should buy her a coffee what do you think Steve?"

"I feel the same as you. I'll go up and order three coffees and get the boy behind the counter to take one over to the old woman." Steve returned with two on a tray.

"Time goes so fast when you're having fun, it's almost eleven thirty I'll have to get going once I've drunk this. Before I leave Steve which part of the country do you come from? You seem to have the same accent as that old woman. "

"Don't say that Mary, in a minute you'll be telling me that she used to live in the same city as my parents or even worse the same street."

"Where's that?"

"Birmingham."

"Steve you're telling me you came all the way down from Birmingham to a bedsitter in Hammersmith to work on the production line at the factory down the road in Ealing Broadway, have I got that right?"

"Yeah afraid so."

"You could have got a job in a factory doing what you're doing here back in Birmingham."

"Mary don't embarrass me. If we meet up again I'll tell you the reason for me moving to London."

"I thought meeting up this evening was going to be a one off, tell me now why you moved down here." Steve starred at me.

"If I tell you why, you must promise to keep it to yourself."

"I promise on my life."

"I left home to get away from a woman."

"Fancy moving right down here, you could have packed your bags and moved to the other side of Birmingham. It must be cheaper to live up there."

"If you can stay for another coffee I'll tell you what happened but please don't laugh or repeat what I'm about to tell you."

"I've just promised you I won't say a word to anyone, if I say I won't, I mean I won't." Steve went on to explain how he met a woman called Jean at the factory – she worked on the same production line as him. "We got chatting in our break and she invited ME out for a drink at the local pub after our shift finished that day. Like a fool I agreed to go why I don't know as I didn't fancy her. We got on like a house on fire and as I hadn't got a girl friend at the time and I guessed she hadn't a man we arranged to go for a drink after work - once a week. This went on for a couple of months until eventually we were meeting up three evenings a week. Jean didn't ever mention having a boyfriend and when I suggested we should get into a sexual relationship she didn't say no."

"What happened then?"

"I booked a hotel room where we stayed one night a week she never seemed in a hurry to go home, in fact she often suggested we should spend two nights a week at the hotel."

"I'm going to guess something went badly wrong come on tell me."

"It went wrong all right, Jean arrived at the factory one morning looking worried to death – she reckoned she was pregnant. Over coffee she explained that she was married to a black man."

"What. How the hell did she manage to stay at the hotel over night?"

"That was easy enough she didn't have any children and her husband worked as the night porter at the local hospital, there was no way that he'd realise she was out all night, he imagined she was tucked up in bed."

"God all mighty Steve what happened next?"

"I did a runner and the rest is history." Steve sat dreaming. "Anyway she was far too old for me, I shouldn't have got involved, she was in her late thirties and I was only twenty two at the time. The stupid woman didn't tell me her age until she told me she was pregnant. How could I suggest she got divorced and marry me?"

"Steve I reckon you did the right thing, the baby could have popped out black and you would have been lumbered with it for the rest of your days – how embarrassing."

"She told me she hadn't had sex with her old man - as she called him - for a good two years."

"Did you believe her?"

"No I didn't. If I had I wouldn't be sat here now - I'd be in Birmingham." I laughed.

"Have you heard from her since?"

"No thank God. My worry is that she knows where my parents live. Like a fool I gave her their address. That was the stupidest thing I've ever done." I held out my hand to catch hold of Steve's which he took willingly.

"I feel sorry for you Steve in fact I feel so sorry for you that I would love to meet with you again."

"You're going to meet me because you feel sorry for me. I won't meet you for that reason I'll meet you because I wouldn't mind having you as my girl friend." I looked shocked.

"I never thought I'd ever hear that from you."

"Well you have, let's have a snog." Steve pulled me towards him and gave me my first lingering French kiss with him.

"Was that because we've had one too many or to seal the beginning of our relationship?"

"The latter you silly devil." Steve moved his chair closer to mine and sat with both arms enclosed around my waist. Before we knew it we were being asked to leave as the boy behind the counter was shutting up shop.

"What are we going to do now?" asked Steve standing up and looking at his watch "the night is young."

"Am I hearing right. You of all people are asking me what we're going to do now? it's past midnight Steve" Steve ignored my comment.

"Mary do you fancy coming back to my place or shall I come over to yours? or are you going to go home alone?"

"Let's catch the tube over to Hammersmith as you're having the day off tomorrow and I can always go into work from your place." Steve looked at me strangely. "I have everything in this bag" I said holding it up "including a spare pair of knickers."

"Mary if you are happy with that lets go and catch the last tube." I held on to his arm.

"Being serious Steve, I think I ought to go back to my own bed and meet up with you later in the week."

"Who is chickening out now after a couple of drinks. You're being the spoil sport Mary."

"I don't mean to be, I'm just being sensible. The thing is Steve I can't have men staying the night at my place unless I'm engaged to the bloke so you coming home with me is out of the question. Going back to your place in theory sounds fine but the trouble is the girls may be sat up wondering where I am and may call the police if I don't return home."

"God all mighty Mary I never thought I'd hear all this rubbish coming out of your mouth. It seems from where I'm standing that you've moved into a convent. When and where do you suggest we meet up and where do you reckon we should consummate our relationship, up some back alley? If we were out in the country I'd suggest performing in a field now." Steve laughed.

"Don't embarrass me or make me feel a fool Steve for God's sake or I'll go on my way and not meet up with you again. What's wrong with you booking a hotel room? You managed to afford that when you were seeing the WOMAN in Birmingham so you should be able to get one here for us. What about booking a room for Thursday night? I get home from the office around six so I should be out and about by eight. If I bring an overnight bag with my bits and bobs I can go to work from the hotel. I know of a private one up the road from here which may suit us. I can give you the phone number – I have it in my bag. You could phone them before we meet on Thursday, if there aren't any vacancies I promise I'll come back to your place." Steve was silent while he watched me find the number. "Speak, say something Steve before I scream and run home."

"Mary, hand over the number then I'll sort something out for us. It's a pity we can't meet up before Thursday, it will a long week for me."

"You can always phone in fact you could phone most evenings as I'll be in."

"Okay I'll phone you tomorrow at seven to let you know if I've managed to book the room. Let's say we'll meet under Nelson's Column at eight o'clock Thursday. Mary, please don't be late as I won't have eaten so I'll need to go for a meal."

"Steve, going for a meal is easy we can always come back in here and have sandwiches and a bun, we don't need a heavy meal before performing."

"You must be joking Mary I'm never putting foot in this place again. It has been bad enough drinking coffee in here and seeing a down and out over the other side of the room. I can't sit and eat in here. One thing I must say Mary is I enjoyed the coffee - it seemed to suit my palate. It's the company in here I'm not so keen on. I reckon like you that the old woman visits here most evenings before making her way to Waterloo Bridge."

"I bet you're right Steve, in fact I'm sure you are."

Then whispering in my ear he went on to say that he wouldn't be able to get a hard if he had to start the night off in this joint. I laughed at him.

"I'll finish you off dear Steve, think about this, I'm wondering if the old woman has drunk out of these mugs." I said picking one up and looking at it closely "as I'm sure they don't have special mugs for the down and outs and I doubt if they have a dish washer. I bet every dish is washed by hand with a dirty old dishcloth."

"For God's sake Mary shut up. I can't take any more of your stupid nonsense, let's leave before the boy throws us out." We staggered out on to the pavement where we had a quick snog before parting company.

179

Chapter 22

Arriving back at Westbourne Terrace I found the building in darkness. There wasn't even a light outside, I found it difficult to find where to put the key to open the door. Once inside I had to take care not to trip over anything while I hunted for the light switch. I know what I ought to have done and that was to take note of the position of the switch before going out - I didn't. After about ten minutes of feeling around the walls I found the switch and was able to turn the light on then stagger up the stairs to my room.

I slept well thank God. Monday morning I was up and running by six thirty as I was scared I wouldn't be ready to walk to the tube and get to the office on time. I had visions of having to wave down a cab. How I imagined I could afford one all the way to Oxford Circus from here - I don't know as I'm running out of money. Tomorrow I'll be given my last pay packet from the office, whether there'll be enough in the kitty to keep me going for the next few weeks I don't know. I'm keeping my fingers crossed that the escort agency pays weekly if they don't I'll have to visit the bank of mum whether she'll give me any money – I'm not sure.

My morning at the office went peacefully in fact none of us had much work to do which made a change from last week when we were far to busy. Lunch time came and Joyce suggested that we should all stop work and go out for lunch together.

"Whatever has come over you lot, none of you have ever suggested coming for lunch with Ruth and I before. Thinking about it we've never invited you or wanted you to join us."

"You've got that right Mary, if and when we have suggested lunch with the pair of you one or other of you have said we couldn't go with you. Whether you like it or not we girls have decided to take you out for a boozy lunch hour today. Mary the weather is fine today, next Monday which is the day before you leave it's just as likely to be raining and none of us would want to go out. This is our last chance to have a meal plus drink with you."

"I've two things to say to you lot. One, I'm not hungry enough to go for a meal and two I'm not drinking alcohol if we do go out together."

"Mary, I can't imagine you having a soft drink when we're on the hard stuff." Said Ruth looking puzzled.

"Whatever you lot say it's definitely going to be a soft drink for me and a snack like a packet of crisps." The girls looked shocked.

"I'll tell you what the matter is with Mary." Said Liz grinning to herself, "she has had too much alcohol over the weekend. Saturday night she slept on the floor in the corner of the sitting room as she couldn't get up to go into bed. Last evening Mary was out with Steve. I saw you from my bedroom window when you got back, how the hell you managed to walk to the door without tripping over your feet I'll never know."

"Liz, if you saw me why didn't you come down and unlock the door?"

"Mary, the truth is I couldn't be bothered. I thought perhaps you would give up the alcohol if you found it difficult to get into the flat while you were under the influence."

"Me give up alcohol that's a joke and a half, I doubt if I'll ever do that." Immediately Liz started to tell us all about her aunt that drank far to much and how Liz's mother who was the aunt's sister had to call the police as she didn't have a key to get into her sister's house. The police were the ones that found the aunt laying on the bedroom floor in a pool of urine, apparently she'd been there for a couple of days after drinking a few bottles of red wine.

"That must have been terrible." Said Joyce.

"Mary that could be you if you don't try to give up the booze." added Ruth.

"That won't happen to me, I don't drink that much. Anyway what happened to the aunt after that?" I was annoyed.

"She was persuaded to join AA by her doctor."

"What the hell is AA?" asked Joyce.

"That's Alcoholics Anonymous, it's a fellowship for people with drink problems." answered Liz.

"I'm not that bad, I don't need to join them." I replied sounding more annoyed than ever.

"Mary you appear pretty bad from where we're standing, any way for God's sake don't get so obnoxious." called out Ruth.

"If someone was telling you that you should join AA you would get annoyed like me, especially when all your mates in the typing pool are stood around listening and cheering each other on."

"Mary you know damn well what I'm saying is the truth. When you were living above Steve you used to drink far too much for your own good. Steve always said he wouldn't take you out on a date because of your drinking habit."

"If you must know I've another date with him Thursday evening." I was near to tears. Then Joyce decided to put her spoke in.

"My granddad drank too much for his own good and finished up doubly incontinent due to the fact that he couldn't get to the lavatory in time because he was drunk."

"Shut up all of you. This is the last chance you lot have to come out for lunch with me unless one of you bothers to phone and invite me once I've left. I'm going to enjoy myself this lunch time even though I'M ONLY GOING TO HAVE A SOFT DRINK. To keep the peace I'm going to give alcohol up. I reckon it will be easy enough as all I need to do is think of Liz's aunt or Joyce's grandad.   Today is the start of the rest of my life – alcohol free. Before we go for lunch I must go to the lavatory, coming with me Ruth?" I put my nose in the air and started to walk out the door. Ruth followed, once in the corridor she put her arm around my shoulder.

"Mary if you take care of yourself you won't finish up going to AA. Try not to take any notice of the girls. You know as well as I do that it's none of their damn business how much you drink. After next Tuesday I doubt if you will see any of them ever again."

"I thank God I'm leaving. I can't cope with the girls keeping on at me about alcohol. Anyway Ruth you drink as much as me given half the chance."

"I realise I drink a lot, the difference is they haven't found out about me and the demon drink and they're hardly likely to unless you tell them, please don't spill the beans."

"Ruth don't be daft I wouldn't tell them. Do you know much about AA?"

"Only that if you go along to a meeting you don't have to tell them your real name you can keep it secret."

"That's something."

"The meetings are held at halls in towns and cities across the country, each meeting lasts about ninety minutes. Some alcoholics go to the meetings every day and some go more than once a day. Mary if you finish up having to go remember it's free. I have a feeling the person that organises the meeting may pass a hat around for the alcoholics to put a few pence in to help pay for the hire of the hall."

"You know more about AA than I do."

"I suppose I do, I had to find out about it when dad was drinking far too much for his own good. He was a bit like your mum he also fell down the stairs. Dad falling down the stairs was the last straw for my mum, she got herself in such a state about dad that I went and found out about AA. He never went to any meetings, all he did was promise mum he would never drink again but you know very well that people that drink a lot have a job to give it up and he hasn't."

"Ruth I'm never going to drink alcohol again." I replied with tears in my eyes.

"I hope that comes true Mary. I'll try and give it up as well. When we go out with the girls for lunch I'll keep you company with a soft drink, most probably I'll have a bitter lemon."

"Thankyou. When we go back in please don't encourage the girls to talk about my drinking habit."

"I won't Mary. I'm going to tell you something as long as you promise not to repeat it to anyone."

"You're my friend why should I repeat what you tell me?"

"A couple of years ago the three of us – that was dad, mum and I – set off to a cousin's wedding, it was the most embarrassing day of my life and mum's."

"What happened?"

"Dad hadn't had a drink for quite a few weeks as he promised mum that he'd give it up and he did until the wedding reception when the waiter offered him alcohol. He took the drink and once he had a taste for it he couldn't stop. The outcome was that he fell over at the reception making a complete fool of himself."

"Ruth, I don't want to hear any more about the effects of drinking alcohol, let's go and find the others and get this lunch over with."

Out in the typing pool the girls were putting on their lipstick. "You lot look as if you're getting ready to go on a pick up."

"Don't be daft." shouted Liz sounding annoyed. At least Ruth's comment stopped the girls from continuing the conversation about me and my friend Alcohol.

"Joyce have you decided where we're going as this is your grand idea?" asked Ruth

"I thought you or Mary would come up with somewhere."

"Well you thought wrong. This was your idea Joyce so you need to suggest a pub." silence reigned,

"Any ideas girls?" shouted Joyce.

"I know a place down Marlborough Street. I haven't been there for a while but they used to make wonderful sandwiches at a reasonable price. If the place is full we can always go on to the pub on the corner of Wardour Street, it's a bit of a dive - it would do at a push." suggested Marg.

"Let's go to Marlborough Street." called out Audrey from the other side of the office.

We set off leaving our boss to wonder where we'd all gone. At the Marlborough Street pub we managed to find a table with enough chairs to accommodate us all. The hour in the pub turned into two as Joyce suggested that we should take it in turns to tell a story about men we had been out with and the catastrophes we'd had over the years with them. Everyone was game especially after a few drinks.

Marg was the first to tell her story. "I'd been going out with this bloke for a couple of weeks after a few drinks in a pub he invited me back to his bedsitter. In my tiddly state I agreed to go back for a quickie - I fancied him rotten. After a bit of foreplay HE spewed up over the floor, that was the end of that romance."

"Eh how blinking disgusting." called out Liz, no one laughed.

"Ruth's turn next." Shouted Joyce.

"I'll have to have a think." silence reigned. "Here goes, I was going out with a bloke that I met at the rugby club. After the match he had one to many in the bar. He carried me out to his car and dropped me in a puddle ruining my clothes - he thought it was funny."

"Whatever next are we going to hear. Your turn Audrey." called out Liz.

"Nothing much has ever happened to me but I know of a woman that went to a dance in a strapless dress. A chap asked her for a dance and twirled her around the dance floor and her dress slipped showing her boobs to the world."

"How bloody embarrassing. I would hate to think that happened to me." called out Ruth.

"Joyce it's your turn." I called over.

"This is really embarrassing it makes me blush thinking about it. I was invited to the theatre up the West End with a man that I would have liked to have called my boyfriend. I dressed myself up in my best attire. While walking into the foyer my stockings fell down around my ankles as they were only held up with handmade garters. The thought of what happened makes me blush even now." Joyce went bright red from the neck upwards.

"That will teach you a lesson Joyce, next time buy a suspender belt or a roll on or better still wear tights." I called out while laughing.

"That's bloody boring suggesting Joyce should have worn tights especially coming from you Miss Mary." called out Ruth.

"We only have time for one more, which one of you is going to tell a story? It can't be Mary as we all know about her and that dick head called Derek and Mary's teeth, nothing could be worse than that." called out Audrey.

"It has to be Liz?" shouted Joyce. Liz put her hand up.

"I'll tell you a story, but it's not as good as any of yours in fact its bloody boring, here goes. I went to a pub with this chap I'd been seeing for a couple of months, he left me sat on my own while he went up to the bar to get the drinks but he didn't return he stayed chatting to a mate. He was away for a good half an hour when I decided to go up and ask him when he was coming back to the table as I didn't like sitting alone, especially without having at least a drink for company. His reply was 'Well you're free to go if you don't like the position you've found yourself in' he shouted as loud as he dared."

"What a bloody cheek." I called out.

"His comment upset me as I hadn't done anything to deserve being left on my own. I'm very wary who I go out with now." Replied Liz.

"So would I be." called out Ruth.

"Let's go back to the office."

"Why?" shouted Liz.

"Because I'm fed up with drinking bitter lemon." I replied sounding annoyed.

"I have another story it beats all your stories. You all know I wear false nails."

"So?"

"For God's sake sit quietly and listen to what I have to say – don't interrupt me. I went out with this bloke and he suggested after a few drinks that we should go up a back alley for a bit of the other."

"Hurry up Marg this is boring – I want to leave." I called out.

"Shut up and listen, when I got home I found I was missing a nail. I'd arranged to meet this bloke again and guess what he gave me back my nail. I asked him where he found it - 'in my pants' he said, I was so embarrassed." The girls laughed and laughed as we got up to leave the bar. On our way out the men that were sat at the bar followed us with their eyes.

"No wonder it was quiet in here that lot have been listening to our stories." said Joyce nodding towards them. We all blushed.

"I hope they got a good ear full." called out Audrey as we walked out the door.

We must have laughed all the way back to the office where we crept up the stairs only to find Mr Robbins sat on a chair in the middle of the typing pool with his head in a newspaper - waiting for us to return.

"Well, well ladies, you have decided to return from lunch." We all looked in shock as we never expected the boss to be sat waiting for us. Ruth and I were the only ones sober, the others were holding each other up. "Thank goodness I haven't much work for you today, if I had I have a feeling you would still be here at midnight as it would take you a while to sober up before you could start typing. As I'm the boss of this joint and you all worked very hard last week I'm going to let you go home."

"HOME." We called out in harmony.

"That's what I said, go before I change my mind. See you all tomorrow at nine o'clock." laughed Mr Robbins.

Chapter 23

Liz and I were back at the flat by three thirty which meant I could spend couple of hours phoning the escort agency to get work for a week on Wednesday and also ring mum to give her my phone number.

I rang mum first she was pleased to hear my voice and said how much happier she was since dad had moved out and that she was filing for a divorce.

"Are you sure about doing that?"

"Of course I'm sure. He's found himself a girlfriend. I doubt if you'll believe this but the woman is younger than you. He's bloody disgusting."

"You know damn well it won't last, he'll be crawling back home before you know it."

"Mary, I'm NOT having him back. The best bit about it all is that his floozy has an eighteen month old baby."

"What! how the hell will he manage with a baby. He had a job to cope with me when I was young especially if I cried. Mum you told me how he used to go for a walk around the block and if I was still crying when he returned he went out again."

"Yeah that's right Mary, sometimes he was away for a good hour."

"I reckon this floozy is after the money - he hasn't got. Perhaps she imagines he'll pay for a nanny so she'll be able to go out and about without the baby. I know one thing the baby will cramp dad's style - serves him bloody well right." mum didn't answer. "Mum are you still there, are you listening?"

"Yeah, I'm still here."

"Perhaps the baby is his, ever thought of that?"

"I had wondered. My solicitor suggested that perhaps it was."

"Well if the baby is his it's a very good reason for getting a divorce. Does dad know you're thinking of divorcing him?"

"I told him the other night."

"What do you mean the other night?"

"Your father came around. The thing is he has a key. He walked in on a soiree, I was holding."

"When you told him to get out I thought he left the key on the side Mum."

"He was supposed to but he didn't."

"I hope you got it back from him the other night."

"No he still has it. When I came back from shopping the other afternoon he was sitting here."

"He may be my dad but I wouldn't put up with that. I'd change the locks."

188

"He told me I couldn't, you see the flat is in both our names and he can come and go as he wishes."

"I wouldn't care about him saying that load of tosh. In a minute you'll come home and find that he has been around to the flat with his floozy and taken some of the furniture."

"He wouldn't do that he isn't that bad, for God's sake Mary remember he's your father."

"Well don't tell me what he has been up too unless you want me to tell you what I think of his behaviour."

"Mary, change the subject. I have a pen, tell me your phone number and address." I told mum the number but not the address. I made out I was moving again in a week or two which is true – I'm moving down stairs. Before saying goodbye I explained to mum that I'd visit her in a couple of weeks and most probably it would be on a Monday as that is the day I plan to have off each week.

After I put the receiver down I immediately picked it up again and rang the escort agency. Celia Bates answered and explained that she had work for me starting Wednesday week at lunch time, apparently I'm to meet Rodney Davis who liked the look of my photo and has booked me for three Wednesdays on the trot to go out for lunch. Celia also booked me for Thursday lunch time to meet someone called Dave at my local pub which is very convenient. Celia finished by asking if I could meet up with a Jonathan James at the Cora Hotel for dinner at seven thirty on the Friday of the same week.

"Will you be able to keep all these appointments Mary? I'd hate to think you may let these men down at the last minute, tell me now if you can't keep all three."

"I'll be there, I won't let anyone down." obviously Celia along with her clients hadn't noticed from my photo that I have two false teeth - thank God.

In the excitement of getting work and after I had put the receiver down I rushed up the stairs and found my bottle of Gin that I'd hidden under my bed and had a quick swig of it – giving up the booze has gone by the board for the rest of today.

Late afternoon and evening became a blur to me - at least I didn't have to cook supper. My turn to be cook is Wednesday which is a good day for me as it doesn't interfere with the weekend. During supper we sat around the table and ate our food in silence, neither Enid or Margaret noticed that Liz and I had been on the drink. I'm sure if they had they would have had something to say and I doubt if it would have been kind words.

Once I'd finished eating I decided not to hang around for coffee but go to my room and have an early night with my friend called Gin – I finished the bottle. I woke early Tuesday morning with the most awful hangover. I staggered out into the kitchen to find a couple of Panadol. Liz was up and about and was surprised at seeing me.

"Mary you look bloody awful what's the matter with you?"

"I suffer from migraine. I need a couple of Panadol I've run out of them, then I'm going straight back to bed. I don't reckon I can come into work today. Do you think you can tell the boss that I'm spending today in bed PLEASE."

"Mary I'll tell him, I doubt if he'll believe you have migraine. I bet he'll say you've been on the Gin again."

"Well I haven't, you know damn well I haven't. I only had a soft drink when we all went to the pub yesterday."

"I reckon last evening you had a full bottle of Gin under your bed and you have drunk the lot overnight. Alcoholics often do that. I know as I have a cousin who enjoyed a G and T. He took his friend Gin to bed every night instead of a glass of water."

"I bet he took water like I do."

"Well he definitely didn't. He was taken into hospital after falling down the stairs having drunk too much and I found the empty bottles under his bed."

"I'm going back to bed to recover from my migraine. I will see you later today." I blushed.

I slept all morning thank God. When I woke I felt a lot better but wished I had more alcohol. I was stupid as I got dressed and went over the road to buy another bottle of Gin. When I lived in Hammersmith the Off License was quite a distance from my flat, which stopped me from going out to get more Gin -especially if it was raining. When I returned I undressed to my nightdress and got back into bed to pretend to be a sleep when the girls returned from work. I put the new bottle of Gin inside my bed just before my bedroom door was knocked "Come in." I called out hoping that I didn't sound drunk. It was Liz. "How are you Mary, I hope you are feeling a bit better?"

"I'm not too bad, I haven't been up and about as every time I take my head off the pillow I feel terrible."

"Mary I went down to see Mr Robbins he understands and has suggested that you stay home for another day. He's not going to deduct any pay from you as he knows exactly what migraines are like - awful, his wife often has them."

"Please thank him for me and say most probably I'll be back at work on Thursday. I am going try to go back to sleep."

"I won't disturb you again this evening. I know I'll call in tomorrow evening that's if you're not up and about."

Wednesday came and went I spent most of my time lounging around the flat drinking tea and coffee and trying to avoid my friend Gin. The girls arrived home by six o'clock and were pleased to see me up and about. As soon as I'd eaten my supper I went into bed as I didn't want anyone to notice I had the shakes due to not having any alcohol.

Thursday was a very quiet day at work, I didn't even see the boss - Mr Robbins, as he'd taken the day off - thank God. Liz and I caught the tube home together. When we arrived at Queensway and were out on the pavement I suggested that we should go into a pub for quick one. "I wouldn't mind that." replied Liz looking across at me "When did you last have a drop of Gin?"

"Three days ago when I was out with Steve."

"Mary the last alcoholic drink I had was last Friday, I think we both deserve one."

After having a couple of doubles in the pub we both staggered home for supper. When I left the table to get ready for my night away with Steve Liz looked at me strangely, I don't think she could make out why I left the table before having a coffee. She obviously didn't listen when I told the girls I had a date with Steve, if she had she would have realised I was in a hurry to get ready to go on my way to Trafalgar Square.

191

I arrived at the square just before eight where I found Steve sat on the bench by Nelson's column. I have to admit he looked pleased to see me which was a surprise as I thought it was the drink talking when he suggested I should become his girlfriend, obviously I was wrong thank God. After greeting each other with a kiss on the cheek we discussed what we were going to do about food as I'd already eaten. "I'm starving Mary I can't live without food."

"Let's visit the Chandos pub. I've seen people eating in there and they never seem to leave any of their food which is a good sign." Steve looked at me blank as if he'd never heard of the place. "Steve can't you remember we went in there the other evening when we came out with Ruth."

"Oh there, I remember, I didn't know what it was called. Come on then." We wandered over to the pub along the way I made a comment "Steve, I hope your manners are perfect and you don't pick your nose or teeth while you're eating like a dirty old man."

Looking annoyed Steve turned towards me "Don't start thinking like that Miss Mary because our relationship will finish before it begins. I was brought up properly like you were. Mary we ate a meal together Sunday night and you didn't complain about my manners."

"Sorry." I felt terrible as this was the drink talking and I shouldn't have said what I did.

Once inside the Chandos Steve ordered himself a pint along with pie and chips. I had a Gin and Tonic which Steve thought was my first of the day but of course it wasn't – it was my third.

"Steve now we're sat down quietly tell me a bit about your family. Have you any brothers and sisters?"

"I have one sister – Mandy. I only meet up with her when I go back to Birmingham to see mum and dad. I can tell you now she's not worth meeting, she's an obnoxious bitch. Mum and dad spoil her rotten. When she was a child they never told her off about anything, now her behaviour and manners are diabolical."

"What does she do for a living Steve?"

"Not a lot, as little as possible, she'd like to think she was a director of ICI but she isn't, she works in the British Home Stores in Birmingham. There's nothing the matter with her job, it's Mandy and her manner that's the problem"

"Steve, you're joking?"

"No I'm not. She still lives at home and doesn't help with anything unless dad gives her one of his looks then she may jump up from watching the television and do what is asked of her. If Mandy is in one of her moods she won't even get up and make anyone a cup of tea. I always reckon if anyone fell down she'd walk over them rather than help pick them up."

"Bloody hell Steve, I'm definitely not like that. I wouldn't dream of behaving like her."

"If I thought you were just a tiny bit like her I wouldn't have even considered having you as my girlfriend."

"The only thing that upsets you Steve about me is my drinking habit and that isn't as bad as some peoples'." I laughed.

"Mary don't forget your job."

"Oh yeah, I forgot about that." I looked down at my feet.

"I hadn't, as long as you only go for meals with men and there isn't any kind of sex involved I can cope with it - at least I think I can. How about you Mary how many brothers and sisters have you?"

"I'm an only child. I always think my parents had sex the once and I was the result."

"Mary I'm sure that can't be true. At the time when our parents got married there was no sex before marriage unless they managed to get a quick grope in the bushes. When they eventually did get married the only thing on the husbands mind was rampant sex. I've been told by many people that once they had tied the knot they performed for breakfast, lunch and tea. Mind you they needed to make sure they had a store of johnnies in the house. It would have been no good them only having a pack of three because the forth time they performed the wife would have got pregnant. Perhaps that's what happened with your parents – it was forth time lucky." We both laughed.

"I'll change them having sex to four times instead of the once. Mind you if you met the toffee-nosed pair you'd understand what I'm on about."

"Excuse me saying this Miss Mary but arrogant people are often a bit thick when it comes to sex or making love. They always seem far too embarrassed to go to the chemist for their johnnies."

"That would have been them as there was no such thing as the contraceptive pill in there day. I reckon they chanced it rather than go to the chemist to buy a pack of three. Thinking about them and johnnies makes me laugh Steve, I bet if they did go to the chemist they'd go to a different one each time as they'd be too embarrassed to go back to the same one twice as they would be thinking the shop assistant could guess how many times they had sex that week."

"Mary, I bet if you worked in the chemist you would be thinking the same and find it amusing."

With that Steve's meal arrived, it didn't look bad in fact it made me feel hungry. We sat in silence while Steve ate, I watched until I decided I would pop to the loo. Once in the cubicle I settled down to wee, before long there was banging on all the cubicle doors it was a woman asking where I was "Who's asking for her?" I said jumping up from the seat.

"Me I'm the barmaid. Are you Mary Huggins?" I didn't reply I looked at my watch and found that I must have fallen asleep on the throne as I'd been in the cubicle for at least twenty minutes. "Your boyfriend has been asking where you are - he's worried about you."

"Well I'm in here weeing for England, tell him I'll be out in a few minutes." I replied.

"I'll let him know you're safe and well."

After a while I wandered back only to find that Steve had bought another round of drinks a Gin and Tonic for me and a Whisky chaser for him.

"What happened to you? I thought you'd been flushed away or even run home leaving your bag behind."

"Steve, I better come clean, I fell asleep on the throne."

"That's a new one, you're saying you sat down on the seat of a public loo and fell asleep?"

"Yeah that's what I said."

"God all mighty Mary, I wouldn't dream of putting my bum down on a public throne let alone fall asleep on one, the thing is you never know what you may have caught, anything could have jumped up and given you the pox especially if you stayed there longer than a minute." I felt stupid.

"Let's forget about what I did, thanks for my Gin and Tonic." I picked the glass up "Cheers Steve." Steve didn't look very happy but he did pick up his glass and take a swig.

We stayed put in the pub for another hour chatting about everything and anything including the hotel we had planned to spend the night in. "I couldn't get a room in that private hotel you recommended - it was fully booked."

" Steve I can't believe it's full."

"Well it is. I've provisionally booked the cheapest room in a hotel down Shaftesbury Avenue. It's very basic but it does have a wash basin in the room, the loo is down the passage. If you don't fancy that we'll have to go back to my place." I didn't answer I just carried on sipping my Gin and Tonic while Steve stared at me. "Why are you giving me one of your looks?"

"I didn't think I was. I'm waiting for your answer to my question."

"Let's go to your place."

"That's settled, my place it is Miss Mary. Going back to you falling asleep on the throne I'm sure it wasn't because you're tired I reckon it was to do with your alcohol input. I bet you've had quite a few Gin and Tonics today. Come on Mary tell me how many you've had?" My face must have gone the colour of a beetroot once again as this was the last thing I thought Steve would be thinking about let alone asking. "Hurry up Mary tell me. If you won't tell me I'm going to guess, I bet this is your fifth today."

"Yeah, afraid so."

"You've had three here with me and two before you left home is that right?"

"Yes." I felt stupid as Steve stared towards me then out of the blue he ranted and raved at me.

"Mary, I've told you before that I'm not in the habit of having a girlfriend that drinks like you. Jean only drank soft drinks, she didn't even suggest having anything stronger – that was one good thing about her."

"Steve, Jean wouldn't dare drink alcohol as she was married to a black man, most probably he was a Muslim." Steve tutted away to himself.

"Look at you Steve with a whisky chaser." I pointed at the glass. "I reckon there is one rule for you and another for your girlfriends. I believe in equality even if you don't."

"I needed to have a whisky chaser to get the confidence to tell you off about your alcohol input."

"When we met up Sunday night you drank almost as much as I did - in fact you may have drunk more than me."

"I suppose I did, it was for Dutch courage Miss Mary to ask if you'd like to be my girlfriend."

"My answer was yes. You remember this Steve I can change my mind any time especially if you keep on about how much I drink. You always seem to find a stupid excuse for you drinking too much. At least I admit to liking alcohol any time day or night." Steve looked at me strangely.

"Mary I'm not addicted to alcohol like you, me having one too many Sunday night was a one off."

"That's the second time you've been on the verge of being drunk when out with me. I wonder how many other times you've had one to many?" I said looking annoyed, Steve looked like a naughty school boy.

Chapter 24

By the time we arrived at Steve's flat we were both quite squiffy, in fact Steve couldn't understand why I'd come home with him.

"Mary, why are you here? You don't live here anymore, you left a couple of weeks ago." He laughed. I felt daft and wished the floor would swallow me up. I couldn't understand if he meant what he was saying or just teasing. His sense of humour didn't appeal to me but I decided to take the bull by the horns and undress to my bra and knickers.

"Steve you invited me to stay the night to consummate our relationship." I said falling on the bed. Steve looked shocked but didn't take long to get on to the bed in his birthday suit. What a night! The sex was pretty good for a first time with my new man, in fact it was far better than I ever dreamt it could be.

Steve was up and running by five. I was left in bed alone with a promise from Steve that he would ring me this evening, whether he will or not I'll have to wait and see.

I arrived in the office to find the girls with their heads down just like they were the other morning but today they looked like thunder. They didn't seem to have a spare moment to say good morning to anyone let alone me.

"Thank God I'm leaving this dump on Tuesday. I'd hate to think I was going to spend the rest of my working life writing up documents." silence still reigned. "What the hell have I done to deserve you lot not even saying good morning to me?"

"Nothing. We're keeping our heads down. Mr Robbins has been up and given us all as much work today as he gave us last week, we want to finish it all by lunch time as we've other things to sort out this afternoon."

"There's no need not to say good morning to me, if I didn't speak to you when I came into work there would be hell to play."

"Sorry my dear. Now you've stopped us working I've news for you." Said Joyce smiling to herself.

"Are you pregnant?" I asked

"Don't be daft I haven't got a bloke let alone one that has a dick which works so I'm not pregnant." replied Joyce sounding annoyed.

"I didn't think you had a bloke. I always thought you used a carrot or may be a cucumber, then again Joyce you could be very modern and use a vibrator to satisfy your needs."

"Don't be disgusting Mary." shouted Joyce.

"I've known women to use a carrot and a cucumber but the most popular thing these days is the vibrator. Women get their husbands to put it up their fanny, it saves them having the bother of trying to get a hard." laughed Audrey.

I joined in the conversation. "Talking about husbands or men in general most have difficulty performing after they've been with the same woman for years. It's nothing to do with being ill in the dick they're just bored floppy so they go elsewhere." the girls laughed. "Before you start to think I'm going to have sex with Tom, Dick and Harry that I meet socially for a meal – I'M NOT. I may wear something seductive to encourage the men to want to book me again, there won't be any sex unless the blokes are a turn on for me and I doubt if they will be." I laughed. "The more clients I go out with for meals the more money I'll earn, also the less food I'll have to buy to eat at home. Hopefully I'll be quids in."

"Mary, how much money do you reckon you'll earn in a week?" asked Liz.

"Enough to have a decent life style, at least as much as I've been earning here."

"I wouldn't want to eat out every day with some old boy, by the end of a couple of weeks I'd be as fat as a pig." called out Marg who was trying to get on with her work in between listening to our conversation.

"Joyce I'm going to change the subject back to you and your news, what have you got to tell me?" I asked.

Joyce told me how Mr Morgan had found his daughter Suzanne living in Soho with a girl she'd met up with. "They're sharing a bedsitter in Old Compton street above one of the restaurants. Mr Morgan is worried sick about the way she's living, he's wondering how she can afford the rent let alone buy any food." continued Joyce.

"None of us can afford to live around here. I bet she's found herself a pimp and is on the game. How old is Suzanne, does anyone know?" asked Ruth.

"Coming up to sixteen," replied Joyce, "apparently she looks a lot older especially now she is wearing makeup and has had her hair cut short. She's refusing to go back home to live and she's made up her mind that she definitely isn't going back to the boarding school."

"What the hell's going to happen to her?"

"God only knows. Mr Morgan is in some state he thinks Suzanne is walking the streets for customers even though she's not sixteen. He imagines she's telling everyone that she's a lot older. Once she's reached sixteen which is in a few weeks' time Mr Morgan can't do much about how Suzanne lives her life."

"Walking the streets is quite dangerous but the pay can be as good as picking up clients in the hotels."

"Mary I don't reckon what you're going to do for a job is very wholesome. I'd rather stay working here." added Audrey.

"It's not as bad as you seem to imagine, at least the agency knows where I am and who I'm with. No one knows where Suzanne is unless she cares to tell a friend. I don't have to have sex for money. Suzanne poor girl has to perform or at least give a blow job. Unless she satisfies the bloke she won't get paid a cent let alone a pound note." I called out to the girls that were still listening.

"I feel sorry for old Morgan he doesn't deserve a daughter that has walked out of boarding school to go on the game. You'd have thought Suzanne would have known better. Any way how the hell did you find out about Mr Morgan and his problem with Suzanne?" I asked.

"He called in after we came back from the pub the other afternoon. In the excitement of the moment you and Liz rushed off. You must have only missed him by five minutes. He looks like he's aged ten years in about ten days."

"Poor man, did he mention when he was coming back to work? Not that it matters to me as I won't be here."

"In a month's time. He hopes to have sorted Suzanne out by then." answered Joyce looking down in the mouth.

199

"I'm going back to my desk to concentrate on my typing. Once it's midday I'm going over to my normal haunt the sandwich bar. Ruth are you coming with me?"

"I usually do and as today is no different from any other day, I'll go with you."

It was soon lunch time and Ruth and I sat at our favourite table in the sandwich bar. Normally when Ruth had finished her ham roll she was in a rush to get back to the office but not today. "I've a question for you Miss Mary, Liz came in this morning saying you stayed out all night. Is that true?"

"Afraid so." I blushed.

"I thought you were seeing Steve for a drink you didn't say anything about spending the night with him, anyway I don't reckon he'd ask you so who did you stay with?"

"That's for me to know and you to guess." this annoyed Ruth.

"I'm supposed to be your best friend and best friends don't keep secrets from one another."

"They do if they don't want their best friend to know."

"Mary don't be so horrible, I don't keep secrets from you. I never have and never will. Tell me one thing was the bed comfortable? I hope the mattress wasn't worn out having been used for too much sex."

"What's it to you if it was?"

"Nothing except you'll get back ache if it's worn out."

"It was very comfortable - one of the best."

"Are you going to tell me who the lucky man was?"

"No, not yet any way. If it lasts a few weeks I may tell you his name and perhaps I'll introduce you." I smirked.

"I hope he's not like that Derek."

"Don't be daft Ruth, I'd never go out with anyone like him again."

"Mary, never say never. Just because you enjoyed what this bloke had to offer doesn't mean he wouldn't hit you about - given half the chance."

"Ruth, I fancy going to the dress shop at the top of Regents Street before we go back to work. We promised one another we'd go there on pay day, this last Tuesday was pay day, not that I have enough money to buy one of their creations let alone two." I said changing the subject.

Once inside the shop Ruth started to collect up armfuls of dresses and made her way towards the changing rooms. I only found one dress suitable for me, it was a short red kaftan type with a gold thread running through the material.   Standing outside the changing room waiting to be ushered in Ruth started to talk nonstop.

"The dress you've got there isn't bad, I reckon it will suit you down to the ground. I can see you wearing it when you meet up with one of your clients. I wonder what the bloke will be like that you're seeing next Wednesday. I hope for your sake he's tall dark and handsome - not short, fat and ugly."

"Ruth, all you seem to be doing today is firing questions at me or make comments about my life. To keep the peace I'll answer your questions this time but whatever you do don't ask me anymore or I'll go mad. I don't think you've ever seen me in a temper?"

"Only that morning at the flat when we'd drunk to much alcohol the evening before."

"I can get crosser than I did that morning, especially if you bombard me with questions. I don't like being questioned about anything, just you remember that."

"I won't ask you anymore. If you don't want to answer the ones I've asked already - don't."

"I'll answer this time, let's move over to the corner or we'll have people listening in." I said sounding annoyed. "My first appointment is for lunch next Wednesday at twelve thirty at the pub down the side of Fortnum and Masons. Knowing my luck the bloke will look like the back of a bus they usually do or the complete opposite, handsome like a film star. I doubt if he'll be in between the two - they never are. The ones in between seem to stay at home with their wives – they don't stray."

"I reckon they're the ones with the most sense. When I'm on the lookout for a boyfriend I'll be a complete and utter bore and go for one in the middle. Mum has always said that they're the most stable. Mind you dad was handsome when he was young, that's what mum thought - he wasn't an in between man."

"You've only got her word for him being handsome, Ruth remember, handsome is in the eyes of the beholder."

"Mum showed me some photos of dad, he was good looking for his era. Mind you Mary the photos didn't look anything like he does now. For all I know mum could have shown me a different man. I'll have to ask to see the photos again."

"Getting back to me and my new job. I may as well tell you my rota for the next week, if I don't you'll keep on until I do. Listen to what I say because it will give you an idea about what you're up against when you start working as an escort. Talking about escort agencies have you phoned and arranged an appointment?"

"No."

"Ruth, you better phone soon, as you'll be out of work once you leave the office, also Celia – who is the owner/manager, may have too many girls on her books and won't take you on, then you'll finish up having to find a job in another boring office."

"For God's sake Mary, don't worry me about that. I'll phone as soon as I come across a telephone kiosk, that's if you give me the phone number."

"I'll give it to you when I come into work on Monday."

"Mary, whatever you do don't forget to bring it in."

"If I forget it on Monday there is always Tuesday. If I forget it then I'll give it to Liz to give to you Wednesday morning."

"Getting back to you and this new job, tell me about the work you have next week – that's if you have any. I bet you haven't!"

"Of course I've work. Ruth I've already told you what I'm doing on Wednesday, I'm meeting up with a client called Rodney outside the Chequers Tavern, hopefully he should be sat on the bench waiting for me to arrive. Thursday is a drink at the local pub in Westbourne Terrace at one o'clock. I doubt if this will be anything more than a drink as the agency has told me that this particular man who is called Dave hasn't much money. He needs female company for an hour, apparently it's to prove to his mates that he has a girlfriend as they don't believe he has. They'll never realise that I'm from an agency as I'll wear clothes similar to what I'm wearing now in fact I may wear these." Ruth laughed.

"Friday is the big one - dinner at The Cora Hotel, Upper Woburn Place at seven thirty with a Jonathan who is supposed to be loaded with dosh. Celia told me he lives in Eaton Place which is not far from mum's flat. This

Jonathan may have been to one of her Soirees which is a bit of a worry for me as I look like a younger version of mum. I feel I ought to change my image before next Friday in case I look familiar to him and he asks if we're related or even worse realises I must be her daughter. I dread the thought of mum finding out I'm working as an escort."

"God Mary, I wouldn't want to be in your shoes, however much money you get for having dinner with him. I would be going down to the nearest Boots for a pot of dye before Friday to change the colour of my hair. I would dread the thought of him realising I was related to my mum."

"Ruth, it's a bit of a worry for me but you never know what may come out of the date. I'm hoping Jonathan will take me on to a club like Annabel's or The Scotch of St James for a dance. Saturday is a day of rest - at least at the moment. Sunday I'll be spending my time washing my smalls etc. Monday is officially my day off – I'll visit mum if she's at home." I smiled.

"Mary, thank God you have work to keep you out of mischief for a few days.'"

"By the weekend I should have clients booked in for the following week. If Jonathan and I get on well over dinner next Friday he may ask the agency to see me again. I wouldn't mind going to the Savoy for dinner especially if it's on a Saturday night. I've found in the past that middle aged single men with money in their pockets don't like sitting at home alone in front of the box Saturday evenings. They often say there's nothing on the telly worth staying in for. I always reckon the truth is they like visiting hotels or restaurants on a Saturday to show off any attractive lady they've managed to pick up during the week. I'm hoping if I play my cards right next Friday Jonathan will invite me out for another meal on the Saturday."

"Mary let us get back to the changing rooms to try on these dresses or we'll never get back to work." We managed to get into a cubicle without having to queue. Ruth looked good in all six dresses but could only afford to buy two. The ones she eventually chose were suitable for her new life as an escort. The dress I chose looked as if it had been made especially for me – no one would guess that I've bought it off the peg.

Chapter 25

After paying for the dresses we made our way back to the office. "You've returned then." Said Joyce laughing to herself. "Marg has gone out to get some doughnuts as it's your last Friday."

"I love doughnuts." I replied. "You all look as if you have stopped work for the afternoon."

"We have. Mr Robbins came up earlier to say he was going home and wouldn't be in again until next Tuesday so we have decided to have a doughnut party today and on Monday we're having a Gin party especially for you Mary. We won't get caught as Mr Robbins is taking his wife over to Paris for the weekend and they're not returning until late Monday night."

"I never expected to hear this when I returned from lunch."

"If Mr Robbins was tall dark and handsome, I would have said he was going with his mistress as he's not, it must be his wife that he's taking. I know someone who went abroad for a dirty weekend leaving his wife in England. On the BBC TV news at six o'clock this man was seen at an airport holding hands with a woman who was definitely not his wife."

"Oh my God, I wonder what happened when he returned home."

"I have a feeling there was a divorce." said Marg carrying two boxes of cream and jam doughnuts in to the typing pool - they looked yummy. After eating at least 3 doughnuts and drinking enough cups of tea to keep me running to the loo till tomorrow breakfast time, we discussed what we planned to do over the weekend - everyone seemed to be going to a pub for a heavy night.

"Liz, I'm coming out with you tonight but I'm definitely going to be careful how much I drink, I may only have a soft drink as I don't want to spend all the weekend in bed recovering,"

"Girls what time shall we shut up shop as I'm sure we don't need to stay here till five o'clock?" asked Audrey.

"I reckon we can leave now as it's almost four o'clock." replied Marg.

"Monday I'm not coming in till after lunch, there's no point if we aren't going to do any work. Even I know we can't sit and drink Gin all day. Shall we come in at one o'clock then open up the first bottle at two?"

"That sounds good. Who is locking up?"

"Old Robbins gave me the key and asked me to lock up." Said Joyce looking a bit worried.

"Liz, are you leaving now with me or are you going to be a goody, goody and stay on until five?"

"Let me get my things together then I'll come and go straight home as we need to get ready for our night on the tiles."

We were lucky to get on the tube before the rush hour and were home by four thirty. Enid was already in the flat as she has a half day on a Friday.

"Mary I'm pleased you've come home early, Steve has phoned three times this afternoon, he said he would phone again at five o'clock."

"What did he want?"

"He wouldn't say but he sounded anxious."

"Perhaps it's to invite me out over the weekend."

With that the phone rang, I rushed down the stairs and yes it was Steve. He was wondering if I would like to go up to Birmingham to meet his parents. "I'm going up tomorrow morning and coming back on Sunday after lunch."

"This is a surprise, this is the last thing I expected you to phone about."

"Mary, would you like to come with me? I better tell you that we won't be able to sleep together as my parents are narrow minded and also they don't keep alcohol in the house so you'll be tea total."

"Yes, I would love to go with you. I've never been to Birmingham I understand the market's wonderful."

"I'll come around to pick you up at nine o'clock. Make sure you are outside as I'll be in a taxi so I won't be able to hang around."

"Are we going all the way by taxi?"

"Don't be daft the taxi will take us to the railway station then we'll go up by train."

I don't know what I expected but both days were very boring. Steve's parents seemed to like me but were not very good at entertaining. All they wanted to do was to sit in the sitting room drinking cups of tea and ask me questions about my family. For supper we had fish and chips from the chippy. On the Sunday we had roast dinner which Steve's mum cooked. I couldn't wait to get on the train back to London. Both Steve and

I were upset as we didn't think the two days went very well. "Mary we'll have to see if mum rings to tell me if she liked you. I know they bored you – I'm sorry."

"The one thing I liked was the roast dinner, your mum is a very good cook better than mine. Don't forget to tell her that"

We arrived back in London at four o'clock. "I'm sorry Steve but I feel worn out, do you think the taxi could drop me off at my flat as I need to go in and have a sleep." Steve looked at me as if his world had come to an end. "I'm not fed up with you I'm just exhausted with doing nothing much."

"I'll phone you tomorrow to see how you are and to tell you if mum has phoned." I kissed Steve goodbye and got out of the taxi. I went straight up to my room and had a swig of my Gin which I'd hidden in my bed. I was in bed by nine o'clock and asleep by ten. I slept all night thank God, I must have been tired due to the fact that I didn't sleep very well in Birmingham as the bed was uncomfortable.

I arrived at the office by one o'clock, on the way I went to the off License and bought a large bottle of Gin to share with the girls. They didn't expect me to buy anything as this was their treat. On the table they had lined up quite a few bottles of wine as well as Gin. They promised if I drank the alcohol they would not keep on at me about being an alcoholic. Between us we drank all the booze and went home tiddly.

Tuesday came, we all arrived in the office with headaches and wondered how the hell we were going to get on with our work. Luckily for us Mr Robbins was nowhere to be seen so we were able to sit around all morning drinking coffee. Ruth and I went out to the sandwich bar at lunch time to have our normal ham roll. By the time got back the girls were sorting out nibbles and sandwiches to put on the large table.

"What the hell's going on here, it looks like you may be having a tea party?" I asked while Ruth pretended nothing untoward was happening.

"You silly devil Mary, we're having a bit of a do as you're leaving." I felt daft as Ruth hadn't said a word even though she knew all about it.

"You're good at keeping secrets Ruth?"

"It was easy, I couldn't get a word in edgeways as you kept yapping so I didn't have a chance to tell you even if I wanted to."

"Would you like me to set up another table?"

"No," called out Joyce, "we don't want you to help with your own tea party, go and sit down and put your feet up or you could go out again and come back at four o'clock when the party begins."

"I'll go for a walk. Anyone coming with me?"

"I'll come." shouted Ruth before anyone else could answer.

We left.

"I haven't got any money to call in anywhere for a cuppa." mentioned Ruth.

"I'm not going in anywhere for anything as I don't want to spend more money than I need as my wages from this job may have to last me a couple of weeks. The thing is Ruth I'm not sure how much money I'll be taking home from the agency after handing over a percentage of my wages to them, for organising everything. Remember I have to pay tax and my insurance stamp out of it."

"Let's walk down Regents Street to Piccadilly to see what's going on, we're sure to see something of interest. We can walk back up Carnaby Street, by the time we've walked that distance it'll be four o'clock."

"That sounds okay we may pass the pub we went in the other week, you know the one Ruth, where we sat up at the bar. You never know we may be in luck the barmen could be sat on the doorstep and may invite us in for a free drink."

"Don't be daft Mary, closing time was at two thirty and it's almost three o'clock. Even if the pub is open I'm not having an alcoholic drink as I don't want to be made a fool of when I get back to the office. Mary just because you're leaving doesn't mean the girls won't tell you off today for drinking and smelling of booze."

"Ruth I need booze for Dutch courage. Even if it's the smallest tipple available, I need alcohol. I hate parties especially if I'm the centre of attention and sober."

"Mary you know exactly what I think of you and alcohol. YOU NEED TO GIVE IT UP. I've told you this on many an occasion, just because we all drank some yesterday you still need to GIVE IT UP. Going in for an alcoholic drink before going to your own tea party is not a good idea. Yesterday you told the girls and me that it's easy to give it up. A day later you're needing a tipple to get to your own tea party." said Ruth sounding annoyed.

After this upset we walked to the bottom of Regents Street hardly saying a word to one another. When I made a comment Ruth replied with either a yes or a no. It was not long before we were turning round and making our way back via Brewer and Carnaby Street.

We arrived at the office looking more morose than we did before we left. "What the hell's the matter with you two?" asked Joyce looking puzzled. "You look as if the end of your world has arrived."

"Nothing is wrong with me." Shouted out Ruth before I could get a word in. "Mary is the problem – Mary and her friend called ALCOHOL."

"Have you been to the pub?" asked Liz "If you have we won't be very happy."

"No we haven't but if Mary had her way we would have. She wanted to go for a tipple in the Carnaby Street pub we went in the other week, didn't you dear Mary?"

"I would have enjoyed a small tipple for Dutch courage."

"I dread to think what would have happened if you'd gone to a pub, as we have visitors."

"What the hell do you mean Joyce by visitors?"

"Both Mr Robbins and Mr Morgan are coming to the tea party." continued Joyce.

"Apparently you're there favourite typist. If they can persuade you to stay, they will." laughed Audrey.

"I've told you all many times that I'm not staying at this dump and I mean it. I'M NOT STAYING."

"Mary, both Mr Robbins and Mr Morgan seem to know what you're going to do for a living - they're shocked."

"It's none of their bloody business what I do to earn money, in fact it's no ones' damn business except mine."

"I've a feeling old Robbins may offer you a pay rise to tempt you to stay."

"He won't tempt me, I've told you all a hundred times I'M NOT STAYING. The pay I should get as an escort will be far more than the pay rise he may be thinking of offering me. Girls imagine getting paid an arm and leg for sitting with an old boy for a drink plus a meal. Putting my bum down on a chair will cost an old boy money and feeding me will cost him even more. I don't even have to go by tube, they have to pay for me to arrive by black cab - I'll feel like royalty."

"That's enough." called out Audrey "here they come." In walked Mr Robbins carrying a bouquet of flowers along with Mr Morgan who looked a bit subdued.

"These are for you Miss Huggins." Said Mr Robbins handing over the flowers to me. "It is a very sad day."

"What do you mean a sad day Mr Robbins? I'm pleased to be leaving. Thanks for the flowers - I love flowers." I said smelling them. "I love their perfume."

"Mr Morgan or I are not happy about you leaving we thought that you'd be staying here for the rest of your working days."

"You know damn well what thought did Mr Robbins, I'm not staying. I'm leaving today whether you like it or not."

"Miss Huggins, I'd like to think you would stay if I gave you a pay rise."

"Pay rise. Why the hell do I need one of those?"

"To tempt you to stay." laughed Mr Morgan.

"I've told you all I'M NOT STAYING, you can double or treble the bloody pay but I'm not staying." Mr Robbins and Mr Morgan looked across at each other in surprise.

"I'll go and put the kettle on." said Joyce butting in to defuse the situation.

"Miss Huggins, I'm upset to think you're going down the same road as my daughter." continued Mr Morgan.

"I'm not going down any ones' road, except my own. Mr Morgan, what I do for a living is up to me. I'm going to work as an escort not a tart. I will not
be having sex with any of my clients, not like your daughter who needs to have sex to earn any kind of money. Sex is out of the question for me."

"I can't imagine you not considering sex if the bloke asked and he looked reasonable." said Ruth who was listening into my conversation.

"You don't know me very well Miss Ruth. I'm very fussy about my men and I won't be having sex with any clients however much money they offer me."

"I thought that was part of the job." continued Ruth.

"Sex is an extra that I won't be partaking in." I replied looking embarrassed.

The food which was delicious. All of us ate far more than we should have, by six o'clock we were sat belly up. Once we'd recovered from over eating I said my goodbyes and went on my way with Liz. This was not until after Old Robbins had attempted to make a pass at me while I was walking down the corridor with him to the toilets. When we reached the spare room Old Robbins tried to pull me inside. Thank God I managed to get away, in the process I hit him across the face and told him he was a dirty old man. I remained in the Ladies for quite a while trying to calm down. When I eventually went into the typing pool the girls looked at me strangely, not one of them asked what the matter was so I managed to say my goodbyes and leave without causing any embarrassment.

Once outside the office and as we were walking along the pavement to the tube station Liz asked why I looked embarrassed when I returned from the loo. "Liz why are you interested, if it was important to you why didn't you ask before we left to come home?"

"I thought it was better to keep quiet. Before you returned Mr Robbins came in with a bright red mark across his face as if someone or something had hit him."

"That was me, I hit him across the face, when he made a pass at me. He attempted to pull me into that stinking dusty spare room, you know the one half way down the corridor on the right."

"What! Mary, Old Robbins seems worse than Morgan, at least he tries it on in his office where it's clean. Neither of them have ever tried it on with me, thank God. Are you sure you didn't encourage him?"

"NO I DID NOT. I was walking down the corridor to go for a wee when he caught me up and put his arm around my shoulder, I never dreamt it was to try and push me into the spare room. I thought he was being friendly the way he was chatting to me."

"Fancy him attempting to take you of all people for a bit of the other in that filthy room. Where the hell did he think you'd hang your knickers if you had agreed to perform in one way or another."

"Liz, I don't know, also I don't care. Change the subject to something more respectable."

We were soon sat on the tube speeding along to Queensway and home when Liz told me she was going to visit a girlfriend in a bed sitter above the tobacco shop across the road from Queensway tube station.

"I'm going to call in to see a friend in a bedsitter across from here, I need to find out when she's coming for supper. You can come with me or you can go on your way." I stared at Liz wondering what I should do as I'm expecting a call from Steve this evening and I don't want to miss it. "Make your mind up Mary or I'll go on my own."

"I'll come with you."

"That's good as it will mean that you will meet Heather before she comes for supper. She was one of the first people I met when I arrived in London. Now we meet up regularly, at least once a week."

"What does she do for a job?"

"She's a clerk in the Westminster bank at Notting Hill. She used to live and work in a market town in Wiltshire, apparently she always wanted to work and live in London. She was a bit like me she couldn't get to London quick enough once she was offered the transfer."

"How the hell did you meet her?"

"At the entrance to the Queensway tube station. We were both waiting to get tickets out of the machine. We got talking and I found out that we were both going to the sales at Marble Arch so we got on the tube together. We've been friends ever since."

"I look forward to meeting her as she sounds as if she could be a bit like us especially if she enjoys city life. I hate it when I meet people who keep moaning about London life. If they want to live in the country they should pack their bags and move. I met a girl who was fed up and moaned like hell about living here, she moaned about everything to do with London. I told her straight to move out into the country. I didn't see or hear from her again whether she left I have no idea."

"Mary how the hell anyone can get fed up with London I don't know." said Liz looking puzzled. "If Heather isn't in we should find her at the pub down the road on the left."

Once the tube stopped at Queensway we made our way to the lift. Before we knew it we were crossing the street.

"Mary, you may make new friends tonight especially if we need to go over to the pub. Heather is very popular and always surrounded by people. After the pub closes she often entertains her friends in her small bedsitter, it's so small that we have to squeeze in like we're in a tin of sardines. We have fun and the alcohol flows, sorry I shouldn't have mentioned booze as you have given it up or at least you're trying to." Liz rang the doorbell, we waited in silence for a good ten minutes. Liz sighed, "Heather always takes ages to answer. I reckon she's hiding someone under the bed or tidying the place up before she dares to answer the door. I don't know who she thinks is standing out here that would care about the state of her place."

"Her mother I expect, if her's is anything like mine. I wouldn't answer the door until I had hidden what I didn't want mum or anyone else to see."

"I hadn't thought about her mother. Thank God mine can't arrive without phoning first and then I'd have to meet her at the station."

"You don't know how lucky you are Liz. I haven't given mum my address as she'd arrive like royalty in a taxi to have a nose around." Liz looked at me strangely. "She has my phone number but that's all."

"I thought you were going to say you'd deserted her."

"No. I wouldn't do that. She wants me to go and live back in Chelsea. If I did she'd help me with the rent. She won't consider helping out with the rent on a flat or bedsitter in any other part of London."

"She sounds a bit daft to me, how the hell could you afford to live in Chelsea?"

"I've told you mum would help me out – she's loaded with dosh." I don't think Liz believed a word I was saying, she looked at me as if I was telling a load of lies, when the door opened and their stood Heather in a complete and utter fluster.

"I didn't expect to answer the door to you Liz."

"Who the hell did you expect, your boyfriend?"

"I haven't got one of them. Anyway who's this you've brought along to meet me?" Heather asked pointing her finger towards me.

"Mary, she's moved into Andrew's old room." replied Liz

"Pleased to meet you." said Heather holding out her hand for me to shake.   "Come in the pair of you, remember you have to take me as you find me - with no frills."

"We don't mind that do we Mary?"

"No as far as I'm concerned it's up to you how you live, remember I have only come to meet you not to criticize how you live." We both followed Heather up the stairs to her bedsitter where she offered us a coffee. Once we'd settled down Heather started to fire questions at me. She managed to back me into a corner and I had to come clean about becoming an escort. I explained how I'd left my office job this afternoon and the boss gave me these flowers as a goodbye gift, hence the reason I have flowers with me.

"We've called in on the way home from work to ask if you're coming to supper tomorrow, as you haven't been over for a few weeks?"

"Who's cooking and what's on the menu Liz? I'm not keen on Enid's food, if it's her cooking I'd rather stay away thank you."

"It's me that's supposed to be cooking on a Wednesday starting tomorrow. I was thinking of cooking liver and onions that's if everyone is agreeable."

"I'll say yes. It'll depend if I like how you cook whether I'll come over again on a Wednesday, I may change my day to a Monday."

"Heather you've got a bloody nerve saying that." Said Liz looking annoyed.   "Mary's cooking will be far better than yours she's been on a cookery course and past an exam not like you." She said winking towards me. "I'll never forget the first time I came for supper here, I had to show you how to bake a jacket potato as you had no idea." Heather looked sheepish.

"Mary don't take any notice of what Liz is saying as it's not true. Have you ever cooked lambs liver with bacon and onions? My gran used to cook it for me. If she got the right bacon to go with the liver – not too fat or

213

salty, it would taste brilliant. Remember to always make thick gravy to pour over, then it will taste bloody good."

"Heather is there anything else Mary should remember?"

"Yeah, sausages they go well with the liver and bacon – they're yummy my gran used to add them."

"Perhaps we'll try the meal with sausages one day but it won't be tomorrow." Replied Liz.

"Going back to you Mary and your job as an escort. A couple of years ago I joined an escort agency as I'd over spent and my bank account didn't look to healthy. It was a quick way for me to make a bob or two. Like you I only socialised in restaurants and pubs with the men, I didn't perform with any of them."

"That is exactly what I intend doing, no hanky panky of any kind unless the bloke is extra dishy."

"I know of one escort who quite fancied one of her clients, apparently he had plenty of dosh, walked well and was handsome. He invited her back to his flat in Knightsbridge. While he made the coffee she went for a wee, in the corner of the bathroom she found his spare leg." Both Liz and I looked shocked.

"What the hell happened?"

"It was a bit sad as the client hadn't mentioned that he only had one leg. Suddenly the escort didn't fancy him and made a quick exit."

"I don't know whether to laugh or cry."

"Nor do I." said Liz looking down in the mouth. "I would hate to think I only had one leg. Obviously he must have found it difficult to find a girlfriend. That must have been the reason he went to the escort agency and paid for female company."

"I would have been in some state if I was like him. It would have been far better if he'd come clean with the agency about his situation before he meeting up with any girl?"

"I agree but he didn't."

Chapter 26

By the time we'd finished drinking our coffees it was time to say goodbye to Heather and walk back to the flat. I was exhausted from the day's events but before going into my room I called out to the other girls to ask if I'd had a phone call – the answer was no. This upset me as I'm quite sure that Steve is serious about our new found relationship. I was in bed by ten thirty, it was a long night, I saw every hour until six o'clock when I must have fallen asleep until I woke at nine. Half a sleep I went into the kitchen - silence reigned. The girls had left for work which was a blessing as I could iron my dress in peace without being told by one or other of them which dress I should or shouldn't wear to lunch with my client - not that they would have known as none of them have ever worked for an escort agency. I'm wearing my black and white geometric mini dress which fits to perfection – it's not too tight and when I sit down it doesn't ride up to show my knickers.

At around eleven thirty I set off by black cab to meet my first client who should be sat on the bench outside Chequers Tavern. Instead of chatting to the cabbie I sat and thought about my night with Steve. If he'd enjoyed himself like he said he did why hadn't he phoned? Once outside the pub I asked the cabbie to hang on while I went and asked a middle aged man if he was Rodney Davis, looking anxious he admitted to being him. I introduced myself and asked if he could pay the cabbie which he did without hesitation.

Once inside the pub we sat ourselves down at one of the tables for two. "Sorry if I look embarrassed and anxious I've never booked or met up with an escort before."

"There's nothing to worry about, escorts don't bite. Meeting up with you is like going on a blind date, in fact it is a blind date for both of us as we don't know anything about one another, the only difference is we're not going Dutch, you're paying for my company and we're hardly likely to meet up again unless you ask the agency for another few hours with me."

"Mary I hope you haven't forgotten we're meeting up again next Wednesday." Said Rodney looking worried.

"I have it down in my diary I believe we're meeting at the same time as today but you'll have to tell me where. Now that's sorted tell me a bit about yourself like your interests Rodney?"

"I'll get our drinks in first, what do you fancy?"

"A Gin and Tonic please – my favourite tipple."

"Okay, G and T it will be. I'm a beer man myself - I'll get a pint." Rodney went over to the bar it seemed ages before he returned carrying our drinks plus two packets of crisps.

"Rodney, I thought we're having lunch in a restaurant not eating crisps in a pub?"

"We are, these are to keep us going until we find some where suitable to eat."

"Sorry, I don't eat crisps as they're full of salt which isn't any good for me."

"That's okay I'll eat both packets." He said looking at me as if he'd never known anyone to refuse a packet of crisps.

"I'm sorry Rodney, crisps put my blood pressure up."

"Mary are you telling me you have high blood pressure at your age?"

"No, I'm being careful with my health. I don't eat any salt if I can get away without it. My parents have high blood pressure, I don't want to join them on tablets. The thing is once anyone is on blood pressure tablets they usually need to take them for life."

"Mary, please don't worry about not eating the crisps as I said I can eat both packets." Rodney opened them up and started to eat as if he hadn't eaten for a week. "While I was up at the bar I had a look at the menu it's not very interesting. I don't know about you but I need a proper meal not a scotch egg with salad. I'm wondering if you'd like to walk to Piccadilly and go into the Indian at the bottom of Regents Street or would you prefer to pop into Fortnum and Masons and have something English?"

"I'd prefer an English lunch perhaps when we meet up next Wednesday we could go for an Indian. The only trouble is Rodney the Indian you're talking about at the bottom of Regents Street only opens in the evenings and I'm booked to meet you for lunch."

"If you're able to come out in the evening Mary, I can always tell your agency that we have changed our plans and are meeting up for dinner."

With lunch sorted along with next Wednesday we chatted away about different things including Rodney's wife who has Multiple Sclerosis. Rodney explained how he was unable to take Miriam out any more as she could hardly move and spent most of her time in bed and also needed help with eating her food. "Miriam can't get out of bed without help and once she is out she can't walk more than a couple of steps and that is on a good day."

"Has Miriam got a wheel chair?"

"Yeah she has but that's another story she's over weight, it takes two of us to get her in and out of bed. One morning the nurse and I decided to get her out and I forgot to put the brake on the wheel chair and it moved. The three of us ended up on the floor in a heap – thank God none of us were hurt."

"That must have been terrible."

"It was, it shook Miriam up so much she doesn't like getting out of bed - she would rather stay put."

"I don't blame her."

"Getting back to you, the reason you're here is because I enjoy socialising. The nurse who looks after Miriam during the day suggested I should phone an escort agency to sort out someone to go out and about with as I don't have many friends who are free to socialise during the day and I'm fed up with staying in. I phoned your agency and the manager suggested after a long chat that she would send me photos of young ladies. I showed these photos too Miriam who picked you out saying you looked kind and pretty." Rodney looked embarrassed.

"I don't believe that this is the first time you've been out with an escort, I'm damn sure it isn't? I've a feeling Miriam has been ill for a couple of years if not longer" I said looking perplexed.

"I better come clean as eventually you'll find out. Women are good at getting men like me to own up to things they wouldn't normally admit to."

"Come on then Rodney tell me. I bet you arrange to meet someone most days if it's not for a meal it's for a drink." Rodney looked shocked to think I realised.

"I meet up with an escort every day except Mondays. I thank God I'm well off and I can afford to employ a nurse for my wife from ten am - six

217

pm. I manage to look after her myself during the night as she's no trouble, once I've settled her down."

"Don't you go to work?"

"I've a business in Oxford Street that I need to keep an eye on. I go in a couple of different days each week to keep my employees on their toes."

"Sorry Rodney, I have one more question. What will happen to Miriam next Wednesday if we meet up in the evening?"

"That's easy enough to answer. I'll get a nurse to come in from seven till about eleven. It didn't take you long to finish your Gin, do you fancy another before we move on?" I looked down at my empty glass then across at Rodney's beer mug which was still half full.

"Okay, yes please but only a single. I enjoyed the last Gin but I'm sure you bought me a double."

"Mary, I only asked and paid for a single unless spirits are extra cheap here and I'm sure they're not – the barman must have made a mistake with the price and size." Rodney went up to the bar, he soon returned with my second Gin. We continued chatting without any long silences, I made Rodney smile about an uncle of mine that lives up north and is a bit of an alcoholic who enjoys a few Gin and Tonics every day. "My parents went to stay and uncle offered them a drink dad said 'Gin and Tonic please' 'a man after my own heart' answered uncle. With that uncle went into the kitchen to pour the drinks, when he returned he handed dad what was supposed to be a small Gin and Tonic. It turned out to be a large glass of neat Gin - dad drank it all. I don't think he has touched a Gin since and that was a few years ago now."

"I don't drink spirits - never have, I find it better to keep to beer or lager they don't affect me in the same way that I think spirits would. I don't mind watching other people drinking spirits as long as they don't encourage me to drink them."

"I've never had either a lager or a beer perhaps I ought to try one, obviously not after a Gin." I laughed.

"It's a longer drink and not as strong as Gin – you may enjoy half a pint on a sunny day."

"When I go out with my girlfriends I may try one." I looked down at my watch. "Rodney it's getting on for one o'clock we better get going if we're to find some where for lunch." We drank up and left.

"Mary we don't need to go into Fortnum and Masons we can always turn left at the top of the road and walk towards Green Park. I know of a family restaurant down one of the side streets, I often call in for lunch when I'm out and about."

"I know London well but not the Green park area. It may sound strange to you Rodney, I've never been past the Royal Academy. If this restaurant is where you fancy eating let's go there, as this meal is about you and where you want to eat. I'm coming along as an escort to keep you company."

"Before we get to the restaurant I better tell you that it doesn't look much from the outside in fact it looks pretty grim. The food is English and is cooked to order and usually tastes delicious, not like some places that sell rubbish in a building that looks perfect from the outside."

"I have been in lots of restaurants like that and you can hardly eat the food."

"The waitresses at this one are quite accommodating, I'll ask if we can have a table in one of the bay windows, then we can watch the sights out in the street."

"I'm going to guess that you're quite a bit older than me and I'm wondering if you have ever been to Scots of St James which is up their?" I said stopping to point up the lane.

"Yeah but years ago why do you ask?"

"I understand from the adverts in the Evening Standard that Jimmy Hendrix and the Stones play there some times."

"They weren't there when I took Miriam, that was a few years ago now. If you can afford to go it's worth going even if you only go the once. I remember that it didn't cost much to join but the drinks were expensive. The other thing is the dance floor, it's a bit small and it gets full."

"I've got a boyfriend perhaps I can persuade him to take me. I'm going to guess that the best night to go is either Friday or a Saturday."

"I don't know as it was back in the mid sixties when I took Miriam. I remember the evening well as Miriam started to feel strange and couldn't walk properly. That was the beginning of Miriam and Multiple Sclerosis. The symptoms worsened until she couldn't do very much for herself. At least she was in her late 30s when this happened. Many people get symptoms in their early 20s, anyway that's enough about Multiple Sclerosis."

We wandered on in silence until we reached the restaurant. On entering we found all the tables were taken except for one which was situated at the back of the restaurant. Rodney looked around then waved a waitress over.

"Is this the only table available Liz?"

"I'm afraid so Mr Davis."

"If we stay you're saying we'll have to sit at this table which is between the doors to the toilets?"

"Yeah." replied the waitress looking embarrassed. Rodney looked towards me as if I should make a comment.

"I was looking forward to eating here. Is there any possibility of you moving the table to a different area? I'm sure you could move the tables around to accommodate this one." I said in my private school accent. "It will be very embarrassing eating next to these toilet doors and seeing customers come and go also we may hear them weeing which would make it even worse."

By this time the customers sat nearest to us had stopped talking and were listening into our conversation which embarrassed the waitress and made her stutter while talking.

"I can offer to get this table moved to the middle of the restaurant Mr Davis. I know you really like to sit away from everyone in a cosy corner."

"Yes I do. Come on Mary we'll leave. I'll eat here another day" I followed Rodney out into the street. "Rodney, what are we going to do, as time is marching on and you must be hungry?"

"I'm not sure where to go, have you any suggestions?"

"Let's take a cab to the Strand and go into the Queens, it's a pub, the food's not bad. I've eaten there many times and I haven't been ill."

"Come on then." Replied Rodney waving down the first cab that came around the corner.

We arrived at the Queens just before last orders. We found a table at a side window looking out towards the Strand. "This is very pleasant Mary. I'll get the menu and while I'm up at the bar I'll get the drinks in. What do you fancy?" I sat and thought. "Stop your day dreaming girl it'll be closing time and they'll be kicking us out before we've had a drink let alone a meal."

"I'm not sure what to have as I've already had a double plus a single Gin and Tonic."

"Another won't harm you. It's not as if you have to walk home in a tiddly state, all you have to do is walk out of here and wave down a cab – before you know it you'll be walking up to the front door of where you live."

"That may sound okay to you but I'm not used to drinking more than a couple of Gin and Tonics in one sitting and I've had three already. I'd far rather be safe than sorry and have a soft drink"

"Okay a soft drink it is, I'll get you a coke." Rodney stormed up to the bar and returned plonking the menu down in front of me. "Have a look at this while I go back and pick up our drinks, see what you fancy eating but don't take all day to decide." said Rodney looking flushed and annoyed.

"Why are you behaving like you are, I can tell you suffer with a short fuse?" I called after him, "It's no wonder you changed escort agencies. I bet the one you used to use was completely fed up with you and your mood swings. I bet the girls phoned into the manager most days to complain about your behaviour. I reckon you were given the boot, I bet I'm more right than wrong." Rodney looked stupid while carrying the drinks back from the bar.

"Hold your hair on girl don't annoy or embarrass me. Just you remember I'm paying for your lunch, your cab home plus your wages. I can get up and walk out of that door leaving you to pay the bill." he said laughing and pointing towards the door "I've done it before and I can easily do it again - don't make a fool of me. Getting back to the food have you decided what you're eating Mary?"

"I'll have the same as you - whatever that is. Hurry up and choose Rodney or they'll kick us out before we've eaten as its past two o'clock." I said looking exasperated.

"They won't kick us out as I've been chatting with the barman. He would like us to choose our meal as soon as possible then he'll give us plenty of time to eat our meal without choking. I'm having steak and kidney pudding with fresh vegetables."

"That'll do." I said looking a bit sad as I'm not keen on kidneys. After the order was placed we sat in silence. Both of us had the shock of our lives when the food arrived in less than ten minutes. "I thought the meals here were cooked to order. These two meals look as dry as chips. I reckon they've been warmed up in the microwave. What do you think Rodney?"

"The same as you Mary but we'll have to try and eat them or we won't have any lunch - I'm starving. If it doesn't taste any better than it looks I'm not paying. I hope you're listening Mr Waiter." The waiter looked shocked and embarrassed as if no one had ever complained about the meals.

"Yeah I'm listening alright. I'll let the boss know what you've said." The waiter wandered back to the kitchen. Rodney must have been starving as he managed to eat all of his, while I only ate a small amount. "Mary you'll never grow big and strong." said Rodney smiling towards me. It was as if his short fuse had been caused by lack of food as after eating he'd gone back to being sociable.

"That's one thing I don't want to be, I'd rather be small and lady like." I said looking down at my body. "You look a bit of alright in fact you look bloody good from over here." He said as if he was undressing me with his eyes from across the table.

"Enough of that Rodney, I'm here to keep you company not to be chatted up or looked at like I'm a tart."

"What the hell do you expect me to say or do when you've come out looking like a sex bomb." he laughed.

"That's definitely not what I am."

"I'm going to call you Tease. That's my new name for you, Tease instead of Mary." After having drunk three Gin and Tonics in the other pub his comment made me grin.

"Thank God I've said something to cheer you up," said Rodney, "if I hadn't my face would have got longer and longer and eventually I would look like thunder. I'm going to get myself another pint. I reckon you should have another G and T it will do you good." I was so surprised at the

222

offer that I agreed. Rodney was up and over at the bar before I had a chance to change my mind.

"Here you are Tease." Rodney said while putting both glasses down on the table. He immediately moved his chair closer to mine. In the beginning I pretended not to notice as I didn't want to cause a fuss. It wasn't until Rodney put his arm around the back of my chair that I asked him politely to take his arm away and to move his chair back to where it was originally.

"What's the matter with you Tease? I thought you were an escort because you enjoyed men. I've wined and dined you now it's my turn to ask for afters."

"There's no afters from me, I'm not that easy in fact I'm not easy at all." This time it was my turn to get annoyed. "There never will be any afters for you with me."

"Surely being an escort you should realise that a man needs sex in some form for afters. I don't mind if you only give me a blow job – I wouldn't take long to come. I'm desperate and you look as if you may be good at it. The thing is I haven't a wife at home who is well enough to do the honours. I need you to help me out."

"IF I say yes and it's a big IF where the hell are you going to take me to perform and how much are you prepared to pay me as this would be an extra?" I asked in my tiddly state.

"First of all Tease it depends what you're offering?"

"I'm not cheap. If I give you a blow job it's going to be quite expensive as I would hate to get caught by a copper while performing up a back alley. If you're desperate as you call it we could chance it but it will cost you a hell of a lot for the risk I'd be taking or we can leave it till we meet up next Wednesday evening when you could book a hotel room and have rampant sex with me, the choice is yours Rodney but I need to know which it's going to be."

"How much is the blow job?"

"Ten pounds."

"Rampant sex in the hotel room?"

"Twenty five pounds."

"Done and dusted I'll have both." To be honest I couldn't believe what I was hearing.

"Rodney you're saying you want a blow job for ten pounds today and next Wednesday you'll have rampant penetrating sex in a hotel room for twenty five pounds?"

"For God's sake Tease that's what I said. I'll pay the thirty five pounds when we meet up next week."

"Rodney, I don't work like that, you'll have to pay the ten pounds before I perform the blow job."

"It was a good try on my part." He said laughing at me. "I'll pay up once we find some where for you to do the deed."

"Have you any idea where we can go?"

"No."

"Over in the corner are stairs that go down to the toilets we could take a chance and go down to the ladies. If you look around there are only a couple of women in here and its closing time in a minute so they'll be going on their way." I said meaning we won't get caught. "If you don't fancy that Rodney we can always walk down Drury Lane as there are plenty of alley ways along there. I'm sure it won't take me long to get you to come."

Silence reigned. I was thinking about my two false teeth and whether I should admit to Rodney about having them or should I chance my luck and not mention them but take them out before performing and pop them back in after and hope that he doesn't notice. What he was thinking about I have no idea.

"Drink up Tease, we better start walking. I hope you know the way to Drury Lane."

"Of course I do I wouldn't have suggested going there if I didn't. We turn left outside here go along to the theatre Royal turn right then after a hundred yards or so turn left again and we're in Drury Lane – fifteen minutes from here." After Rodney paid up for what I thought was a disgusting meal we plodded along the road until we arrived in Drury Lane where we looked for a convenient alley way.

It didn't take long before the deed was done and dusted and I was ten pounds better off. Rodney waved down a black cab for me. I told the cabbie where I needed to be dropped off then Rodney paid.

224

Chapter 28

It was five o'clock by the time I put the key in the door to the flat. Joan was stood at the bottom of the stairs calling up to get my attention. "Oh there you are Mary, a woman called Celia rang ten minutes ago to say you aren't needed tomorrow lunch time - whatever that means." said Joan looking towards me, as I walked through the door.

"Does she want me to phone her back?"

"I don't know, she didn't say and I didn't think to ask. She sounded a bit annoyed as if you'd upset her in some way."

"I can assure you I haven't. I'll ring her back once I've found the number, unless she gave it to you."

"No." replied Joan looking stupid. "Before you go upstairs I must tell you I'm moving out of the flat next weekend."

"Good."

I answered then immediately stomped up the stairs to my room where I found the agency's phone number and went straight back down to ring. Celia must have been sat next to the phone as it only rang the once before she answered. "Miss Celia speaking."

"Mary Huggins here, I've just received your message saying you don't need me tomorrow."

"Yeah that's right the bloke you were meeting has cancelled." Replied Celia sounding exasperated. "I'm pleased you've phoned back as I've a question for you. Have you got two top front false teeth?"

"Why do you want to know that?"

"Miss Huggins, don't answer me with a question, please say if you have a couple of false teeth, I need to know."

"Celia, I don't need to answer that as it's not in my contract saying I mustn't have false teeth. It's none of your damn business whether I have or I haven't." Sounding annoyed Celia went on to tell me how a Derek had phoned a few days ago to book a young lady to take out for a meal.

"I sent him some photos and one was of you. When he rang back he wasn't very complimentary about you in fact he was quite rude, as well as other things he told me that you had two front top false teeth. Is this

225

true? You may as well own up if you have, come on Miss Huggins come clean tell me the truth."

This was a shock to my system as I never thought in my wildest dreams that Derek would phone around escort agencies. Mind you it could have been worse as Derek could have changed his name and asked if he could meet me for a meal and I turned up what would have happened I dread to think. When Celia mentioned the false teeth I thought perhaps Rodney had seen me taking them out of my mouth and put them in my pocket before giving him the blow job then phoned into the agency. Thank God he hadn't as I would have had the sack immediately. I went on to explain to Celia in no uncertain terms how Derek was the cause of me having the false teeth.

"Celia you didn't notice my false teeth when I came for the interview also no one else has mentioned them. Rodney who I met earlier today for lunch didn't say a word about me having two false teeth. I don't think it makes a difference whether I've false teeth or my own as long as they don't rattle around in my mouth."

"Okay Mary, I'm going to see how you get on with Jonathan on Friday, he's a very fussy man. If he notices your false teeth he won't be very happy especially if they move out of position while you're eating. If Jonathan gets back to me about your false teeth rattling around in your mouth, you'll be on your bike."

"It's not my fault that I have two false teeth."

"Who do you think should be blamed for your false teeth Mary? If you hadn't gone out with Derek most probably you'd still have your own teeth. It seems from what he said you went out with him for a year. It's not as if you went out with him the once and he punched you in the mouth, if that had been the case I may be feeling sorry for you but I definitely can't feel sorry for someone stupid enough to go out with a man that hits them about." by this time I was almost in tears.

"Now you have told me that I shouldn't be working as an escort as I've false teeth I'm going to put my receiver down as I'm about to start crying. I guess you haven't any more work for me this week other than me having dinner at the Cora Hotel with Jonathan?"

226

"You have that dead right Miss Huggins – no more work this week. I'll give you a call Saturday morning after I've had a chat with Jonathan to see how the pair of you got on, hopefully he won't have noticed your false teeth. If you get on with him and he has enjoyed your company he may invite you out again, keep your fingers crossed." bang went the receiver.

This conversation upset me so much that I don't feel like cooking for myself let alone the girls along with Heather if she turns up. I'm going to offer to buy fish and chips for everyone.

I plodded up the stairs to wait for the girls to return home from work. The first to arrive was Liz she started to rant on about how I looked. "Mary, you look like you've been pulled through a hedge backwards and finished up crying. What's up? Remember when Margaret came home from the paper shop the other evening."

"Yeah what about her?"

"Well you look like she did. Has some one upset you? I bet the bloke you met for lunch has something to do with the way you look. I bet he forced you into a corner and got you to do something you didn't want to do, like giving him a blow job."

"He offered me good money - I couldn't refuse."

"I hope you had a johnny to put on his dick." I went the colour of a beetroot as soon as Liz mentioned johnny as I didn't use one. Liz shook her head and told me exactly what she thought of me for even agreeing to do a blow job let alone performing without a johnny.

"I had too much to drink, I wasn't thinking straight."

"You told the girls and me on your last day at the office that you were going to try and give up the booze and now you are getting drunk when you're out with clients. I wouldn't have had one alcoholic drink let alone the few you have had with someone you hardly knew. Once you were drunk this bloke could have raped you."

"Don't be daft Liz, Rodney wouldn't do that."

"How the hell do you know he wouldn't you silly bugger you didn't know him from Adam. He could have told you any old rubbish about where he lived and worked, it could have all been lies. You tell me how you know he was telling you the truth and wouldn't have raped you given half a chance, once he got you down a back alley."

227

"Liz don't make me feel worse than I do already. I know I shouldn't have got cosy with him then agreed to give him a blow job - I feel a fool."

"Mary, I'll put the kettle on and make us both a mug of coffee. I hope you realise it's your turn to cook supper tonight. How you'll manage, I don't know as you look as if you'll fall over in a heap if you don't go and sit down." said Liz as if she was completely fed up with me. "Before you go in the other room have you been to the butchers to get the liver?"

"NO I HAVE NOT. I have been too busy getting drunk." I laughed.

"I don't find getting drunk very funny. What the hell are we going to have for supper Mary?"

"I may have had too much alcohol but I have managed to think up a plan, I'm going to treat you all including Heather, if she turns up, to fish and chips." I said slurring my words.

"That sounds wonderful in theory but the girls won't think much of that even though you plan to pay, as they're looking forward to having liver."

"Well they'll have to put up with fish and chips unless they go to the all night butchers and get the liver and cook it themselves as I know damn well that I'm not in a fit state to cook for myself let alone five of us." I hiccupped. "Liz, do you think you can keep me being drunk to yourself?" I said before plonking myself down on the nearest chair. "Okay, it will be our little secret Mary. Make sure it doesn't happen again, if it does I'll tell the world."

"Thanks Liz." I gave her a hug. "Once I've finished drinking my coffee I'm going into bed. I'll leave out the money for the fish and chips, don't bother to buy any for me. I almost forgot to tell you I met Joan downstairs in the hall and she told me that she's moving out next weekend, which means I can move into the flat, that's if you're agreeable." I said trying my hardest to look coy.

"It's okay with me as long as Ruth moves in at the same time as I reckon you need someone to keep an eye on you and your drinking habit. I'll have a chat with Ruth tomorrow and let you know."

"I've told you a hundred times Liz that I'm giving up the demon drink. By the way Joan also told me that she has finished painting the flat." Liz looked at me as if she didn't believe a word I was saying.

"Mary I don't reckon she's painted one room let alone all of them as I haven't smelt any paint coming up the stairs from her place."

"She told me all the rooms plus the ceilings have been painted Magnolia."

"What, am I hearing right the walls plus the ceilings are Magnolia?" Liz sounded very annoyed.

"Apparently."

"I told her the ceilings had to be painted white."

"Liz, you must remember Joan hasn't much money, it's far cheaper for her to paint everything one colour. I bet she got the paint from Woolworths. The other night she said something about Woolworths having a sale and she was going to buy the cheapest paint she could find and didn't care about the colour."

"When I see her she'll start to care about the colour or she won't get her deposit back. If she's not careful she'll find herself sleeping under Waterloo Bridge."

"Poor Joan."

"I'm not saying poor Joan it serves her damn well right." After I finished drinking my coffee I staggered into my bedroom leaving Liz to her own devises.

Chapter 29

Thank God I slept all night without being disturbed, I didn't wake until around nine o'clock. I haven't a client until tomorrow at seven thirty pm so I stayed put wondering how I should spend my day and decided I would go for a walk to get used to the area.

I'm going to keep walking until I find some where to call in for a drop of the hard stuff. Mind you I must only have a small glass of whatever I fancy and it must only be the one or I'll be in the same state as last night – drunk, then Liz and the girls will get annoyed and may suggest that I find somewhere else to live and that place will not be the flat downstairs.

Eventually I got myself out of bed made myself presentable, ate my breakfast then went on my way to Queensway tube station where I decided to walk along Bayswater road until I got to the entrance to Hyde Park. Once inside the gates I found a bench to sit on to watch the sights before walking across the park to Brompton road then into the first pub I came across.

By the time I arrived in the pub the bar staff were very busy with the lunch time customers and most of the stools and chairs were taken up by the locals. After a few minutes of looking around I found an empty stool at the end of the bar, once I'd made myself comfortable I ordered a single Gin and Tonic when a man came in through the main door and gave me a strange look before coming over to confront me about the stool.

"The stool you're sat on belongs to me." said the man pointing down at it. "It's mine, I always sit here."

"No one was sat here when I came into the bar, also none of the bar staff have asked me to move, surely if this is a customer's own stool one of the barmen would have told me to sit somewhere else. I've never been in a bar where the customer has his own stool."

"Well you have now. If you used your eyes which you obviously didn't you would have noticed that this stool belongs to Charlie. Have a look at the back, it says Charlie's stool – Charlie is me." In shock I jumped down to take a look and yes it said Charlie's stool whether the stool belongs to this bloke I don't know as the barman wasn't over friendly towards him. Surely if this bloke is Charlie the barman would have a chat with him instead he seemed to be avoiding him.

"I'll have to stand here to drink this." I said holding my Gin and Tonic in the air.

"Yeah you will unless you go and pinch one of the chairs from over there." He said pointing to the other end of the bar while smirking to himself. I'm very good at blushing and blush I did. Then out of the blue the bloke came out with this statement.

"I'll let you sit on the stool as long as I can keep you company." He said tapping his hand down on the stool. I took him up on the offer.

Once I'd settled myself back on the stool I explained to the bloke that I'd never been inside this pub before, in fact I told him the biggest lie I could think of. "I don't know what made me come in here as I only visit pubs on high days and holidays – today's neither."

"Perhaps you were bored and decided to come in to see what this dear old place has to offer. This is my favourite pub. I'm in here most days unless I have a date and today I haven't. Have you a boyfriend?" I pretended to be deaf as I didn't know what to answer also I had to think about my relationship with Steve, is he my boyfriend or just a mate? If going to bed regularly with one particular man makes him my boyfriend I haven't got one as Steve hasn't even suggested getting cosy let alone us having a quickie.

"Hurry up and answer my question I haven't all day. If you haven't got a boyfriend I'll buy you another Gin and Tonic, that's if you'd like one. If you have a boyfriend I'll say goodbye and go on my way." He shouted down my ear.

"I haven't got a boyfriend and yes I wouldn't mind another Gin but please don't get it in until I've finished this one." I answered sounding annoyed.

"A question for you, why did you take so long to answer such a simple question?"

"I don't know." I answered sounding stupid.

"You can't tell me why you didn't answer my question quicker than you did. You come over as if you're as thick as two short planks." I felt so daft that I wished the floor would open and swallow me up. With that the man

231

called over to the barman who immediately came to serve us. "Charlie what can I get you?"

"A pint of brown split for me – make sure you put it in my pewter mug and a Gin and Tonic for the lady." At least he was telling the truth about his name and I'm going to guess that the stool must belong to him and not some other Charlie.

"Mr Barman, there's no need to pour my Gin yet as I haven't finished this one." I said nodding towards my glass. "I'm not used to alcohol so I'm going to take it slowly." The barman smiled at me while winking towards Charlie.

"This pub doesn't close for another couple of hours then sometimes if the barmen aren't in a rush to get home we're able to stay a bit longer. Now I've ordered you a drink and we have settled down to have a natter what's your name and what do you do for a job?"

"I'm Mary, I haven't much of a job in fact I haven't got one at the moment. I used to work in an office at Oxford Circus but I was bored out of my skull - I left on a whim, now I'm in between jobs." Charlie looked at me as if he didn't believe a word I said – I wonder why people think I lie? "Once I've finished these Gin and Tonics I'm going to take a walk along Brompton road towards the Knightsbridge tube stations to see if there are any job vacancies in the shop windows. Harrods and Harvey Nicholls are always advertising for staff in the Evening Standard, I may call in and see what they can offer me. Working in a shop would make a change from typing letters." I said lying through my teeth once again.

"If you like I'll walk with you as that's the direction I go to get home."

"Charlie, you're telling me you walked all the way down past Harvey Nicholls to here for a pint of what you fancy?"

"Afraid so."

"I imagined you lived around the corner from here especially as this is your local."

"You've got that wrong darling it's only my local for this week." Charlie replied laughing at me. "I live quite a few yards from here in fact this pub must be a good mile from my flat. Whatever you do don't show an interest in me."

"What do you mean by that? It hasn't entered my head to fancy you."
By this time I was getting annoyed. "Before you call me darling again, I'm
no one's darling so don't call me by that name. I'm Mary to anyone and
everyone and especially you."

"Sorry, I won't call you that again. I'm pleased you don't fancy me as I
get bored quickly and change women as often as I change pubs which is
weekly. The day I decide to move pubs I pick up this stool along with my
beer mug and leave never to return. This week I'm here next week I could
be down the Kings road in the 6 Bells living it up with the Stones road
manager."

"Do you know him?"

"Don't be daft, that's just something I say to impress." He said laughing
at me. "My stool and I move most weeks to different areas of London.
Don't be surprised if one day you bump into me the other side of the city,
as I said earlier I get bored and like you, I move on a whim."

"Answer this one Charlie, do you keep moving flats or do you stay put
and just go out and about visiting different pubs with your stool?"

"I couldn't be bothered to move home, it's easier and cheaper to pick
up my stool and take it along to the next pub, I fancy spending time in."

"The barmen must question you arriving with your own stool plus beer
mug."

"No they don't care. When I'm not sat on the stool other customers can
use it – my stool helps the pubs out with seats. If I found someone
drinking out of my pewter mug I wouldn't be happy."

I hadn't eaten much for breakfast and started to feel woozy. "Charlie I
don't reckon I can drink a second Gin and Tonic. Perhaps you could explain
this to the barman then he may give you your money back as he hasn't
poured the Gin out yet."

"You're not very good company in fact you're a complete and utter
bloody bore Mary, no wonder you haven't a boyfriend." He said slurring
his words as if his pint of brown split was not the first he'd had today.

"What the hell do you mean by that, I've had one G and T that's enough
for me at lunch time in fact this one alcoholic drink will keep me going for
a week. I'm not an alcoholic and don't intend turning into one?"

"I was hoping you may be one then we could drink our lives away together."

"Only a minute ago you were telling me not to fancy you and now you want me to drink my life away with you. I'll tell you now that I'm not going to have another drink. You can call me what you like but you won't persuade me to have more Gin." I could feel myself blushing while getting annoyed with Charlie and his attitude that I decided to get down from the stool then ask him to point me in the direction of the Ladies so I could go and cool off. "I've a feeling it's over there." He said pointing towards the back wall then he immediately turned to look the other way. "Perhaps it's over there and down the stairs, I don't know where the bloody bog is, I haven't a clue." He answered laughing in my face. Waving his hand in the air Charlie shouted along to the bar man "Where's the bog barman?"

"Over there." Said the barman pointing to the far end of the bar and at the same time he walked down towards the pair of us. "Charlie we don't call toilets bogs. If you want to call them that you better find some where more suitable to your language as this is Knightsbridge not the East End."

"I don't see why I should have to leave because I called the toilet a bog."

"I'm sorry Charlie it's obvious to me that you've had more to drink this lunch time than that one brown split, you have to leave."

"Okay, I'll go, but only because I don't like it here, the company is rubbish. I'll leave as soon I've drunk this." Charlie said holding his mug in the air. "Don't think I'll be back tomorrow because I won't, I'll never return to this dump."

"Good." I shouted joining in the end of the conversation. Picking up my handbag I went across to the Ladies hoping by the time I returned Charlie will have left.

Chapter30

After leaving the Ladies I had to go back through the bar to get to the main door that led out to Brompton road. To avoid eye contact with Charlie I focused on the door just in case he was still stood at the bar and was waiting for me to return. Once outside I escaped across the road into Hyde Park then hurried across to Bayswater road where I bumped straight into Enid who was coming out of the local butchers. "What have you been buying?" I said looking down at the carrier bag.

"The supper we didn't have last night, LIVER." She shouted in my face. "We were looking forward to this last night and what did we get fish and chips and not one of us finished eating them in fact most of the meals went in the dust bin."

"That was a waste of my money."

"It serves you damn well right Mary if you feel you wasted your money. We all know why we had to have fish and chips it was because you were in a tiddly state again and couldn't cook." I felt stupid.

"At least I didn't go to bed and leave you all starving, I did leave money on the side for food."

"That was very good of you Mary." Answered Enid while looking me up and down. "Mary, getting back to today where the hell have you been while we have all been working our socks of? I bet you have been to a pub." I blushed. "Liz has told us all about you and how you can't resist a G and T whatever time of the day or night it is. Ruth told Liz back along how you drank a G and T for breakfast the other weekend." Enid laughed.

"That's not true it is a lie. I've never drunk a Gin before lunch time."

"Ruth was adamant that you did, she told Liz she would swear on the bible that you had G and T with your cereal."

"I will have to have think about what you have just said but if Ruth said I drank it perhaps I did, I can't remember. Before I lose my temper with you for God sake shut up about me and my drinking habit. I'm trying hard to give it up, in fact I'm making sure that I'm only having one alcoholic drink a day. If I was invited to a party I would only have one glass of whatever they had to offer and that would be because I had my back against the wall." Enid laughed at me as if she didn't believe what I was saying. We walked along the street together until we came across a café and decided to go in for a coffee. Once we had made ourselves comfortable at the table I asked Enid a question about her childhood, this started her chatting non stop.

"Enid, you've told me about your job in the city but I don't know a thing about your home life or your childhood."

"I'm not a very interesting person, I was brought up by my mum in a council flat down the East End. Dad left home when I was eighteen months old. The story goes that the man who was supposed to be my dad only married mum because she was pregnant. When I was about ten years old and mum was in a temper she told that she was not sure if dad was my dad as she had lots of men and he was just one of many and also I was lucky to be white as she had loads of black blokes over the years." I sat with my mouth open wide in shock.   Enid continued to chat and tell me about her grandmother that had two children, one being Enid's mum.

"I'll give you a shock my grandmother had a boyfriend who visited two or three times a week for a bit of the other, this was when grandad was down the pub. Mum told me that grandad visited the pub every day in fact twice a day if he had half a chance – lunch time and evening. Apparently gran made mum and her sister sit in the window looking out for their dad to return, when they saw him coming along the road they shouted up the stairs to gran and the bloke."

"That must have been terrible, I would have hated to have to do that. Did they ever get caught?"

"No, they always managed to get back down the stairs, then the bloke ran out the back door into the lane, long before grandad opened the front door."

"How long did this go on for?"

"Years, it continued until grandad died then the bloke moved into the house and took charge of the family."

"That must have been awful."

"Mum hated him especially when he moved in, they were always having rows, he often hit out at her. I felt sorry for mum as she went through all of this before having me so looking after me without a husband was a piece of cake."

"Where is your gran now?"

"Digging up the daisies, she'd be ancient if she was alive today."

"What about your mum where does she live?"

"She's dead as well. You remember what I'm about to tell you Mary. Mum was an alcoholic on Sherry."

236

"Eh I couldn't drink that stuff, my favourite tipple is Gin and Tonic – I love it. Alcohol can't be that bad it makes my life worth living, it puts a smile on my face."

"It may do that at the moment but if you carry on drinking like you are, you could finish up with pancreatitis, incontinence and seizures – I could go on for ever."

"Oh God don't tell me anymore." I started to cry.

"I'm going to frighten you into giving up the demon drink if it is the last thing I do. I'm going to tell you what happened to mum. In the end she had diarrhoea and finished up with cirrhosis of the liver – she was only forty five when she died."

"How long ago was that?"

"Four years ago I was sixteen when it happened they allowed me to stay living in the council flat until I decided to better myself by coming to live in the West End."

"I moved out from snooty alley years ago, as my parents and I were not getting on."

"What do you mean not getting on Mary? You should always try and get on with your parents."

"I was fed up with mum drinking far too much for her own good then arguing with dad about the women he was seeing on the side. I used shout at them to try to stop the arguments but it never worked so I walked out. I didn't go back to see them for eighteen months – I didn't even phone. When I eventually plucked up the courage to call around they were still arguing about the same old things."

"They're still together? I couldn't stand that I'd rather live on my own in a bedsitter down the East End than put up with a husband that was fucking some one else and still expecting me to sleep with him."

"Mum eventually lost her temper and kicked him out – thank God. The strange thing is he only moved to the other side of the street into his mate's flat. If he wanted to he could watch mum in her flat from his front room especially if he bought a pair of binoculars."

"Eh Mary, that would make your dad a dirty old man."

"Oh God, he would be like Jeff in the Alfred Hitchcock's film Rear Window the only difference being he wouldn't see mum murdering someone." We both laughed. We finished our coffees and went on our way to the flat. On entering the flat I asked who was cooking

237

"Me worse luck, last night it was ME that went to the chippy. There is no peace for the wicked." Enid replied looking fed up.

"It's my turn to cook next Wednesday that's if I'm still here."

"What do you mean by that – still here? If it's your turn to cook you'll be cooking whether you want to or not Miss Mary. Even if you're drunk next Wednesday you'll be cooking." I explained about the flat and how I may be downstairs with Ruth. Enid wasn't very happy.

"If you move down there I doubt if you'll have anything more to do with us up here. Most probably you'll become a snob like Joan she hasn't had anything to do with any of us since the day she moved into the flat. Mind you she does take messages if anyone phones which is something – I hope you'll do the same."

"I'll take phone messages, I can't speak for Ruth but I think she will if she is in. Getting back to me being a snob I'm not one and I'm hardly likely to become one now. I may call my parents Mr and Mrs Snooty behind their backs that's because of the way they behave – I don't behave like them. I wish I'd been born into a working class family – all my friends are working class which suits me fine."

"Mary from where I'm stood you only seem to go out with blokes from snob alley."

"That's not true Enid you have definitely got that wrong. I only spend time with snobby blokes because of my work also they're the ones with plenty of dosh to spend on meals and entertainment. If they want more than a meal with me and I feel hard up I would agree to go along to a posh hotel like the Hyde Park for a bit of the other – I close my eyes and think of the money or as others say think of England."

"The money can't come in regularly so how the hell do you pay your bills?"

"Enid you have a nerve to ask but as you have I'll tell you. My mother is as rich as shit, she pays most things for me - I don't need a proper job." I said lying through my teeth for about the fifth time this week.

"I told you that you're a snob from snob alley and I'm right."

I put my nose in the air and walked off to my bedroom but not until I told Enid to mind her own business. Once I was in my bedroom with the door locked, I got my bottle of Gin from under my bed and took a swig. It was not long before Liz was knocking on my door to say that Ruth had arrived home for supper and to look at Joan's flat.

"I'll be out in a moment." I called from behind my door, I immediately took another swig of Gin before going out into the kitchen for supper. The girls were sat staring at me when out of the blue Ruth started to rant on about me and my drinking. "Mary you look a bit squiffy."

"What do you mean?" I replied pretending not to understand.

"You look drunk have you been on the bottle AGAIN?"

"No I have not. Why do you always think I've been drinking?" I answered sounding annoyed.

"Because you usually have."

"I have been told to give up alcohol and I haven't had a drop for a couple of days. I'm finding it bloody difficult, look at my hands shaking." I shook my hands as if I had with drawl symptoms – the girls seemed to believe me thank God.

"Mary you know damn well what is going to happen to you if you don't give it up, you'll die like mum."

"What happened to her Enid?" asked Ruth.

"She was an alcoholic, she drank Sherry. Eventually she died as her liver gave up the ghost."

"I'm fed up with you lot talking about my drinking habit, you ought to look at yourselves in the mirror. I reckon you all drink more than me in one sitting especially when you go out together on a Friday night. I'm so fed up with you lot yapping on about me and booze that I'm going to take my supper into my room and eat it on my own in peace."

Chapter 31

I woke Friday morning with my head spinning. I found dirty dishes along with an empty bottle of Gin in my bed, also I was still wearing the dress I wore to the pub and my false teeth were rattling around in my mouth. I'm shocked as I can't remember finishing off the Gin or even eating my supper in bed. All I can remember is how Enid had explained to me about her mum drinking sherry and how she'd died of cirrhosis of the liver. I laid in bed wondering how the hell I was going to get out of this mess and stop drinking and why I had become a drinker in the first place.

I stayed in bed for a good hour before deciding to move and sort myself out. Once up and running I took the dress off and replaced it with my dressing gown before wandering into the kitchen where silence reigned, all the girls had gone to work – thank God. On the side was a note from Liz telling me that Ruth will be moving into the flat with me but not until she leaves her office job in three weeks. Liz also asked if I'd be moving downstairs on my own and paying full rent for the next three weeks or was I going to stay put up here with the girls.

After reading this all I could think about was having a large Gin and Tonic for breakfast, but I'd run out of Gin so I had to make do with a mug of coffee and a couple of Panadol for my headache. By the time I'd finished drinking the coffee it was getting on for lunch time so I decided to have a lick and a promise and go to the local café for a bite to eat. Along the way I went into the Off License to buy the largest bottle of Gin they had - this will be hidden under my bed. I know damn well that this is definitely a stupid thing to do but at this moment alcohol is my friend and I need a drop as soon as possible. Once back in my room I immediately took a swig.

"That's better Gin, I love the taste of you." I said out loud to myself, before I knew it I had two more swigs. Staggering around my room I sorted out a dress to wear to dinner with Jonathan this evening – whether it's the right thing to wear I don't know but it will have to do as I have nothing else unless I wear something dated. This sorted I took an afternoon nap. I was woken at five by Liz and Margaret who were chatting loudly in the kitchen about their day. I was annoyed with myself for drinking the Gin that I took it out on the girls by storming into the kitchen and telling them to shut up. They looked at each other as if they were completely fed up with me but didn't say a word. Embarrassed I returned to my room and prepared myself for the evening.

At seven o'clock I crept along the landing, down the stairs and out into the fresh air, hoping not to fall down – thank God I didn't. As usual I waved down a black cab. it wasn't long before the cab was being driven with me sat in the back along Upper Woburn Place to the Cora Hotel where who I thought was Jonathan was standing patiently on the top step smoking what looked like a manikin cigar. If it's him he's just like I was expecting, short and fat in a navy blazer with grey flannels along with a white shirt with a colourful tie. To me his looks made him appear boring whether he is or not is another matter. The cab stopped and waited while I hobbled up the steps to ask if the cigar man was Jonathan - he was. The one thing he had going for him was his smile he beamed from ear to ear. Like all my clients before him he immediately went down the steps to pay the cabbie. While he was paying I stood and had a dream about my alcohol input and wondered if Jonathan was a boozer and would expect me to keep up with him in the drink department or was I going to be in luck and find he would rather drink water. The thing is I don't feel in a fit state to have any more alcohol today.

Jonathan soon returned and before we knew it we were both being ushered into the dining room by the head waiter who sat us at a table in the window looking out over Upper Woburn Place and St. Pancreas Church. Sitting across at one another Jonathan looked as if he was the cat that had got the cream, while I looked down in the mouth and was wondering how the hell I could get out of giving afters, if asked. I decided the best thing to do was to suddenly feel ill after eating the pudding which may be far too sweet for me. This sorted in my mind I started to chat for England making sure Jonathan could hardly get a word in.

"Mary do you think you could stop yapping for a few moments so we can discuss the drink and food menu." asked Jonathan - looking annoyed.

"Sorry, I got carried away. I haven't had anyone to talk to all day. I forgot who I was with." I blushed.

"I'm thinking of ordering champagne – to celebrate."

"What's the celebration? I haven't anything to celebrate." Jonathan looked like he was in shock. "Jonathan if you buy the champagne I won't be drinking much of it as I'm NOT a drinker, I'd far rather have a cup of tea or a mug of coffee. I'll drink one small glass - the rest will be yours. I mean what I've said one glass only you'll never get me to drink a second." Jonathan looked at me very strangely. "Mary, when I booked someone from the agency I asked for a female that enjoyed a drink or two. I didn't want a female that would tut-tut me if I drank one to many, now I find I have you who is gorgeous to look at but virtually tea total." he put his arm across the table as if he wanted to hold my hand and become cosy – I didn't respond.

"My boss didn't say anything about me having to be a drinker to have dinner with you, in fact she has never asked if I drink alcohol."

"Well I drink quite a bit, I enjoy an alcoholic drink. The stress of my job makes me drink."

"What the hell do you do for a job if you need alcohol to get you through the day?"

"I'm a lawyer and work down the road from here and also in the Old Bailey."

"Gosh, I've never had the pleasure of eating dinner with a lawyer."

"You have this evening Mary and if you play your cards right you may spend the night with me."

"What are you on about Jonathan? I've been booked to keep you company while you eat your meal as you don't enjoy eating out on your own."

"Mary, I may need afters."

"Well if you mean something other than a pudding it won't be me providing it." I said sounding annoyed. Silence reigned.
Jonathan started to stutter "I've booked a room for us."

"You better unbook it unless you can find someone else to share it with because it's not going to be me." Thank God the waiter arrived and our order was taken. Jonathan was annoyed because in my tiddly state I told him in front of the waiter that I didn't know whether to have a starter or a mains as I couldn't eat both. It was a wonder he didn't notice I'd been drinking and send me packing. He just ranted and raved about what I said and told me not to make a fool of him. I apologised.

Jonathan immediately changed the conversation over to whether he'd met up with me before as I looked familiar to him. "I reckon you have been to one of my dos over in Chelsea, you look very familiar."

"I never go to Chelsea - in fact I wouldn't know how to get there."

"Mary from where I'm sitting I would put all my money on you socialising in Chelsea. In fact you look like a younger version of a woman I know that lives near Sloane Square and often comes around to my place for a drink or two in an evening." Luckily for me our food arrived, while eating I kept my head down hoping if Jonathan had to talk it would be about something other than me looking familiar to him. Once the meal was over and the Champagne had been drunk we made our way to the lounge where we sat on one of the large sofas and had our after dinner coffees.

While drinking our coffees I started to get worried about Jonathan expecting me to spend the night with him as he hadn't been over to the reception desk to cancel the room and he seemed to be getting more and more excited. He even pretended to forget that I didn't drink and ordered a couple of cocktails from the waiter that visited the tables in turn.

"I told you earlier, I'm not a drinker."

"Mary, I've been listening to you all evening and your words are getting more and more slurred by the minute. You either had a drink before leaving home for Dutch courage and the Champagne you drank over dinner has made you tiddly or you're a boozer and trying to pretend not to be, which ever it is keep me company with a cocktail - please."

"Okay I'll try and drink it, if I fall over it will be your fault as I'm NOT used to alcohol and the Champagne we had with our meal was strong, I thought it may be like lemonade but it wasn't" I said picking up my glass "Cheers Jonathan."

"Chin chin." said Jonathan smirking away to himself as if he was in charge and getting his own way. Jonathan soon finished his cocktail and was calling the waiter over to order another. I took my time to drink mine as I was determined not to have another as I didn't want to be in a position where I didn't know what I was doing and before I knew it I would be in the lift speeding up to the bedroom. "Why are you looking at your watch?"

"It seems to have stopped, it says nine forty. I thought it must be past eleven."

"Are you fed up with me rambling on that you want to retire to the room for a bit of excitement?"

"No, I'm enjoying sitting here chatting about nothing much." After listening to Jonathan's ramblings I decided to ask him a question. "Have you ever been married?"

"Once, never again. I'd rather be my own man and do what I want, when I want to do it. If I was married I wouldn't be able to meet someone as gorgeous as you from an escort agency as the wife would soon find out what I was doing. One evening I was out and about when I saw my wife sat at the bar of the Hyde Park Hilton having a drink with an old boy - old enough to be her grandad, I didn't confront her. I thought if you're going to play silly buggers I'm going to chance my luck and meet up with someone from an escort agency and I did and I got caught by my wife. I can only thank God that the woman I was with looked respectable and around my age. I never dreamt Molly (that's my ex) would ever suspect she was from an agency but she did."

"Was that the end of your marriage?"

"Yeah afraid so – the divorce cost me an arm and a leg."

"I must visit the Ladies – I won't be long."

"While you're away I'll get another round in." I didn't answer. I thought it best not to cause an upset by refusing another drink. In the past I have known men to loss their cool if one refuses anything - I have a feeling that Jonathan may be one of them.

I sat on the throne in the cubicle and contemplated about Jonathan and came to the conclusion that if he had any more to drink he wouldn't be capable of having sex in any form. I went back to the sofa smiling. "What have you got to smile about? Someone or something must have excited you in the Ladies as you look as if you've won the pools. Before you went out there you looked as if you'd eaten sour grapes."

"A woman in the loo made me smile she told me what I'd call a lady joke – like men have private men jokes. Let's get back to these cocktails they're a different colour from the last ones we had. What flavour are these?"

"The Waiter recommended them, they're supposed to be very popular and taste delicious. They're made from Campari, mixed with a little gin and lemonade."

"I must take a swig, cheers Jonathan."

"Chin, chin."

"I don't like chin, chin, I much prefer cheers." I said slurring my words.

"Alright Mary cheers it is." After a swig Jonathan went on to tell me how he only drank shorts and cocktails when he was in female company.

"I much prefer a beer and most evenings I drink at least seven pints."

"How the hell do you get home? I would be so tiddly having drunk all that, I wouldn't be able to tell the cabbie my address."

"The same way as you by cab unless I trip over the pavement then I usually get picked up by a copper and taken to a cell to sober up. I have been known to sleep under Waterloo Bridge with the down and outs before now." He smiled.

"God almighty that must be terrible especially waking up and finding yourself laying on concrete."

"It's bloody awful as the area stinks of urine as there are no toilets so they all wee anywhere and everywhere. Some even shit themselves if they can't hold on long enough to reach a local lavatory which is a good half a mile away. Now you know what happens if you carry on drinking alcohol till you fall down."

"What do you mean?" I asked "why do I need to know about what happens if I drink too much? I've told you I don't drink enough to worry about falling over."

"Don't think I haven't noticed you slurring your words and not being able to walk in a straight line Mary because I have. You turned up half drunk and you haven't refused an alcoholic drink all evening." I felt daft as I honestly thought I appeared sober. "I booked a room as I thought I'd be civilised tonight and spend the night here with you." laughed Jonathan.

"You know what thought did. Even if I agreed to spend the night with you I doubt if you'd be capable of performing." I grinned.

"What the hell do you mean Mary I can always perform?" I couldn't stop laughing. "Anyway if I can't I can always use a vibrator, I have one in my pocket in case I get caught out."

"Jonathan, I can't imagine anyone wanting sex with you at a drop of a hat. God you've got a very high opinion of yourself."

"Sorry Mary, I've been teasing you. I haven't had sex for years. I wouldn't know where to start let alone finish." I felt stupid, I couldn't wait to get out of the hotel. Jonathan carried on yapping. "The thing is Mary I have a catheter so it would be a bit difficult to perform. At the hospital

245

they did tell me what to do if I wanted sex. They said I should tape the catheter up the side of my penis." Jonathan laughed.

"For God's sake Jonathan shut up, you'll put me off sex for life in a minute. I'm going home before I say something I shouldn't."

"You haven't drunk the cocktail."

"I don't want it. All I need from you is the fare to get home by cab in one piece." Jonathan attempted to stand up but immediately fell back down on to the sofa. "If you're used to drinking seven pints a day you must have had quite a lot of alcohol before leaving home as you haven't drunk much this evening and now you can hardly get up."

"Yeah, I had a couple of pints." he smiled to himself then attempted to get up again. "As I have a catheter I've been told to drink a lot of fluid every day so the catheter doesn't block – that's my excuse and I'm keeping to it."

"I haven't a catheter so I can't have that as an excuse for me drinking far too much. Before I leave I must go for another wee or I may wet my knickers before I get home." We both laughed.

I staggered out to the Ladies and weed for England. When I eventually returned I found Jonathan stood leaning against the wall by the main door to the hotel talking to the doorman who was asking if Jonathan would like a cab."I was thinking of staying the night." Jonathan replied.

"Sorry Sir, all the rooms are taken to night. I'll call a cab for you and your lady." The doorman waved down the first empty cab that came along the road, Jonathan immediately started to climb into the back and was explaining where we wanted to be taken. I found it difficult to get in as Jonathan was sitting in the middle of the back seat leaving me hardly any room to sit next to him. Whispering in his ear I asked if he could move over. "There isn't enough room for me to sit comfortably please move over."

"Don't be daft girl there's enough room for you to sit next to me," he said tapping the seat. "I don't mind if your leg touches mine." he laughed

"I mind. I don't want anything of mine touching you."

"For God's sake girl I won't bit."

"Is something the matter Miss?" called the cabbie.

"Yes, I haven't enough room to sit comfortably."

"Move over please sir."

"What do you mean? Mary is my girlfriend, surely I can sit up close to her."

"You can if she agrees but she's not agreeing so please move over." Annoyed Jonathan moved along the seat when his catheter bag burst open, there was urine everywhere including on the seat and down the back of my dress. "What the hell's going on Jonathan my dress is soaking wet I bet it's something to do with that damn catheter bag even your trousers look wet. I don't know much about catheters but the one thing I do know is that the bag needs emptying at least twice a day, surely you could see it was full as there was a bulge down the side of your leg." Laughing Jonathan went on to say that he didn't empty the bag in the hotel because he thought it looked impressive. "Don't be so damn stupid you're bloody disgusting, no one has a dick that comes half way down their leg."

"What's going on back there?" called out the cabbie.

"There has been an accident my girlfriend has wet herself and the wee has gone everywhere including all over her skirt and down my trousers." "You'll be getting a bill for the mess sir as I'm sure it's nothing to do with the young lady. I'm going to take her over to Westbourne Terrace then you and I will have a chat about money and how much it will cost you for me to clean up the mess plus the fare to Chelsea from Upper Woburn Place." Thank God it wasn't long before I was getting out of the cab and walking along the terrace in tears.

Chapter 32

Before putting the key in the door I tried to stop crying - I couldn't. Once inside and up the stairs I bumped straight into Liz. "What the hell has happened to you? You look as if you've been attacked."

"Well I haven't. I've been out to dinner in a posh hotel with a stupid bloke that had a catheter and the bag broke in the back of the cab. My dress is ruined and it stinks."

"What! I thought the blokes you met from an agency were decent?"
"I suppose Jonathan is/was decent, his catheter was the problem, the bag needed emptying and he didn't bother to empty it so it split open in the cab."

"What! that's terrible in fact that's bloody disgusting." Said Liz holding her nose.

"Everything I have on I'm going to take off and throw in the bin and that includes my bra and knickers."

"I don't blame you Mary. I would think of doing the same but it's such a shame to have to get rid of the dress as it looks like it cost a pretty penny."

"It did, it came from a shop in Regents Street."

"Why don't you take it down to the launderette and give it a good wash, you have nothing to lose."

"Perhaps I will. I haven't a clue where the laundrette is."

"Mary are you blind? It's next to Queensway tube station you pass it every day."

"That's easy enough to find."
"Here's a carrier bag to put all your clothes in." said Liz taking it out of the kitchen cupboard and throwing it across to me. "Catch, make sure you don't put any clothes on the bathroom floor. I'd hate to think I was standing where urinated clothes had been placed."

"For God sake Liz don't make it seem worse than it is already."

"Mary it can't get any worse, from where I'm standing it's as bad as it can get."

"If we had a shower I would suggest you got in it, as we haven't the next best thing is a bath – I'll provide the smellies to put in the water and hopefully cheer you up."

"Thanks Liz. I'm going to have a couple of baths one to get rid of the stink and the second to make me smell lovely again."

I took the carrier bag and stormed off to the bath room where I stripped. Thank God all the other girls had either gone to bed or were still out gallivanting so they were not around to make a fool of me.

While in the bath I had a think about my drinking habit and decided I'd join AA as soon as possible. At the same time I'm going to continue working for an escort agency but I'm only going to meet clients for lunch. I'll be avoiding any form of alcohol or sex like the plague. Whether I'll be able to keep this up remains to be seen.

I slept like a baby which was good but strange. I was up and running by eight o'clock Saturday morning. By ten I was on the phone to Steve to ask if we could meet up but not in a pub. "What the hell's wrong? Something must be seriously the matter for you NOT wanting to meet in a pub."

"I'll explain everything when I meet you."

"I bet it's something to do with the demon drink, come on tell me. Have you been drunk, had sex with some old boy then to crown it all I bet you or the old boy tripped over your knickers?" we both laughed.

Chatting on for a few more minutes we arranged to meet at my favourite haunt –Trafalgar Square. "Okay Steve I'll meet you under Nelson's column at twelve noon I'll bring my overnight bag then I don't need to come back here until Monday." Steve seemed happy that I was staying over. I put the receiver down and started to walk back up the stairs when the phone rang again, as no one else is up and about I went back down to answer. It was Celia from the agency to tell me exactly what she thought of me wetting my knickers in the back of the cab which of course was not true.

"That is a complete and utter bloody lie Celia. Jonathan has a catheter and the bag broke and urine went everywhere including all over my dress which is now only fit for the bin. MY DRESS IS RUINED." I screamed down the phone. "I never want to see him again he's bloody disgusting." Celia attempted to calm me down by explaining that Jonathan enjoyed my company and was quite sure that wetting myself was an accident and he would like to meet up again.

"Celia you must be bloody joking. I wouldn't meet up with him again even if the catheter hadn't broken. You remember this Celia as far as I'm concerned he isn't worth getting out of bed for – snooty, disgusting little man. Now we have got that straight and you're still on the phone I have something to tell you I'm only going to meet clients at lunch time from next Thursday. I'm going to keep my appointment with Rodney, Wednesday evening. After that I'm not going out with any clients in the evening. I hope you understand what I've said."

"Yes I understand, but why Mary?"

"Celia, you've asked so I'll tell you, because I don't need to wear a cocktail dress for meeting up with clients at lunchtime."

"Mary, you'll need one for Wednesday evening."

"I know I will. I'm going to try and wash the dress I wore last night. If it shrinks or still stinks of urine I'll be back on this phone to arrange to come over to your office to get money for my dress. It cost me an arm and a leg from a shop at the top of Regents Street. I've kept the receipt, I'll bring it over with me then you'll be able to hand it over to Jonathan and ask him for the money or you'll be paying me from your bank account, the choice will be yours."

"Mary you better pray that your dress washes up just fine, if it doesn't after Wednesday you won't get any work from me especially if I've had to pay you for a new dress. I've plenty of girls who are willing and able to go out in the evenings and also I have a few that are looking for lunch time work. I'm afraid you'll be on your bike."

"I have my diary by my side, it says I have three appointments with Rodney, one to go out for an Indian meal next Wednesday evening, I'm looking forward to that as I love Indian food. Then I have a couple more dates at lunchtime with him on the following Wednesdays. The thing is Celia he enjoys my company and will be up in arms if I don't turn up."

"You can keep those dates as the other girls on my list find him very awkward."

"I found him very easy to get on with."

"That's okay, you meet him for the next three Wednesdays. In three weeks' time I'll chat with him and see if he still wants to meet you on a Wednesday or whether he wishes to meet up with a different girl."

"Most probably he'll want to meet me. He seems to like everything about me —at least he did when I met him last week."

"Men are very fickle and often change like the weather. Mary, I'm going now as this call is costing me money. I'll speak to you on Thursday May 4th to let you know what Rodney has to say about you meeting up with him on a permanent basis."

"Bye Celia."

Once upstairs I went straight to my room to have a serious think about whether I should get a full time job in another office as I need regular money to pay my bills as It seems like Celia isn't going to give me much work if any. After quite a bit of thought I decided I would commiserate with Steve.

Chapter 33

Steve was already standing under Nelson's Column when I arrived at Trafalgar Square, he looked pleased to see me and welcomed me with open arms which cheered me up no end. After a chat we decided to walk to the South Bank which meant walking across the Strand into the lane which took us to the Thames and Steve's favourite coffee bar. It wasn't long before we were stood outside the coffee bar wondering whether to go in or not.

"The coffee in there is excellent far better than the coffee we had in that dive behind the portrait gallery." Said Steve nodding his head towards the door.

"I wouldn't call that place a dive - I like it in there."

"To me it was a complete and utter dive, a better class of person visits here. It's also far too expensive for the down and outs to visit."

"Are you trying to make out that you're a snob to impress me because that's one thing I'm not, you can't impress me with that rubbish. I can guarantee I'm not going to become one either. Just because I was unlucky enough to be born to parents I call Mr and Mrs Snooty and I say they live up snob alley that'll never make me a snob - I'm down to earth." silence reigned for a few moments.

"Sorry Mary, let's go in and see what we can get to eat and drink."

"Okay but don't try and impress me again or I'll walk and that'll be the end of this relationship."

Once inside we ordered a couple of toasted sandwiches plus coffee then settled ourselves down at a table where I explained to Steve about the problems I was having working for the agency. He was not surprised and thought it a good idea if I gave up the escort work and went back to working in an office. "I won't be able to give it up until I've worked the next three Wednesdays as I'm booked to see Rodney once for dinner and twice for lunch."

"If you manage to find an office job you could always be sick. The office manager wouldn't realise you were working elsewhere on those days unless you were daft enough to tell one of the girls and she reported you to the manager. If you're not hard up for extra money pretend to be sick with the agency the choice is yours Dear Mary."

"What you have suggested is a good idea I've plenty of time to think and sort it out as I have to find the office job first." Our food and coffee arrived. Steve was right about the toasted sandwich it was delicious and coffee was very good much better than we had the other night even the waitress looked more respectable not like the scruffy boy who imagined he was the manager of the joint behind the Portrait Gallery.

We sat in silence while we ate our toasted sandwich. Once finished I started the conversation about how pleased I was that I'd met him.

"Steve I'm pleased you came knocking on my door back along if you hadn't we wouldn't be sat here together now. You're the only good thing that has happened to me in years. It has taken all these horrid things going on in my life to make me realise that I'm very fond of you."

"Mary you come over as a very nice girl especially when you're sober."

"Thank you Steve. I'm sure I've told you a hundred times before that I'm going to try to give up the booze."

"Yes Mary you've told me quite a few times and you haven't given it up. If you don't give up the booze I'm afraid you'll finish up having a very sad and lonely life in fact I doubt if you'll live to old age. Have you ever thought of going to AA there is a hall in most areas of London where they hold meetings for recovering alcoholics."

"Steve a question for you. If I manage to give up the alcohol do you think we could make a go of it together?"

"Don't rush things darling, we're spending this weekend together, let's see how we get on. At the moment you have this problem with a friend called Alcohol and I think that this friend needs to be sorted before you can think about any kind of future with anyone."

"Steve if I had a purpose for going to AA like a future with you I think I'd go."

"Mary let's leave it there and enjoy a booze free weekend."

"Okay, I must go to the Ladies before we leave here." I said getting up from my seat.

I soon returned only to let Steve know that I'd caught the waitress that served us our food cleaning the toilets.

"What! that's not true, I'm sure it's not true, it can't be. It's one of your sick jokes. The waitress must have a twin sister"

"Well I swear to God it's true. I couldn't believe my eyes when I saw the waitress kneeling over the lavatory holding the toilet brush to the ready, mind you she did have her marigold gloves on. I don't know who was the most shocked me or her being caught." Steve sat with his mouth open wide as if he was catching flies.

"Haven't you anything to say Steve?"

"I shouldn't have been so hasty in saying how much better this place is to where you took me the other night. All I can say is SORRY and hope and pray that we don't get some rotten bug and end up in hospital. I'll go up and pay."

"Don't be so bloody daft Steve you don't pay for anything after what I saw - let's do a runner." As there was no one up at the counter we picked up our bits and pieces and made a quick exit never to be seen in this dive again.

We hurried down to the Thames and stood looking towards the Houses Parliament from Hungerford Bridge. "Thank God we got out of there without getting caught." said Steve looking worried to deaf in case we'd been followed.

"You make me smile Steve, if I hadn't been with you you'd have paid up, you wouldn't have done a runner."

"What shall we do now?" asked Steve changing the subject and trying not to look embarrassed while looking into my eyes.

"I know what I want to do, I want a snog." With that I threw my arms around Steve's neck and gave him a long lingering French kiss. "Now I've had what I've wanted from the minute we met at Trafalgar Square, what do you want, what shall we do? - think of something Steve." whispering in my ear he suggested that we should catch the tube back to his flat as he felt randy and couldn't wait much longer to get inside of me. My face must have been a picture as I never thought I'd hear the day when Steve would say this. "If you can't think of anything to do other than taking me home to bed I'm suggesting before we go back to your place that we stroll across this bridge then along the river to Westminster Bridge, back over to this side to catch the circle line to South Kensington where we can change on to the Piccadilly line for Hammersmith. The exercise will do me good. What do you think?"

"Mary, I'll agree to that, along the way we should pass a pub I'm going to take you in and buy you a soft drink while I have my normal pint."

"Steve, how the hell can I go into a pub and have a soft drink. If I smell alcohol I'll want some of it."

"Well Mary I'm not going to buy you any, it's as simple as that. Hopefully this is going to be your first day alcohol free. I think it's better for you if you try to confront the demon drink with me rather than with one of your drunken mates who will tempt you to get pissed instead of encouraging you to stay sober. Tomorrow I may take you to Jack Straws."

"Steve, where the hell's that?"

"On the top of Hampstead Heath – it's a very popular pub most people have heard of it even if they haven't been inside."

"Getting back to me and the booze, I agree with what you're saying Steve about me giving it up. The trouble is I've tried before and within a day or so I was shaking as if I'd suddenly got Parkinson Decease. I couldn't even put my make up on without my hands shaking. I was a complete and utter mess so guess what Steve - I had a drink." I laughed. "Mary I'm going to attempt to help you and hopefully the shakes won't happen again or if they do they'll be very mild." Steve said throwing his arms around me

"Come on Mary let's go for this walk and see what we can find." Holding on to Steve's arm we made our way over the bridge in silence, in the distance I could see what looked like a pub. "If we have to go into the pub that is coming up on my left Steve I'm going to have a tomato juice with Worcester sauce. I haven't had one for years in fact the last one I had was when I lived at home and had to help mum at one of her snooty cocktail parties. God, Steve if you could have seen the snooties that turned up just to nose around my parents' apartment, you would have cringed."

"I can imagine there are a lot of people out there that do that then go home moaning that they don't have what other people have." We plodded on and were soon outside the pub. After a lot of deliberation we went in and managed to find a couple of stools up at the bar where I could hear what the customers were ordering. "I hate it in here Steve, I'd rather go home than sit here listening to the customers conversation about alcohol, as well as that I can smell the beer you're drinking. Unless you take me out of here now I'm going to order myself my favourite tipple - Gin."

"Let me finish my pint then we'll go. I promise I won't bring you into a pub again as you definitely have a problem with drink."
"You know damn well I have, you didn't need to bring me in here to realise that."

255

Chapter 34

It wasn't long before Steve and I were sat on the tube and he started whispering in my ear about my drinking habit.

"Mary if we're going to go steady you need to do something about your alcohol input. The thing is when you start drinking alcohol you don't seem to know how to stop or when to stop. My problem is that I enjoy a pint and if you can't come into a pub with me to have a drink without getting drunk out of your mind there can't be a future for us. When I was eighteen I met a girl who had parents that were mega rich they gave Emily money to spend on anything and spend it she did. One lunch time we went to the pub and before I realised it Emily had drunk herself silly. It was the worse day of my life as on the way home she hit out at a greengrocers shop window with her umbrella, glass went everywhere we both finished up at the police station. Eventually we had to go to the local court where we were both fined. "

"God Steve that must have been terrible."

"It was bloody awful. Emily's parents paid her fine but I had to pay mine out of my wages as my parents wouldn't help me out. I don't want this to happen again especially with you."

"I promise if we go steady I'll go along to Alcohols Anonymous. I may need to go a few times before I come to terms about going into a pub without having alcohol."

"Mary, now you've told me you'll definitely arrange to go to AA, I've news for you about my firm wanting me to move out of London to a new factory in Essex."

"What do you mean Steve? Is this happening soon?"

"I'm not sure they have to decide on a date but they've said it could be in about eight weeks' time. If you're serious about giving up the booze and wanting us to be a couple you could move with me to Essex."

"What the hell will I do in Essex?"

"In the first instance you would be able to sort out our home then perhaps find an office job. The factory where I'll be manager will need office workers you may be able to get a job there." I didn't know what to reply as I was happy but in shock. "What have you got say to that Mary?"

"If I hadn't agreed to try and give up the booze I'd say ' get me a glass of my favourite tipple' but you couldn't do that as we're on the tube and there's no bar here." I laughed.

"Say something sensible Mary."

"Here goes, something as serious as moving out of London has to be thought about. I have never put foot over the border into Essex. I don't know a thing about Essex except the girls have a reputation of being very glamorous."

"I'll take you over to Ilford next weekend to see what you think of it." I was silent for a few minutes.

"Steve I'll find it a wrench leaving London, it's the only place I know. I have never lived anywhere else. I haven't even had a holiday away from London."

I looked into Steve's eyes. "I've an idea instead of you moving straight over to Essex why don't you move to my place and share the flat with me that's available downstairs then go to work from there it wouldn't take long to get over to Essex by tube." Steve looked at me strangely.

"I thought you were going to live downstairs with Ruth before I mentioned you coming over to Essex?"

"I was but Ruth could take over my room and live upstairs with the girls. I'm sure she wouldn't mind as she'll be pleased about me setting up home with you."

"I'll have to see how far it is to Ilford by tube before I can agree, I'll look in my A-Z. If it's further than twenty miles it won't be happening, then you have to make the big decision come and live in Essex with me or stay in London living in the flat with Ruth."

"As you haven't answered my question by saying definitely YES to moving over to Westbourne Terrace I'm going to have a snooze. Steve please wake me once we get to South Kensington as we have to get off and go over to the Piccadilly line." It wasn't long before Steve was nudging me awake.

"Mary, you don't half snore."

"You're the first man to tell me that, I'm sure you're teasing – it can't be true."

"Sorry Mary, it's true and you seem too be able to snore in unison." By this time I was stood up and looking in every direction.

"What the hell do you mean Steve?" I said sounding annoyed.

257

"See the bloke with the long hair who's getting off the tube?" Steve nodded towards him

"Yeah, what about him?"

"He was sat behind you and snoring along with you." Steve laughed.

"For God's sake Steve don't embarrass me."

"I'm not meaning to, let's get off the tube – I can't wait to get you home." Steve tapped me on my bum.

It wasn't long before we arrived at Hammersmith and were walking past Derek's flat. Thank God he was nowhere to be seen, as I'm sure if we had bumped into him he would have made a point of telling Steve exactly what he thought of me, whether Steve would have believed him is another matter. Hopefully my relationship with Steve will be calm and we will live happily ever after but that remains to be seen.

Once we were inside the flat Steve put the kettle on to make pot of tea. "I thought we would have jumped into bed for rampant sex before having a cuppa?"

"I always have a cuppa before doing anything."

"Anything?"

"That's what I said Mary." laughed Steve.

"So it's a cup of tea first then sex for afters?"

"Yeah, you've got it right."

"I would have had it the other way around."

"Well I don't, you'll have to get used to my way or it will be the highway for you."

"Cup of tea it is then, I hope it's as good as the coffee you made the other day – that was very good."

I sat on the end of the bed looking down in the mouth wondering what other stupid quirks Steve may have and thinking that this is why he's on his own. I finished my tea long before he did. I couldn't understand why he was taking so long perhaps he's avoiding having sex with me. He must have taken a good half an hour to finish his tea then to crown it all he insisted on washing the mugs before getting into bed.

"What the hell is the matter with you Steve? At Westminster Bridge you were saying how you couldn't wait to get me into bed, now you're trying to avoid the inevitable."

"Nothing's wrong with me - I like to take my time."

"The other night when I stayed we didn't have any of this stupid nonsense."

"Well today we have, I sometimes have a complex and today is one of those days." I looked at him as if looks could kill, then I started to shout.

"You want me to try and give up the booze by going to Alcoholics Anonymous and I have agreed to do that. I need you to sort yourself out by getting rid of the stupid complex."

"Surely you don't have to scream at me so everyone in the building can hear you."

"Sorry Steve, I didn't mean to shout I'm usually a quiet sole but you have made me lose my cool. What with you telling me to go to AA and you behaving as if you don't care about me by insisting on making a pot of tea as soon as we got back here. You haven't even put your arms around me to have a snog let alone get into bed with me. Perhaps if I take all my clothes off you'll jump into bed. Before I do that I have to tell you that I'm NOT going to instigate sex or love making – whatever you want to call it - every time - I enjoy a man being in charge especially in the bedroom."

"Well I'm the opposite I love a woman to be in charge." Steve laughed.

"Come on then get your clothes off, hurry up, chop, chop." I said clapping my hands. I don't know what happened but before I could blink Steve was stood in his birthday suit waiting for me to take advantage of him. "Get on the bed Steve, I don't want you standing up I want you laying down."

"Mary I love it when you're telling me what to do."

"That's good just lay back and enjoy everything I do – I won't bite."

Once the deed was done Steve mentioned how much he enjoyed making love with me. "God I did enjoy that, the best love making I've had in years. Now I must get up and wash the dishes, then go and get our fish and chips." Steve started to get up, I pulled him back down on the bed.

"Steve it couldn't have been that good if you're getting up. I thought we would be staying put and having a snooze together till morning. I'm not moving, you don't need to either as you only have a few dishes to wash and we can do them together sometime tomorrow."

"What about food? I'm starving, I need sustenance. I always need food after making love. I'm going to get fish and chips."

"Steve I'm staying put. I shall still be here when you return with your fish and chips waiting for you to instigate making love, you better think what you're going to do and how you're going to do it." I laughed

259

"God Mary you're a bossy little madam."

"No I'm not, I'm just saying what I want. Remember not to get me fish and chips because all I need is YOU." After a long lingering kiss Steve got out of bed and made his way down the road to the chippy.

It was a good half hour before he returned "The queue must have been at least a quarter of a mile long, any way I'm here now. Once I've eaten this lot I'll be game for anything."

"Anything?"

"That's what I said Mary." I'd never seen anyone eat so fast.

"God, Steve you'll choke in a minute eating that fast."

"I don't want to waste precious time eating as it seems like you're gagging for more of me."

"I won't deny that, to me you're the best thing I've had since sliced bread. I've got it bad, in fact I think I'm falling for you in a big way."

"All the girls fall for me and they get hurt, take a step back Mary as I don't want to hurt you. Remember what I said earlier today that I won't get serious with you unless you give up the booze."

"Well I haven't had any alcohol today and I don't intend to have any tomorrow or any other day. How long I'll be able to keep it up for I don't know. I'll just have to try my hardest and when I think of having a Gin I find something else to do or think about like jumping into bed with you." we both laughed.   "One thing I must say is that I promise I'll join Alcoholics Anonymous as soon as possible."

Our love making lasted for most of the night it was brilliant. Whether Steve enjoyed it as much as me remains to be seen as he has only told me the once how much he enjoyed jumping into bed with me - that was the first time we made love.

Chapter 35

Sunday we spent most of the day walking on Hampstead Heath where we found a seat to have a quiet chat. Steve was first to start the conversation. "Mary I've enjoyed this weekend especially as you've managed to stay off the booze that I'm thinking of taking the day off tomorrow to be with you, then I could come over to Chelsea to meet your mum. What do you think Mary?"

"God, Steve that's a shock to my system you asking to come over to meet Mrs Snooty – I mean mum."

"Why not? If we're going to be a couple I think I should meet her and tomorrow is as good a day as any." I wondered what the hell had happened I thought perhaps he'd had a funny turn. "Is something wrong with you Steve?"

"Should there be?"

"Asking to meet mum is the last thing I thought I'd hear coming from you." We carried on chatting about things in general until Steve managed to change the conversation back to the one and only question. "Mary can I come over to Chelsea with you tomorrow? I need to know so I can phone in sick."

"I suppose you can but in the morning I have to go back to Westbourne Terrace, if you come with me you can inspect the flat I've told you about."

"That sounds good to me."

Monday we got up early and were over at Westbourne Terrace by ten only to find Liz had taken the day off and was sat in the kitchen drinking a mug of coffee. I'm not sure who was the most shocked her or me at seeing one another.

"All of us here have missed you over the weekend. I guess Mary has been with you. What's your name and where do you live?" asked Liz holding out her right hand for Steve to shake.

"Hello I'm Steve, I live over at Hammersmith and you are?" silence reigned for a few minutes.

"I'm Liz. Are you Mary's boyfriend?"

"Afraid so, we're planning to live together." Liz looked surprised.

"You're a dark horse Mary where the hell did you meet? Are you one of Mary's customers?"

"No I'm not. I live in a flat in the building where Mary used to live."

"You're not that landlord she used to tell us about?"

"NO. I'm a respectable man that has fallen in love with your friend. Eventually I plan to make an honest woman of Mary." I felt embarrassed as this was the first I'd heard of this. "You're not a one night stand?"

"No, I don't agree with having them. We've known each other for quite a few months."

"Steve has come over to look at the downstairs flat. I'm thinking of renting it with him – that's if you're agreeable and Steve likes it."

"Mary this is such a shock you could knock me down with a feather." Liz smiled, "Getting back to you renting the flat, you have to remember I collect the rent weekly and if you don't pay up or behave I'll kick you out without thinking twice about it. The girl that used to live in the flat I kicked out the other week Steve, for smoking and not keeping the place clean."

"It was in a filthy state and it stunk of fags." I said holding my nose.

"I guess you have had the place decorated since she moved out?"

"I'll give you the key then you can have a look for yourself." Liz handed over the key to me.

Down we went I unlocked the door Steve went in first he inspected every room including the bathroom "This isn't bad especially at the price and furnished. What do you think of it Mary?"

"I like it, in fact I've always liked it but when I came to see it before it was in a disgusting state. I wouldn't have wanted my worst enemy to live here"

"Mary shall we arrange to rent it?" asked Steve smiling away to himself "I've brought my cheque book with me so I can put a deposit down on it today."

"Are you sure Steve?"

"As sure as I can be. I told you upstairs in front of Liz that I've fallen in love with you, in fact from day one when you opened the door to me I thought I'm going to marry this girl." I threw my arms around Steve's neck and stayed put for at least ten minutes before telling him I felt the same. "Steve there's one big problem, how the hell will you get over to Essex from here?"

"Don't worry about that darling I'll find a way, the only thing that matters at the moment is you and I being together. Let's go upstairs and give Liz the cheque." We both plodded up and found Liz still getting over the shock of me finding a serious boyfriend. "Mary must have done something right that made you feel the way you do."

"Mary is a lovely girl who deserves to have someone to look after her." said Steve looking the happiest I've ever seen him. After a lot of chatting and laughing I went and phoned mum to see if she'll be in this afternoon.

"I can be if you're definitely coming over."

"Yes I am, with some news."

"I hope you're not coming to tell me you have the pox or you've got a bun in the oven because if it's either you may as well stay away."

"Don't be stupid, I'm your daughter not a tart."

"Have you got yourself married off behind my back?"

"NO I HAVE NOT. You'd be the first to be told if I'd found myself a husband."

"Well whatever you have to tell me it better be good news which will make your father and I happy."

"I don't care about making Dad happy as he hasn't bothered with me since the day you kicked him out, he won't care about my news - good or bad."

"Mary what time are you thinking of arriving as I'm visiting Jonathan for lunch time cocktails?" I almost dropped the receiver.

"Three o'clock."

"That sounds okay to me. I may bring Jonathan back to meet you, I'm sure you'd like him. He's a very honest bloke, he's a lawyer - a very good catch. Far nicer than your father he has plenty of money, if I get cosy with him he won't need to pinch my cheque book."

"Mum I don't want to meet Jonathan. I don't care how much dosh he has or how nice he is to you, please don't bring him back to your place especially after
you've had a few drinks. If Dad is still living across the road from you perhaps you could invite him to come over but I definitely don't want you to ask Jonathan to come to meet me."

"Mary you sound a bit annoyed about me having drinks with a man from around the corner. You must remember I'm getting divorced from your father and I don't intend staying single and celibate for the rest of my days."

"Well, I hope you're not considering marrying this Jonathan."

"Not at the moment, I'm still married to your father."

"Has Jonathan mentioned getting married to you?"

"He said something about marriage one evening after he'd had a few to many, I didn't take any notice of what he said."

263

"I think you're better off on your own than married to someone that drinks far too much."

"Are you trying to tell me something?" silence reigned. "Mary I'll continue this conversation when you come over. I reckon you've met Jonathan when you've been out and about." I banged the receiver down in shock, then ran back up the stairs.

"All done and dusted." I said clapping my hands

"You look as if you're in a bit of a fluster dear." Said Steve looking at me as if something's up. "Nothing's wrong Steve. I've arranged to get over to mum's by three o'clock - it'll take us a good half an hour on the tube. I'll go and have a wash and brush up and change my dress as I've worn this old thing all weekend, then we can go on our way. Before I do that tell me, have you given Liz the cheque?"

"Yes, Liz put it in her hand bag. She's gone out for lunch with friends, she said cheers to you"

"I'm looking forward to living with you, I can't wait. While I get ready go and sit in the sitting room I'll only be a few minutes."

Within minutes I was standing in the doorway of the sitting room.

"How do I look Steve?" I gave him a twirl.

"Great, if we were not in such a rush I'd suggest spending an hour in bed with you." I laughed as I'd heard this many times before from different men.

"Let's get going or we'll be late."

We soon arrived at Sloane Square and were walking along to mum's flat.

"God, Mary this is a posh area are you sure we're in the right street?"

"Of course I'm sure, I know this road like the back of my hand. I was born here."

"Mary how much further is it?"

"We're here." I ran up the steps and rang the doorbell. Within seconds mum answered.

"I've only just got in." said mum eyeing Steve up and down. "You must be my surprise?"

"Yes Mum. This is Steve a very good friend of mine."

"Steve you're very welcome here, remember any friend of my daughter's is a friend of mine. Both of you go up to my flat." Mum seemed to look sober, I doubt if she is especially if she's been for cocktails with Jonathan. Once we were sat in the sitting room mum explained how dad had moved out from across the road and was now living in an up market flat on the corner of Fulham Palace and Kings Road. "Mum I can't imagine how he can afford to live there, he must be quite poor now he can't get his hands on your cheque book."

"Mary that is exactly what I said to myself when I found out. He's still with his floosie who has this eighteen month old baby."

"Have you found out if the baby's Dad's?"

"No, my Solicitor said it would cost a lot of money to find out and it would be sending good money after bad. I doubt if I'll ever know unless you call around to see him and the floosie happens to be there."

"I won't be doing that as I haven't heard or seen him since you kicked him out."

"That's that then because I haven't got his address to give you."

"Good riddance to bad rubbish" I said clapping my hands and laughing.

"I'm going to make you a cup of tea unless you would like a glass of something stronger?"

"Mum I've told you many times I don't drink alcohol and Steve only drinks beer and you never keep beer in the flat so that's that. We will have nice cup of tea please Mum."

"Before I go and make it I have something to say to you Mary about how you have been spending your time picking up men in the West End hotels. You listen to this Steve my husband's best friend picked darling Mary up in the bar of a hotel."

"How the hell do you know that?" I said looking shocked.

"After he left you my darling he came straight round here and told your father and I all about you and how much you charged."

I felt so embarrassed that I sat with my head in my hands while mum went on to explain to us both how she gave the money to dad's best friend to give to me for the sex he had with me once a week for eight weeks.

"Come on Steve you may as well spill the beans and tell me which hotel you met my daughter in."

"I didn't meet Mary in any hotel she was a neighbour and a very good neighbour she was."

"I bet she was."

"Mum, why be so horrible to me? It's either because you've had too many Gins and it's the drink talking or you're jealous as you haven't a man and you're GAGGING for one." I laughed out loud.

Immediately Steve told us both to shut up and act like adults. Silence reigned for a few moments then out of the blue mum apologised for her outburst - what she had said about me was true. I also believe her when she said she gave dad's friend the money to pay me. Looking back on the situation I'm sure he didn't have much dosh to pay me from his own bank account.

"The only reason I became an escort was because I had no money for food. What else could I do as it wouldn't have been any good coming to you for a few pence. At least I was working in posh hotels, not walking the streets and being picked up by men with little sense and hardly any money. Mum you would have had something to moan about especially if I came home crying with the pox."

"Mary I'm going to make the pot of tea before one of us say something we may regret."

"Mum before you go out to the kitchen a question, why did you pay for dad's friend to have sex with me?"

"I needed to make sure you only met him I gave him a lot more money to give you than you deserved. Your dad and I knew that you couldn't catch the pox from him as he was what one would call celibate, until he met you. He never had sex with anyone other than his wife and he only had sex with her the once." Once mum was out of hearing distance Steve had something to say.

"Mary I reckon she's a heavy drinker and it's the drink talking – none of what she has said can be true."

"I told you she drank far too much and that she may be drunk due to going for cocktails with Jonathan. When she comes back I'll embarrass her about Jonathan then mum and I will be sort of quits."

"Mary don't have a row with her, remember she's your mother and you only have the one."

"I know that, I'll be careful how I speak to her but I am determined to get my point over. I know mum, she won't let it rest about dad's best friend, she is like a dog with a bone. I'm going to put the mockers on her and Jonathan and tell her about his catheter."

"For God's sake Mary be careful how you tell her. If I was in your shoes I wouldn't say a word about him, as I wouldn't want to rock the boat."
Steve looked quite annoyed with me

"Okay, I promise I won't mention it, I'll keep it to myself as I don't want to embarrass you or finish up falling out with you over something stupid."
Mum returned carrying a tray with cups of tea and fancy cakes from her favourite store – Harrods.

266

"Steve, have you come to meet me because you're serious about my daughter or is it to say you're Mary's pimp?"

"Mum for God's sake shut up being horrible about me. I gave up working in the hotels at least eighteen months ago. I'm a typist in an office at Oxford circus." I winked at Steve. "Steve is serious about me in fact we're in love and are planning to live together and eventually Steve hopes to make an honest woman of me."

"Are you telling me we're going to have a wedding in the family?"

"Yes Mrs Huggins, I hope to marry your daughter."

"Are you engaged? Have you bought the ring?"

"It's no to both questions Mrs Huggins. We only decided all of this over the weekend. We both thought I should come over to meet you before announcing our engagement."

"Am I the first person to be told about this?" asked mum.

"Yes." We both replied in harmony.

"I am shocked and pleased at the same time. I must give my future son in law a hug. Come here Steve." Once the hug was over mum suggested that we should drink a toast to us both. "Whether you drink alcohol or not I'm getting a bottle of wine out to toast you both. What would you like red or white?"

"Neither thank you." Said Steve "Let's toast our engagement with a cup of tea."

"That's a bit boring Steve but if that is what you would prefer, Cheers to you both. I hope you have a long and happy life together."

"Thankyou."

After celebrating with a cup of tea we chatted to mum about our plans, then saying I would ring to keep her abreast of things Steve and I left. Thank God Steve seemed to get on okay with mum even though she kept talking about us having an alcoholic drink and couldn't understand why we wouldn't.

On the way home and feeling elated I suggested to Steve that we should have party to celebrate our engagement.

"We could invite my ex work mates and my new flat mates along with your friends."

"Mary, that's a brilliant idea I look forward to it. We'll need to ask our friends about dates in case some of them are on holiday then we can arrange a place for holding it."

267

Putting the key in the door at Westbourne Terrace I could hear the phone ringing, I answered, it was mum to tell me how much she liked Steve and how she would like me to have Gran's engagement ring.

After thanking mum for the ring I realised at last my life is making sense and meeting someone like Steve and settling down with him is what I'd always wanted.

I'm pleased to say after living with Steve for the last six months that we're still in love and are living happily together in Joan's old flat. I've given up the drink and go to AA once a week also I have a job in a different office, not far from our flat. Steve and I are planning to marry in the spring with all my girlfriends coming to my big day. Mum will be giving me away as no one has seen dad since he moved to the corner of Fulham Palace and Kings Road.

The end

About the Author

I was brought up in Buckinghamshire but was born in Devon during the Second World War.
After leaving school I trained as a nurse. Now retired I spend my time writing articles for various magazines. This is my 3rd book, 2nd novel. I share my life in Exeter, Devon, UK with my husband Terry. I have a son Quinton Winter who lives in Kent with his family.

Printed in Great Britain
by Amazon

54549278R00153